I0572295

In loving memory of Cathy.
She encouraged me to write this novel.
I'll be grateful to her for the rest of my days.

Impetuous

The Odyssey of a Solitary Man

Novel

T.S. Aguilar

IMPETUOUS - The Odyssey of a Solitary Man
Second edition: 2022

Text design: T.S. Aguilar
Cover design: T.S. Aguilar

For information: T_S_Aguilar46@yahoo.com

ISBN: 978-0-9687711-7-4

The economic system has a natural law: supply is determined by demand. When cocaine stops being consumed, when there's no demand... that's going to be the end of this business.

Pablo Escobar Gaviria, May 1990

I think we're going through the most critical time of the cocaine culture. I also believe that this phenomenon needs to be viewed from a global perspective. It is true that the American people are being harmed by cocaine. It is also true that the producing countries suffer indiscriminate terrorism, contract killings, kidnapping and government corruption.

But what is the difference between exporting a kilo of cocaine from a producing country and exporting an AR-15 rifle and ammunition from the US to murder innocent people in developing countries? Why are countries like Germany free to export chemicals used for cocaine production? Why do countries like Switzerland, Luxembourg, the UK and even the US protect funds of dubious origin?

Gilberto Rodríguez Orejuela
during an interview with Time magazine, June 1991

As long as the government does not take decisive action to eradicate poverty, social injustice and hopelessness, the police force will fight a losing battle against drug-related crime.

Extract of the US police chiefs' annual meeting resolution,
Washington, D.C., June 1991

1

The first rays of sunshine pierce the murky light of a false dawn. Moravia, sleepy suburb of Costa Rica's capital city San José, hasn't yet come to life on Friday, 15th September 1989.

Tall trees cast their shadow across the lawn of a park and dewdrops glisten on the blades of grass. The park is deserted except for two men rushing towards the rotunda in the centre. Dressed in traditional, embroidered shirts over baggy trousers they appear to be local businessmen on their way to work, which is true in a way. They are the wholesale drug dealer Bernal 'El Burro' Villalobos and his hitman Mario Brenes.

They meet the retailer Benito Vargas who likes to sport a cowboy look in denim shirt, jeans, and riding boots. Bernal shows him a transparent plastic bag of half a pound of cocaine and quickly stuffs it back into his trouser pocket. Benito wants proof that the bag is sealed and contains cocaine. Bernal extracts it again, and Mario applies a small cut with the tip of his stiletto.

A few crystals ooze out. Benito picks them up with a moistened finger and licks them. Satisfied, he agrees to pay the demanded price and takes a thick bundle of US-dollars out of his shirt pocket.

But before he can peel off the agreed amount, Mario rams the stiletto into his chest and Benito collapses fatally wounded. Bernal wrests the bundle of money from the clutches of the dying man and together he and his executioner get away in haste.

***

Not far from the park in a quiet side street squats an architecturally uninspiring old-style guesthouse, a posada. It looks run down. Paint peels off its rampart in large flakes and weeds grow out of the cracks of the grim and forbidding wall. An arched gateway with a wooden gate of solid oak and two small, square windows on either side are the only signs of character of the barren bulwark. Not a shingle or a plaque declares 'Room for Rent'. Neither is there any indication that the posada actually houses some tenants. Thus, it appears to be a rather neglected residence of an extended family, although it has been rumoured to be a safe house of the secret service. But that is just hearsay and anyone wanting to enter the posada can pass through a small, unlocked door in the gate. No need to rap the doorknocker. It is there only for decorative purposes.

The small door opens up to the expanse of a cobbled yard. Glued to the rampart to the left of the gate is the residence of the owner, Doña Flora. The plump, that is to say obese landlady shares her quarters with her very old mother and a dog, three cats, a rooster, and six chickens. Her main activities amount to keeping the peace among the canine, feline, and fowl lodgers, watching the comings and goings of her tenants and their visitors, and, once a week, collecting the rent in advance.

Doña Flora inherited the posada from her third husband, who, it is said, died under the same mysterious circumstances as his two predecessors. They consumed toxic mushrooms Flora had picked 'accidentally' on the slopes of the nearby Poás volcano.

Rumour has it that there had been a fourth husband who kicked the bucket as a result of suffering a broken neck when he refused to eat her mushroom fricassee.

The yard is bordered to the left by a tall concrete block wall, three single storey dwellings at the far end and five more on the right. Four of the eight lodgings are occupied by a motley crew of tenants.

The digs in the centre of the three dwellings at the far end of the yard is the present home of the thirty-one-year-old Oscar Antonio Ortiz Acosta. He is a Cimarrón, a scion of African slaves who escaped the Caribbean Islands many years ago and found freedom in Colombia. He is a stout fellow who stands out in Moravia, a community of squat descendants of Spanish settlers, not only because of the colour of his skin but also on account of his height of six feet. Officially he is the representative of various patent medicine companies. But his real professional activities are known only to his intimate clients, or so he thinks, and a sheltered residence is important to Oscar.

His neighbours have similar reasons for seeking the seclusion of the posada. The one to his right is a hulky, balding guy who goes by the pseudonym of Don Alfonso. He has a penchant for worshipping Hitler and similar mass murderers, all of whom he considers to be deities. He claims to be a travelling salesman in ladies' underwear, which always leads to the question if a big guy like him doesn't feel uncomfortable strutting around in bra and panties. In reality he works as an evangelist giving daily hellfire sermons to a growing congregation. The clergy of this arch catholic country is mad as hell and would like to see him hang from a lamppost for proselytising their flock of sheep and pocketing the offertory, the money tossed on his collection plate, without giving a fair share to the local diocese. Small wonder he has good reason to fly under the radar.

The neighbour to Oscar's left is José León, a young, wiry guy with a crescent shaped scar from the left eyebrow to the tip of his chin, and long hair he subjects to an oil change every two weeks, apparently. None of his neighbours know what he does for a living, but it is thought that he is a petty thief and cat burglar responsible for the many cases of breaking and entering in the neighbourhood. He just chuckles and nods whenever someone voices this rumour and tries to lift the veil of secrecy surrounding his activities. He is very reticent and does not let anyone see his arsenal of silenced guns, stilettos, and razor-sharp knives. If Oscar had an inkling of José being an undercover agent of the secret service and a member of the feared Rapid Reaction Force, he would distance himself from this strange character. But as things stand, he hasn't just befriended José. He calls on him and pays him handsomely for protection when it is time to deal with seedy underworld characters and resolve territorial disputes with dealers of all sorts of banned substances.

Kitty-corner from these three tenants lives a gaunt man everybody calls Bert. He is in his forties, has a full head of grey hair, and wears glasses. On behalf of the national tourism institute, he writes glorious reviews of the national parks, although he has never seen one. Actually, he is an investigative journalist much more interested in the national politicians' crooked business deals and their corruption, as well as the country's environmental pollution. He writes devastating reports about it under several pseudonyms for press agencies around the globe. Should his cover ever be blown, his neighbour José would know how to let him disappear without a trace.

***

A light breeze blowing through the open window of Oscar's abode rustles the front page of yesterday's newspaper on a nearby table. Oscar glances at the headlines while putting on a tie. Having read the paper the night before, he is familiar with the news but still has to chuckle about the report concerning an old man who ran naked out into the street, danced, and sang sexually explicit songs after he had been given hash oil instead of his regular cough syrup.

Oscar takes a look in the mirror, adjusts his tie, pats his slicked back, curly black hair, and splashes some aftershave on his clean-shaven, heavy jowls. He puts on his jacket and looks down at himself - navy blue blazer, light grey slacks, sky blue shirt, red and blue diagonally striped tie - yes, he is ready to face the world. He shuts the window, picks up his rectangular business briefcase, steps out, and locks his abode.

The door in the posada's gate opens with a squeal and Oscar walks out onto the sidewalk.

He hesitates for a moment and checks the variety of his business cards he takes out of the breast pocket of his shirt. Satisfied, he puts them back and wants to proceed to the bus stop on the corner with Moravia's main drag when Bert, clad in a white cotton shirt, black leather bomber jacket, and blue jeans, steps out and lights a cigarette.

They acknowledge each other with a nod and Oscar says, "Bert, you shouldn't smoke so much. It'll kill you."

Bert shrugs. "Yeah, but only if my work doesn't kill me first."

Oscar nods and responds, "I know what you mean."

Bert smiles and asks, "Really? It wasn't you who sold the hash oil to the old guy who made the headlines in the papers?"

Oscar whispers, "Psst! Not so loud! If Doña Flora hears you, it won't be a rumour any longer. She will pass it on as a fact that I'm a drug dealer and the cops are gonna be up my ass like a pack of bloodhounds."

Bert pulls back his head and gives Oscar a doubtful look. "Is that a fact, eh? And why would that be?" he asks quietly.

Oscar looks bewildered, gropes for words and blurts out, "Pushing drugs is a scourge! It's illegal! A crime! That's why!"

Bert takes a puff, blows the smoke in Oscar's face, and grins. "No kidding. You realise you're givin' yourself away, bud?"

It's Oscar's turn to pull his head back. "What do you mean, I'm giving myself away?"

Bert answers quietly. "You said what every drug pusher says to deflect from his activities. The more they condemn the drug trade as illegal, the deeper they are involved in the business."

Oscar puffs up his cheeks. "If you know that much about the drug trade, you should tell me about it. Wanna join me for lunch?"

Bert pulls a face. "Where? At the Mercado Central? Forget it. I'm allergic to cockroaches paddling in my soup. But we could've a beer at the Salsa Palace tonight."

He turns when Oscar points his chin in the direction of the door and waves to José who leans in the frame. Bert acknowledges his presence with the words, "Mornin', José, up to no good as usual?"

José grins, nods, and gives a thumbs-up.

Bert slaps Oscar on the shoulder. "Take care, eh? I'll see you tonight."

He gets behind the steering wheel of a dented Mazda, starts the engine with the roar of its busted exhaust pipe, and takes off with squealing tires leaving behind a stinking cloud of bluish smoke.

Oscar walks to the bus stop, waits in line, and enters the rickety public bus. It is jam-packed. He squeezes into the standing room behind the driver's enclosure face to face with a young, buxom woman. Straight dark hair frames her pretty face. She wears a blouse with a plunging neckline and a wide skirt with side pockets. She looks up at him seemingly embarrassed every time the bus stops and flings her frontally against Oscar. He doesn't mind and innocently looks out the window. When it happens, he relishes the pressure of her large breasts on his belly and the touch of her warm hands on his sides in her struggle to maintain balance and composure. He can hardly wait for the next full stop of the bus that grinds to a halt about every hundred metres to his great delight.

She tries to squirm out of the tight enclosure in the last moment before the bus starts to move again. Oscar pats down his jacket in a flash and feels the empty pocket that contained his wallet. He holds the woman by her arm and pulls her back ever so gently but firmly. He looks at her and shakes his head. Without uttering a word, he slides his hand swiftly into a pocket of her skirt that turns out to be just a slit and his hand slips down the front of her panties where he retrieves his wallet and three more. A scream of protest gets stuck in her throat when he holds them close to her bosom. He leans forward and whispers in her ear. She nods and tears well up in her eyes. He stows his wallet back in its pocket, opens the others, takes out the banknotes, and drops the wallets under the driver's seat. He folds up the money and tucks it into her cleavage. He hands her a business card that shows his real name and address, pats her behind, and lets her get out at the next stop.

Oscar stays on the bus until it arrives at the Mercado Central, the central market terminal. He walks along the narrow streets to the White Horse Bar on Avenida Central. The barkeeper, a balding man in his fifties, invites him to sit down. He points out two Gringos and whistles sharply to draw their attention. Oscar opens his briefcase and puts a cough syrup bottle filled with hash oil and two inhalers containing twelve grammes of cocaine each on the bar. The two guys mosey on up to him. He hands one of them an inhaler who puts it up to his nose, sucks, and grimaces joyfully. The Gringos buy the two inhalers and the bottle, hand over four hundred and twenty dollars, and rush out. Oscar pushes a twenty-dollar bill to the barkeeper, salutes, and leaves as well.

He goes to a small jewellery store in a narrow side street. The saleswoman hands him a piece of paper. He reads the note, pays her a hundred dollars, and leaves the store in the direction of the Grand Hotel located next to the National Theatre.

He enters the hotel's Arcade Café, takes the note out of his pocket, reads it once more, looks up, and approaches a middle-aged couple sitting at a table in the corner. He greets them, introduces himself, and they invite him to sit down. He puts a leather pouch on the table, exchanges a few friendly words with a waitress, and orders a coffee. The tourist couple stares at the pouch. Oscar takes his time putting six spoons of sugar into his coffee and stirring leisurely. He takes a sip and then unties the string of the leather pouch to reveal cut emeralds of different sizes glittering in the sunshine. He pushes the open pouch across the table for the couple to take a closer look. He encourages them to pick up a precious stone each and hold them up to the sunlight.

The woman swoons and the man chuckles. The woman picks the biggest clunker and two smaller ones. The man picks two of identical cut and size and starts to negotiate with Oscar. They come to an agreement and shake hands. The man gets out his wallet and hands Oscar nine hundred dollars. Oscar pockets the money and gives the man his emerald dealer business card with fake name, business address, and telephone number. He stows the pouch in his briefcase, points to his watch, and bids farewell. He hurries back to the Mercado Central and disappears in the maze of stalls and restaurants.

Oscar sits down at a small table in the corner of a lunch bar. He orders a 'casada', a simple meal of boiled beef, rice, and three vegetables. While he waits for his lunch, he reads the events column 'Sucesos' in the newspaper 'La Nación'. He circles a small news item about the worldwide seizure of cocaine and tens of millions of drug dollars.

He ponders the reported news while he eats his meal and engages in some mental arithmetic. He shoves the plate aside, takes a clean sheet of paper from his briefcase, and writes down numbers. The first column concerns his take so far minus the material cost and bribes. He has cleared almost eight hundred dollars. That's not bad for a morning's work but he wants to make some more cash, jots down '4-I, 2-HO, Tunnel', indicating that he wants to pass by a disco called Tunnel to sell at least four inhalers and two bottles of hash oil, his wonder elixir that can be smoked, drunk, used as an additive in cookie and brownie dough, or, so the rumours have it, to fry pork sausages for the heavenly experience of getting a buzz and satisfying the munchies at the same time.

The second column is a calculation of the losses of five per cent of the global cocaine trade based on the information in the news item and the drug money lost to seizure and confiscation. He arrives at a loss of a staggering twenty-eight million dollars per month.

Oscar sighs and wonders how he could lay his hands on just ten per cent of the lost revenue. With so much dough he could buy his parents a decent home in Buenaventura on the Colombian Pacific coast, pay for his sisters' dowry, invest in a lucrative legal business, and retire.

He turns the sheet of paper over thinking about what just flashed through his mind - investing in a legal business, if he had the money. He doodles a bit and then starts to draw a chart. It takes several corrections before he is happy with the result. It is a plan to avoid the seizures of cocaine and the confiscation of the hard-earned money. He takes two more sheets of paper and an envelope from his briefcase and wipes some crumbs off the table with the back of his hand. He must forge the iron while it is hot, he thinks, and wants to write a letter to someone in power who can initiate changes to the way business is conducted at present. That person is Pablo Escobar in his opinion. Oscar wants to suggest a plan of letting the entire business disappear in a global network of legit businesses. But it turns out to be more difficult than he anticipated formulating a letter that shows respect for the big cheese. He chews on his pen for a while before he writes:

Boss, much esteemed Pablo Escobar,

With great concern I read almost daily the reports about the seizure of immense quantities of cocaine and millions and millions of dollars of your hard-earned money. I have given this problem some thought and developed a plan to solve it.

My plan involves the creation of a global network of

legal companies that would allow us to let our entire trade disappear into a fog of legality, assure the arrival of our goods at their destination, and transfer our earnings without a loss due to confiscation.

Also, the smuggling of cocaine as it is conducted at present with brutality instead of skill leads to conflict and bloodshed and should be changed. Again, I have some ideas how to do that. Please give me an opportunity to present my plans and discuss them with you.

With respectful greetings,

Oscar A. Ortiz A.

Oscar stuffs the letter into the envelope. He takes off his blazer, turns it inside out, puts it on again, and wears now a burgundy-red silk jacket. He changes the red and blue necktie for a yellow one. Then he gets a box of contact lenses out of his briefcase as well as some coke bottle glasses. He puts the contact lenses in and the glasses on and can see again.

In this changed getup he feels safe not to be recognised by his customers of 'emeralds' that are in fact cleverly cut green beer bottle shards.

He gets up, pays for his lunch, and leaves the market. Outside he hesitates and checks his watch. It is too early for a visit of the disco. He turns west and walks past the children's hospital until he reaches the small hotel 'Casa Azul' in a residential street. He enters the front yard of the hotel and greets the owner, a Colombian by the name of Carlos, who is busy pruning a bougainvillea bush. They shake hands and Oscar entrusts Carlos with his letter.

Oscar whispers, "Pablo Escobar."

Carlos looks critically at the sealed envelope, raises an eyebrow, sniggers when he gets a proper eyeful of Oscar's getup, and holds up two fingers. Oscar understands, gives Carlos two hundred dollars, and they shake hands again.

A moment later Oscar is walking away in an elated mood. It shows in the light and almost bouncing steps he takes.

***

At the end of his successful business day, Oscar affords himself a taxi ride from downtown to the shops near his home. He buys a fresh baguette from the baker and at the cold-cut counter of the butcher next door a pound of smoked ham, some sliced cheese, and butter, as well as a couple of 'salchichas', the spicy smoked pork sausages he loves to have as a snack.

Loaded down with his purchases, he enters the posada. Right behind the door sits Doña Flora on a stool and awaits his return.

Holding out her claw, she expects to get paid the rent. Having his hands full, he nods towards his abode trying to indicate that he will pay her later - but no such luck. She wags a finger under his nose and points to the floor. She expects to get paid here and now. Groaning with disgust, he puts down his briefcase, digs a wad of Colones, the national currency, out of a trouser pocket, and thumbs off the four hundred she demands.

Oscar trundles off to his digs. He wants to take a shower. But first he puts away the coke bottle glasses and contact lenses, locks his take of the day in the briefcase, and then makes himself a ham and cheese baguette.

After the snack, he closes the window curtain, switches on a lamp, gets undressed, and struts into the shower in his birthday suit.

He has barely rinsed off the soap when he hears a knock on the door. 'Oh shit,' he thinks, 'who could that be? I hope it's not Doña Flora, who noticed the Colones bills I passed her were counterfeit.'

He shouts, "One moment, please!" and rushes into the bedroom looking for a towel. He grabs the first one he finds, a small hand towel, and wraps it around his waist barely covering what he wants to have essentially covered.

Cautiously he opens the door a crack and to his immense surprise sees the pickpocket woman of this morning on his doorstep. He opens the door wide and says with a big grin, "Hello, flower of my soul. What a pleasant surprise it is to see you."

Although a bit grubby looking after her day's work on the busses, there is something about her that captivates him and stimulates his desire for her. Is it the look in her eyes that says, 'I am happy that you are happy to see me'? Is it her dishevelled appearance that says, 'I want to get out of these clothes'?

He holds the door open with his left hand, waves his right bidding her to come inside, and in his enthusiasm the towel drops to the floor.

A bit stunned seeing him in the altogether, she moseys past him while eyeballing his stirring groin. She enters the room with a peculiar grin on her face while he is picking up the towel and wrapping it around his hips.

"Sorry, so sorry," he mumbles. "That wasn't my intention at all. But believe me, I am over the moon seeing you."

"I've noticed," is her response. "You're very physical expressing your desires. This morning I thought you had a long banana in your pocket."

Oscar needs a moment to digest her remark. "Really? I didn't think it was that noticeable."

"Are you kidding?" she shoots back. "You're a couple of inches short of a baseball bat, I think."

"You think," replies Oscar in the spirit of her banter. "Uh-huh, you don't know the size of a baseball bat. Right?" She giggles and he says, "Have a seat. Please, sit down. Uh, I'll get dressed."

"You don't have to on my account," she retorts. "Just a bigger towel would do the trick."

He casts his visitor a surprised look. She is still standing when he disappears behind the curtain that separates the bedroom from what passes for living room and kitchenette. He takes a shirt and underwear from a chest of drawers when she asks, "May I take a shower, please? I feel so dirty after working on the buses."

"Yes, go ahead," he replies. "I'll get you a towel."

He drops shirt and underwear back in the drawer, wraps a bath towel around his hips, and picks another one that he hands her in the shower.

He notes her blouse, skirt, bra, and panties are dropped carelessly on the easy chair. Either she is very quick getting out of her clothes or got undressed before asking to take a shower.

He picks up her clothes, drapes them over the backrest of a chair at the table, and looks at her enormous pink bra. He picks it up and puts it with one cup on the back of his head. It's a snug fit. He looks in the mirror and raises a hand to bless an imaginary congregation. He smiles at himself and wonders if he could pass for a bishop if he cut the bra in half and removed the remaining straps. All he would need then is an ankle length plain white nightgown with long sleeves, a pink tunic, and pink shoes to complement the beanie.

He listens to her warbling in the shower and gathers her loot of the day of five wallets and a pile of banknotes lying on the easy chair. He puts it all on the table.

Obviously, she didn't follow his advice of taking the money out of the wallets and discarding them. He opens one wallet after another and looks for any identification of their owners.

The third wallet, stashed with a thick wad of US-dollars, almost gives him a heart attack. It belongs to Bernal 'El Burro' Villalobos with whom Oscar had a territorial dispute recently. It was thanks to José's presence that he escaped that altercation unscathed.

Oscar puts El Burro's wallet aside with the intention of using it as a bargaining chip for the next foreseeable quarrel with him. He takes the money out of the other four, tosses it on the table and the wallets in the garbage bin.

Then he opens his little fridge, takes out a bottle of rum and a couple of cans of soda, and places them and two glasses on a side-table next to the easy chair. He turns on his radio and twiddles with the dial to a station that broadcasts rhythmic salsa music.

The shower is turned off and a little while later the curtain is pulled back.

His visitor appears in all her jaw-dropping splendour with the towel wrapped around her head to dry her hair. Oscar is thunderstruck by the sight of the radiant smile on her almond shaped face, her enormous perky breasts, her flat belly, rounded hips, shaved pubes, strong legs, and ivory skin. It is a woman whose photo he would have expected to see in a porn magazine but never in real life.

She dances towards him to the rhythm of the music playing on the radio and looks more huggable with every step she takes.

He reaches out to her hand but then gives in to his urge, takes her in his arms, hugs her, kisses her neck and shoulder, lifts her off her feet, and warmly presses her against himself. She responds in kind, wraps her legs around his hips, and rips off his towel. She reaches down to feel his swelling appendage. Heat rises from her hot spot, and she says, "It's time to put your meat into my burrito."

She lowers herself to draw in his full length, moans with joy, moves up and down, and opens her eyes to look at Oscar's face. She stops her motions and snickers.

"Monsignor, do you service all your nuns like this?" she asks unable to contain her amusement.

Seeing her laughing face and wondering why she calls him 'Monsignor', a thought flashes through his mind: 'A woman bursting with laughter during copulation normally kills a man's performance instantly as it raises his level of insecurity resulting in the immediate withdrawal of his endowment and the shutdown of all operations due to a sudden flaccidity of the workforce.' Yet, his joystick indicates no let-up in its function.

When she reaches up to adjust the beanie, he understands what she meant by addressing him with the title reserved for religious dignitaries. He laughs with her and wonders about the strange phenomenon of the most congenial encounter of a man and a woman being usually accompanied by miserable facial expressions similar to singers who kvetch about the greatest love of their life with a grimace that hints at a severe case of stomach cramps or painful haemorrhoids.

"No, you are my first and only nun," he replies, takes a couple of steps to the easy chair, and sits down with her squatting in his lap.

She grumbles, "These armrests are hard. They hurt my shins."

Having her behind firmly in hand, he carries her to the table, clears it with one swipe, lays her down and asks, "Is that more comfortable?"

She sighs. "Oh yes, very comfy. You don't mind standing up?"

"Not at all," he replies, "gives me more room for movement. May I demonstrate?"

"Oh yes, please," she shouts in response and clutches the edges of the tabletop to keep up with the quickened rhythm.

A bit out of breath he asks, "What is your name, sister?"

"My name is Silvia Robles, Monsignor. What is yours again?" she asks and puts his hands on her breasts.

He starts to massage her melons and replies, "My name is Oscar Antonio Ortiz Acosta, Sister Silvia."

She sniggers. "I've noticed by your accent that you're not a local boy. Where are you from, Oscar?"

"I'm from Colombia," he replies and adds, "I've noticed that you shaved your pubes, Silvia. Any particular reason?"

"Yes, after I had a bikini wax, it looked down there like our president on a bad hair day. So, I removed it all. You have a problem with that?"

"Removing the look of the president on a bad hair day? No, not at all. I like it."

"You do? Good!" Silvia takes the bra off his head and flings it away. "You don't need that anymore."

"Neither do you."

"Oh yes, I do. My puppies are just too big to be let loose. They could knock me out cold if I ran after a bus. That's why I wear that contraption. Do you think they are too big?"

"No way! A woman's boobs can't be big enough for me."

"That's too bad," she mutters breathlessly.

"What do you mean?" he asks.

"If boobs can't be big enough for you, I can't introduce you to my mother," she answers with a smirk. "She's a horny old slut and has much bigger ones than me."

"Sounds intriguing," mumbles Oscar. "When did you say I could meet her?"

Silvia's shouts of protest and his exuberant laughter are audible well beyond the walls of the abode. But they don't have a care in the world and enjoy their encounter. So what, thinks Oscar, if his immediate neighbours put a glass to the wall to listen and shave their carrot to the rhythm of the creaking table.

***

After three Kama Sutra sessions on the table, Oscar carries Silvia to his bed in a state of exhaustion. He plunks himself down next to her. She fiddles with his assets in the hope of getting him going.

"Give me a break," he pants. "You've had three orgasms. Isn't that enough for a start?"

"Three isn't bad," she replies. "But ten is such a nice round number."

"You are insatiable," he mumbles. "Let me recover and then we carry on. Okay?"

With his left arm around her shoulders and holding her close, he dozes off. A short while later she moves his arm and gets up. She goes to the bathroom, washes herself, and puts some oil from a little bottle on her tender parts. She wonders about its sticky quality and earthy smell but is pleased with its arousing effect.

She moves cautiously, silently to his wardrobe and goes through all the pockets. When she doesn't find anything of interest or value, she looks around and eyes Oscar's briefcase and the bedside table. On the kitchen counter she finds a knife with a sturdy blade. She tries to open the briefcase, but the number locks are securely shut. The bedside table appears to be a different matter. She squats in front of it and inspects the door. It looks easy to pry open. Carefully she inserts the blade into the narrow space between door and frame and wants to force the door open, but the frame won't budge.

Oscar is still dozing. He moves his left arm in search of that cuddly companion who kept him warm. He squints and sees Silvia with the knife in her hand. In a daze and panic stricken, he flings his arm at her, grabs her wrist, and shakes it until the knife clatters to the floor. Silvia struggles to get out of his grip, but he holds on and pulls her on top of him.

"What the devil are you doing?" he asks and holds her tight.

"Ow, ow, ow," she wails, "You're squeezing my tits."

Unimpressed, he gives her barely enough room to move a bit but continues to hold her firmly. "You wanna rob me?"

"No, no, no," she whines. "I'm sorry. I don't know who you are or what you do."

"Horseshit," he cuts her off, "if you want to know who I am and what I do, just ask. Crawling around my bed with a sharp knife in your hand looks more like you want to kill me."

"No, Oscar, no," she wails and tries to wriggle out of his hold.

"Calm down," he says firmly. "I'm not angry, just surprised."

"Let me go, please," she begs. "I don't want to rob or hurt you. Please, believe me."

He scoffs at her feeble assurance and mulls over what she does for a living - picking other peoples' pockets, stealing wallets. Why shouldn't she try it with him? A leopard can't change its spots.

His initial craving for her satisfied, he looks at her without the rose-coloured glasses of sexual desire. She is obviously not the perfect woman he assumed her to be when she first stepped out of the shower.

He loosens his grip on her and is taken aback by what she says next with a muffled voice.

"Punish me."

"What? Punish you? What do you mean?"

"Hit me or do whatever you want."

"Hit you? Are you nuts? I've never hit a woman in my life. I think you're just trying to distract me from finding out why you crawled around the bed with a knife in your hand."

She looks at him with dewy eyes. "I've been a bad girl."

Oscar feels a chuckle rising in his throat. "How old are you?"

"Twenty-two."

"Uh-huh, and at the age of a grown woman you call yourself a bad girl," says Oscar with the chuckle bursting out. "What is it with women even at an advanced age referring to themselves as girls?"

He needs a moment for his amusement to subside and carries on in a serious vein, "Listen, no more trying to weasel out of answering what you were doing with that knife."

Silvia sits up and says in an accusatory tone of voice, "When I don't get enough orgasms, I do stupid things sometimes."

It is Oscar's turn to sit up. Bemused, he points a finger at his chest. "Oh, I see! It's my fault! Do you kill every fucker who doesn't give you the satisfaction you feel you deserve? Or do you just rob them blind before you piss off?"

In the silence that follows, her eyes shift about with a far-away look. Not expecting to get answers, he gets up, pours two drinks, and hands her a Cuba libre. She takes a sip and reaches for his hand. "It was a stupid mistake to poke around," she says with a little voice and tears in her eyes. "I'm sorry. Can we start over?"

Oscar sighs and sits down next to her. She appears to be aglow in the dim light of the lamp in the living room and looks again as desirable as she did when she stepped out of the shower.

He ponders the fact that she is a little criminal, but then, so is he. He asks himself if he should adhere to the little criminals' code of honour, trust her, and be completely honest with her about his work or just off-load a pack of lies and pretend to be what he never was and never will be.

He puts a hand around her hips, pulls her a little closer, gives her a kiss, and decides to stick to the code of honour by telling her everything about himself.

***

In the course of the night, Silvia and Oscar tell each other their life stories. Thus, he finds out that Silvia is from a small town in the central valley.

Her father is a pickpocket who taught her his tricks to follow in his footsteps. Her mother, the local tart available for a leg-over to anyone willing to pay the demanded price, took Silvia out of school with the argument that a woman doesn't need an education beyond the basics of reading, writing and minimal arithmetic to avoid getting ripped off by her johns. She suggested work in a brothel to her and wanted to teach her all the tricks of groaning and moaning and pretending to have an orgasm. But Silvia had other ideas. She wanted to go back to school and ran away from home when her mother wanted to rent her out to a disgusting john.

Stranded in San José without money, she was abhorred by the idea of working in a brothel, remembered the tricks her father had taught her, and started picking pockets. She did well for herself in her chosen profession but not at all well in her relationships with men. Her life so far had been a ride on a rollercoaster with no certainty of a secure future.

Oscar gives Silvia the lowdown of his life and even mentions the plan he had formulated in a letter to a big cheese. He tells her that he is full of hope of having his big break in the near future. It would provide him with enough moola to buy a hotel somewhere in the Caribbean and live the good life away from the drug trade.

As a result of their conversations, he recognises that Silvia is not just a pretty face. He suggests she stop working on the busses and instead become his assistant. He would forego his most profitable day of the week to show her how to fill inhalers with cocaine and replace cough syrup with hash oil in the little bottles.

Silvia is intrigued by his offer. She is certain that Oscar is not the kind of guy who would ask her to become a prostitute to support his bad habits, as all the other guys in her life had demanded once they found out that they couldn't satisfy her sexual appetite. She looks back at her life, figures that she has nothing to lose, and agrees to stay and work with him.

2

Pablo Escobar tosses a baseball up and whacks it with a bat into a large flexible screen on the far side of the large office in his Hacienda Nápoles in Antioquia, Colombia. A TV-screen to the left flashes 'Homerun!!!' Pablo dances with joy and punches a clenched fist into the air.

His lieutenant, Juan Diego Arcila Henao, opens the glass-panelled door and steps into the office. He holds a copy of the Miami Herald dated 21st September 1989, as well as Oscar's mugshot and his handwritten letter. Pablo grabs the newspaper. He reads the headlines, "Major Blow Against Drug Cartel" and looks up angrily. Juan hands him Oscar's letter. Pablo reads it and gets even angrier. He shouts at Juan while tapping the marble top of a large desk with the baseball bat, "Who is this son of a bitch? Does he think he can run my business, the sack of shit?"

"Calm down, Pablo, calm down. This, uh, Oscar doesn't want to run your business. He's merely suggesting..."

Pablo cuts him off sharply. "Shut up! Who is this Oscar?"

Juan looks at his boss. "As far as I can determine, he is a small-time dealer in Costa Rica."

Pablo is surprised. "Costa Rica? The motherfucker is a Tico?"

Juan shakes his head, "No, Pablo, he is a Cimarrón from Buenaventura, here in Colombia."

"Cimarrón?" asks Pablo with a crooked smile. "Really? Got a photo of this feral dog?"

Juan hands him the letter size photo. "Yes, here. I found it in the police files. It was taken about six years ago."

Pablo looks at the unflattering mugshot of Oscar printed on paper, places it on the desk, and taps it with his bat. "Oscar, eh?"

He brings the bat down with considerable force. A chunk breaks out of the marble tabletop and the photo flutters away.

Pablo rages and lashes out at the fluttering photo, "I'm gonna kill you, you sack of shit! Kill you!"

Without much luck, Pablo continues lashing out at the photo floating through the air. Juan bobs down to escape the swinging bat, grabs the letter, and leaves the office in a waddling duck walk.

Two hours later, Pablo calls Juan back. Sitting at the repaired desk, Pablo wants to know what happened to the letter.

"I filed it," is Juan's short response.

"Good, keep it handy. I want all lieutenants to read it. They will agree that a guy with highfalutin ideas about running our business is more dangerous than ostentatious street dealers, freelance middlemen and pushers, or Mexican mules."

"I don't follow," mutters Juan.

"Look, Juan, it's obvious," explains Pablo in a magnanimous mood. "We get over ninety five percent of our product to market and retrieve over ninety six percent of our earnings. That is an outstanding result in comparison to any other business. Of course, it is annoying to read that a quantity of our product was seized or that a cache of cash was confiscated. But remember that all the seized drugs worldwide are never more than five percent of what is consumed in any given country. A street dealer or that greedy stewardess, what was her name again, Mary Roseann, uh, whatever, who got caught in L.A. last week with a suitcase full of cocaine, they don't know how we run our business. When caught they can't tell the authorities anything beyond their own activities."

He pauses briefly and wags a finger as a warning, "But a guy like this Oscar who has worked out a plan to improve our business, just imagine he gets caught and spills the beans. It could blow the lid off our entire operation! And one more point, Juan. He could be working for the boys in Calí, our biggest competitors, and try to damage our organisation with a diversionary plan. Think about it."

"I see, yes, I understand now. Thanks for bearing with me and explaining it."

"You're welcome, Juan."

Pablo claps his hands and orders the servant entering the office to bring them coffee and mineral water.

Once he has a sip of the brew, he looks more relaxed, and instructs Juan, "Now that you understand the letter's implication, you will understand that you have to have this Oscar dispatched. And do it without delay. Okay?"

Juan finishes his coffee and gets up to leave. "Of course, Pablo. I'll get on it right away."

"Excellent," responds Pablo. "I know I can rely on you."

3

Oscar is a happy man after having spent almost three weeks with Silvia. Also, he has come to trust her explicitly. She is punctilious in cleaning out the inhalers and filling them with exactly twelve grammes of cocaine, draining and refilling small cough syrup bottles with hash oil, and selling them to a new clientele.

She is very honest with the money accounting for every centavo she has earned. In turn, Oscar encourages her to have a makeover including a facial and a hairdo of her choice. He bought her a complete professional wardrobe and expensive jewellery that allow her to enter the upscale places of San José without hindrance or raising suspicion. Consequently, she brings home tons of cash and starts pestering Oscar about moving to a nicer place and buying a house.

In anticipation of a positive response to his letter to Pablo Escobar, he asks her to be patient. He assures her that an upcoming deal would lift them right into the realm of the upper class of society or even allow them to move to a country of their choice and realise his dream of owning and running a hotel.

Wednesday, 4th October 1989, is Oscar's big day. He received Escobar's response from Carlos and one half of a 500 Colombian Peso Oro banknote that was torn to serve as an identifier.

In the morning Silvia kisses him farewell and wishes him good luck. Knowing that he is on his way to the Caribbean port city of Limón and will have to rely on the assistance of his neighbour José, a guy she wouldn't trust as far as she could throw him, she gathers their money, cocaine, and hash oil, and puts the goods into two briefcases.

She is ready to be on her way to the bank and stash them in his safe deposit box.

***

It is late afternoon when Oscar walks past the Parque Vargas in Limón. On the wrought-iron fence around the park sit black chicken vultures waiting to rummage the piles of garbage the ambulant vendors leave behind after cleaning out their stalls. The street is clogged with smoke-belching trucks and busses. Oscar holds a white handkerchief over mouth and nose while he approaches a café near the corner of the park.

José sits at a small table by the sidewalk. Oscar taps him on the shoulder, sits down, and places an order of coffee and mineral water with a young waitress. José rubs the crescent shaped scar in his face and throws his hands up in a questioning gesture. Oscar checks his watch, peers along the road towards the fishing harbour and signals José to be patient. The waitress places his order in front of him. He pays and gives her a generous tip. She appreciates it and does a little dance down the aisle looking back at him with a big smile.

Oscar has barely taken a sip of coffee when a grizzled, old man in baggy trousers arrives and tips his grimy cap. It is the craggy-faced, barefoot captain of a fishing boat, Arturo Aquije.

"Oscar? José? How are you?" he greets them.

Oscar pulls up a chair. "You are Arturo? Please, sit down."

Arturo declines the invitation to have a seat and puts half a banknote on the table. It is the other half of the 500 Colombian Peso Oro Oscar takes out of his wallet and lays next to it. The two halves are a perfect match along the jagged edges of the tear. It identifies Oscar as the legitimate partner.

Arturo and Oscar exchange envelopes. Arturo rips his open and thumbs a wad of cash. Oscar takes a crudely drawn map out of his and passes the envelope to José who dips his little finger into it. He licks off a powdery substance and nods approvingly.

Oscar shakes hands with Arturo who whispers, "Tomorrow morning at five, okay?"

Oscar nods and Arturo waves to the driver of a pickup that has a fish tank mounted on its back. The brand new, white truck pulls up at the curb. The driver gets out and walks away. José clambers onto the fish tank, opens a flap, checks the water level, and gives a thumbs-up. Arturo tips his cap, turns, and walks away towards the fishing harbour.

***

At 4:00 a.m. on Thursday, 5th October 1989, José and Oscar barrel along a dusty road in the pickup on their way to Cahuita, a small tourist resort. They stop on the beach of the bay near some cabins and a small shop, the pulpería that is still shuttered at 5:00 a.m.

José changes into swim trunks, puts on flippers, diving mask, and snorkel. He waddles into the water and swims to a buoy bobbing on the waves of the calm sea.

He dives around the buoy and comes up empty. He waves to Oscar indicating that he will take another dive a bit further out. A moment later, he resurfaces and holds the end of a rope. He swims back to shore pulling the rope.

On the beach, Oscar and José pull a net full of fish onto shore. Among the wriggling fish are ten rectangular, plastic wrapped parcels. The two men pull the net to the truck. José climbs up, mounts a winch on top of the tank, lifts the net, and dumps its contents into the tank. He recovers the parcels and Oscar stashes them in a travel bag that he puts behind the driver's seat. Their job done, they high-five each other and José changes back into his street clothes.

All the while throughout their activity, an old man in checker shirt, baggy trousers, and straw-hat leans against the wall of the pulpería and watches them. José spots him, gets out a cigarette, and pats his pockets looking for a lighter. He comes up empty and looks to the old man. The old man smiles, nods, and holds up a box of matches. José conceals a razor-sharp knife for gutting fish in the right sleeve of his shirt and goes over to him. The old man steps out of sight into the wind shadow of the shop and lights José's cigarette. Once he has taken a puff, José slashes the old man's throat and kills him instantly. He dumps the corpse behind the shop. On the old man's checker shirt, he wipes the knife clean, and holding it by its sharp point with his fingertips he walks back to the pickup truck.

Unawares of what has been going on, Oscar takes the knife by the handle when José asks him to stash it. They get into the truck and drive off, leaving behind a huge cloud of dust.

Back in Limón, José and Oscar stop on Avenida 2 where Arturo's driver is already waiting for their return. Oscar takes his belongings and the travel bag out of the pickup and walks into a hotel across the road. José puts his murder weapon, the knife, into a plastic bag, hides it among his belongings, and follows Oscar.

Shortly after lunch, Oscar and José leave the hotel dressed in suits. They carry small suitcases and the travel bag, walk to a compact rental car, pack their luggage into the trunk, and depart on the highway to San José.

***

It is already dark in the early evening when a checkpoint is set up with police cruisers across the main street into Moravia. A young Rapid Reaction Force officer, Miguel Arías sits in one of the cruisers next to Alfredo Calderón, Costa Rica's major drug baron. They have a lively discussion about their favourite football teams.

Miguel holds a photo of Oscar. It is identical to the one Pablo Escobar tried to hit with a baseball bat.

Miguel looks at every driver and passenger in the cars that are stopped and checked. When he recognises Oscar in a car with José at the wheel, he whistles sharply to draw the policemen's attention and points at the car.

In a flurry of action, the policemen drag Oscar and José out of the car and handcuff them. The trunk is opened, the suitcases are tossed out, and the travel bag is ripped open. Swim gear flies onto the street and a policeman holds one of the plastic wrapped parcels triumphantly up in the air.

Oscar is pushed into the back of the police cruiser to sit next to Alfredo who gives him a disparaging look.

Oscar looks down at the black rubber mat on the floor, but he might as well stare into an abyss. He can't quite figure out what went wrong and why the biggest drug pusher, a wholesaler, is sitting next to him all smug and superior looking.

Why isn't that guy Calderón under arrest? Does he have the protection of the police and the Rapid Reaction Force? If so, why? Who is behind the set-up? The questions drive Oscar nuts. He has no answers but is certain that his arrest is the beginning of a descent into hell.

4

The Colombian TV station Canal 6 counts on a massive public interest in the round table discussion 'Diálogo del Día' presented by the hard-hitting investigative journalist Julio Betancourt as part of the current news program 'Noticias Corrientes'.

That applies on Tuesday, 10th October 1989, as well when Julio's guests are Senator Benito Uribe of the governing party and General Adolfo Fernández of the national security forces and commander of a paramilitary organisation known as a death squad.

The dialogue is well advanced. Uribe squirms and pulls on his collar while Fernández tries to demonstrate resolve with a grim expression and hammering his fist on the table.

He shouts, "... and we will crush Escobar and his vermin. We will defoliate coca plantations and destroy them. We will find and burn coca labs and fight Escobar's killers to the death. We will hunt Escobar down and deliver him to the United States where he can rot in prison for the rest of his life. That's what we're going to do. Yes, Sir!"

Betancourt gives him a sardonic smile. "In short, General, you follow the same strategy you claim to follow since 1975 - without success, I may add. You want to destroy coca plantations in Colombia although there are none that are suitable for producing cocaine. Of the nineteen species of coca plants only three produce the cocaine alkaloid. None of these three species grow in Colombia. Coca paste for the production of cocaine is imported from Bolivia and Peru."

Uribe butts in, "Nonsense! We have proof of massive coca plantations in the south that were destroyed with a defoliation agent."

Betancourt sneers at the senator and holds up a report. "Sorry, Senator, but this report by an independent investigative body provides evidence that our American friends only destroyed food crops. They sprayed the internationally condemned and banned defoliate Agent Orange. Witness statements confirm that it resulted in death and suffering of the rural population and livestock in the affected areas."

Fernández barks, "Witness statements? Don't make me laugh! I demand the names of those witnesses and will deal with them."

Betancourt looks scornfully. "Yes, of course, General. You want to arrest and interrogate those witnesses, force them to retract their statements, and make their lives utter misery. But allow me to point out that the witnesses are farmers who suffer a fate worse than death already."

Uribe, having regained some of his normal pompousness, speaks out. "Sorry, Julio, but you are walking a very fine line here. You are defending vermin and assassins that are on Escobar's payroll, as you should know."

Betancourt responds quite incensed. "Vermin, Senator? The people you call vermin are hard-working citizens of Colombia. You and the General have the obligation to protect and support them and not to accuse them of collaboration with Escobar for which you don't have a shred of evidence. But on another topic, General, let's talk about your drug war. Do you follow the directives of the United States government or the dictate of Colombia's 'Mil Familias'?"

Uribe looks rattled and asks, "Mil Familias?"

Betancourt smiles and explains, "Yes, Senator, the families better known as the 'Mil Familias' to which you and your family belong. It is the one percent of Colombians who own ninety-five percent of the country and want to lay their hands on the billions of dollars Escobar and the Ochoa brothers are alleged to have accumulated!"

Uribe's blood pressure rises visibly when he shouts just the one word, "What!?!"

Betancourt continues with a smile, "Please, Senator, don't pretend to be surprised. It is a well-established fact that the drug war is not about drugs. It is all about money, that is, the money the 'Mil Familias' claim as their share of the drug money."

Fernández interjects, "You better have some solid evidence for that ridiculous claim, or you may face a very long time in prison."

Betancourt's contemptuous look is actually enough of a reply, but he says, "I am deeply touched by your concern for my personal well-being, General, although you seem to forget that I am an investigative journalist. I would never dare to say or claim something that I could not back up with facts and the solid evidence my research yielded. Permit me to refresh your memory with a morsel of Colombia's recent past and remind you of the meetings in Puerto Boyacá at the end of 1981 in which you, General, as well as you, Senator Uribe, participated. These meetings of the Colombian legislature, the Colombian military, and the Medellín cartel served the purpose of forming the paramilitary organisation MAS, 'Muerte a Secuestradores', that was supposed to hunt down and kill kidnappers. The Medellín cartel, your partner in these meetings, was founded by Pablo Escobar and the Ochoa brothers in response to the kidnapping of the Ochoa brothers' sister, Martha Nieves Ochoa Vásquez. You knew at the time of the meetings that the Medellín cartel had accumulated billions of drug money dollars and you saw your chance to extract a fair share of the loot via the formation of MAS that was financed by Escobar and the Ochoas.

"Once MAS was established, you diverted millions of dollars into your pockets with Escobar's tacit agreement. In the course of your personal enrichment with drug money and by some fantastic coincidence, Pablo Escobar was elected as an alternate member to the Chamber of Representatives for the Liberal Party. He was sent as the official representative of our government to the swearing-in ceremony of the elected prime minister of Spain, Felipe González, in December 1982. Are you going to deny these facts, or do I have to show you copies of official documents and your bank records?"

Uribe looks ready to faint and pulls again on his collar. Fernández clenches his fist, points a finger at Julio Betancourt and barks, "That is a most outrageous pack of lies! You are on Escobar's payroll, aren't you?"

Uribe gets up, sways and states, "This interview is over!"

Julio Betancourt chuckles. "I'll say!"

The sound is switched off when the general and senator shake their fists at Betancourt and curse him before they leave the studio.

Rushing along the hallway to the exit of the broadcast building, Uribe asks Fernández in a low voice, "What are we going to do? How did he get a hold of secret government documents and my bank records?"

"Don't worry," replies Fernández. "I will take care of him."

Shortly after the news broadcast, Julio receives a phone call from his source in the Senate. He is congratulated for blowing the lid off the government and military's collaboration with the Medellín cartel. He is invited to come to the Senate the next day to discuss further revelations.

***

In the early afternoon of Wednesday, 11th October 1989, a black Audi sedan is parked in a no stopping zone on Calle 9 near the intersection with Carrera 7 in the vicinity of the Senate of Colombia building in Bogotá.

A white notice board behind the windshield proclaiming 'TV - Canal 6 - Noticias' does not impress a traffic warden, a young woman in uniform. With a foot on the bumper, she gets out a pad and a pen and writes a ticket.

Julio can see her from afar and risks his life rushing through the traffic on Calle 9 to reach the warden in time. The meeting with his confidential source took much longer than he had anticipated. He greets the warden courteously and shows her his press pass. She points to the no stopping zone sign. He tries to charm her by asking why a pretty young woman like her would be working as a traffic warden when she should be on TV. He gives her his business card. She tucks it into a breast pocket and gives him his ticket. Resigned to the fate of having another ticket in his collection in the glove compartment, he gets into the car and turns down the window. She leans with a hand on the roof of the car and continues their chat. Both enjoy the exchange while Julio puts the key in the ignition lock and starts the engine.

A massive explosion rips the car apart and kills Julio Betancourt and the traffic warden instantly. A dense shower of glass shards, mortar, and metal frames from nearby buildings rains down on dead and severely injured pedestrians including men, women, and children on the sidewalk and in the street.

***

The patrons of a café in the centre of Bogotá sip refreshments while they chat or watch the soap opera on a TV-set above the counter. Suddenly the screen turns black and breaking news are announced in white letters on a red background.

An appropriately sorrowful looking announcer appears on the screen. "Ladies and gentlemen, it is my tragic duty to inform you of the death of our colleague Julio Betancourt. He was assassinated with a car bomb in the vicinity of the Senate building an hour ago. Eighteen dead and over sixty injured, pregnant women and children among them, is the deplorable result of this heinous attack. We have a first reaction from General Adolfo Fernández of the Colombian Security Forces."

After a brief flicker, the general's mug appears on the screen. "Citizens of Colombia, this horrendous act of violence is proof that the killers of Escobar's drug cartel know no limits in their murderous pursuits and have no mercy for the good people of

Colombia. I am particularly distressed by Julio Betancourt falling victim to this dastardly crime."

He swabs his eyes pretending to wipe away a crocodile tear and continues, "He was a fine investigative journalist. I respected and greatly admired him for his courage. It is now our duty to avenge the death and suffering of all victims by crushing Escobar and his killers."

Fernández slams a fist into his open hand to underscore his statement. Some of the café patrons express their doubts about the veracity of the General's claims. They know that Escobar had no reason whatsoever to kill Betancourt and very likely had nothing to do with the car bomb attack and assassination.

Other patrons don't seem to care about the general's claim, are simply overcome by genuine grief for the victims of yet another car bomb and worry about the drug war their beautiful country has to suffer. They wipe away tears and blow their noses.

A photo of a smiling Julio Betancourt appears on the screen. The announcer's voice narrates, "Julio Betancourt, our esteemed colleague of the past eight years, dead at age thirty-six. He is survived by his widow and three children. We will observe a moment of silence before we return to our regular program."

After ten seconds of silence, Bach's 'Ascension Oratorio' drones out of the loudspeaker, fades together with Julio's smiling face after forty seconds and the soap opera continues.

5

Oscar and José sit in the dock of a court in San José facing Judge Juan Cordero on Thursday, 14th December 1989 at 11:30 a.m. Evidence is piled on a table to the right of the judge. It includes ten parcels of plastic wrapped cocaine, some cash, swim gear, and the knife that has Oscar's finger and palm prints on the handle. It was used as the weapon in the heinous murder of an old man, a life-long resident of Cahuita. It has been concluded that José León, a day labourer of limited mental capacity, was inveigled by Oscar Ortiz, a highly intelligent and ruthless character, into participating in a drug deal gone sideways but had nothing to do with the capital crime. The proceedings are about to conclude with Oscar's defence attorney Jorge Bolaños, a man in his thirties with tussled hair and wearing a crumpled suit, delivering his final statement on behalf of his client.

Not a trace of drug dealing activity was found in Oscar's abode, he says and adds that his client has no criminal record. His character profile states that he is a peaceful man incapable of committing a capital crime. Bolaños concludes his plea for mercy, walks back to his client, and shrugs.

The prosecutor Antonio Arías, whose brother Miguel sits behind him, snorts at the defence attorney's assertions. He listens to his brother, who hands him a note on a small piece of paper.

Judge Cordero clears his throat. "Very well, the defence rests its case. Is there anything the prosecutor wishes to add before I pronounce sentence?"

The prosecutor rises and points at Miguel. "Your honour, Miguel Arías, a witness and government employee in the security sector, has received information in reference to this case, a matter of national security. He wishes to approach the bench."

Cordero nods, waves his hand, and Miguel approaches. He hands the judge the note, '20 years, $100,000'. Cordero rejects the note and hands it back. Miguel scribbles '25 to life, $250,000' and passes the note to the judge. Cordero nods and puts the note into his file. Miguel returns to his seat.

Bolaños gets up, raises a hand, and demands to be heard.

"Your honour," he says deferentially, "The defence wishes to review that information and have it entered in the court records."

Cordero has nothing of it. "Señor Bolaños, you may not review the information, or have it entered in the court records. It is a matter of national security and, therefore, it has to stay off the record."

Bolaños persists, "Your honour, it is highly irregular that information allegedly referring to the accused is presented just before sentencing. My client has the constitutional right to be informed in matters that may affect his sentence negatively and speak in his own defence regarding that information."

Cordero gives the defence attorney a stern look. "Señor Bolaños, citing your client's constitutional rights is correct. However, in a matter of national security these rights are suspended, as you know very well. However, on condition that you will keep the information secret and won't reveal it to anyone in public or private, I will let you review it."

Bolaños approaches the bench and reads the judge's note, 'Life for your client / $50,000, a new suit and a decent haircut for you'.

The defence lawyer gives the smiling judge a bug-eyed look, shrugs, and returns to his seat.

Judge Cordero clears his throat and drones on about going to pronounce sentence. He lists once more the skimpy evidence, including the rigged knife, describes José as a poor misguided soul who became quite innocently an accessory to a crime, and sentences him to three years in prison less time served with a chance for parole. Oscar on the other hand he describes as a monster hiding behind a meek, peaceful exterior. He is the ruthless murderer of an innocent bystander who happened to have observed the smuggling activity. Without providing any evidence, the judge claims that Oscar smuggled vast amounts of illicit drugs into the country for the purpose of distribution and sale to children on school grounds. He sentences Oscar to life imprisonment without parole and brings down his gavel. Thus, the proceedings come to an end, the case is closed, and the courtroom is cleared.

Oscar and José are shackled, handcuffed, and dragged out. Just before they leave the courtroom, Oscar looks back and sees Bert waving to him from the public gallery.

Bailiffs are packing the evidence into cardboard boxes and carry them outside where Miguel Arías is waiting for them. He takes care of the box with ten kilogrammes of cocaine, tells the bailiffs to wait, goes into a small office, and slams the door shut.

Alfredo Calderón sits on the desk. His hand rests on a blue travel bag with ten packs of plastic wrapped baby powder. He exchanges the cocaine for the identical packs of powder and hands Miguel a bundle of one-hundred-dollar bills.

Miguel returns the box with baby powder to a bailiff who carries it dutifully to the evidence lockup.

***

Meanwhile, Bert presents his press pass to an officer of the guard of the court. He states his wish to interview the prisoner Oscar Ortiz, a convicted murderer and drug dealer for a report of Costa Rica's criminal justice system. The officer suggests he interview Oscar in the high security prison Cárcel de Guadalupe tomorrow morning, but Bert argues that it is practically impossible for the press to get a visitor's pass. The officer scratches his head and his nuts, accepts the one-hundred-dollar bill Bert offers him, waves, and marches ahead of Bert to the holding cells in the basement. He gives Bert fifteen minutes.

Oscar cowers in a corner of his cell and rocks to and fro. When he sees Bert enter, he quickly wipes away tears with the sleeve of his shirt and gets up. Before they sit down together, Bert looks around and checks the walls. He spots a small microphone in a crevice, takes the chewing gum out of his mouth, and plasters it over the listening device. He conducts the chat with Oscar in a subdued tone of voice.

"How the fuck did all this come about, Oscar?" asks Bert in his opening salvo. "I suspected you were a cocaine pusher - but a murderer? I just don't see that."

Oscar nods. "I'm not a murderer, Bert. I can't kill anything, and I haven't. I have no idea who the victim was. I never even saw anyone getting killed in Cahuita."

"Hmm, but you did the drugs, right?" asks Bert and when Oscar nods, he adds, "Did you always get the coke in Cahuita?"

"Uh-uh, no," responds Oscar. "It was a new route based on information I received from Colombia. I thought it was going to be my big break. Instead, it was a big mistake. I should've stayed with my approach of dealing with the local wholesaler and pay the premium he demands."

"So, what was that information from Colombia that inspired you to change course?" asks Bert.

"It was a setup. When I think about it now, I should've become suspicious and not take the bait."

"What do you mean?" asks Bert. "Come on, give me the details."

"Well, it started with a news item about the losses of the drug trade. I had worked out a plan to prevent the losses and wrote a letter to Pablo Escobar."

"What?" Bert looks exasperated. "You wrote a letter to Escobar telling him how to run his business? Are you nuts?"

"No! I didn't tell him how to run his business. It was a plan to prevent the losses and I wanted to discuss it with him. That's all."

"Cheese-whizz, Oscar. You're some naïve klutz! I bet that Escobar took it the wrong way and figured that a dealer like you wanted to meddle in his business model. So, instead of an invitation to discuss your plan, what did you get?"

Oscar looks embarrassed and stares at the floor. "My contact gave me the message that Pablo was grateful and sent me ten kilogrammes of cocaine as a sign of his appreciation. I was given a 500 Colombian Peso Oro banknote torn in half that would match the other half the delivery guy presented. It was the identification that I was the legitimate recipient of the coke."

Bert lets out a groan listening to Oscar. "And your greed dictated to switch off your instincts and your brain and go for it." After a brief pause, he continues with a pressed voice, "Man, how could you? You expected to get an invitation! How could you fall for an offer that was ruse? Shit! How many years have you been in the trade? I'm not and I wouldn't have stumbled into that trap!"

Oscar props his head into a hand. "Yes, I was impetuous, but I was also under pressure from Silvia who bugged me constantly to move out of the posada and buy a house."

Bert rejects that remark waving his hand. "Come on, Oscar, leave Silvia out of your equation. She turned out to be quite the smart cookie." He lowers his voice and whispers, "When you and José didn't return that night in October, she smelled a rat and cleared out your abode of everything pointing to you being a drug dealer. She came knocking on my door and asked for help. Together we moved everything into my place except a few clothes and a box of legit cough syrup. We even exchanged your locked bedside table for mine. Then she broke into José's room and came back with a bag full of knives, two silenced guns and his badge of the Rapid Reaction Force."

Oscar is stunned. "What? The son of a bitch is...?"

"Yes, nobody even suspected him to be an assassin for hire. In all likelihood, he had you under observation since the day you arrived at the posada."

“But, but...” stammers Oscar, “if he knew all along about my business, why did he provide protection when I had to purchase coke and hash oil? Why didn’t he strike earlier?”

“Search me. I have absolutely no idea. Anyway, Silvia took care of your possessions lock, stock and barrel and stayed at my place for a few nights.”

“Did she now?” interrupts Oscar Bert’s flow of speech. “And did you...?”

“What?” Bert sighs and looks up to the ceiling. “Oh, well, yes. You know how Silvia likes to express her gratitude.”

Oscar stares at the wall. “You lucky bastard!”

“Well, yes, I suppose. But she hasn’t forgotten you. She’ll take care of your possessions and money wherever she’ll go to continue your line of business, I’m sure of that.” He checks his watch. “Listen, Oscar, the time I’m allowed for the interview is almost up. What you faced today was a kangaroo court. I’m sure José killed the old man. The evidence was rigged, and the judge and the prosecutor probably accepted huge bribes to sentence you to life in prison. I want to know if you can appeal your sentence?”

Tears well up in Oscar’s eyes. “No, I can’t, and I’m surprised you ask. You should know that the judicial system in Costa Rica is based on half the Lex Napoleon.”

“What the hell is half the Lex Napoleon?” asks Bert.

“They bastardised the law to suit their understanding of justice,” explains Oscar. “Under the Lex Napoleon you can be accused of anything, and you will be considered guilty until you prove your innocence.”

“Yes, I know that,” interjects Bert. “But what’s half a Lex Napoleon?”

“Well, Napoleon stipulated that if you prove your innocence then your accuser has to suffer the punishment you would have received had you been found guilty. You follow?”

Bert nods and Oscar continues, “This latter part of the accuser suffering your punishment has been eliminated. That means that anyone can accuse you of anything with impunity and get off scot-free despite you proving your innocence. So, even if I could provide evidence that would get me off the hook, they wouldn’t sentence the officers of the Rapid Reaction Force, the police, the prosecutor, as well as the judge to life in prison. An appeal is useless. You have to commit the far worse crime of killing your accusers to get justice in this country.”

Bert swallows hard and wrings his hands. "Is there anything I can do for you? I mean, life in prison on a trumped-up charge of murder - you'll die in the slammer."

Oscar whimpers, "I know, I know, and I'm already scared to death."

There's a knock on the door, it is opened, and the guard gestures for Bert to come out of the cell. Bert takes out his wallet and quickly passes some money to Oscar.

"Take this. That's all I have on me. It may help you a little bit. Are you sure there's nothing else I can do?"

The guard taps his baton impatiently on the open door. Bert gets up and hears Oscar say with a pressed voice, "Talk to Carlos at the Hotel Casa Azul. He can establish contacts for you."

Bert nods, leaves, and the cell door is slammed shut.

6

In the morning of Friday, 15th December 1989, a black prison truck drives into the yard of the medieval looking prison Cárcel de Guadalupe. The truck's back door is opened. Oscar and José climb out, handcuffed, and shackled. A guard removes José's manacles. Oscar holds out his arms to have his removed. The guard gives him a scornful look and shakes his head. José greets some of the guards with ritualistic handshakes and hugs one of them. He leaves the yard entering a low building through a door with the inscription 'Administración'.

Oscar shouts, "Where are you going, José? Come back here!"

In response, a guard raises his truncheon, brings it down hard across Oscar's back, and shouts, "Shut up, you filthy dog!"

Oscar screams out in pain and sinks to his knees. Two guards pull him up and push him to the gate of the cellblock.

They take Oscar up some stairs, along a hallway, and stop to unlock and open a cell door. Oscar is shoved inside. The door is slammed shut and locked. The two guards outside bend double with laughter.

Oscar stands by the door and stares at three inmates on two bunk beds. They are the cousins Bernardo and Mario Cardenas and their boss Raúl Chinchilla. They are younger than Oscar, slim and muscular, have shaved heads, and piercing eyes in their unfriendly faces.

Raúl gets out of his bunk with a grin. "Look what we got here, boys. Fresh meat. A marshmallow arse!"

Bernardo and Mario get up and crowd Oscar by the door. Mario pinches Oscar's behind. "Nice and soft like a big, wet cunt."

Bernardo giggles and splutters, "He's two cunts in one. Just look at his inviting lips. We can give him a spit roast."

Raúl unbuckles Oscar's trousers. "Let's have a closer look at what we got here. Bend over, son of a bitch!"

Oscar resists but with his hands cuffed he can't fight off the strong grip on the back of his neck. Raúl winks at Bernardo who twists Oscar's nose and ear until he bends over. Raúl rips down Oscar's trousers and drops his own. He jerks his penis until it is erect, spits on it, and shouts, "Mario, hold him in a headlock! This is a big fucker who'll struggle. I don't wanna have an accident."

Mario does as ordered, puts his arm around Oscar's neck, and twists until Oscar stares straight ahead. Oscar screams out in agony when Raúl penetrates his rectum. Bernardo gets aroused by the screams and pushes his erect penis into Oscar's open mouth. Mario struggles with the bucking Oscar but still manages to masturbate. Bernardo reaches his climax and fills Oscar's mouth.

Oscar spits out the jism. Bernardo shouts in his face, "You have to swallow my pride, bitch! It's all you'll get to eat around here!"

Raúl reaches his climax, extricates himself from Oscar's rectum, and slaps his behind. "That was very good, man, better than defiling a ripe papaya or doing push-ups over a bowl of lukewarm minestrone. But now I stink of his shit. Make room, I have to clean myself. Hold him, Mario, hold him!"

He shoves his penis into Oscar's mouth and roars, "Suck, baby, suck! All the morsels are yours! Lick it clean!"

When they are finally finished with their orgy, Oscar spits, chokes, and cries. He is shoved onto a lower bunk bed. Raúl grabs his ear and twists it. "Welcome to hell, son of a bitch!"

Then he bangs on the cell door until it is opened by a guard. "We are finished with his initiation for today. You can take his shackles off. Thanks for putting him in our cell."

"It was our pleasure, Raúl. You owe us one," answers the guard, takes Oscar's handcuffs and leg-irons off, and leaves the cell slamming and locking the door behind him.

7

Eighteen months have passed since Oscar's trial and the heat is on in the drug war in the middle of 1991. The government of Colombia in collaboration with the Calí cartel run by the Orejuela brothers and José Santacruz Londoño gives death squads and vigilantes a free hand to kill anyone associated with Pablo Escobar and do whatever they deem necessary to get what they consider their fair share of his loot. Also, the guerilla armies FARC and ELN have come to realise that the cocaine trade is an excellent way to finance their war. They extract whatever money they can from whoever they assume to be involved in the drug trade - farmers, cocaine lab operators, and the gangs that smuggle the stuff into any country where there is a demand for it. Getting a share of the loot is after all what the drug war in Colombia is all about, how it started, and continues ceaselessly.

The organised cocaine trade started with a few guys from the lowest echelons of society. The Ochoa brothers, previously known to the police only for stealing horses, as well as Pablo Escobar, who scraped by selling stolen gravestones out of the trunk of his car, had found a way to organise the drug trade properly and make billions of dollars by satisfying the noses of millions of Americans greedy for a snort of cocaine. Problem is that these sudden billionaires are absolutely unwilling to hand over part of their hard-earned cash to the upper one percent of Colombian society, the 'Mil Familias' as they are commonly known.

Simplified put, these 'thousand families' consider it their birthright to demand a share of the earnings or gains of the ninety-nine percent of Colombians they regard as their underlings. When Pablo Escobar gives them the middle finger instead of tons of cash, the families, in effect also being the government, declare war on the drug bosses. They use their personal bodyguards, essentially the armed forces and police, in a bombing campaign that could easily be blamed on Escobar. He had used a similar campaign to rescue the Ochoa brothers' sister who had been kidnapped by security forces. His offensive established him as the top honcho of what became known as the Medellín cartel.

As a result of the enduring conflict, Medellín, Colombia's second city, acquires the reputation of murder capital of the world with thousands of victims to mourn every year. The drug war is on the verge of turning into a civil war, which to no small extent is due to the fact that Pablo Escobar spends more money on social housing in the region of Antioquia alone than the government spends on social programmes for the entire country. Thus, there are on the one hand people who don't understand why Escobar, a philanthropist with a social conscience, apparently, is hunted, and on the other, there are those who believe the official pronouncements of him being a bloodthirsty monster and want him killed.

The ongoing carnage scares other drug bosses and some of them go underground with their assets but practically all of them send their kids abroad to study at the best universities and prepare them for a profession other than pushing drugs.

These sons and daughters of drug bosses came together in a group as the result of circumstance. Several of them studied at the same university or at different universities in the same city. Being far away from home they were looking for the company of compatriots and became friends with other Colombian students quite independently of and contrary to their fathers' animosities towards each other. At the same time, they stayed in touch with old friends. All of them watched with differing degrees of horror the bloodshed that was going on in their home country.

Several students met on occasion with old and new friends after they had completed their studies and returned home. The insights they had gained during four to six years in foreign lands provided the impetus for ignoring their fathers' animosities, go beyond seeing things in black and white and develop a common goal of pursuing their fathers' business better and more effectively than they had ever done. Problem was that every son and daughter had a different idea of how to go about achieving such lofty goal.

***

It is Sunday, 23rd June 1991, a day of sunshine and mild temperatures in the historical city of Calí. Two young men, Alejandro Muñoz, whom his friends call Alec, as in 'smart Alec', tall and slender, yet athletic, and Igor Guttiérez, stocky and muscular, sit at a table under a parasol in the manicured garden of the Muñoz family's luxurious Spanish colonial style house. Alec, scion of a family with links to Escobar, and Igor, youngest son of an independent family, are the descendants of two drug bosses who over time have grown quite hostile towards each other. Despite that, these two young men have become friends. Having returned home after completing their studies in England and the United States, respectively, their conversation centres on their studies at first.

Alec talks with pride about his studies at the London School of Economics where he earned his MBA summa cum laude, while Igor uses pretty foul language to relate his experience at Princeton University. It irritates Alec to hear Igor's constant use of gutter language. He approaches the problem cautiously, being fully aware of Igor's short fuse and how quickly he flies off the handle when confronted by criticism.

Alec raises a hand. "Igor, did you really go to Princeton?"

Confronted by doubt about his honesty, Igor sputters, "Fuck, man, yeah! You think I'm a lying, cock sucking asshole?"

Alec shakes his head, "No, but I'm wondering if all students at Princeton talk like you do."

Igor looks agitated and spits out the question, "What the fuck d'you mean, talk like I do?"

Alec leans back and answers quietly, "Well, all I hear is fuck, fuck, fuck and other expletives. You don't sound like a man of higher education."

Igor jumps up, leans on the table, and barks, "You can go fuck yourself, you pseudo-English twat! I speak like my father taught me to speak – in any language, you arrogant prick!"

Alec struggles to suppress an urge to laugh. He takes a moment before he retorts, "Speak like your father taught you to speak? For your edification, our fathers speak the 'paisa' dialect of Antioquia. It is laced with expletives and hardly understood outside our region. Perhaps that's the reason most of them hide like rats in a sewer - nobody understands them. We, on the other hand, should speak a language that is understood everywhere, if we want to succeed. English is the accepted lingua franca around the world today, but nobody will listen or take you seriously when addressed in a slew of foul language – in any language! Kindly curb your expletives! Please, sit down and pipe down!"

Still pumped, Igor won't sit down and asks, "Oh yeah? Anything else?"

Alec answers calmly, "Plenty! Please, sit down!"

He waits for Igor to slump into his chair before he continues. "We didn't get our education for nothing and can't carry on business as usual."

Still pissed off about being called on the carpet, Igor asks, "Oh yeah? What you gonna do about it?"

Alec sighs. "We could go into politics to attain power."

Igor snaps, "Money is power! We got plenty of that!"

Alec wags a finger. "No, money isn't power. It's an exchange medium without intrinsic value and quite arbitrarily used to give value to tangibles and intangibles. One can use it to attain power, but we can't even do that."

Igor leans forward. "We can't do that? Why not?"

Patiently Alec explains, "Igor, the billions of dollars in cash our families sit on were gained with the trade of an illicit substance. If we use the money, it will be confiscated."

Igor scoffs, "So? We'll launder it with investments or real estate deals."

Alec rejects that suggestion. "No, we can't invest it or buy anything legally, and it loses value due to inflation."

Igor waves that comment off. "Come on, man. That loss is minimal."

Alec looks surprised. "Minimal? Are you kidding? Inflation in the US is three percent. Three percent of one billion is thirty million. In Colombia, our families sit on over fifty billion bucks in cash. That's a combined loss of one and a half billion each year!"

Igor is stunned and spouts, "Don't fuck me! Are you for real?"

Alec nods. "Yes, do the math! And that's just inflation! Another five to six billion dollars are lost each year to rats, mice and chemicals eating into our stockpile of cash."

Igor whispers, "Shiiiit! That's over seven billion bucks! Each year! Can't we stop that?"

Alec shrugs. "As I said, we have to go into politics by some wily method and use some of our money to get elected. Once in power, we can legalise our product and all our money."

Igor sputters, "Legalise cocaine! Yeah, right! Dream on, President Alejandro."

"Dream on?" asks Alec and taps a finger on the table. "Let me explain something to you. Cocaine was a regulated and licensed substance in 1922. As far as I know it could be bought in legal outlets until one of the most foulmouthed and stupid presidents of the US, Richard Nixon to be precise, decided in 1971 that cocaine was an illegal narcotic and declared his War on Drugs.

"Compare that to the alcohol prohibition in the 1920s when some stupid American politicians gave in to the pressure of various holier-than-thou groups like the Temperance Society and the Daughters of America and declared alcohol illegal. The result was a rise of crime to unprecedented levels, assassinations, murder, and corruption almost identical to what we have in Colombia and neighbouring countries today. It was stopped with a stroke of the pen by repealing prohibition in the 1930s.

"The same could apply to cocaine, which in essence is a stimulant like coffee or tea and is also used as a local anaesthetic. In its raw form, the coca leaf isn't even addictive. So, don't you think that the status of cocaine as a restricted substance could be lifted with a stroke of the pen as well by declaring it for example a regulated substance that would be obtainable legally by prescription?"

Igor listens and mutters, "Hmm, you got a point there."

Alec leans forward and says, "Exactly! This process of lifting the illicit status of cocaine and regulating it has to be started by someone and that should be us. Once one country has declared cocaine not to be illegal any longer, others will follow like sheep follow the ram. And that one country to take the lead should be Colombia."

Igor nods in agreement, "I see what you're getting at but how are we going to achieve that?"

Alec leans back. "That's the fifty-billion-dollar question. I think we have to get all of us together for a brainstorming session. One of us may have a bright idea to get a project going. The alternative to legalising cocaine is continuing our fathers' business as usual. And that would not lift the curse of being criminals and hunted all over the world."

He pauses for a moment before he concludes in a low voice, "As I said, we have to get all of us together for a brainstorming session. Perhaps someone has the sound idea of an alternative to pursue our business safely."

8

Oscar has somehow survived the time in prison since his conviction although he still suffers the occasional sexual abuse bestowed on him by his cellmates when they are full of drugs and alcohol. Yet, despite trying to stay as healthy as possible, Oscar's body turns to blubber, and his legs swell due to water retention. Often, he feels sick after eating the scraps of food tossed his way. He has no money to buy healthy food or favours. He is allowed one hour in the exercise yard every day, which is not enough to help him improve his condition. He suffers from depression as well and feels that there is no hope for him because he doesn't receive any visitors or for that matter any news.

On Tuesday, 25th June 1991, Oscar sits on one of the lower bunk beds in his tattered clothes. He watches a rat that scurries around and disappears in the hole in the ground that serves as the toilet. The rat has become something of a pet to him. It only comes out of hiding when Oscar is alone in the cell and waits for him to share some of the stale bread he has often as his only food. The door is unlocked and opened while Oscar watches the rat disappear.

A guard waves his truncheon and tells Oscar to step outside. "You better clean up a bit. You have a visitor."

Having learned his lesson of getting punished for asking questions, Oscar just stares at him, shrugs, and shuffles off to the showers. He looks for soap in the sinks, finds a few flakes of washing powder, and twiddles with the taps until a trickle of water drips out. He lathers his face. He bends down to rinse off the suds when the trickle of water ceases. Oscar curses, twiddles with other taps and turns to the showers. He presses a button and with a farting sound a jet of water sprays his face and clothes. The stream of water stops with a burp as suddenly as it had started.

Dripping wet, Oscar walks out, and the guard says in a sarcastic tone, "Washing your hands and face would have been quite sufficient."

The guard pushes Oscar with the truncheon in the small of his back along the hallways, down some stairs and into the bare visitor hall. Oscar is understandably nervous in view of this being the first visit in eighteen months. He paces to and fro, then sits down on the floor and drums a beat with his sausage fingers. He looks to the visitor's entrance when the door is pushed open.

Bert steps into the hall carrying two large shopping bags. He walks towards Oscar with a worried look.

Oscar is a bit puzzled, then breaks into a broad smile and gets up. "Hello, Bert, my old friend. How are you?"

Bert drops the bags and gives Oscar a brief hug. "Hello, Oscar. It's good to see you." They sit down and Bert continues, "You don't look well and smell worse. It's tough in here, eh?"

Oscar mumbles under his breath, "Man, it's a shithole." After a pause he adds with a smile, "But I feel so much better just seeing you. You're my first visitor since I got here."

Bert is startled. "What? I'm the first? In eighteen months? What's with your friends? Have they forgotten you?"

Oscar looks pensively. "I've never had friends in this country. I thought José... but... oh well."

Bert sneers and mutters, "José, that swine. He never returned to the posada since he was burgled. Silvia did the right thing."

A smile creeps across Oscar's face. "Silvia, yes, is she still around? Do you see her? How is she doing?"

Bert touches Oscar's arm in a reassuring gesture. "She's doing alright, bought a house in Escalante, and has two women working for her doing the material acquisition and selling inhalers. She came to my place a few times when she needed a hug."

"And?" asks Oscar with a big grin on his face.

"Yes, that, too," answers Bert. "You know how she is, all loving and that very physical. I'll keep her warm for you, which reminds me to tell you that she can't forget you. You pulled her out of the ditch, she said and will be waiting for you."

Oscar shakes his head. "Nobody is going to wait for a lifetime."

Bert reaches for the bags. "How's the food in here?"

"Food?" asks Oscar. "The slop they serve can't be called food. You must have family to bring you food or you trade for it."

Bert looks puzzled. "Trade? What have you got to trade?"

Oscar rubs his forehead to hide his face and mumbles, "Blowjobs and the occasional reaming."

Bert is aghast. "I don't believe it! You're kidding! Right?"

Oscar scoffs and asks, "Do I look like I'm kidding? That's Costa Rica for you, a country of violent bumfuckers!"

Bert shakes his head in disbelief. He opens the bag containing a baguette, ham, cheese, cans of corned beef, and sweets. The other holds shirts, trousers, underwear, socks, a pair of sneakers, a towel, as well as soap, shampoo, toothpaste, toothbrush, and a shaving kit.

Oscar has a look in the bags. "Wow! Look at all that stuff! Thanks, Bert. It must have cost you a bomb."

Bert chuckles. "Yes, it did. As a matter of fact, this stuff cost me all the money I made selling your emeralds."

Oscar whispers, "My emeralds? Man, they were fake!"

"I know," says Bert with aplomb. "But the tourists liked them. They wanted a bargain and got it - buying finely cut Colombian green beer bottle shards thinking they were emeralds."

Oscar chuckles and digs into the bag with food. He stuffs a slice of ham into his mouth and rolls his eyes while chewing the smoked delicacy. He takes a shirt out of the other bag, strokes the smooth cloth, and smiles happily.

Content with the result of his shopping for Oscar, Bert watches him for a while. He lowers his voice. "Listen, Oscar, my visit at this time is for other reasons besides getting you food and clothes. I would have come earlier but it took me a long time and a few bribes to get a visitor's pass."

Oscar nods and says with a full mouth, "I can imagine. Ask Silvia to reimburse you."

Bert waves off the suggestion and continues his whispered sermon. "A lot has been going on in Colombia. Pablo was captured and put in the slammer. He escaped after they wanted to extradite him to the States. He and his lieutenants were hunted down, and they gave up a couple of weeks ago. They stay in the prison La Catedral near Pablo's hometown Envigado. Reportedly, he had a reformatory converted to something resembling a luxury hotel at a cost of eighty-five million bucks. It is alleged that he still runs the business from his prison, but most big bosses have gone underground. There's also been a massive increase in the seizure of drugs and cash. I think there are big changes in the works, changes along the line of the old farts' sons and daughters, the second generation taking over. These kids are not known to the authorities, at least not in any criminal context. They could carry on the business without being suspect. But another development is more important. You told me to contact Carlos. Took me one heck of a long time to find him. His Hotel Casa Azul was firebombed and burnt to the ground. When I got a hold of Carlos and mentioned you, he wasn't helpful at all. He dodged every question as if he was afraid of me. He gave me a Calí telephone number to call from within Colombia, if I wanted inside information and suggested to contact your brothers. Here's my question, why should I contact your brothers and how can I contact them?"

Oscar nods but takes a moment to come up with his answer, "I think Carlos was trying to be helpful. I suppose that Pablo blew a fuse when he read my letter and wanted to have me killed. The drug deal was a setup, and I was never supposed to come out of it alive. I guess José screwed up if he was my assigned killer. And here's the crux. Pablo didn't understand or didn't like my letter, but others may see it differently in light of the increased seizures of drugs and cash you mentioned. If there's indeed a change of operators in Colombia then Carlos was trying to tell you to make my brothers aware of my letter, let them know of my plan and ask them to contact one of the families."

Bert is perplexed. "Okay, and how? How do I contact your brothers? Also, whom are they supposed to call with the news that you wrote a letter to Pablo? And finally, what's in it for you, if the new operators, assuming that there are any, look at your plan favourably?"

Oscar smiles. "Easy. I'm sure Carlos referred to my older brother Benigno. He's a pharmacist in Buenaventura and owes me. I paid for his university studies. He has a drugstore and should be easy to find. He should be able to figure out which family to call. Give him the Calí telephone number Carlos gave you. I don't have an answer to your last question. If the new operators find the letter, which is doubtful, and like what I wrote, which is questionable, they may want to visit me to hear my plan. If they like what I tell them they may pay a judge a huge bribe to open my case again and set me free. But that's in the stars."

Deep in thought, Bert gets out a cigarette, lights up, and takes a puff. "I've been planning to fly to Europe via Colombia in a few days. I guess I could have a stopover in Bogotá and call your brother."

The guard enters the hall and taps his truncheon against the wall indicating the end of the allowed visiting time.

Bert and Oscar get up and Bert says, "Gotta go, Oscar. Try to stay healthy, okay?" He hands Oscar some money. "Take this. It's not much but may allow you to buy some stuff. And don't let yourself get reamed any more, you hear? I fear you may pick up this new disease called AIDS."

“Aids?” asks Oscar. “Sounds nice. I need all the aids I can get.”

“Not this one,” is Bert’s hasty reply. “It’s an acronym spelled A-I-D-S.”

“Oh, I see, and what does that acronym mean?”

“It stands for the deadly Acquired Immune Deficiency Syndrome, but the popular interpretation will make it clearer to you in how much danger you are if you don’t stop getting reamed. It’s called the Arse Injected Death Syndrome. Think about it.”

They embrace briefly. The guard leads Bert to the exit door and lets him out. Oscar is still mulling Bert’s explanation of AIDS, picks up his bags, leaves the hall, and is brought back to his cell.

9

Alec is talking on the phone in the dimly lit library room of his family's home on Saturday, 29th June 1991 at 7:45 p.m.

"Yes, yes, I understand. And your name? Benigno Ortiz, uh-huh. A letter? A very important and urgent letter, you say. Well, that's your opinion. Why is it so important? What's in the letter? A plan. What? Your brother Oscar wrote the letter and sent it to Pablo Escobar. Oh, I see. Of course, I'll look for it and if... Yes, yes, thank you..."

Igor sits in a chair behind a desk and listens to Alec but can't make any sense out of the one half of the conversation. He watches Alec hang up the phone, stare at it in deep thought, and turn to him, "That was the third strange call I got in the past couple of days."

"Strange call?" asks Igor. "What's strange about it?"

"It's the third call pertaining to a certain Oscar Ortiz. Have you ever heard of him?"

"No, never. Who called? Perhaps he's important."

"It starts to sound like it," surmises Alec. "See, the first call was from somebody called Carlos. My father told me that he is a kind liaison man on our behalf in Central America who keeps an ear to the ground to let us know about any developments and activities. He mentioned this Oscar in regard to some journalist who was going to call and wants us to help Oscar. Then as predicted this journalist calls from Bogotá yesterday and wants to talk to us about Oscar. I invited him to come here to find out what he wants to know. If we find out that he snoops on behalf of the DEA, we'll let him disappear."

"Hold it," interjects Igor. "Letting him disappear could lead investigators of his disappearance right on our trail."

"I've taken care of that," Alec reassures him. "I bought an airline ticket for a fictitious Fernando Butragueños and told him to ask for it. If he follows up on it, he'll be here tomorrow morning. I asked my father's bodyguards to pick him up and take him to a luxury hotel where I booked a suite for him under the same name. Should he turn out to be a snoop, we'll let him disappear and nobody would be any the wiser, right?"

"Yeah, that's safe," agrees Igor. "And who was that last caller? Don't tell me it was Oscar."

"No, it wasn't. It was his brother Benigno Ortiz. He's a pharmacist in Buenaventura. He told me to look for a letter Oscar wrote to Pablo Escobar almost two years ago. It contains a plan, supposedly very important and of great interest to us."

Igor sits up. "A letter he sent Pablo almost two years ago?" He slumps back. "Huh! Pablo probably wiped his arse with it. And anyway, how could a two-year-old plan be of interest to us? So many things have changed in the past six months alone."

"I agree, I agree. But often the time has come for old ideas. We should at least look for it."

"And where should we start looking?" asks Igor. "Get serious. You're suggesting a paper chase with no beginning and no end."

Alec shakes his head. "No, a couple of weeks ago, after Pablo gave up, I went to Hacienda Nápoles ahead of the security forces. It was already a mess because Pablo had given orders to clear out and destroy all records. But I managed to salvage two boxes of papers Pablo's lieutenant Juan Arcila had filed. He saved every shred of paper." He kicks a couple of cartons that stand beside the desk and tips them over spilling the contents on the carpet. "There you are. We can start looking here and if we don't find the letter then that journalist can possibly tell us what the plan is all about."

Igor gets up, kneels on the floor, and starts sifting the papers. "So, what are we looking for?" he asks. "A yellowed sheet of paper with a brown streak that smells of Pablo's shit?"

Alec looks piqued while he sifts through papers of the second box. "That would be based on your assumption that Pablo used it for hygienic purposes. No, from what I understood, it is a handwritten letter without a brown streak."

Putting all typed papers aside, Igor finds a handwritten one and asks, "Could this be it?"

Alec gets up, takes the yellowed sheet, and flattens it on the desk. He skims it. "Yes, that's it. It's signed Oscar A. Ortiz A."

Igor snorts, "Oscar A? Ortiz A? Does 'A' stand for asshole?"

Alec looks really annoyed and says, "Get serious, man! He states that his plan involves the creation of a global network of legal companies that would allow us to let our entire trade disappear into legality, assure the safe arrival of our goods at their destination, and transfer our earnings without a loss. That sounds pretty good, wouldn't you agree?"

"Yes, and where is this plan to achieve that goal?"

"It doesn't say. He wanted to discuss it with Pablo."

"Then let's call him up and discuss it with him."

"Yes, right, but there's the hitch. His brother told me that he is in prison, the Cárcel de Guadalupe in Costa Rica."

Igor scratches his head. "So, uh, what're we gonna do?"

Alec looks a bit worried and replies, "Off hand? I don't know, but we have to contact him somehow and talk to him."

"Yeah, but he'll have no reason to reveal details if we leave him in the klink. We have to bust him out."

"Bust him out? How?" asks Alec. "Walk into the prison in Costa Rica, say we are Colombians and walk out with him?"

Igor chuckles. "That may work in Costa Rica. That country is such a fucking joke."

Alec wags a finger. "Please, show some respect, Igor, and watch your language! Let me think."

Impatiently Igor walks to the door. "Alright! You do your thinking, Alec. I'll make a couple of phone calls, see what develops, and take some action. Okay? I'll see you."

"Wait! Don't do anything hasty! You..."

Alec stops short of admonishing him against reckless action when he realises that Igor is gone, and the door closed behind him.

10

Two beefcakes in black leather jackets and blue jeans are standing in the arrival area of Calí's Alfonso Bonilla Aragón International Airport on Sunday morning, 10:45 a.m., 30th June 1991. One of them holds up a sign with the name 'Fernando Butragueños' scrawled on it in big letters.

Bert picks up his travel bag from the luggage carousel and sees the two men with the sign. He is not impressed to be welcomed by a couple of meatballs with greasy hair. He hesitates. They don't know what he looks like. He could just walk past them, forget about his planned encounter, take a taxi to a hotel, stay for a night, and fly back to Bogotá and on to Europe the next day. But then he considers that he is dressed just like the two greasers in black leather jacket and blue jeans, decides to go on with the visit as planned, waves to them, and is strangely touched by the reception he gets. They greet him with bear hugs and a lot of shoulder slapping as if he was an old friend. They grab his travel bag and guide him to a van waiting outside with engine idling.

After a speedy ride they arrive at a luxury hotel. One of the guys picks up the key to Bert's suite at the reception and shuffles him into an elevator. On the way up, he asks Bert if he has formal attire in his travel bag suitable for a business meeting. When Bert responds in the negative, the guy checks his watch, says that there is enough time, and instructs him to go to the gent's boutique in the lobby of the hotel and pick out a suit, shirt, tie, socks, and shoes to his taste. And he shouldn't worry about paying for the stuff. Señor Muñoz has already taken care of that.

It is the first time Bert hears the family name of his host.

He follows the instructions to the letter but also acquires a new and very expensive watch presuming that in a roundabout way some cocaine snorting fools in the States have already paid for it. Once dressed in suit, shirt, and tie, he hardly recognises himself in the mirror. He feels uneasy about the upcoming meeting when he takes the lift down to the mezzanine floor.

Bert opens the door to the conference room, looks around, sees a group of youngsters standing around holding plastic beakers, and wants to pull back. But one young man calls out and bids him to come in. "Are you the journalist who called on Wednesday?"

"Yes," confirms Bert surprised about the young man's pronounced British accent. "I'm Bert. Did I talk to you?"

"Indeed, I am Alejandro Muñoz. My friends call me Alec. Pleasure to meet you, Bert."

"Thank you and it's my pleasure meeting you, Alejandro, uh, Alec."

Bert looks around at the faces of the other fourteen young men and women and asks, "Are these the, uh, participants of the business meeting I was advised to attend?"

"Yes," confirms Alec. He has to smile about Bert's doubtful stare. "Permit me to introduce you."

They make the round shaking hands. There are too many names to remember, except the few that stick because they remind Bert of famous actors, musicians, politicians, or criminals like Penelope Saenz, Jorge Guzmán, Gerardo Restrepo, and Armando Rójas. He is offered alcohol free fruit juice and encouraged to help himself to the snacks laid out on a sideboard. He sips a drink, takes out a cigarette, and lights up to the horror of some of the youngsters. Unperturbed by the ensuing gasps and whispers that are familiar to him from North America, where people poop their pants when someone smokes tobacco, but hype smoking marihuana as if it was a health promoting remedy. He keeps up the small talk with Alec and Penelope until they all sit down around the large oval table for the meeting.

One of the women sitting opposite Bert looks at him critically and asks, "Excuse me for being blunt, but what is the actual reason for your stay in Colombia? You are a journalist, right?"

Bert smiles at her and answers, "My actual reason for being in Colombia is to change planes in Bogotá on my way to Europe. Does that answer your question?"

He smiles when he sees her getting royally pissed off about his flippant response. She glowers at him but before she can spit out the bile gathering in her throat, he continues, "I would like you to forget that I'm a journalist. I am not here to ask questions or snoop around, and your business, simply put, is none of my business. And the less you tell me about your business, the better. I prefer plausible deniability when cops apply the third degree. Okay?"

He gives that woman opposite an icy stare to underscore his words and notices a smile creeping across Alec's face. The woman swallows hard and tosses her hair. Bert continues, "I came to Calí upon the invitation of Alec to plead the case for my friend Oscar

Antonio Ortiz Acosta. He has a plan to help you, and he needs your help - desperately."

"What does his plan to help us entail?" asks the man to his left.

"I don't know the details," answers Bert. "It's a plan to let your business and money transfers be handled through a global network of legitimate companies. I assure you that the plan is well thought out because Oscar is a very smart man. I've known him for almost four years. He was my neighbour in Costa Rica until the day he was arrested and thrown in prison on trumped up charges from what I understand."

"What were the trumped-up charges?" asks the man to his left.

"Smuggling drugs and killing an old man."

"Smuggling drugs and killing someone?" asks a woman to his right. "That doesn't sound trumped up or very smart."

"Superficially it doesn't," agrees Bert and drops a stink bomb. "But I wonder what you would say if you had been framed by Pablo Escobar."

Gasps and horrified faces are the response to mentioning Pablo Escobar's name and accusing him of framing Oscar.

Bert realises he kicked a hornets' nest and quickly continues, "It was all a misunderstanding on Don Pablo's part of Oscar's most well-intentioned suggestion to discuss his plan of avoiding the seizure of coke and cash. Perhaps Don Pablo had a lousy day and misinterpreted the letter thinking that Oscar was trying to tell him how to run his business. He actually ordered Oscar to be killed. But Costa Ricans being what they are, the hired assassin probably forgot to kill him."

Some of the horrified faces actually relax and manage a vague smile when Bert uses the honourable term 'Don Pablo' and makes a hired assassin sound ridiculous.

Yet, Alec expresses some doubt when he asks, "But Oscar killed the old man you mentioned, right?"

"No, he didn't, I'm sure of that," is Bert's immediate response. "It is easy to frame someone when you hand that person the murder weapon to hold, especially when that person is unawares of a murder having taken place. Fingerprints on the handle of the murder weapon was all the evidence the court had to sentence Oscar to life in prison." He pauses to light up another cigarette and continues, "In my opinion and based on how well I know Oscar, he is totally incapable of killing another human being. Let me tell you a little anecdote about Oscar. Almost every morning and to the great amusement of his neighbours in the posada where he lived, he was chasing flies and cockroaches with a newspaper out of his abode. He can't stand the sight of a squashed bug. Can you imagine him cutting the throat of an old man?"

The response of the men and women ranges from amused to doubtful expressions. Amused expressions say, 'I'm with you', doubtful expressions on the other hand seem to say to Bert, 'Who the hell are you and what do you really want?'

The young man whose name Bert recalls as Gerardo Restrepo because of his uncanny resemblance to a leading Colombian politician of the same family name is one of the guys with a doubtful look. He says, "I see that you are smoking a lot, Mr. Bert. Are you addicted to other drugs? Do you take any drugs for recreational purposes?"

Bert takes a puff, inhales deeply, and stubs out the cigarette. "First of all, don't call me mister. Bert will do just fine. Second, you use the relative term 'a lot' to refer to my habit of smoking tobacco. 'A lot' means nothing. Compare it to one dollar that may mean nothing to you while it means a lot to somebody who has no money at all. Third, I have to wonder, why you mention drugs and recreation in the same breath. I consider recreation to be an activity like taking a walk in a forest or painting a picture, a different activity from whatever you do habitually or professionally to help you relax and gather your thoughts. Taking drugs doesn't do that. Consequently, I have to ask you, Gerardo, do you take drugs for recreational purposes?"

Stunned that Bert addresses him by his name and turns the table on him, Gerardo stammers, "No! No, no, I, uh, I don't take drugs at all. I never touch the stuff. It, uh, it is dangerous and criminal."

Bert chuckles and fixes Gerardo with his gaze. "You don't sound very convincing. Truth be told, you sound like a drug dealer who states that drug dealing is the scourge of humanity."

Embarrassed silence follows until a smiling Penelope asks, "Is that what Oscar says?"

Bert nods. "Well, he did on one occasion although at the time I didn't know that he was dealing drugs. He worked under the cover of being a representative of patent medicine companies and was pushing cough syrup and inhalers. Only on the day of his arrest, when his girlfriend came to me for help to clear out Oscar's abode and hide his stuff in my apartment, did I learn that the cough syrup bottles were in fact full of hash oil and the inhalers full of cocaine."

The last doubtful faces turn to smiles and one woman raises her voice, "Hash oil in cough syrup bottles and inhalers full of cocaine. That's pretty smart."

Bert agrees, "Yes, it is smart. Here's another little anecdote for you to enjoy. Oscar's girlfriend Silvia carried on his business for the past eighteen months. But she only pushes the goods in upscale circles of society. During a reception for government officials and security officers she noticed that the chief of police had a blocked nose. She gave him one of her inhalers. Ever since, he is after her but not for dealing drugs. He wants only another one of her wondrous inhalers that didn't just unblock his nose but got rid of his clinical depression for a few days."

Everybody is amused. It is the icebreaker Bert had wanted to achieve. Alec waits for the amusement to ebb and asks, "Bert, I presume you have travelled extensively. Have you maintained your contacts in the countries you visited?"

Bert nods. "Yes, of course. I have good contacts to business and governments in the Americas, Europe, Africa and the Middle East."

Alec lets that statement sink in for a second before he asks, "Would you be interested working in Colombia, that is, working for us, uh, with us?"

Now it is Bert's turn to let the question sink in for a minute. He doesn't have any facts about these young people's business. He can only assume that they are what he calls the Second Generation of drug dealers. Should he agree to work for Alec, he could be a very rich man in a very short time, or he could be shot and killed by a death squad in an even shorter time.

He looks at Alec and chooses his words carefully. "As you know, the purpose of my visit is to plead Oscar's need for your help and for you to seriously consider his plan - not more and not less. I appreciate your offer to work for you and with you. But as I stated before, your business is none of my business and we should leave it at that. It is my wish to part with you in the knowledge that we are friends."

Alec's thin smile can't hide his disappointment. He looks at his watch while he gets up. "Alright, folks, I should think that lunch is about to be served. Let's go."

On the way out, he holds Bert by the arm and mutters, "Don't worry about Oscar. One of our guys is already en route to provide all the help Oscar needs."

11

In the early morning of Monday, 1st July 1991, a twin-engine Piper Seneca skims over the crest of the waves of the Pacific Ocean and approaches a landing strip on the peninsula of Matapalo in the region of Guanacaste, Costa Rica. The landing gear is lowered, and the plane touches down.

Ricardo León, José's older brother, sporting a ponytail and neatly trimmed goatee, waits for the plane to stop. Igor gets out and Ricardo takes his suitcase. They get into a limousine with tinted windows and drive away at high speed. The plane turns around and takes off over the ocean.

***

The limousine stops in front of the Grand Hotel in San José. Ricardo and Igor enter the hotel's arcade café and sit down at a table reserved for six. Igor gets out a small writing pad, scribbles a few lines, and explains something to Ricardo. Delgado Miranda, a haggard man with grey hair, and Carlos, Jaime, and Omar Castro, three stocky brothers with identical crew cuts enter the arcade café, shake hands with Ricardo and Igor and sit down. Igor finishes explaining his note to Ricardo, excuses himself, and enters the hotel lobby.

***

Igor sits on the bed of his hotel suite and flips through a notebook. He stops, picks up the phone, and dials a number.

***

In the open plan office of the Rapid Reaction Force some of the men hack away on typewriters, a few of them look at computer terminals, and others speak on the phone.

Miguel Arías looks through a pile of photographs when a colleague turns on a TV-set mounted on the wall. It shows a report of Pablo Escobar and his lieutenants giving themselves up on 4th June 1991 and being transferred to the prison La Catedral, a one-storey building on a mountain slope outside the town of Envigado in Colombia. All heads turn to look at the pictures. The sound is turned off. Some of the officers murmur quietly and a couple of them whistle when they see the layout of the prison with a sports complex, swimming pool, and all the amenities of a luxury hotel.

Miguel's telephone rings, he picks it up, answers in a subdued voice and listens. His expression changes from happy surprise to anger and outrage. Finally, he slams down the phone.

***

Igor puts down the receiver and ends his call. He smiles and murmurs, "What a wanker...!"

He gets a camera with a zoom lens out of his suitcase and leaves his suite.

***

Miguel Arías drives an unmarked police cruiser along Avenida 2, parks the car a distance away, and rushes across the street to the entrance of the Grand Hotel where Alfredo Calderón and José León are waiting for him. Alfredo gives a confused looking Miguel a warm hug and José slaps him on the shoulder. Igor snaps pictures of them from a distance.

Ricardo León joins the trio and hands Miguel a letter. He reads it, takes out an ID-card, and hands it to Ricardo who checks it and compares it to the letter. Satisfied, he hands letter and ID-card back to Miguel. Alfredo and José take him to a limousine waiting at the curb and drive away to the Cárcel de Guadalupe.

José greets the guard at the prison control post and introduces Alfredo and Miguel. Miguel presents the letter and his ID-card. Alfredo passes a business card that identifies him falsely as the Deputy Minister of the Interior to the guard and signs the letter. The guard picks up a phone and makes a call. Alfredo gives Miguel a small camera and indicates with his hands to take portrait photos. The guard puts down the phone, stamps the letter, hands it to Miguel, and lets him enter the prison. José and Alfredo go back to the car and wait for his return.

***

Oscar's prison cell is opened and the guard yells at Oscar, "You have another visitor. Two in less than a week is quite irregular. You got friends in high places?"

Oscar ignores the guard's snide question, gets up, and mutters, "I have another visitor! Who is it this time?"

The guard gives him a bored look. "It's your friend."

"My friend Bert?" mumbles Oscar. "I can't believe it!"

Full of joy in expectation of a fresh baguette, ham, and cheese, and possibly a couple of salchichas, he wants to storm out of the cell, but the guard stops him dead in his tracks and handcuffs him.

***

Miguel Arías looks lost in the visitor hall. Oscar shuffles in followed by the guard. Both Oscar and Miguel stare at each other for a moment before Oscar turns to the guard to protest, "That's not my friend."

The guard pokes his truncheon in Oscar's back, pushes him forward. "Doesn't matter. Get a move on, you fat bastard!"

Oscar stumbles towards Miguel who hands the guard a wad of cash. The guard stashes it, removes Oscar's handcuffs, and leans against the wall.

Oscar is furious about Miguel pretending to be his friend and releases his anger with the opening salutation, "Wha'daya want, you piece of shit?"

Miguel responds in the haughtiest of tones. "Pipe down and cooperate or you'll never see daylight again!"

Oscar scoffs, "Drop dead, chickenfucker!"

Miguel gives that obscenity some thought and wonders if Oscar refers to him having sexual intercourse with a plucked and disembowelled carcass or a plump live chicken in full plumage.

Either way, it is an outrage for this darkie to assume he gets his jollies with fowl as the recipient of his loin juice. He can't think of anything else but to say, "Watch your lip, Sambo!"

That remark gets Oscar all riled up and he shouts, "Sambo? You're calling me a nigger, you bleached sack of shit?"

Miguel realises that his visit is getting a bit out of hand and may lead to failure of achieving the objective. He lowers his voice and pleads, "Pipe down already! I'll just take a few pictures of you and leave. Okay?"

Oscar growls, "Fuck off! Asshole!" He watches Miguel pull a small camera out of a trouser pocket and turns away.

When Miguel sees Oscar shuffle towards the guard, he hisses, "Hold it right there, you fat pig! Don't you want us to get you out?"

Oscar stops and asks, "Who is 'us'?"

Miguel snaps pictures of him and mutters, "That is confidential."

Oscar sneers at Miguel, "Confidential? Bullshit! You don't know! The killers that sent you don't trust you with such info."

Miguel mutters, "No, I know exactly who wants to get you out!"

Unimpressed Oscar says aloud, "Oh yeah? Who is that? The CIA or Escobar's killers?"

Miguel asks, "What's the big idea anyone of them want to get you out?"

Oscar scowls at Miguel. "They protect Escobar and want me dead. You're just a little snitch, you dumb shit."

Miguel responds in his haughty tone, "Nonsense! I got orders from high up."

Oscar hisses, "Bullshit!" He takes a step forward and strikes at the camera. But Miguel sidesteps the blow and quickly pockets it.

Oscar points a finger at him. "Listen, asshole. The rule is 'plata o plomo'. You got plata, a lot of money to get me in here. Now it's time for you to get plomo, the bullet."

He motions a flat hand across his throat, turns abruptly, shuffles towards the guard, and says in a firm voice, "Please, get me out of here. I want to go back to my cell."

Having heard Oscar's warning, Miguel turns pale. He knows all too well that 'plata o plomo' is a reality and wonders if his colleagues from the Rapid Reaction Force would provide him the protection he needs. He wishes that he had not got involved with the drug barons and accepted the ten thousand dollars to provide false testimony. He can't wait for this episode with Oscar to blow over. All he really wants is a return to his task of letting recalcitrant and obstreperous citizens disappear without a trace.

***

Delgado and Ricardo walk along a sparsely lit, narrow street in the suburb of Tibas. The asphalt glistens after a rainfall. The heady smell of the beautiful nightshade 'Reina de la Noche' fills the air. It is the perfect time of night for a stroll in the neighbourhood. The quiet is only broken occasionally by the drivel oozing out of the TVs, the lonely, bored, and brain-dead residents are watching. But these two men are not out for a stroll. They are on a mission.

Arriving at Delgado's house, he unlocks the door, turns on a dim light in the hallway, bids Ricardo to enter, shuts and locks the door, and secures it with a couple of heavy iron bars.

At the end of the hallway a door opens to a printer's workshop. It is located in a solidly built, soundproof extension of the house. Delgado flicks a switch, and the workshop is dipped into blinding, glistening light. There are Heidelberg printing presses, a silk-screen set, and a studio with cameras and computers. A darkroom is open and enlargements of Miguel's photos of Oscar hang on a string. On a workbench in the centre of the room is a framed matte silver cloth.

Delgado picks a rag laced with thin copper wires out of a basket and wipes the wall behind the printing machines. Silently the wall slides open and reveals a large safe. Orange letters in a display window above a keypad announce that the safe is locked. Delgado types three lengthy codes until the window announces 'Warning - Safe Unlocked'. Delgado pulls the handle and the heavy safe door swings open. He selects documents and blank sheets with letterheads from several drawers. He shuts the safe and wipes the rag over the wall that closes as silently as it opened.

Delgado spreads the documents and sheets onto the matte silver cloth. He pulls a bright desk lamp with a powerful magnifying glass in its screen down from above the workbench. He motions Ricardo to have a look at the blank sheets with seals and letterheads of several ministries as well as USA and Peru passport, ID-card, and birth certificate blanks.

Ricardo points to a sheet with the letterhead and signature of the Minister of the Interior when the doorbell rings. Before Delgado goes to answer the door, he pulls the upper edge of the matte silver cloth frame calmly towards him and pushes it back. The papers and documents slide out of sight and are replaced by the title page layout of a woman's magazine.

Ricardo stares at the title page, tries to find out where the papers and documents went and looks under the table. He can't find the vanished items, straightens up, and bangs his head into a handle of a printing press. He dances around cursing, rubs his head, and adjusts his ponytail when the door opens, and Delgado enters the workshop in the company of three policemen.

Ricardo takes a step back and in shock cracks a resounding fart. It takes a moment for him to recognise the three brothers Carlos, Jaime, and Omar Castro who hold their noses and wave their caps to spread the evil smell.

Carlos hands over a small envelope with passport photos of the three brothers and a woman. Delgado compares the photo of the woman to Oscar's in the darkroom. The other men have a look and show their approval with a thumbs-up. Oscar and the woman look like twins. The men whisper excitedly amongst each other when Delgado pushes and pulls the lower edge of the frame of the matte silver cloth on the workbench and the blank documents and sheets of paper reappear. He places the photos of the brothers on blank ID-cards, the woman's photo on the Peruvian passport blank, and Oscar's photo on that of the USA.

The four men nod their approval and Ricardo peels fifteen one-hundred-dollar bills onto the workbench. Delgado holds up five fingers and smiles sardonically until he gets another thirty-five bills laid out on the table.

Delgado leads the four men down the hallway and unlocks the front door. Before he opens it, he says in a low voice, "Tomorrow morning at six everything will be ready for pick-up including all required visas and entry and exit stamps in the passports. Okay?"

"At six tomorrow morning?" asks Ricardo. "Don't you ever go to sleep?"

"No, insomnia," explains Delgado. "I can't sleep since my wife was murdered."

"Insomnia?" asks Omar. "Sleep with the fat woman that looks like Oscar. One weekend with her and you'll sleep like a baby."

The three brothers and Ricardo cackle. Delgado smiles and opens the door. "Get out of here!"

***

Miguel Arías sits in the arcade café of the Grand Hotel. He drains a glass of beer and orders one more bottle.

It is getting late, but the café is still packed with locals as well as tourists who speak a variety of languages. It adds to Miguel's discomfort. He hates it when people speak a language he doesn't understand. He peers across the open space fronting the hotel and waves a hand when he sees Ricardo stroll towards him at last.

Before Ricardo sits down to join him, Miguel whines, "Man, I've been waiting for hours! What's going on, man?"

Ricardo gives him a blank stare and says in an icy tone, "Big problems. Your snapshots of Oscar are blurred and out of focus."

Miguel barks back, "What'd you expect? That camera is a piece of junk."

Ricardo responds calmly, "You're drunk, Miguel. Keep your voice down. You fucked up! Couldn't get Oscar to hold still for one second."

Miguel gripes, "What could I do? The fat bastard raged. Accused me of sticking him in the klink."

Ricardo grins at him. "Well? You did, didn't you?"

Miguel protests vehemently, "What a crock of horseshit! I only diverted attention with my testimony. He deserved what he got."

Ricardo counters, "You got big bucks for the perjury that put him away for life. Now that we ask you to do a real job, you fuck up. Does the entire Rapid Reaction Force operate like that?"

Miguel waves him off and complains, “Aw, shut up. A good camera would’ve taken good pictures. That’s not my fault.”

Ricardo gets up and tosses a one-hundred-colones bill on the table. “Alright. If you say so, here’s your pay, you useless prick!”

He walks away. Miguel jumps up, knocks over his chair, and bumps into a frail, elderly man at the next table who got up at the same time.

Miguel grabs the banknote, crumples it, throws it to the floor, and shouts, “Son of a bitch! That’s not our agreement!”

A waitress puts a bottle of beer on the table in front of Miguel. She bends down, picks up the chair, grabs the crumpled colones bill, and stashes it in her money pouch. The elderly man hands her Miguel’s wallet behind his back and sits down again. The waitress stashes the wallet and holds out her hand to get paid for the beer.

Miguel looks at her with alcohol-glazed eyeballs and gropes for his wallet. He comes up empty and squints at the waitress who squints right back. Panic-stricken, Miguel scans the floor and crawls around in search of the one hundred colones and his wallet.

Two pairs of thick-soled lace-up boots appear in his field of vision. He looks up and stares into the faces of Carlos and Jaime in police uniform. They demand to see positive identification. Miguel slurs that his wallet has disappeared. Jaime grins, puts the cuffs on him, and marches him together with Carlos to a waiting police cruiser where brother Omar is at the wheel.

***

Omar stops the car in a lay-by on the highway through the Braulio Carrillo National Park shortly before midnight. Carlos drags the struggling Miguel out of the car and marches him a long way up a muddy forest path to a four-foot deep, seven-foot long, and three-foot wide hole in the ground. Carlos removes Miguel’s cuffs and holds his arms behind his back while Jaime comes up the slope with a razor-sharp machete slung over his shoulder. Jaime pulls Miguel’s head back and without hesitation cuts his throat to the bone. They dump the body into the shallow grave and push soil and leaves over it with their boots.

Carlos and Jaime high-five each other and walk back to their car. Omar has already removed all the insignia and fake license plates as well as the red, white, and blue flashlights that marked it as a police cruiser. They take off their bloodied police caps and shirts, change into regular shirts and drive home for a good night’s sleep after a hard day’s work.

12

A long queue of visitors waits in front of the Cárcel de Guadalupe's main gate early in the morning of Saturday, 6th July 1991. At the head of the line stand Carlos, Jaime, and Omar in the company of Oscar's 'twin', a tall, rotund woman by the name of Rosalía Hernández. She wears a long peasant style skirt, a blue blouse, grey cardigan, and a black mantilla. She carries a blanket and a large hamper with food, a thermos, cartons of cigarettes, and clothes.

As soon as a prison guard signals that the gate will be opened, Carlos rushes forward and hands a Peruvian passport, three national ID-cards, and a letter from the Minister of the Interior to the control officer. The documents are checked and handed back with a list on a clipboard. Carlos signs it, and the quartet enters the prison.

Jaime scans the visitors' hall. He points to a corner about halfway between the prisoner entrance and the visitor exit. They spread the blanket on the floor and settle down.

It is Rosalía's first visit to a prison. She is excited, looks at the men, women, and children entering the hall and wonders who the distant relative of hers is that had been asking for her to visit him according to her three companions. Are there any other members of her extended family who might want to visit their relative?

Carlos notices Rosalía's display of nerves and pours her a cup of tea from the thermos. She drinks the drugged infusion and falls fast asleep.

***

Oscar lies on his bunk bed and watches Raúl, Mario, and Bernardo getting dressed in anticipation of being called to see their visitors. He watches them pacing around as much as the narrow cell permits. He looks forward to the time he will have to himself and can feed his pet rat. He has some bread at the ready and knowing that his pet is partial to corned beef he opened a can.

The cell door is unlocked, and Oscar is surprised to hear his name being bandied about. A guard pulls the door open and shouts, "Oscar Ortiz? Get dressed and step out! You got visitors!"

Oscar sits up and asks, "Me? Again? Is it another friend?"

The guard shouts back, "No, it's your family!"

Oscar rolls his eyes while images of his father, mother, brothers, and sisters float around in his mind. Finally, he mutters, "My family? Oh!"

He gets up, puts the corned beef on a plate and pushes it with the bread under the bed. Quickly he puts on shirt and trousers and steps out of the cell leaving his three gawking cellmates behind. At speed he is pushed along the hallway and down the stairs.

Overwhelmed by the crowd in the visitors' hall, he stops and looks around in search of any familiar face. He sees neither friend nor foe and wants to ask the guard of the whereabouts of his alleged family.

Omar sees Oscar standing by the entry gate. He rushes up to greet him, gets a firm hold of his arm, and half pushes and half drags him to the corner where his 'family' is waiting. Carlos and Jaime get up to greet Oscar with bear hugs. Jaime forces him to sit down next to the snoring Rosalía.

Oscar looks with great suspicion at the three men and Rosalía. He points at her and asks, "Who is that?"

Omar chortles. "Don't you recognise her? It's your Aunt Ana from Peru. She came to see you, but her long journey really tired her out."

Oscar whispers, "Bullshit. I have no Aunt Ana. Who is that?"

Instead of giving him an answer, Jaime stuffs a smoked salchicha into his mouth. "You should eat something. You look famished."

At the first delectable taste of the sausage that he missed for over eighteen months Oscar feels in heaven. His eyes bulge out when Jaime takes pudding filled tartlets, a ham and cheese baguette, and a bag of 'chicharrónes', fried pork crackling, out of the hamper and spreads the goodies out in front of him.

Oscar wonders how these guys he has never seen before and who are obviously not his family know all his favourite snacks. Perhaps Bert is behind this charade, he thinks and keeps on stuffing his mouth.

Omar opens a can of orange drink and drops a load of LSD into it. He hands it to Oscar who takes a swig. Within a short time, Oscar has eaten four salchichas, the bag of pork crackling, three tartlets, half a baguette with ham and cheese, and washed it all down with the orange drink.

When Oscar takes a break from his pig-out, his face starts to twitch. He opens his eyes wide in an attempt to focus, smiles in a stupor, points a finger at a couple of guards walking by and bursts into outrageous laughter. He follows it up with a rendition of a bawdy song about the pawnbroker's three balls he displays outside his shop.

Another prisoner has noted the facial and physical similarity of Oscar and the woman sleeping next to him. When he hears Oscar sing the pawnbroker song he chuckles and takes out a cigarette. He gets up and approaches Omar. He flicks his thumb to show that he needs a light. Omar hands him a lighter and tells him to keep it. The guy lights his cigarette but does not leave. Jaime gets up and gives him a menacing look. The guy smiles, looks at Oscar, and whispers, "Farewell, Oscar."

Carlos can see Jaime getting all tense and ready to do something hasty and stupid. He tugs on his sleeve and hands him two cartons of cigarettes. Jaime relaxes noticeably and passes the cartons together with some rolled up banknotes to the guy.

The guy winks at Jaime in appreciation of the gifts. He turns, opens the cartons, waves to the inmates in his vicinity to come closer, and hands out the packs of cigarettes until Oscar and his 'family' are screened off from the looks of the guards.

Oscar's condition appears to have deteriorated somewhat. Instead of laughing and singing, he picks his nose, wipes snot on his shirt, burps, and farts. Jaime and Carlos take action. Against Oscar's feeble protest they pull him flat on his back and take off his shoes and pants. Omar hands them a shirt of identical colour to Rosalía's blouse. They take off Oscar's shirt and dress him in the new one. Next, they take Rosalía's skirt and cardigan off and put them on Oscar. They pull away Rosalía's black mantilla, squeeze a baseball cap on her head and fit her in Oscar's pants and shoes. There is a problem with Rosalía's shoes - they don't fit Oscar. Against his growling protest they squeeze his feet into her shoes and cover his head with Rosalía's mantilla. Finally, Omar shoves a thick wad of money and Rosalía's real identity card into a pocket of the pants she wears.

The smoking inmates are in awe about the brothers' swift job of rolling two fat persons to and fro and exchanging their clothes. They acknowledge the perfect change of identity and disperse.

Jaime and Carlos get Oscar up on his feet that hurt him immensely. Oscar bellows in agony while being dragged along, which makes it all the more believable that there is something seriously wrong with him.

Omar takes out a vial, breaks off the top, and dribbles the liquid onto Oscar's back, the blanket, and the floor. An infernal stench starts to spread in the visitor hall. Inmates complain about the foul smell and shout that the guards should open some windows.

Omar waves to a couple of guards who keep a safe distance holding their noses. Omar shouts at them over the din of loud protests, "Sorry about the stink, gentlemen. It's cholera, yes, I'm sure our aunt has a bout of cholera. She's from Peru, you know?"

Upon hearing the word 'cholera', bedlam reigns in the hall. Inmates and visitors get out of the way to give Carlos, Jaime, and their 'aunt' a wide berth. Omar apologises constantly, goes ahead, and demands the exit door for this emergency to be opened.

The guards stand clear and watch the quartet reach the prison gate. An officer of the guard checks the identity papers Carlos presents to him, gives the photo in the Peruvian passport and Oscar's face a fleeting glance, approves everything and orders the big gate opened when he gets a whiff of the 'aunt'.

Oscar is dragged into the parking lot where he is put into a van. The prison gate slams shut.

Skirt, mantilla, cardigan, and the nice little lady's shoes are dropped in the parking lot before the van speeds away on the road to the international airport west of San José.

***

A couple of hours later the prison visitors are leaving. The hall is almost empty before anyone notices the lonely figure sleeping on the blanket in the corner surrounded by food wrappers, tartlets, half a baguette, a couple of sausages, empty soda cans, some clothes, and an empty hamper. The loud snoring draws the attention of prisoners lining up on their way back to the cells. Those men who witnessed the switch and know that Oscar was busted out keep quiet. Oscar's cellmates are not part of the men in the know. Fortunately they had been seated with their visitors far away from the action and suffered only the stink.

Mario nudges Raúl and murmurs, "Look over there. Our marshmallow arse fast asleep."

Raúl redirects Mario and Bernardo over to the corner and gives the sleeper a light kick in the butt without attaining a change. The sleeper keeps on snoring and Bernardo bends down to have a closer look under the baseball cap pulled low into the face.

He straightens up with a strange expression, points a finger at the figure and whispers, "That isn't Oscar."

Raúl gives him a doubtful look and asks, "Are you sure?"

Bernardo whispers, "Yes, Oscar doesn't wear makeup."

Mario wrinkles his brow. "You mean that's a woman?"

Bernardo nods and Raúl orders him to put a hand down her pants to make sure.

"What? Are you fucking crazy?" protests Bernardo. "I'm not gonna put my hand on her whatsit."

Raúl asks, "Why not? You're afraid to get bitten by a snappy pussy?"

Mario belts out a laugh that draws the attention of a couple of guards. They come over truncheons at the ready to sort out these three amused guys and to wake up the sleeper.

"Hello, hello, hello," says one of the guards, and enquires, "What's going on here then?"

"We thought this was our cellmate," answers Raúl with a grin. "But it isn't. It's a woman that looks like Oscar."

"Yes? And?" asks the guard. "It's a relative. Fell asleep. It happens."

"Is that so?" enquires Bernardo. "Then where is Oscar?"

The guard shrugs. "Back in his cell? Perhaps?"

"Back in his cell?" barks Raúl. "Are you blind? Look at all that food. You think Oscar would have gone back to the cell without sucking up the last crumb of food like a vacuum cleaner?"

The guard looks baffled and without another word starts poking Rosalía with his truncheon until she wakes up.

She rips off the baseball cap to get a better view of her tormentor, pats her head and wails, "Where's my mantilla?"

She looks down at herself and whimpers, "Where's my skirt? What happened to me?"

The guard orders her to get up and shouts, "Who are you and what are you doing here?"

Rosalía gets a helping hand from Mario and Bernardo. Instead of answering the questions, she gives the worn-out shoes she was bequeathed a dazed look and whines, "These brothel creepers aren't mine. Whose are they and where are my nice little shoes?"

The guard stops her complaints by poking her with his truncheon and repeats, "Who are you?"

Rosalía grabs the truncheon and rips it out of the guard's hand. Tears roll down her cheeks when she shouts, "Stop poking me with your wooden dickie, you ugly little man. I'm Rosalía Hernández from Limón."

The guard tries to retrieve his truncheon that Rosalía swings over her head. When he bumps into her, she gives him a push with her paunch, and he lands on his backside.

The other guard helps his colleague to get up and asks Rosalía, "What are you doing here?"

She relinquishes the truncheon and answers, "I came to visit my nephew Aurelio who is imprisoned here. He wanted to see me."

"Who told you that?" asks the guard.

"His cousins José, Juan and Jacinto," she replies and asks, "Where are they? Have they left without me? And where is my nephew, Aurelio? I never got to see him. Is he alright?"

Raúl butts in, "There is nobody here by the name of Aurelio. And I've been here long enough to know, I assure you."

"No? No Aurelio?" asks Rosalía and starts to weep. She shoves a hand into a pocket in search of a tissue. She shrieks and pulls out a bundle of banknotes and her identity card. "What's all this?" she asks and holds up the booty.

"It's not yours?" asks the second guard.

"No!" she calls out and shoves the bundle into his hands. "Oh wait. There's my identity card," she squeaks and picks the card stuck between the banknotes before he pockets the money. She holds up the card. "You see, that's me."

Bernardo has a peek and turns to Raúl. "Looks just like Oscar."

"What?" asks the guard, "Who looks like Oscar?"

"She does." Raúl points at the photo on the card. "Look, same cropped crinkly hair, skin colour, thick nose, heavy jowls. But I think Oscar has bigger tits."

When the guard looks at Rosalía and nods in agreement with Raúl, she snaps her identity card away with an insulted look.

The first guard pipes in, "I think I know what's been going on here. Come on, madam, let's go, and clear up this mess."

He and his colleague take Rosalía between them and walk to the exit when Bernardo asks brazenly, "Can we come along? You know, we could help you identify Oscar."

The second guard turns on his heel, raises his truncheon, and says with a smirk, "Likely you could identify his arse, but not his face." Then he shouts, "Now get back to your cell, you bums!"

As they turn, Mario can be overheard to say, "Shit, when that screw has a bit of money in his pocket, he gets ever so cheeky. We only offered to help."

"And perhaps sneak out of the gate in the muddle," adds Raúl.

The matter is resolved at the gate after checking the list of visitors. Since Rosalía is obviously a victim, she is released and told to leave.

Looking down at herself, she complains that she can't go out into the streets like that in ill-fitting trousers and brothel creepers. She insists on finding out what happened to her skirt and mantilla and would at least like an appropriate replacement. The officer in charge responds that the Cárcel de Guadalupe is a men's prison, and a skirt and mantilla is hard to come by because none of the guards are cross-dressers as far as he knows.

He opens the gate, has a look outside, and says, "Look, there's a skirt, shoes, cardigan and mantilla, out there in the parking lot. Now get lost, madam."

He grabs Rosalía by the arm, shoves her out, slams the gate shut, and the sirens start to wail announcing a prison break.

***

A Twin Commander 1000 lands on the Tierra Altas airfield of the town El Hato del Volcán in western Panama in the late afternoon.

Igor and the co-pilot have to help Oscar get up. He is still flying high on LSD. Decked out in a cowboy outfit of large white Stetson held up by his ears, pale-blue, rhinestone decorated denim shirt, jacket and jeans, and alligator boots, he looks utterly ridiculous.

The two men transfer him swiftly to a Mercedes 560 SEL waiting at the landing strip and the car speeds away along narrow mountain roads, through forests, and past lush meadows.

***

The Mercedes comes to a stop in front of a bungalow of the Buena Vista Health Resort & Spa in the town of Boquete in a valley of Panama's central mountain range. It is a well-appointed five-star hotel with luxury suites, bungalows, and a golf course. It caters to well-heeled Panamanian and foreign clientele.

Amerigo Cardenas, the boss of a fitness crew, a muscular man in T-shirt and jeans, angular face, moustache, and cropped hair, opens the door of the car. Igor and Oscar get out. Amerigo shakes hands with Igor and looks amused when he gets an eyeful of Oscar.

He greets Oscar. "Welcome to Buena Vista Resort and Spa, Mister Oscar Meyer. This is your home for the next eight weeks."

Oscar wrinkles his brow, sways in the light evening breeze, and turns to Igor. "Who's Mister Oscar Meyer?"

"That's you," says Igor poking a finger into his chest. "And don't you forget it."

Oscar stares at him with glazed eyeballs for a moment and breaks into derisive laughter. "Oscar Meyer? Do I look like a big hot dog weenie to you? You couldn't have thought of a different name, could you?"

Igor looks him up and down. "I did and considered the names Dan Druff, Willy Nilly, and Seymour Butts but decided that Oscar Meyer suits a fat American weenie like you much better. I give you eight weeks to correct that, lose weight and get fit."

Oscar stares at Igor. "Eight weeks? Why eight weeks?"

Igor gives Oscar a stern look. "That's my estimate for Amerigo and his team to get you into shape and fit for work."

Oscar sways to and fro. "Fit for work? What work?"

Impatiently Igor barks, "Any work!"

He turns to the car to get back in and says in a threatening tone, "Listen, Oscar, uh, Meyer. You look bad, smell worse, and worst of all you talk rubbish. Healthy body, healthy mind is our credo. You have eight weeks to get fit or it's back to Guadalupe."

In a state of shock, Oscar watches the car drive away with Igor in the back. Amerigo points to the door of the nearest bungalow. He pushes it open and invites Oscar to enter. He watches Oscar staggering around the comfortable rooms.

Amerigo leans in the doorway and cleans his fingernails with a flick knife. He clears his throat. "There's everything you need, clothes, toothbrush and paste, soap and towels, and all that."

Oscar nods and sits down on the bed. "Is it true that it's back to Guadalupe if I don't get fit in eight weeks?"

Amerigo shrugs and looks away. "I doubt they'll go to that much trouble. There's alternatives to let you disappear. The Pacific is a big ocean full of sharks and the jungle here is pretty dense. But don't worry, my team will get you fit."

Amerigo puts away the flick knife and is ready to leave. When he sees Oscar slump back on the bed, he says, "That's the idea. Sleep a couple of hours. I'll get you up for dinner."

***

The dining room of the hotel is crowded with dinner guests. The indirect lighting on the walls and ceiling gives the room a cosy atmosphere, which together with the comfortable chairs and soft background music entices the patrons to stay for more to eat than they had planned or to have one more drink. It appears to have that effect on Oscar. He had changed into a tracksuit and gobbles yet another helping of his dinner.

Amerigo and his team of Liam Hickey, an Irish human resources consultant, Felipe Martínez, a medic from Honduras, and the Californian weight training coach Rafael Castaño have finished and face their empty plates. In disbelief they watch the amount of food disappear down Oscar's gullet.

Liam manages a smile. "Oscar, is that your fifth pork chop?"

Oscar has some problems answering with his mouth full and only manages to mumble, "Don't know. The portions are so small."

Felipe asks, "When did you have your last bowel movement?"

Oscar looks up, mouth open, food spilling out and asks, "What?"

Rafael doesn't put too fine a point on Felipe's enquiry and asks, "When did you have your last shit? Man, if I had your figure, I'd be on the can twelve hours a day blocking the sewage system."

Oscar swallows the last bite and wipes his mouth. "Decent people don't talk about that at the dinner table. Anyway, my mother always said, when your stomach is full, your heart is happy."

Rafael chortles, "Then you must have a really happy heart now."

Oscar holds his belly. "No, there's still room. Waiter!"

Amerigo slaps his forehead and shouts, "Aw, for crying out loud! Will you stop it already! You have eaten more than the four of us together. That's it, you understand?"

Oscar looks at him apologetically and whimpers, "I was only going to order some dessert."

Infuriated, Amerigo barks back, "Like what? Ten caramel puddings and Black Forest cake, but a whole one, please?"

Liam, Rafael, and Felipe whinny with laughter. Oscar looks ready to cry.

Rafael turns to him and says, "Let me tell you a funny story about another fat man."

Amerigo protests, "Please, Rafa, not another one of your stories. I'm trying to keep my food down."

But Rafael insists, "This story involves you, Amerigo. You better listen."

Amerigo groans, "Oh my. Then tell your damn story but be quick about it."

Rafael leans on the table and fixes Oscar with an unwavering stare. "See, Oscar, there was this fat guy at the fat farm where we did a job a few weeks ago. He was supposed to run at least ten laps on the indoor track every morning, but he was only interested in eating. So, one day our fitness coach Vanessa, a beautiful young woman in hot pants and a tight tank top, comes in and says, 'If you catch me, I'm gonna be all yours.' Well, you should have seen that fat guy run after her around the track, but he couldn't catch her. This goes on for several weeks and he gets quite fit. One day he misses her only by six inches before she slips out of the hall and he says to himself, 'Tomorrow is the big day. Yes, tomorrow I gonna catch her.' And the next morning he's ready with a well-greased loin to have a go at her when the door opens. But it's not the young woman that comes into the hall. It's Amerigo, stark naked and also with a well-greased loin, who barks, 'When I catch you, you gonna be all mine!'"

Everybody cracks up - except Oscar. He looks scared when Amerigo leans over to him and says, "See, what's in store for you?"

Amerigo gets up and stands behind Rafael ruffling his mullet. "I think somebody will get a haircut tonight."

Amid the laughter and Rafael's shriek of protest, Amerigo directs Oscar to get up. "Time for you to go to bed, Oscar. If you want a beer, there's some in the fridge of your bungalow."

Together they leave the dining room.

The other members of the team also get up. Rafael winks at two middle-aged women at the next table. They wink back, join him, and leave with his arms around their waists. Seeing it, Felipe looks ready to cry.

Walking to his bungalow, Oscar asks Amerigo, "Where's Igor?"

Amerigo mumbles, "Had to catch a plane, is busy with changes."

Oscar stops and asks, "Changes? What changes?"

Amerigo shrugs, "Who knows, I'm not part of his group."

His curiosity aroused, Oscar asks, "Group? What group?"

Amerigo mutters, "Second Generation. They gonna change everything."

"Second Generation," repeats Oscar and thinks of Bert having used that term.

He is certain that Bert contacted his brother and got the ball rolling that led to him getting busted out of prison this morning. But how is it possible that a term used by Bert only a few days ago is already in use for the sons and daughters of the old drug barons? Or is it just a generic term that Bert used when he met the Second Generation? They may have liked it since it is neutral and not a give-away like the misnomer 'drug cartel' for a group that is not even a cartel.

Amerigo snaps him out of his thoughts. "Your fitness coach, Vanessa Camacho, will join us tonight. Then the team is complete."

They stop in front of Oscar's bungalow. He thinks of Rafael's story with dread. "Fitness coach? Vanessa?"

"Yep, that's her alright, Vanessa, your fitness coach," confirms Amerigo. "She'll get you fit in less than eight weeks, uh, if you cooperate. But never mind that now. Go to sleep."

Oscar looks anxious. "Sleep? I can't sleep. I'm all wired up."

"Ah, just keep your window open," suggests Amerigo and chuckles. "The cicadas will sing you to sleep. Good night."

Abruptly Amerigo turns and walks away.

Oscar shuts the door and looks at himself in a wall mirror. He tries to suck in his enormous belly but doesn't succeed.

13

The sun rises in a cloudless sky over the mountain range of Boquete. It holds the promise of yet another glorious day with sweltering temperatures on Saturday, 20th July 1991.

Vanessa Camacho does her callisthenics right in front of Oscar's bungalow. She is wearing a loose, red tank top, white terry cloth shorts, and grey and red-hooped socks. A white sweatband holds back her auburn hair. She is waiting for Oscar to join her in doing some stretching exercises and go for their morning power walk before a light breakfast of toast and herbal tea.

Vanessa applies a strict regimen of exercises for Oscar every day, also on weekends, cajoling him into swimming after breakfast, followed by weight training, and two hours on the rowing machine before lunch. When he protested on his first weekend after his arrival about exercises on Saturday and Sunday, she said with a smile that there is no rest for the wicked and then cracked her verbal whip to get him going.

The first few days were awfully difficult for the team and for Oscar. He was given gallons of diuretic herbal tea to combat the water retention in his legs. It took a whole week of drowning in tea combined with relatively light power walks for any visible effects of the treatment. He was on the can practically every fifteen minutes to piss away the water retention or take yet another dump. When he said that his anus and penis would be worn to a frazzle unless the treatment was stopped, he earned nothing but laughter.

The fitness crew was ruthless in his opinion but after a week he could actually touch his toes without falling flat on his face.

The noticeable weight loss allowed Oscar also to get on the rowing machine without breaking the little wheels under the seat. Furthermore, he underwent the sensible change of not resisting Vanessa's regimen any longer and accepted a small salad, and soup and sandwich as enough for a lunchtime meal. He exercised with gusto and as a result was often so bushed at the end of the day that he didn't even join the crew for dinner. He crawled into bed for a restful sleep and enjoyed getting up early in the morning feeling good about himself and his improved physical condition.

Although his prison experience still weighs heavily on his mind, which expresses itself by avoiding physical contact with anyone including Vanessa, outwardly he appears to be a happy man. His happiness with himself and the lack of contact with the crew beyond what is absolutely necessary contributes to him failing to notice the tension among the crewmembers.

Amerigo is the boss and wants to be respected as such. He is patently unhappy with Vanessa taking over with her strict regimen and having contact with Igor whom she called to get his approval for her rule of the roost. Rafael is hot to trot to get Vanessa laid and grumbles about her rejection of his advances. Felipe is gay and in love with Rafael since he first met him. Consequently, he is upset about Rafael taking a different woman or even two or three women at once to his quarters almost every night.

The only person that stands out is Liam, the guy from Ireland. He is in Boquete upon the insistence of Igor but no one, except Vanessa, has figured out why he is part of the crew.

During their power walk she tells Oscar that today is the day when he will have to forego his exercises after breakfast and sit down with Liam for his professional assessment. Oscar has no idea what a 'professional assessment' might be but lets it pass and doesn't ask for an explanation.

***

Oscar and Liam sit at a table on the lawn near the bungalow. Liam sorts a batch of papers and is highly irritated by Oscar resting his head on his hands on the table and snoozing. Liam wakes him up by rudely poking his elbow with a pencil.

Liam snaps, "Wake up! I have to ask you some questions."

Oscar gives him a dazed look and asks, "Is that so? And what questions might that be?"

"You'll find out as we go along."

Oscar props up his head and starts to snooze again.

Liam barks, "Pay attention! This concerns your future."

Utterly unimpressed, Oscar opens one eye and asks, "Really? And what future did you have in mind for me?"

Liam squints at Oscar and adopts a haughty tone. "Well, Oscar, your future hinges hugely on your answers. If they're good, you will get the red-carpet treatment. If they're not, you are finished. I guess Amerigo and Igor have made you aware of what a failure to pass the assessment entails."

Oscar sits up ramrod straight eyes wide open. Liam is certain that it is Igor's Sword of Damocles effect, and says, "Okay, the first set of questions concerns your formal education."

***

Amerigo hides behind a laurel bush between the bungalows to spy on Oscar. He knows that Liam is supposed to assess Oscar and wants to be assured that everything is done by the book. He disliked Oscar since he first laid eyes on him and would be only too pleased to see him fail, not only for personal reasons but also for monetary gain. Should Oscar fail, the crews' job would be done, and they would still get paid the full amount for the eight weeks of work they were hired to do.

Amerigo bends low to get a view through a couple of branches of the laurel bush. Vanessa peers around the corner, sees Amerigo sticking out his bum, sneaks up, and gooses him.

He leaps, turns, jabs an open flick knife, and stops a hand width from her abdomen. Angry about the sudden attack, he folds his knife, and whispers, "Are you crazy? I could ha' killed you!"

Unfazed by his reaction she retorts, "I was only pinching your bum. What are you doing?"

Amerigo nods in the direction of the garden and mumbles, "Keepin' an eye on Oscar. If he fails the assessment..."

Vanessa cuts in with, "... then what?"

Amerigo puffs up his cheeks. "He's goin' south, and we'd have done our job. We get paid in full and can go home."

Vanessa asks calmly, "What's more important? Oscar going south or you getting paid despite not having done your job?"

He is flustered by Vanessa questioning his motives. "What's the difference? I didn't care much for the slob in the first place."

Vanessa is ready to drop the subject but states, "You should care. Oscar's not a bad guy."

Amerigo almost bursts out laughing but controls himself and asks, "Him? Not a bad guy? You got the hots for him already?"

She rejects that question out of hand. "Don't be ridiculous!"

Amerigo puts on an air. "Aw, come on, missy. Everybody knows you're a nympho."

Vanessa protests, "Oh, I see. When I say that a man is not a bad guy, I'm a nympho. But when you screw a different woman whenever you can, you're only proving your manhood."

Amerigo shoves a hand under her tank top and grabs her breast. "That's how nature designed us. I squeeze your tit, get a hardon, and you drop your pants. Men hunt and women want to be hunted."

Vanessa is stunned and doesn't move. Her eyes turn to slits, and she hisses, "Take your hand off, Amerigo. I'm warning you!"

Amerigo tweaks her breast and asks, "About what? What ya gonna do?"

Amerigo has hardly finished his dumb questions or time to withdraw his hand when Vanessa jabs two fingers into his eyes and knees him in the groin. He bends double in agony. She does a quick turn and rams an elbow into his face busting his nose. Amerigo falls to the ground clutching his groin and face.

Vanessa picks up the knife that slipped out of his pocket and mutters, "Time to grow up, Amerigo!"

She tucks the knife into the waistband of her shorts, steps over Amerigo, and goes to join Oscar and Liam. They look up and smile when they see her coming around the bungalow.

Liam gets half-way up out of his seat in some form of acknowledgement. Cheerfully he greets her, "Hello, Vanessa. What a pleasing sight you are. Will you join us? Have a seat, please."

Vanessa bows and responds in the same spirit, "Well, thank you, Liam. I might just do that. How are you doing, Oscar?"

She sits down next to him and rubs shoulders with him. Oscar blushes, nods, and shrugs.

She imitates his nod and shrug. "What are you trying to say?"

Liam sighs. "Oscar means to say that we have a serious problem. He's not qualified to continue the programme. He's finished."

Vanessa leans back and looks at Oscar and Liam. "What? He's not qualified? Nonsense! Oscar's not finished. He's here to get fit and get ready to do his job. Look at the progress he's made."

Liam twists in his chair hearing Vanessa's objection and grasps for words. "Well, uh, yes, he's made some progress, uh, physically. However, I was sent a questionnaire to assess his qualifications objectively and subjectively. Oscar just doesn't fit the required profile for the job, which poses yet another problem. It is simply, uh, that I don't know what his job is going to be. Whatever it is, Oscar gave all the wrong answers."

Oscar has some difficulty breathing and bursts out, "That's because you asked all the wrong questions."

At that moment Vanessa sees Amerigo staggering towards them. Quickly, she takes the knife from her waistband and pushes it with a foot vertically into the soft sod.

Amerigo towers over the trio. They see his bloodshot eyes and out of joint blood-dripping nose.

Amerigo stares at Vanessa and asks with a nasal twang, "Where's my fucking knife, you bitch?"

Vanessa looks left and right in a theatrical move. "Bitch? You're looking for your bitch? Sorry, but Rafael isn't here."

Amerigo leans on the table in a threatening pose and shouts, "For the last time, you cunt! Where's my fucking knife?"

Vanessa gets up and aims two outstretched fingers at Amerigo. "I don't know where you lost your potato peeler. Perhaps you dropped it when you ran into a kitchen door."

Amerigo flinches and holds his hands in a defensive position in front of face and crotch.

Vanessa recognises his fear and provokes him. "You wanna search me? Go ahead. Search me. But be careful. I'm ticklish."

Amerigo blinks at her with his bloodshot eyes and walks away.

Vanessa mocks him by saying, "Ask Felipe to fix your eyes, nose and balls. Perhaps the chef can spare a potato peeler for you."

She sits down again with a crooked smile.

Liam cackles. "He ran into a kitchen door? Isn't that reserved for housewives and mothers in domestic disputes?"

Vanessa gives him a scathing look. "That's not funny, Liam. Now, where were we?"

Oscar says hastily, "Liam asked me all the wrong questions."

"Right," says Vanessa, holds out an open hand to Liam and demands, "Gi' me - the questionnaire, please."

Liam hands it to Vanessa. She scans the papers and nods. "Who wrote the questionnaire? Do these guys in Colombia know Oscar?"

Liam shrugs. "I, uh, don't know. I don't think so."

Vanessa puts the paper down. "Then there's no problem."

Liam looks ready to jump over the table. He bellows, "What are you saying? Of course, there's a problem. Oscar has no..."

Vanessa completes his sentence, "...formal education. Right! Do you know the education system of Colombia?"

Liam looks flabbergasted. "Uh, no."

Vanessa smiles impishly. "So, there you are. Oscar can be quite eloquent, has good table manners, knows arithmetic and the laws of physics, and speaks at least two languages. That's more than you normally learn at a school in Colombia and can use in life."

She asks Oscar, "Are you familiar with international business?"

Oscar nods, beams a big smile, and assures her, "Oh yes - import, export, wholesale and retail of medications and precious stones. Also, banking and international money transfers."

"And you learned all that on the street, so to speak?"

Oscar nods and Vanessa gestures her agreement with raised eyebrows and open hands.

Her evident support of Oscar infuriates Liam. He protests, "Vanessa! That is exactly the problem. It is street education."

She counters, "Who cares? On the street you learn to survive and apply immediately what you learned or you're dead. Igor and his cohorts need somebody with crucial survival skills. You can bet your ass on that. So, equate Oscar's skills to formal education. The guys in Colombia will never check the details. They want to be assured that Oscar's the guy for their business. So, assure them."

Liam gets all jittery. "No way! If they check the details and find out that my assessment is fudged, they'll have my guts for garters."

Vanessa rejects his objection. "No, they'll have Oscar's balls for cufflinks. But that won't happen if Oscar does a good job, and he will do that. Won't you, Oscar?"

He nods and Vanessa gets up. She leans on the table, reaches out, puts a hand under his chin, and raises his face until he looks into her eyes. "If you have any questions, Oscar, just open your mouth and ask. I'll help you."

She looks at the papers to the left of Liam, sees a blank questionnaire, and tears the one he filled out into shreds.

"I guess you are back at square one. Get cracking," she says and walks away.

Liam picks up a blank form and a pen and sighs. "Alright, Oscar. Let's give this another shot and see if you qualify."

14

It is late morning on Monday, 22nd July 1991, and Igor and Ariana are still in bed. He is exhausted from his extensive travels the past three weeks that concluded with a visit of several drug barons. He agreed with Alec that they had to determine the support they could expect to get from the heads of their associates' families to run the business or, for that matter, to assess the degree of opposition to such an idea. His activities were all in all successful with twelve of the sixteen families not opposed to the idea and the remaining four willing to go along with whatever directive Pablo Escobar would issue. He is pleased with himself and sleeps soundly.

Ariana on the other hand is worried that her family might disown her if they find out that she and Igor are lovers. Her family is not on a friendly footing with Igor's family and her father opposes the takeover of the business by a troop of greenhorns that includes Igor. She tossed and turned all night and couldn't sleep despite being awfully tired.

In response to a knock on the door, she shakes Igor by the shoulder to wake him up. She slides out of bed and lies out of sight on the floor as a precaution in case somebody opens the door and looks in. Igor looks around and wonders what happened to Ariana when he hears a second and more intense knock on the door.

He sits up and calls out, "Yes! Who is it?"

Igor recognises the voice of the barely audible response and whispers, "Shit! It's my father!"

Hearing Igor's curse, Ariana grabs her clothes and rushes into the bathroom.

He puts on a pair of shorts and opens the door. His father, Osvaldo Guttiérez, crumpled face, balding pate, stands in the hallway holding a fax message. He cranes his neck to look into the room and flares his nostrils.

Igor asks with due respect, "Yes, Sir? What is it?"

His father looks at him torn between agony and ecstasy and mutters, "This message arrived for you." He sniffs and asks, "Do you have someone in your room? I can smell pussy."

Igor blushes, grabs the fax, and stammers, "Uh, no, Sir."

His father looks at him sternly. "Don't lie to your father." He starts to grin and adds, "Is she pretty?"

Igor wants to protest his father's assertion but is prevented by him spotting Ariana coming out of the bathroom dressed in a dark green silk dress.

Osvaldo's jocular greeting is punctuated by a series of hiccups, which happens when he has a laugh. "Ah, Miss Ariana Andráe - the chemist. Have you analysed - my son's chemistry or - taken only his temperature? Hot stuff, what?"

Ariana looks embarrassed and blushes but manages a vague smile. "Hello, Don Osvaldo. How are you?"

"I'm fine," is Osvaldo jovial response. "But don't let your father know that you spent - the night in our house or - he'll explode. Just imagine the predicament - of his bits and pieces splattered all over your recently redecorated lounge and - your mother scraping them off the wall - with a teaspoon to preserve them - in a jar to keep on the mantelpiece!"

He holds on to the doorframe when his uproarious guffawing interspersed with powerful hiccups throws him off balance.

Igor has enough of his father mocking Ariana's family. "That's quite enough, Sir! Please!"

He shuts the door on his cackling father, looks at Ariana apologetically, and goes to sit down on the bed to read the fax message. Ariana squats next to him and looks over his shoulder.

"What are you reading?"

He wants to say something, looks at her, and laughs right in her face. Nervously, Ariana looks at him, then down her dress, and touches her face in search of the reason for his guffaw. She gets annoyed seeing him rocking to and fro unable to control himself. She's had enough and gets up. "What's so funny, you clown? Get a hold of yourself or I'm leaving!"

He tones down his amusement a notch and reaches for her hand. "I'm sorry but you are the spitting image of your mother, and I had the vision of her scraping bits and pieces of your exploded father off the wall with a teaspoon and putting them in jar to preserve him for posterity."

Ariana punches him in the shoulder. "My mother wouldn't use a teaspoon. That leaves streaks. She'd use a spatula."

Igor can hardly fend her off in the ensuing tussle. Finally, they calm down and he says, "Just blame my father. He has these crazy ideas. You should hear him tell his story about Elvis Presley who wasn't cremated because he was so full of drugs that the addicts of Memphis would have dug up his urn to sniff his ashes. My father had us rolling in the aisle many times. He's a goofball. That's why I like the crusty old fart."

Ariana leans on his shoulder sitting down next to him. "Then what's this message about? Tell me."

Igor reads, nods, and begins to smile. "It is the professional assessment of that guy Oscar."

"Is he any good?"

"Oh yes. Already in high school he got exceptional marks. Have you ever heard of the Germán Obejo Lyceum in Bogotá?"

"No, but I can tell you that a lyceum is generally a very expensive private school."

"Really? Wow! His parents must be loaded."

"Downloaded with debts more likely."

"Downloaded with debts?"

"Yes," asserts Ariana, "you told me that Oscar was a small-time dealer in Costa Rica. Why would he do that if his parents were loaded?"

"Okay, but his brother is a pharmacist," parries Igor. "That means he went to university. That is damn expensive. Nobody loaded down with debts can afford to pay their kids' university and lyceum education."

"Some people do, when they work like a tag team."

"What's a tag team?" asks Igor with a wrinkled brow.

Ariana sighs quite bemused to have to explain 'tag team' to him. "They help each other. The whole family chips in to pay for the education of one kid. Once he or she has achieved the qualifications and runs a profitable business, like Oscar's brother does, that kid pays for the education of the next sister or brother. You could find out what's what in no time if you checked on Oscar's family."

Igor thinks about that for a moment and then discards it. "Yeah, I suppose, but look at all his other qualifications and his job experience. Oscar's our guy."

He picks up the phone and calls Alec to tell him that he received Oscar's professional assessment. Then he adds a special request.

"Listen, the pictures I took in Costa Rica, yes, send them to the DEA with a fake message. Why? I want them to know that their own liaison agent is in bed with the drug dealers. It will draw their attention to Central America and cool their activities in Colombia a bit when they are forced to investigate their own people and have to restructure. Okay?"

15

It is a cloudy, grey morning in Arlington, Virginia, on Wednesday, 24th July 1991. Dennis Adams, a grey figure in a grey suit, section head of the Drug Enforcement Administration's cartel investigation unit, walks into the DEA Headquarter building's vestibule. He passes the security check and steps into an elevator.

Before he enters his office, he greets his secretary and asks her to please bring him a coffee. He drops his briefcase, checks some papers, reads a note, sits down in his high backrest swivel chair, and looks out the window. He turns in response to a knock on the open door and greets one of his team leaders, the agent Sean Murphy, who is holding a case folder.

"Hi, Sean, whatcha got there?" is Dennis' opening question.

Sean, a finicky young man with accurately parted dark hair, takes the formal route to greet his boss, "Good morning, Sir. How are you this splendid morning?"

Dennis casts him a contemptuous look. "Splendid morning? Whatcha talking about? It's cloudy and there's a gale-force wind bearing down on us. But otherwise, I'm fine. One day closer to retirement and very little to show for."

Unimpressed by his boss' gloomy mood, Sean continues, "Well, Sir, I got something that may change your outlook."

He opens the case folder and spreads out some photos for his boss to see.

Dennis puts on his reading glasses, picks up one of the photos, and points at one of the men in it. "I know that guy. That's Alfredo Calderón, the slippery drug boss we've been trying to nail for years. Who's that he's got his arms wrapped around? Looks familiar."

Sean comes around the desk to see which person his boss is talking about. "That, Sir, is Miguel Arías, our liaison man in Costa Rica, an officer of the Rapid Reaction Force."

Dennis scoffs. "Rapid Reaction Force, ha! Tell me, Sean, why do we keep financing the training and supply military equipment to a paramilitary force of one thousand two hundred men whose job it is to let recalcitrant citizens disappear in a country that claims to have no standing army?"

"I wouldn't know, Sir. National security, perhaps?"

Dennis shakes his head. “Are you sure? So, you share our former United Nations ambassador Kirkpatrick’s view that we have to finance a gang of murderous bums to prevent some three million moochers threatening our national security by throwing overripe bananas at us.”

The secretary serves a mug of coffee and enquires if Sean wants one, too. He declines. Dennis takes a sip and looks again at the pictures.

“Right, just imagine, Central America’s most elusive drug pusher hugging our liaison officer. Son of a bitch!”

Sean points to another picture. “There’s more, Sir. Look at the next photo.”

Dennis picks up the photo of a corpse partially eaten by animals. “What’s that?”

“That’s him, too, Sir,” Sean hastens to say. “It’s Miguel Arías according to the autopsy report that came with the photo from the Costa Rican police. The corpse was found by a group of tourists. A landslide coughed it up near a road through a national park.”

Dennis leans back. “You’re shittin’ me.”

Sean pulls his head back somewhat aghast. “I wouldn’t dare, Sir. The picture and autopsy report are an official communication from the police in San José. The other pictures were sent last night by fax with a short note from a General Adolfo Fernández.”

“Fernández? General Adolf? He’s Colombian. What’s he got to do with a dead agent in Costa Rica?”

Sean shrugs. “I wouldn’t know, Sir. I don’t know the general. I traced his fax-call to a police station in Calí, Colombia. That’s where the story takes on a strange twist. When I contacted the station, the sergeant said that the general has never been there and that they don’t have a fax machine - never had one.”

Dennis tosses the photo of the corpse back on the desk and grunts, “Now that’s just marvellous! I betcha the bear hug photos are a diversion. The Calí cartel is up to something, I’m sure.”

Sean looks confused. “I don’t follow you, Sir.”

Dennis leans back with his hands folded behind his head. “Okay, Sean, put the two messages in the proper sequence. The pictures of Arías in the embrace of the Costa Rican drug pusher Calderón come from Colombia. Since neither Arías nor Calderón have reason to go to Colombia, we have to assume that the pictures were taken in Costa Rica meaning that someone from Calí went to Costa Rica.

“Without a doubt it wasn’t General Adolf on the cartel’s behalf after years of his alleged fight against the drug cartels. Furthermore, would General Adolf have any reason to send us the pictures? Had he got a hold of them, he would have gone public with his find on TV and in the press to provide proof of the cooperation of drug dealers with the security forces in other countries, and he would have demanded an increase in his budget to fight the menace of the cartels. But he didn’t do that, did he? So, we can discard the notion of him being behind this ploy. The question is who sent them and why?

“We have to assume that it was someone from the Calí cartel or who has close ties to the cartel bosses. Leaving that aside for the moment, the photos are still of value to us because they show clearly that we have to get reliable agents in Central America. And that’s a funny twist in the developments so far.

“The pictures show that Arías was evidently a reliable partner of the Calí cartel. They had no reason to kill him. His colleagues of the Rapid Reaction Force didn’t kill him either. That’s a cert. Otherwise his corpse would have disappeared without a trace. That’s their specialty.

“In short, some amateurs killed him and dumped his body in a shallow grave where a landslide coughed it up. But who are these amateurs? What was their motive? This question looms large if the sender of the bear hug photos knew that the corpse had been found.

“We can presume as well that the sender doesn’t know that General Adolf is known to us as a liar and a fraud. And finally, the photos are not as important as the message somebody is trying to convey by sending them to us. It is crucial to figure out what that message might be.”

“I see, Sir,” says Sean with eyes closed to figure out what his boss was talking about. “But what if the bear hug photos were a setup? Just look at this one. Arías doesn’t appear overjoyed or happy to see the drug baron and he looks downright awkward when he gets the hug.”

“Good point, Sean. If it was a setup, it could mean that the cartel had him killed after all, but then again, what was their motive?”

“I guess the motive could be related to the message that was conveyed by sending the photos.”

“That is possible, of course, but it is all just conjecture until we have some solid evidence to back up our speculations. Do we have one of our boys in Costa Rica to dig up some facts?”

"No, Sir, there is only one of our agents in Panama investigating the banks' drug money laundering."

"Okay, Sean, write up a report about what we have so far," instructs Dennis. "Send it to our agent in Panama and order him to get a move on in Costa Rica."

"Right away, Sir, but I have one more question."

"Shoot," says Dennis and puts the photos into the case folder.

"How can one send a fax message without a fax machine, Sir? Yet via a telephone line of a police station."

Dennis looks amused. "It's easy with the old telephone systems of wires, cables, and switches. I think they still operate such a system in Colombia. You tap into the line of the police station with a couple of alligator clips attached by wire to your phone or fax machine, dial the number and bingo. As far as the telephone company can see on their records, it was a call from the police station."

"Oh, I see," mumbles Sean.

"Have you never done that? I mean as a kid? My brothers and I did it so many years ago. We scared our neighbours shitless with fake telephone calls."

"What? You did that as a kid?"

"Sure thing, there wasn't much else to do for fun in the small town where I grew up."

Sean sighs thinking about his own boring upbringing as a single child. He picks up the folder. "What are we going to do about this case, Sir?"

Dennis grabs his coffee mug and takes a sip. "Just follow up on it and establish a pattern of facts. Stay on top of the work you've done so far, Sean. I fear that something really big is developing, so big we may never see the end of it."

16

Four weeks into Vanessa's fitness training as well as eating healthy and wholesome food, Oscar is a changed man. He can smile when he looks at his figure in the mirror and his general attitude is almost that of the easy-going guy he was before he was sent to prison. The professional assessment that equated his street education to formal education and the positive response he received from Colombia also helped to lift his mood. He would be an all-round happy man if it weren't for his prison memories. When he is alone, he broods and thinks of revenge. He is wondering how he can ever get even with his tormentors in prison and those corrupt and lying bastards that had sent him there for a murder he didn't commit. He keeps his equilibrium by reminding himself of the Sicilian saying that revenge is a dish best served cold.

Vanessa is also pleased with Oscar's improved disposition. On occasion they engage in good-natured banter and share a laugh, which escalates Amerigo's misgivings about her. His obsession with watching her every move results in neglecting his duties as a team manager. He doesn't notice the deteriorating condition of Rafael, who shows severe signs of illness and a loss of muscle mass. Neither is he aware of Felipe ignoring Oscar and not providing regular medical check-ups anymore.

On Friday, 2nd August 1991, a very sick looking Rafael sits under a large tree in the front garden of the resort. Very gingerly he rubs boils on his face and arm.

Felipe comes out of the lobby of the hotel. He looks extremely distraught, takes a white handkerchief out of his pocket, and waves it in dramatic fashion while walking towards Rafael.

Rafael gets up when Felipe approaches. "What's the verdict, Felipe? What's wrong? Can you fix it?"

Felipe is close to tears and has some difficulty formulating his response. "Well, Rafa, my dear, I've got only bad news for you. What have you been doing, man? The diagnosis looks like textbook S.T.Ds."

Rafael wrinkles his brow. "S.T.Ds? What the fuck's that?"

Felipe looks around and says quietly, "Sexually transmitted diseases. You've got the clap and syphilis. I can fix that but there's something else I can't fix."

Impatiently Rafael shifts his weight from one foot to another. "Tell me already."

Felipe starts to sob and gives a tearful response that turns to uncontrolled anger. "I had to send your blood, stool, urine and swab samples to Mexico for analysis. The results came back this morning. You've got full blown AIDS, man, not just HIV! Full blown AIDS! Who in hell did you fuck, you stupid bastard?"

Unflustered by Felipe's outburst, Rafael shrugs. "Don't remember. I fuck'em and forget'em."

Felipe is appalled at the nonchalant response to what amounts to a death sentence. He emits a muffled cry and blows his nose.

Amerigo comes out of the lobby. He looks incensed and waves a piece of paper. He barks, "Rafa, I got this note at the reception. What the fuck did you do?"

Rafael doesn't like his tone and asks, "What now? What's your problem, dingbat?"

Amerigo barks, "Two high society chicks claim that you infected them with HIV. They went to the police in Panama City and laid charges. We're in deep shit, man. We must find a solution before the cops get here. I hafta talk to you."

He points to the overgrown area behind two bungalows for Rafa to follow him. Felipe senses doom and gloom and wants to go along but Amerigo tells him to get lost.

He leads Rafael through the bushes until they reach a ridge that affords a view of the valley below. It is a peaceful sight with cows grazing on meadows and horses romping through a coppice. In the distance people can be seen harvesting vegetables. The entire scene is underscored by the trills and songs of birds.

Amerigo rubs his forehead and gazes into the far-off distance. He turns to Rafael, "Beautiful, isn't it?"

Rafael is on edge and doesn't share Amerigo's appreciation of the scenery. "Yeah, beautiful. So what?"

Amerigo smiles. "And peaceful and quiet. We're under strict orders to be quiet and not draw attention to our presence in Panama, especially not here. You didn't do that, Rafael. What are we going to do?"

Rafael shrugs, puffs up his cheeks and replies, "Just keep going, I guess. Those bitches in Panama City, I'll just bump them off."

Amerigo is momentarily at a loss for words. "Bump them off? Are you insane? How many more bitches would you have to bump off? How many broads did you infect?"

Rafael sounds rebellious in his response, "I don't know, man. Look, it all started with this horny banker's wife. I showed her my pornos and she wanted to be serviced like the bitches in the films. So, I serviced her - top, bottom, back and front. Then she came back with a friend for a threesome and word got out. It was one after another after that."

Amerigo has only one short question, "How many?"

Rafael is annoyed about the inquisition and whines, "I don't know! Count my videos! I recorded every session."

Amerigo is stumped. "You what? You recorded every session? How many? Fifteen? Twenty?"

Rafael responds with a sense of pride. "Oh, yes. More than that, I'm sure. Man, we've been here for over four weeks."

Amerigo needs a moment to grasp the extent of the damage Rafael has done and tries to figure out how many more complaints he may receive. He turns to look out over the valley and thinks of the long time he has worked with Rafael. Until a moment ago he would have described him as an old and trusted friend but now he feels angry and betrayed. He decides that an end with horror is better than horror without end.

He pulls out a knife with a double-edged blade, turns and rams it into Rafael's chest and stomach. He grabs him by his mullet, pulls his head back, and cuts his throat. Blood splatters Amerigo's face, jacket, and trousers. Rafael collapses two short steps away from the edge of the precipice. Amerigo covers the corpse with a pile of leaves and some branches. He wipes blood off the knife, takes off his jacket, and sees the blotches of blood. He rushes back to the hotel, gets in through a back door and into his room.

He takes a shower and packs his suitcase. His bloodied clothes he discards in the garbage chute in the hallway. He gets into Rafael's room and packs the few belongings into a travel bag.

***

A taxi waits at the hotel entrance in the early evening. The driver gets out and opens the trunk. Amerigo is in the lobby, pays the bills for Rafael and himself at the reception, picks up a suitcase and a travel bag, and walks out to the taxi. The driver stows the luggage and shuts the trunk. They get into the car and drive away.

***

Night has fallen and the taxi stops at the intersection of the road from Boquete with the Pan American Highway. Amerigo points to the left down the highway towards Panama City. The driver shakes his head and points down the road into the city of Davíd. Instead of getting involved in a futile argument, Amerigo stabs the driver and cuts his throat. Blood-splattered he gets out of the taxi, pulls the driver's body out on the passenger side, and dumps it in a ditch. Calmly he gets back into the taxi, grabs some tissues out of a box, wipes his face, hands, and the steering wheel, and adjusts the rear-view mirrors. He waits until the highway is clear of traffic and drives away at high speed in the direction of Panama City.

***

Two police cruisers stop at the entrance to the Buena Vista Resort & Spa main building. Three policemen enter the lobby and talk to the receptionist. She shakes her head, puts the guest register on the counter, and points to an entry. The policemen nod, tip their caps, step outside, and walk over to Oscar's bungalow. They see that nobody is home and return to the lobby.

It takes a while to locate Vanessa and Oscar in the restaurant and inform them that the police would like a word with them. A bit anxious they go outside. They have no idea what is going on or that Amerigo has left. They were surprised to be seated by themselves for dinner but didn't miss the company of the four lunkheads, as they had started to refer to the rest of the crew.

They meet Virgilio Bládes, the burly figure of the police officer in charge and chat with him standing next to one of the police cruisers.

Vanessa explains that she is Oscar Meyer's personal trainer and fitness coach. He is an American citizen, and she is from Mexico she hastens to add. She asks why he wants to talk to her and Oscar. He states that the receptionist told him about their link to Rafael Castaño who is wanted for questioning. When she wants to know what link he is talking about, he mentions that they were booked into the resort by the same agency and that they were seen having breakfast and dinner with the suspect.

Vanessa fires back that he would have to question all the other guests that booked their stay through that agency in Panama City and that the women Rafael was bedding every night could probably clue him in much better than she or Oscar.

Virgilio looks at her with some suspicion. "You talk a lot, Miss. I want Mister Meyer to say something in this matter."

Not intimidated, Vanessa counters, "Yes, of course, but please consider the treatment of Afro-Americans by the police in the

United States. Then you might understand why he feels frightened by your presence and is scared of talking to you."

Virgilio sucks his teeth and asks for their passports. He shines his flashlight on Oscar's passport, flips through the pages, and hands it back to Oscar with a dismissive gesture.

While he checks Vanessa's passport, he is interrupted by his colleague, Romero Cruz. Virgilio listens to him whispering in his ear. His response is almost violent the way he shoves the passport at Vanessa, pushes Romero aside, and gives him instructions.

He is distracted by Oscar shouting to Felipe who walks by at a distance. "Hey, Felipe! Come here for a moment!"

Felipe sees Oscar and the police cruisers and rushes into the darkness towards the overgrown area behind the bungalows.

Virgilio looks up and asks, "Does that guy know the man we are looking for, uh, what's his name, uh, Rafael Castaño?"

Vanessa nods. "Yes, they are really close friends."

Virgilio squints at her. "Why is he running?"

Vanessa shrugs. "I don't know. Diarrhoea, perhaps?"

"Very funny," mutters Virgilio, switches on his flashlight, and gets ready to go after Felipe.

"Why else would he run into the bushes?" asks Vanessa with a grin and Oscar starts to chuckle.

Irritated by Vanessa and Oscar not taking his work seriously, Virgilio bawls, "Aw, shut up!"

He has almost reached the undergrowth when a scream can be heard that grows rapidly fainter and ends with a barely audible thud. Virgilio breaks through the bushes until he reaches the precipice. He points his flashlight down the ridge, turns around, and sees the disturbed corpse of Rafael as well as two deep footprints leading to the edge.

It takes a moment for him to gather his faculties and scream, "Damn it! Manuel, Romero! Come here! On the double!"

Virgilio's two colleagues run into the bushes. There is a lot of discussion between the three policemen before Virgilio reappears and walks back to his cruiser.

Vanessa asks Virgilio what happened. He explains that the guy who ran away very likely tripped over a corpse and probably took a deadly leap over the ridge. It is a very steep precipice of almost sixty meters and unlikely that he survived the fall.

Virgilio places an emergency call on his police radio and a while later the front of the hotel reflects the orange and white flashing lights of an ambulance. Two paramedics take a stretcher to the spot where Virgilio's colleagues are waiting. The searchlight of a police cruiser barely shines through the thick growth to light up the spot where the paramedics put Rafael's corpse on the stretcher.

A pathologist from the town of Davíd has arrived by car and watches the stretcher being carried to the ambulance.

He inspects the wounds on the corpse and inserts a thermometer into a stab wound on the chest.

Virgilio calls Vanessa and Oscar to approach the mutilated body. Oscar looks ready to vomit when he sees Rafael's remains and Vanessa clasps a hand over her mouth.

Virgilio asks her, "Miss, do you know this guy?"

Vanessa nods and tears well up in her eyes. She speaks very quietly, "That's the guy you wanted to question. But I can't say we knew him. Sometimes he joined us for dinner, but I don't know what he was doing here or where he was from. He never talked about himself."

Virgilio turns to Oscar. "But you, Mister Meyer, you knew his friend. You shouted to him before he ran away. What was his name?"

Oscar looks to Vanessa who nudges him to answer. "His name is Felipe Martínez. I only know him as a medic who helped me with some herbal medication to get rid of the water retention in my legs."

"A medic, you say?" asks Virgilio and takes some notes.

"I, uh, I really don't know," stammers Oscar. "He may be an herbalist because he only prescribes herbs and stuff."

"I see," says Virgilio and asks, "Why did he run away when you called him?"

"I have no idea," says Oscar. "He's a foreigner and perhaps he worked here without a licence. I never asked him, though. He was scared of being questioned, I think, when he saw you."

At this moment the pathologist provides Virgilio with a murmured account of his findings. Then he gets into his car and leaves. Romero reaches out from the cruiser and draws Virgilio's attention by tapping him on the arm. He hands him a note and they have a whispered exchange.

Virgilio turns to Vanessa. "We have received the names of the guests that were booked into this resort and arrived on the same day. Among them are the wives of a well-known banker and the surgeon general. They travelled together and laid charges against Rafael Castaño for infecting them with HIV. He and Felipe Martínez, Amerigo Cardenas and Liam Hickey were booked in as a group.

"Rafael is dead, Felipe vanished, and this guy Amerigo checked himself and Rafael out and left the hotel by taxi. That makes Amerigo the prime suspect in the killing of Rafael.

"But let us get back to the guest list, Mister Meyer. You arrived on the same day and according to the receptionist had immediate contact with that group of four men. Do you still claim not to be associated with them, Mister Meyer?"

Before Oscar can answer, Vanessa butts in, "That is pure conjecture, officer, and at best circumstantial evidence."

Virgilio smirks and fires back, "Are you a lawyer, Miss, or do you have a vested interest in speaking continuously on behalf of Mister Meyer?"

Vanessa is furious about Virgilio questioning her integrity. She knows only too well that Virgilio is on the right track of linking her and Oscar to the four lunkheads and tries to think of something to counter his suspicion.

Fortunately, before she can say something impudent, Oscar declares, "Look, officer, I arrived here in a very poor state of health. The first evening, when I went to have dinner, I was seated at the same table as these four gentlemen because the restaurant was crowded. We started to talk. I mentioned my poor health as the reason for coming here. That's when Felipe offered his advice and the herbal treatment to cure the water retention in my legs. The next day my personal trainer Vanessa arrived, and she agreed with Felipe's approach. That is the full extent of our contact with these four men."

Virgilio takes notes during Oscar's discourse. He looks up with a smile, and his hand gesture seems to say, 'Why didn't you say so in the first place?' He snaps his notepad shut, stows it in his breast pocket, and asks, "Do you have any idea of the where-abouts of the fourth guy of that group, this, uh, Liam Hickey?"

Instead of saying anything both Vanessa and Oscar shake their heads and shrug their shoulders. The radio in the cruiser starts to blare again. Somebody shouts something about a corpse in a ditch. Romero adjusts the radio volume, and the caller repeats that the corpse of a taxi driver had been found by the side of the road from Boquete at the intersection with the Pan American Highway over an hour ago. The corpse has a stab wound in his chest and a slashed throat conveys the caller and adds that he had already requested some support.

Virgilio tells the caller to wait for the pathologist who is on his way down from Boquete in a white Buick. It is very important to learn if the taxi driver was killed with an identical weapon, a double-edged dagger, like the corpse they found at the Buena Vista Resort Hotel.

While they are waiting for a report, Rafael's remains are loaded into the ambulance. It leaves without sounding its sirens. Finally, the voice of the pathologist can be heard on the radio. He confirms that the taxi driver was killed in the same manner and in all likelihood with the same weapon as the victim at the Buena Vista Hotel.

Virgilio issues the order for a nationwide dragnet to be activated in search of a taxi from Boquete.

Oscar and Vanessa want to leave but are stopped by Virgilio who asks, "Do you know this guy Amerigo?"

Vanessa shrugs. "Sorry, no! Why do you ask?"

"We need a description. Can you tell me what he looks like?"

"Oh yes," volunteers Oscar. "He's a tall, muscular guy with an angular, craggy face, moustache, and cropped hair. He has dark piercing eyes and cleans his fingernails with a switchblade."

"Thanks," says Virgilio. "It isn't much, but every bit helps."

"Why do you want to know all that?" snaps Vanessa.

"He's presumed to be a serial killer," answers Virgilio. "A taxi-driver was found near Davíd who was killed in the same manner as this guy Rafael."

"Oh my," is all Vanessa will say to that and bites her lip to restrain herself from asking any more questions.

Virgilio gives her a dark, probing look and asks, "Are you going to leave Panama soon?"

"No, Sir," she answers. "We are going to stay another four weeks until Mister Meyer has completed his programme."

"Very well," mutters Virgilio and adds, "Keep yourself available in case we have more questions, Miss, uh?"

"Camacho, Vanessa Camacho," she states promptly.

"Of course, Miss Vanessa, and thank you for your cooperation. You may go now."

He tips his cap and watches them enter the lobby. He is certain that there is something fishy about this odd couple.

***

Amerigo speeds along the Pan American Highway towards the small town of San Lorenzo. Having passed several closed gas stations he is nervously on the lookout for one that is still open. The gauge on the dashboard shows the taxi running on fumes and in desperate need of a fill-up. He sees the flickering lights of a convenience store some fifty metres off the highway and pulls into the gas station in front of it. He stops at the first fuel pump, jumps out of the car, and in his haste drops the key for the gas cap. An attendant sitting on a stool nearby gets up to help him and reaches for the key. Amerigo knocks him down, grabs the key, unlocks the tank flap, switches the pump on, and listens to the gasoline rushing into the tank. The attendant scrambles to his feet, sees the bloodstains on Amerigo's shirt and trousers, and screams. The cashier in the convenience store stops counting the money in the cash register when she hears the scream. She sees Amerigo pull a pistol from the back of his waistband and shoot and kill the attendant. She runs out of the store and is stopped dead in her tracks by a bullet hitting her in the forehead.

Two policemen in a cruiser pass the gas station on their way to Davíd. They are on alert to look out for a taxi with a big, muscular guy behind the wheel. They see the woman getting shot by a guy who is gassing up a taxi. They pull up by the side of the highway, scramble out of their cruiser and rush to the trunk that opens with a pitiful squeal. They grab their rifles and take cover behind their cruiser. Amerigo turns, sees the police car, and opens fire. The policemen shoot back aiming at Amerigo but hit the taxi and the gas pump with several bullets. The taxi explodes first and ignites the gasoline-spewing pump. The convenience store and gas station are levelled in the ensuing inferno of a giant ball of flames.

The bodies of Amerigo, the attendant, and the cashier are burnt to a crisp.

***

Vanessa and Oscar are back in the restaurant waiting for their dinner to be served. Oscar is shrivelled up in a state of heightened anxiety and wrings his hands. Vanessa is a picture of self-confidence and calmness. She drums her fingers on the table in anticipation of a waiter bringing their meals.

Oscar wishes that she would stop drumming the tabletop. "Could you stop doing that, please? That drumming is driving me nuts. I'd like to know what we are going to do?"

Vanessa waves her hands. "We are going to have dinner with a nice glass of wine. We carry on as if nothing happened."

Oscar makes big eyes and almost slips under the table when he asks under his breath, "Nothing happened?"

Vanessa has to smile about his reaction. "Yes, nothing of any concern to us. We'll stay put and continue with your programme. You still have a way to go before you are completely fit. As far as the crew is concerned, I'll give Igor a call and explain the situation. He'll take care of us."

Her voice trails off when the waiter serves their dinner and opens a bottle of Bordeaux. He lets Vanessa taste the wine, gets her approval, fills their glasses, and wishes them a healthy appetite. Vanessa and Oscar eat in silence.

***

Oscar feels very tired after the meal, half a bottle of wine, and also on account of the excitement of the day. He excuses himself, returns to his bungalow, and leaves Vanessa alone in the hotel's garden.

She is talking to Igor on her cell phone. She explains the demise of the crew due to the death of two of its members, the third on the run from the police, and the fourth one not showing his face. She can explain the reason for the chain of events only based on the charge of Rafael having infected a number of female guests with HIV. She states that the police came to the hotel to interrogate him and instead found his corpse.

Igor contemplates stopping the programme and asking Vanessa, Oscar, and Liam to come to Calí forthwith, but his concern for Oscar's fitness ultimately wins the day and he insists that the programme has to be pulled through as intended. He assures Vanessa that he will send a couple of heavies to provide inconspicuous protection. Vanessa ends the call on a note of relief and turns to go to her room.

After a few steps, she notices a rustling hedge and stops.

Liam appears and stands in her path with a large calibre pistol. He mutters, "You bitch!"

Vanessa is on her guard and says calmly, "And a good evening to you, Liam. Or do you actually wish each other a gloomy bottom o' the evening in contrast to the cheerful top o' the morning in Ireland? Never mind, never mind, what's with the peashooter?"

Taken aback by her torrent of words that didn't express any fear of the gun, he exclaims, "Peashooter? T'is a Magnum!"

Vanessa breaks into his Irish brogue. “Oh, t’is a magnum! Are you offerin’ me champagne? Where are the glasses?”

Liam realises that she is taking the piss and asks, “What are you talkin’ about? T’is a gun!”

Vanessa continues her assault of ridicule. “Ah, ‘t’is a popgun. Is the cork attached with a string, so you won’t lose it?”

Liam gets impatient with her foolish talk and threatens her. “Shut up! I’m goin’ to kill you!”

Vanessa giggles to his great annoyance. “Oh, that’s exciting! I’m vibrating in my flip-flops. Now, pray, tell me why you want to kill me?”

Liam hisses, “You’re at the root of the troubles.”

Vanessa cackles briefly and continues in the same vein, “Ey, how poetic! The troubles! You mean Amerigo slashing the throats of Rafa and a taxi driver? How very Irish of you to classify bloody murder as troubles. But what has that got to do with me?”

Liam is at the end of his tether, can’t contain himself anymore, and shouts, “You gave Rafa AIDS! You bloody whore!”

Vanessa ignores the accusation and asks, “What about Oscar?”

Liam fires back, “I’ll kill him, too.”

Vanessa sounds very agreeable when she asks, “Of course, but why? What did he give Rafa? Smelly feet? Acute nose-drip? Chronic flatulence?”

Slack jawed Liam stares at her. “What on earth are you talking about?”

Vanessa takes a step forward a smug smile on her face. “Don’t you know? You must be a terrorist the way you don’t follow your own logic or arguments.”

Liam is totally lost now. Looking up, his eyes wander about from left to right trying to locate some response in his brain. Without alcohol providing the necessary lubricant for even a stupid explanation there is nothing coming forth. He asks, “So, you think you know me, my dear woman?”

That question tells Vanessa that she can land a punch that will tempt Liam into thoughtless action. “Don’t call me your dear woman! I’m not your wife, you ridiculous intermission clown!”

Bullseye! Liam reacts as Vanessa had anticipated and fumbles with the gun while he hisses, “Intermission clown? I’ll show you who’s an intermission clown!”

In his haste to put a silencer on the gun and release the safety catch, he fires a shot into the night sky. The recoil almost flings the gun out of his hand. Vanessa steps swiftly forward, turns, grabs his wrist, and with her back to him wrests the gun from his grip. Just as swiftly she turns again and points the gun at his midriff. He hangs his head, raises his hands, and looks utterly defeated.

Vanessa looks at him in disgust and speaks in a low voice. “Drop your hands and listen. Unless you want the police to investigate your suicide tomorrow, you’ll take a taxi right now to Panama City and fly home to Ireland. You don’t belong here.”

Liam doesn’t move and just stares at Vanessa. She fires a shot in the ground near his feet. He does a couple of leaps not dissimilar to an Irish jig and rushes into the hotel.

Vanessa tucks the gun under her waistband, pulls her blouse over it, and sits down on a bench. She waits patiently for over half an hour until Liam comes out of the hotel.

He wears a dark three-piece suit, white shirt and tie, and carries a briefcase and a travel bag. He stops briefly and looks at Vanessa as if he wants to say something but then walks away on the path into Boquete.

17

The bus from Davíd comes to a gentle stop at the terminal along the southernmost end of Avenida Balboa in Panama City shortly before noon. Weary travellers get out, pick up their luggage the driver has put on the sidewalk, and they are on their way.

The last passenger to exit the bus is Liam Hickey with his briefcase. His suit crumpled, the collar of his shirt soaked with sweat, and his shoes scuffed, he picks up his travel bag and looks around disoriented not knowing where to turn or what to do. That is small wonder on account of the tightly strapped necktie restricting the flow of blood to his already confused brain. At last, he does the right thing in the overwhelming heat and humidity of this Saturday, 3rd August 1991. He drops his travel bag and loosens his tie. He takes it off completely and unbuttons his vest and the stiff, wet collar. The sudden ability to breathe freely and the proper flow of blood to his brain appear to give him a clear view. He looks in amazement at the hustle and bustle of nearby ambulant vendors of snacks and fruit juice, and the men, women and children loaded down with parcels and shopping bags rushing to the numerous bus stops to queue up and go home.

It takes Liam a moment to decide what to do next until he spots a small hotel sign in the distance with an arrow pointing into a side street. He picks up his luggage and slowly walks towards the sign in the hope of a cool shower, an air-conditioned room, and a comfortable bed.

At the hotel's reception he gets the first surprise when the tough looking guy with a scarred face and a glass eye in a steel bar reinforced cage asks him for how many hours he wants the room and if he has a companion. Liam feels too exhausted to simply turn his back on this dosshouse that is obviously the place of work for streetwalkers. He doesn't even get the picture when the guy asks him if he wants fresh sheets and towels, which costs an extra five dollars per night. Also, the question if he wants a room with a working air conditioner doesn't alert him. He just nods and accepts another fifteen-dollar surcharge. A working shower and running hot and cold water cost an additional twenty dollars. Once the receptionist has added up all the charges, the costs per night are over a hundred dollars. It could have afforded Liam a stay in a luxurious five-star hotel just a few city-blocks away. But he doesn't care and pays the total amount for two days. He doesn't even care that the lift is out of order. He has to lug his travel bag and briefcase up the narrow and foul-smelling staircase to the fourth floor. What makes him stop and wonder if he shouldn't have entrusted himself to a taxi driver and asked to be dropped off at a nice clean hotel of which there are plenty in the city of Panama is the condition of the alleged luxury suite he rented. The walls are a mottled brown and yellow, the stench in the room is reminiscent of a toilet the previous tenant forgot to flush, there are empty beer bottles strewn on the floor, and the mattress of the double bed appears to be a well-worn hammock.

Liam drops his luggage and opens the window. He turns on the AC that rattles and clangs but creates a mild flow of air. He gets undressed and takes a shower under the pipe that sticks out of the concrete wall. After barely drying himself off with a small hand towel, he lies down naked on the bed to think of what he is going to do next. While he has to see a travel agent to arrange his flight back to Ireland, another issue has a higher priority. He wants to go to the police and tell his tale. Originally, he wanted to do that in David after the taxi had dropped him off at a hotel but then it was getting late, he didn't know the police station's location, he was tired, and the bus to Panama City was going to leave early in the morning. One excuse led to another and in the end, he downed a bottle of Irish whiskey to drown his fury over the humiliation at the hands of Vanessa and her theft of the gun he had purchased in Miami on his way to Panama.

The fury still gnaws on his psyche, but he wants to take a nap and relax for a while. Before he gets some shut-eye there is a knock on the door, and it is pushed open. His first thought is that the woman with a fleshy face and masses of frizzy hair is a chambermaid who will bring him a proper bath towel until she exposes her floppy breasts. She holds a card the size of a passport, lifts her skirt to show that she doesn't wear anything underneath, spreads her legs, and moves her hips provocatively.

Liam is astounded by the performance of what he thinks must be a voodoo princess. He suffers the brief nightmarish impression of waking up next to that monster in the morning. Hectically, he waves his hands to indicate that he has no need for her obvious services, but she ignores his signals in light of him lying naked and inviting on the bed. Leaving the door wide open, she rips off her

Velcro-fastened blouse and skirt and proceeds to squat on top of him. She shows him the card dated, Friday, 2nd August 1991, that states with stamp and signature that she is free of venereal disease. Liam isn't interested and tries to wriggle out of his awkward position. No such luck! The woman has his stiffening male appendage firmly in hand and inserts it into her cavernous ventral body opening, pins down his arms and starts their joint session by hammering his loins with rapid, machine-like movements of her hips. Just before he reaches his orgasm, Liam thinks that this has nothing to do with making love. It is intravaginal masturbation that lasts less than a minute.

The woman, having had her fill, separates herself with a sucking noise of her crotch, and dribbles their mixed juices over him, the bed sheet, and the filthy floor mat. She holds out a hand rubbing thumb and forefinger showing that she wants some money. The fingers of her left hand spread wide leave no doubt that she wants fifty dollars. He gropes for the wallet in his jacket on the floor, extracts one hundred US-dollars, which is the nominal currency in Panama called Balboa, holds it out to her and slaps the worn-out mattress. She grabs the money, grins, exposes the gaps left by missing teeth, and drops down next to him.

Liam sees in the prostitute a substitute for Vanessa. He will do to her what he wishes he could have done to Vanessa to get even with her. He rips down the cord of the torn window curtain, ties up the woman's wrists and ankles to which she is a willing participant thinking that it is just a kinky game.

She starts to object by voicing her anger and pain when he starts to maltreat her in every possible form he can conceive. He hits her in the face, whacks her in the belly with a fist, twists her breasts, strangles her, and looks for a suitable object to cut her. He settles for hitting her in the head with an empty beer bottle and then shoving it up her vagina where it disappears. Viciously he engages in what he regards as the ultimate humiliation of a woman by having anal sex with her.

Once his manly outrage has been satisfied to an extent, he still doesn't feel that he got even with Vanessa, yet he tells the woman to get out of bed by way of untying her and slapping her ass. As soon as she can move her hands, she lands a punch on his mug and gives him a black eye. A little cut drips blood. He takes it like the man he is, howling and cursing, and pressing a hand on the swelling eye. His assumption that he was done with the rented woman having paid her in advance turns out to be a slight miscalculation.

A bulky guy stands in the open door. He watched the maltreatment of his woman and holds a flick knife in his right hand. It speaks a clear language. The guy enters the room, picks Liam's wallet off the floor, and empties it of almost one thousand dollars. Without a word he waits for the woman to extract the beer bottle and put on her clothes. He salutes and leaves with her.

Liam slumps back on the mattress, groans loudly about the trickle of blood on his face and the pain in his wallet. He wonders if he has enough cash left for a plane ticket to Ireland. He is loath to use one of his credit cards. It would provide irrefutable proof of his visit to Panama, which in turn would bring the Irish Secret Service into the picture because the payment for arms deliveries of the Irish Republican Army to the Colombian FARC guerilla came from a bank account in Panama.

He shuts the door, takes a shower, wipes himself down with the wet hand towel, gets dressed, and leaves the whorehouse with his wallet, credit cards, and passport in his pockets. The first travel agency he enters informs him that the only ticket he can afford to pay entirely with his remaining cash is for a flight with the Russian airline Aeroflot via Managua, Havana, Moscow, and London to Dublin. That would entail a stay of one night each in Havana and Moscow, which would require him to use his credit cards. He is tempted to give Igor a call in Calí and ask for a bonus cash payment for all the good work he has done. But he leaves all of that aside for the moment, hails a taxi, and asks to be dropped off at the nearest police station on Avenida Julio Linares.

Liam enters the station and asks at the front desk to speak to an officer of the drug squad.

The cop looks him up and down and asks with broad grin, "Why? You need some help with a drug deal?"

He keeps on chortling when Liam looks baffled and answers, "No, I have hugely important information about activities of the Calí cartel right here in your lovely country."

Unimpressed the cop keeps on grinning and asks, "Is that so?"

"Yes," confirms Liam. "I have names, place, and activities."

"You have names," mumbles the cop, picks up the phone and talks to someone repeating what Liam said. He puts down the phone and points a pencil down a hallway where a man comes out of an office waving a hand.

Liam follows the direction of the pointed pen, approaches the man, and introduces himself using the name of a former boss who, unbeknownst to him, is wanted by Interpol for big drug deals in the United States, Britain, and Ireland, "I'm Paul Dolan. Are you a drug enforcement officer?"

The man shakes hands with Liam. "Miguel Chavez. I hear that you have some information relating to the Calí cartel, as you call it. Come into my office, Mister Donut."

Miguel points to the rapidly darkening swelling of Liam's eye. "Nice rosette you got there. Where'd you get it?"

Liam touches the black eye. "Oh that! I got into an argument with a prostitute outside my hotel when I declined her offer."

Miguel smiles and Liam feels encouraged to tell his tale of doing human resource evaluation for an international corporation in the town of Boquete. He talks about the outbreak of violence among his employer's representatives that was investigated by the police. In due course he had learned that the international corporation was actually the Calí cartel. He mentions the names of the crew as well as Igor's and points out that Vanessa Camacho is the real boss who should be arrested immediately. About Oscar he can only say that Oscar Meyer is not his real name and that he is a small-time drug dealer originally from Colombia.

Miguel listens and searches through a pile of papers on his desk. He selects two sheets and lays them out on the desk. They are reports relating to Boquete. One is the charge of the two women that were infected by Rafael, and the other is a list of the crewmembers and Oscar as well as Igor and Alec and their telephone numbers. The names of Amerigo, Rafael and Felipe are scratched out and the name Liam Hickey is circled in red.

There is a knock on the door and the policeman Antonio Bládes enters. He is the younger brother of Virgilio Bládes, the officer in Davíd. He drops a couple of files on Miguel's desk and looks at Liam with a grin. "Nice rosette you got there. Where'd you get it?"

He doesn't get an answer but listens intently when Miguel asks Liam, "Do you remember the names of the police officers who investigated the outbreak of violence in the hotel in Boquete?"

"I don't know their names," answers Liam. "There were three officers from Davíd and the first name of the guy in charge was Virgilio. But I can't be sure. I got his name at the reception."

Antonio pulls a face and slowly walks out of the office when he hears Miguel ask Liam, "You didn't talk to him personally?"

"Oh no," confirms Liam. "I didn't want to get involved."

Antonio stands outside the office, leaves the door slightly ajar, and listens to Miguel. "You have mentioned the name of only one applicant you evaluated. It is Oscar Meyer, a drug dealer from Colombia. What are the names of the other candidates?"

Liam didn't expect to be asked so many questions. He wanted to tell his tale and provide the names of the crew and Oscar in the hope that the police would follow up the lead and arrest Vanessa. But now he ended up in a tight spot. "Off hand, uh, I really can't recall the names of all the applicants."

Miguel leans forward and his eyes bore into Liam's when he asks, "Do you recall how many applicants you interviewed?"

Liam looks flustered. "Must have been more than twenty."

"More than twenty," echoes Miguel. "Why were they asked to travel such a long distance to be interviewed in Boquete, a pretty farming community in the west of the country when we have nice luxury hotels and airports right here in Panama City? What do you think, hmm?"

Liam waves his hands about and claims, "I rightly wouldn't know. That was the Calí cartel's decision."

Miguel shuffles more papers until he finds the international arrest warrant for Paul Dolan. The picture shows the stupidly grinning moon face of a balding man with glasses and a neck so thick that he doesn't need to unbutton the collar of his shirt to get in and out of it.

Miguel looks up. "You have used the term cartel several times. Don't you know that cartel is actually a misnomer? A cartel is the collusion of businesses that rig prices and restrict competition. The Colombian drug barons don't do that. On the contrary - they go with the flow, take whatever the market offers, and don't mind at all when others pick up any slack and expand the market."

Miguel keeps an eye on Liam and lifts the phone. "I have to make a call."

He hits a quick dial button and a moment later he is talking to Igor and taking notes. After briefly exchanging niceties without mentioning names, Miguel says, "Here's a guy in my office with a whore wound. What? No, not a war wound, a whore wound. Got into an argument with a hooker and lost. Yes, a rosette turning deep purple on his right eye. Looks funny, I can tell you. Says his name is Paul Dolan. He did human resource work in Boquete. What? Yes, yes. Hmm, no, he told me that Oscar Meyer and Vanessa

Camacho are members of the Calí cartel. What? No, we can't do that any longer since President Noriega is vacationing permanently in the United States. Got any other ideas? Yes, no problem. Of course! What? The fingers and a front tooth? Okay, you know you can rely on us. Talk to you soon. Take care. Bye."

He hangs up, looks at Liam, and asks, "Can I see your passport or any other identification like driver's license or credit cards?"

Liam blushes. "Uh, no. Sorry, I left it all in the hotel for safe keeping."

Miguel murmurs, "Hmm... What's the name of the hotel?"

Liam is highly irritated and raises his voice. "Why do you want to know where I stay? Don't you think it's far more important to follow up on what I told you and arrest that woman in Boquete?"

Miguel answers calmly, "All in good time. I want to send an officer to your hotel to pick up your papers. What's the name of the hotel?"

Liam slumps in his chair and says meekly, "I don't know. I never saw the name of the hotel. It's a few blocks away from the central bus station."

Miguel gives him a puzzled look. "There are no hotels in that area. Only whorehouses."

Liam nods, looks at the floor, and mumbles, "Yes, I know."

He takes his passport out of his back pocket, hands it to Miguel, and says, "I'm not Paul Dolan. My name's Liam Hickey. I just don't want to have my name on any police report. I'm scared of the Calí cartel. If they find out that I talked to you, they'll have me killed."

Miguel flicks through the pages of the passport and calls out, "Antonio, are you still within earshot?"

Antonio pushes the door open and nods. "Yes, boss."

Not surprised about the quick response, Miguel instructs him, "Antonio, take this man to a holding cell. We'll process him in due course."

Antonio puts handcuffs on Liam who shouts, "Why? I provided hugely important information. Why am I being arrested?"

Miguel waves off Liam's outburst. "You're not under arrest. We put you into protective custody. Anyway, we already know what you told me. We're not a bunch of slackers. But you also gave patently false information. You didn't evaluate more than twenty applicants. It was only one, the man you know as Oscar Meyer whose real name is Oscar Ortiz. Furthermore, you turn out to be working for Colombian drug barons. So, you are just as guilty as the people you accuse. Don't worry, though, you won't end up in one of our prisons. You'll be on the next flight home as soon as we have processed you."

Antonio marches Liam out of the office. Although Liam is somewhat relieved, he is also overcome by fear. He feels now that it was a big mistake not to follow Vanessa's advice of taking the taxi to Panama City and the next flight to Ireland. Whatever made him think, he wonders, that he could tell an officer of the drug squad something he didn't know already?

Alone in his office, Miguel gets up, shoves his hands into his pockets, and looks out the window.

He shakes his head and mutters under his breath, "What a stupid bastard. He is the personified insult to Ireland and the good Irish people. I should check the Hickey clan to see how many more idiots there are in its ranks. They could serve us handily as stooges."

***

The processing of Liam takes on the form of having one of his incisors extracted with a pair of pliers and getting his fingers smashed with a rifle butt without the benefit of an anaesthetic. Liam's blood curdling screams are transmitted by phone to Igor who listens with some satisfaction.

Liam is given minimal medical attention. He is shipped to Panama City's Tocumen International Airport with a big tuft of cotton wool in his mouth and his fingers individually bandaged. His first-class ticket for a flight to Dublin via London is paid for with his credit card.

***

Upon his arrival in Dublin, even without glasses the most short-sighted member of the Irish Republican Army group recognises Liam immediately on account of his black eye, missing incisor, and heavily bandaged fingers.

He is given a warm welcome at the airport and taken for a long, leisurely ride in the country. Finally, the guys take care of him with a couple of bullets through his kneecaps and one for target practice in his mushy brain before his earthly remains find heavenly peace in one of Ireland's many bogs.

18

It takes Antonio Bládes almost three weeks until Friday, 23rd August 1991 to find the door to Miguel Chavez's office unlocked and the occupant absent early in the morning. He rummages through the desk drawers until he finds the file relating to the investigation in Boquete. He recognises Miguel's scribbling that implicate Vanessa and Oscar in the business of the Calí cartel. He faxes the entire batch of papers to his brother Virgilio in Davíd, gives him a call as well, and urges him to go after these two culprits.

Upon his return to the office, Miguel Chavez can see that somebody sent a message on his fax machine to the police in Davíd. He wants to investigate the matter but drops the idea when he finds all the papers in place and can't recall the last time he sent a fax to Davíd. But cautious as he is, he calls Igor to let him know that there has been an unidentified communication with the police in Davíd and suggests precautionary measures to safeguard the operation in Boquete.

***

Vanessa swims the length of the pool and touches the rim ahead of Oscar. She dunks him, they splash around and get out of the water. He puts an arm around her shoulder for a gentle hug. She beams a happy smile looking up at him.

Oscar sits down on a bench and towels off his arms and head. He gets up and slaps his flat belly. "This is it. One week to go. You think the guys in Calí will be happy with the result?"

Vanessa's response is almost jubilant. "Happy? They will be ecstatic. You're slim and fit and have a changed attitude."

Oscar is mystified. "Changed attitude? What do you mean?"

"It's positive. You even hugged me."

"You don't want me to...?"

"No, I mean, you never did as if you were afraid me."

"Well, I was."

Her head cocked to the right Vanessa gives him a worried look. "Why? Did I give you any reason to be afraid of me?"

Oscar smiles vaguely. "Plenty with all the stunts you pulled. You busted Amerigo's balls and nose. You gave the police a lot of lip. You scared Liam shitless and took his gun away. I don't know how you do it. You're as tough as nails and your actions go far beyond the call of duty of a fitness coach. Yet with me you were always kind."

"So? Why were you afraid of me?"

"I was scared of touching and being touched after eighteen months of getting beaten up and sodomised in prison." His emotions get the better of him and he needs a moment to calm down. "You've changed all that. How can I ever repay you?"

Vanessa is relieved. "Well, you can start by giving me a proper hug."

Oscar gets up and takes Vanessa into his arms. She puts her arms around his neck and kisses him passionately.

She stops, looks at him with a mischievous grin. "I can feel something moving. You have a snake in your shorts?"

Oscar chortles. "I suppose you could call it that."

"Really? Do we have to call the SPCA?"

Oscar shakes his head. "Not if you know how to charm it."

Vanessa grabs him by the hand, drags him to the massage parlour, pushes him inside, and shuts and locks the door. She puts a hand down his shorts and looks disappointed. "What happened? Did the snake recoil?"

Oscar shakes his head. "No, it's the law of gravity. What goes up must come down."

Groping around in his nether regions, she chuckles and whispers, "Now I will go down on what's coming up."

She hums the Marseillaise while having her snack. Before she intones the third verse, Oscar has his orgasm.

Vanessa stands up with a grin and wipes the corner of her mouth. "That was quite a meal you saved up. What's for dessert?"

Oscar lifts her up to sit on the massage table. "Dessert? What do you mean? You had a cream pie for starters. It's time for the main course."

***

The black Mercedes 560 SEL pulls up in front of the hotel. The driver rushes into the lobby and talks to the receptionist. She picks up the phone and dials a number. After a while, she dials another number and then raises her hands apologetically. She points to the entrance of the hallway that leads to the gym and swimming pool.

The driver follows the directions, looks into the empty gym, and the deserted swimming pool. The weekend guests crowding the resort haven't arrived yet. He spots a sign that points to the beauty salon and massage parlour. He wanders along the corridor and almost freaks out when a female client in the window of the beauty salon with a mudpack on her face stares at him through the holes in the cucumber slices on her eyes.

He is ready to turn around when he hears a muffled, "Yes...! Yes...! Yes...!" followed by a husky, "Oh, yeah!!" He stops at the door to the massage parlour from where the noise emanates and can only wonder what kind of a massage is given to that female customer who yodelled a second ago. He is sure she wasn't given just a gentle backrub and listens with his ear to the door. He can't make out what the woman is burbling except the words 'again', 'my slave', and 'come on'. When the man says, "Okay, you wanna do the wheelbarrow?" he recognises Oscar's voice.

Amid the woman's chiming laughter, he knocks on the door and says in a firm voice, "Oscar? We have an emergency! I have to talk to you! Now!"

In response to the driver's urging, a chair is knocked over, whispering can be heard, and some furniture is moved around. Then the door is opened. Oscar fills the frame wearing his shorts back to front.

He looks at the driver. "Yes? Who are you?"

"Oscar? I'm your driver. A radio communication of the police in Davíd was intercepted. They will be here any minute. You have to leave! Now!"

Oskar makes big eyes. "Oh shit! Vanessa, come here we have to leave!"

Vanessa slinks up by his side still adjusting her swimsuit and puts an arm around his waist. The driver takes one look at her and shakes his head. "No, Oscar, I was ordered to pick up only you."

Oscar snorts. "That's out of the question. She comes with us."

The driver takes an envelope out his jacket and insists, "Sorry, I can't do that. It's against orders. Here's Vanessa's pay. She'll have to make it out of here on her own by taxi or bus."

Vanessa takes the envelope and rips it open while Oscar snorts again. "No way! You understand? There's no way I will leave her behind."

Vanessa pushes past Oscar and holds out the open envelope. "This isn't my pay. It's not even two thousand dollars for seven weeks of work. My fee is six hundred dollars a day."

The driver looks at her sheepishly. "Sorry, it's all I was given."

Oscar declares, “There you are! Vanessa has to come with us to collect her pay.”

Vanessa puts a hand on Oscar’s shoulder. “No, Oscar, it’s alright. I have my own method of collecting what’s due to me. You go ahead. I’ll make my way out of here by myself.”

Oscar pulls her close and shakes his head. “No! I won’t leave you behind. You come with me, or I go with you!” He turns to the driver and stares him down. “You heard me! I won’t go with you if Vanessa can’t come with us.”

Vanessa wriggles out of his hold and voices her fear. “No, Oscar, don’t do that! Go by yourself! You don’t know what these guys will do when you go against their orders. Please, just go.”

Her voice trails off. It triggers Oscar’s stubborn streak. “No, I won’t. I was told that these guys want to change everything. You come with me, and they can prove that they have changed.”

He sees panic in Vanessa’s eyes. She is close to freaking out. “That’s insane, Oscar! You take such risks at your peril!”

Oscar replies completely cool and in control. “That’s okay. I take that risk. Why do you think I was busted out of prison and underwent the programme to get me fit? They don’t just want to hear my plan but want me to realise it, too. If they bump me off, they’ll end up with nothing.”

The driver interjects, “Can you get on with it? Time is of the essence!”

“Oh sure,” agrees Oscar. “You go back to your car and keep the engine idling. We’ll be out in a jiffy.” He turns to Vanessa. “Where’s your cell phone?”

“In my room.”

“Good, let’s go!” He takes her by the hand but when she pulls back and refuses to go along, he grabs her around the waist and puts her over his shoulder.

He gives the driver a push to get going and struts down the hallway. At the door to her room, he puts her down, and says, “Give me your phone. I’ll try calling Igor. You pack your stuff. I’ll change into my track suit and take only my cowboy outfit as a souvenir.”

***

The driver takes side roads past meadows and through forest to the Tierra Altas runway of El Hato del Volcán to avoid running into the police he anticipates will be taking the main road from Davíd to Boquete. He parks the car near the southeast end of the airstrip and makes a phone call. He and his passengers have to be patient for about an hour. When the Twin Commander 1000 has landed, it stops not too far away from where the car is hidden and turns around to be ready for take-off within a minute. The steps are dropped, Oscar and Vanessa run to the plane with her three suitcases, get in, and the steps are pulled up.

The driver comes out of the thicket waving a large white Stetson, a denim cowboy outfit, and alligator boots. Nobody notices him as the plane takes off in the direction west-northwest and disappears from view over the nearby mountains.

***

Oscar looks at the crater of the Barú volcano. Vanessa sits opposite him. Her face expresses relief mixed with worry. Oscar points down and bids Vanessa to have a look. She unbuckles herself and gets onto Oscar's lap. He wraps his arms around her hips.

The plane goes into a wide curve in the direction south-southeast and dips its wings just in time for Oscar and Vanessa to have a full view of the Buena Vista Resort Hotel. It is cordoned off by a contingent of police vehicles. The flashing blue, white, and red lights create an eerie atmosphere around the buildings in the dim light of dusk. The policemen look like ants running in and out of the hotel and Oscar's bungalow.

Vanessa hugs Oscar, kisses him, and looks at him wantonly. "Let's screw. Right here. I know you want me, too. Right now!"

She starts pulling up her skirt and shifts around in Oscar's lap when the co-pilot comes out of the cockpit. His sudden presence puts a crimp in Vanessa's act although she keeps on squirming until the co-pilot says courteously, "Please get back in your seat, Madam, and buckle up. It's just for now. We expect the plane to go through some wild gyrations for the next ten minutes."

Vanessa is ready to kill that young man but follows his directive however reluctantly and buckles up in her seat opposite Oscar.

The co-pilot opens a little fridge and takes out a small bottle of champagne and two glasses. He pops the cork, pours the champagne, and hands his two passengers a glass each. "Welcome aboard, Madam, Sir. I trust we will have a pleasant flight. Everything going to plan, we should arrive in Calí in due course. I will serve you a snack in an hour."

He turns and goes back to the cockpit. The door has hardly closed behind him when Vanessa unbuckles her seatbelt and Oscar's. She rips off her panties and follows through on satisfying her urges. She sounds like a raving mad woman that should alert the pilot, but the door stays shut. The gyrations of the plane don't bother her. On the contrary, the steep descents and ascents of the plane flying under the radar over the mountains promote her movements and give Oscar every reason to sit still to prevent a fallout and let her get on with her actions.

Having achieved some satisfaction, they settle down and wait for the snack to be served while the Twin Commander 1000 flies at its maximum speed of over 700 km/h and the lowest altitude possible above the Pacific coastal waters of Panama.

An hour into the flight the co-pilot comes out and sets up a couple of meals of smoked salmon, beef stroganoff, cheese and crackers, dessert, and a bottle of wine. He clips a table between the two seats and serves the exhausted looking Vanessa as well as Oscar their meals. He winks at Vanessa and returns to the cockpit.

The lights of Panama City flicker in the far distance and ships can be seen on their way to the Panama Canal when the plane takes course over the Bahía Panama on its way to Colombia.

Some hours later the Twin Commander 1000 circles slowly out of radar range of the Calí airport. When a Boeing 737 approaches, the Twin Commander speeds up and flies in its radar shadow. It lands on the taxi runway unseen by the air traffic controllers and right next to the jet landing on the main runway.

At the very end of the taxi runway a matte black GMC Suburban is waiting. Vanessa gets out of the plane and into the car ahead of Oscar. Her luggage is tossed into the back of the vehicle by a young man who gives the pilot the all-clear signal. The plane taxis away in the dark and disappears in a hangar.

The young man runs to a gate in the airport fence and opens it for the car that rumbles across a grass strip and onto the dirt road north of the airport. He closes the gate and jumps into the car that drives away at high speed and turns onto the highway to Calí.

***

Alec, Igor, Sabrina Grajáles, and Ariana Andráe are seated in the lounge of the Hotel Continental and chat.

The digital clock above the reception counter clicks softly and shows 1:15 a.m., Saturday, 24th August 1991.

Igor gets up and goes to the entrance when the GMC Suburban stops in front of the hotel.

Vanessa looks a little shaken and rather pale when she staggers towards the sliding glass doors. She enters the lobby ahead of

Oscar. The young man rushes past with her three suitcases and drops one on Igor's ingrown toenail. Igor jumps around and curses while Vanessa stands in front of him.

He looks at her with watery eyes. "Vanessa? Where's Oscar?"

She giggles and points to the tracksuit-clad guy who stands behind her. "Hello, Igor. Here he is. Happy with my work?"

Looking stunned, he gives Oscar a limp handshake. "Oscar? Wow, what a change. Glad to see you. Welcome to Calí."

Oscar replies, "Hello, Igor. Happy to be back in Colombia."

Igor wipes his watery eyes. "You look fit, Oscar. Amerigo..."

Vanessa interjects, "...is dead."

Igor waves a hand. "Well, yes, of course, but surely Rafael..."

Vanessa interjects again, "...is dead."

Igor gives her an angry look. "Yes, yes, yes! But Felipe..."

Vanessa rolls her eyes and says, "...is dead."

Igor blows a gasket. "Will you shut up, Vanessa! Next you wanna tell me that you did all the work!"

Oscar is happy seeing Igor losing his marbles. "But she did! The guys did nothing! Vanessa did it all and has to get paid for it!"

Igor stares at Oscar. "We'll see about that later. Let me introduce you to some members of our team."

Alec, Sabrina, and Ariana get up. Oscar pulls Vanessa close when Igor introduces him. "Alec, meet Oscar."

When Alec wants to shake hands with him, Oscar points at Vanessa. "Meet Vanessa, my coach. She's responsible for me being as fit as you want me to be."

Alec looks a little embarrassed about his blunder of not greeting the woman by Oscar's side first and gives her a warm handshake. "Welcome to Calí, Vanessa. It's a pleasure to meet you. You did an absolutely splendid job. Thank you."

Vanessa nods and smiles in appreciation of his well-chosen words. "It's a real pleasure meeting you, too, finally. I've heard a lot about you. Only good things, of course."

Alec looks surprised and breaks into a smile. "It is excellent to know that you heard only good things about me."

He looks Oscar up and down. "Oscar, I'm so happy to see you. You look in fine shape. Splendid, splendid! But tell me whose track suit you borrowed."

Oscar looks down at the baggy suit. "Oh, that's mine alright. Seven weeks ago, it was skin-tight."

Alec smiles. "You jest, of course!"

"No, he doesn't," mutters Igor. "It was bursting at the seams."

Alec looks at Oscar in admiration. "Incredible! Please, meet Sabrina, our biologist, and Ariana, one of our chemists."

Once the greetings are over, they sit down, and Igor turns to Vanessa. "So, what's your plan?"

Oscar leans forward and puts a hand on Vanessa's knee. "Vanessa is staying with me, of course."

Igor looks totally floored. "What? No, no, Oscar. Impossible. We have to sort out a serious matter and then she's on her way!"

Oscar looks sternly at Igor. "No, Igor. Vanessa is staying with me, you hear? The serious matter you have to sort out is her pay, isn't it? She did all the work and I expect that you will pay her the sum for the entire team. Is that clear?"

Alec raises a hand in response to Oscar's aggressive tone. "Wait a minute, Oscar. This is neither the place nor the time..."

Oscar interrupts him firmly, "Oh yes, it is the right time and place to sort out any serious matter! I insist that Vanessa will get paid in full and stay with me. Or we're going to walk right out of here. Whatever your plans, you can't separate husband and wife."

Igor slips almost off the sofa when he belts out a mocking laugh. "What? She's your wife? Since when?"

Oscar gives Vanessa a hug and Igor a cold look. "Today! We got married on the plane. As you probably know, the pilot has the authority to conduct such ceremony over international territory."

A moment of stunned silence follows. Vanessa leans her head on Oscar's shoulder and suppresses a giggle about his cheeky lie.

Sabrina and Ariana look enviously at the happy couple. Alec regains his composure first. "That comes as quite a surprise."

Oscar chuckles and dispenses the folksy philosophy, "Yes, life is full of surprises. But at least it's a pleasant one, isn't it?"

Sabrina and Ariana congratulate Vanessa and Oscar, but Igor interrupts the gushing in a high-pitched tone. "Hold it! Hold it right there! Husband and wife or not, we had other plans."

Sabrina cuts him off, "Oh, shut up, Igor! Stuff your stupid plan and blow it out your ass. We'll pay Vanessa, book a suite for the happy couple, and retire for the night. I'm far too tired to suffer any more of your futile arguments."

Ariana chimes in, "You are right, Sabrina. These arguments are so tiresome. Igor, what do we owe Vanessa? I can get the money."

Sabrina and Ariana stand in front of Igor and wait for an answer. He does a quick calculation and whispers with Ariana. She nods and leaves while Sabrina whispers to the stupefied Alec and Igor. "I guess Oscar is not the soft-boiled egg you two expected him to be. Live with it and make the best of it."

She waves to Oscar and Vanessa to follow her to the reception.

Igor looks at Alec and hisses, "What a fuck up!"

Alec raises an eyebrow. "What are you saying?"

Igor says in a low voice, "Vanessa's a fuckin' skank. If you care to know details, my father could tell you. And so could that Irish guy, Liam."

Alec cuts him off. "Liam? He was the real stinker in Panama. Had he not coincidentally run into Miguel Chavez at the Balboa police station he could have blown the lid off our operation."

Igor looks apologetically and mutters, "I know. I've taken care of him."

Alec is surprised. "What? You've taken care of him? How?"

Igor puts on airs. "I had the IRA give him a reception upon his return to Ireland. Hasn't been seen since."

Alec asks even more surprised, "You have contacts to the IRA? Do you think it's wise to cosy up to them?"

Igor tries to look like a man of the world when he shrugs and mumbles, "Why not? They're like our FARC, secretive, effective, and ideal for the dirty work. By the way, I'll have the FARC take care of Vanessa."

Alec gives Igor a long thoughtful look before he speaks in a barely audible voice. "Oh, please, Igor, farc off! It was a masterstroke how you got Oscar out of the klink and set up the operation in Panama. But there's a limit to you going it alone especially as regards Vanessa. Just drop the idea of doing her any harm, Igor. Just drop it."

Igor persists to ask, "Why? Do you know what she did to my family? She has to be taught a lesson."

Alec gives a curt reply. "No! Forget about it. Your family with all due respect takes a backseat to what is ahead. So, forget it!"

Igor shakes his head. "Why? Does family honour mean nothing to you anymore?"

Alec explains, "It has nothing to do with your family's honour. Don't think for a moment that the women in our team let you get away with action against Oscar's wife. You would split our team right down the middle. Let's integrate Oscar and Vanessa. Then we can keep an eye on them and prevent Oscar from becoming another Pablo."

Stunned Igor pulls back. “Oscar another Pablo? You think...?”

“Oh yes,” assures him Alec. “He’s got the chops to orchestrate it! Just think how he put us on our haunches a minute ago.”

Igor wants to say something but holds back when Alec waves to Ariana who comes into the lobby carrying a small black tote bag. She hands it to Vanessa. Sabrina gets a bellhop to take Vanessa’s luggage to the elevator and Vanessa and Oscar are ready to turn in.

Alec has the last word before they all part to get some sleep. “Have a nice two-day honeymoon. Your big day is next Tuesday in the mezzanine conference room. Okay? Sleep tight and don’t let the bedbugs bite.”

19

Vanessa comes out of the shower wearing a white bathrobe. She pulls back the window curtain of the honeymoon suite on the top floor of the hotel to let the sunshine flood in.

Oscar is in bed and grunts, “Please, shut the curtain. I’m tired.”

But she is merciless. “You have to get up, Oscar. It’s already half past six. It’s your big day, Tuesday, 27th August. Remember? We still have to go shopping to get you some outfits. You can’t conduct a business meeting in a baggy track suit and sneakers.”

Oscar turns over and stares at the wall. “Half past six? I can’t get up that early.”

Vanessa retorts, “Yes, you can! Get up and get ready.”

She takes him by the hand and pulls him up. Oscar crawls out of the sack and wobbles to the bathroom.

Vanessa opens a wall safe, takes a bundle of one-hundred-dollar bills, and puts it in her handbag. She picks the least crinkled clothes out of her suitcase, gets dressed, calls room service for breakfast, and sits down by the window to enjoy the panoramic view of Calí.

***

Vanessa and Oscar have some difficulty finding their way in the downtown area. They don’t know Calí and don’t even have a map.

They hail a taxi and take a tour of the city with the specific request to point out the best shops that are already open at the still early hour. The driver is very helpful once he spots Vanessa holding a one-hundred-dollar bill in her hand. He waits for them patiently when they are in a shop to buy suits, shirts, shoes, and everything else for Oscar. He gets a little impatient when Vanessa tries on one dress after another in a brand name boutique and takes even more time to purchase shoes in the shop next door. The trunk is filled to bursting with bags and cartons and they are on the way back to the hotel when Oscar tells the driver to stop near an alley where he spotted some urchins, barefoot and dressed in rags. The driver curses under his breath using a derogatory term for the kids. It gets Oscar riled up and he barks at the driver to shut up and show some empathy. Vanessa wants to know what he is on about, but Oscar gets out and slams the taxi’s door before she can ask him.

Oscar enters the alley dressed in a new suit, shirt and tie, and creaking leather shoes. He scares most of the kids who take off and scatter. Only one crying little boy, not more than five years old, remains. Vanessa watches Oscar chatting with him when a girl, perhaps eight years old, approaches them cautiously. After a while Oscar has the boy and girl laughing. He tells them something while pointing out of the alley, gives them some money, and returns to the taxi. The boy and girl scamper. They cross the street through busy traffic and are soon out of sight. Oscar looks content but not happy as the taxi drives back to the hotel.

***

Oscar sits at a table of their hotel's café and Vanessa joins him after selecting pastries and ordering coffee at the counter.

Surprised she watches him take off one shoe and sigh with relief. She tut-tuts his action, but he takes off the other shoe as well, and starts poking the collar of his shirt. He is uncomfortable in the formal wear and voices his wish to change back into his baggy tracksuit and sneakers.

Vanessa is amused about his discomfort. Looking at him, she realises aware how little she knows about this guy and is still amazed about his transformation from a shy and withdrawn slob to a self-assured, assertive, and even aggressive hunk. He followed her exercise regimen like a lamb for seven weeks and then dared to dictate terms to the second generation of drug barons. And what she thought would perhaps become a nice memory of friendship with him turned into an orgasmic sexual experience that she has every desire to continue for some time to come.

She finishes her pastry and sees that Oscar hasn't touched his light, fluffy snack. "Why don't you eat your pastry? Don't you like it? You have to eat something before we go to the meeting."

Oscar shakes his head. "I've already gained five pounds just looking at it. My former fitness coach, a little dictator told me only four days ago that I have to watch my weight."

Vanessa titters. "Oh, I'm a little dictator, am I?"

Oscar nods earnestly. "Yes, you are. You have proven it over the past few weeks."

Vanessa is amused. "If I'm a dictator, what are you?"

Oscar cocks his head and answers, "I'm just an obedient servant and abide by my dictator's raging desires any place and time."

She reaches for his hand. "You are? Shows how little I know about you. Who are you, Oscar? Tell me about your life."

Oscar looks at his watch. He is at odds about revealing how he came to be what he is. He thinks of her dogged support and their coming together over the past few days. It assures him that whatever he tells her will be safe with her. He takes a deep breath and starts with the question, "You saw the urchins in the alley, didn't you? I used to be one of them. We were called 'Disposables'. That's why I was so pissed off when the taxi driver called abandoned and homeless children by that disparaging name.

"I'm from Buenaventura, a coastal town not far from here. Although we didn't have much and lived in a decrepit house on the harbour front, we were a happy family. My mother, father, two sisters, and three brothers lived with our granny who told us about her days as a slave in Trinidad. She had escaped as a young girl and found refuge in the hostile environment of Colombia of those days. Money was always in short supply because my father is a builder of boats that have the unfortunate habit of sinking when they are launched. He is terrible at his job, but it is the only thing he ever wanted to do. For us kids it was great entertainment to watch a boat being launched and disappear in the mud. We placed bets and I won a few pesos when one of his vessels actually floated.

"Often we had only the fish to eat we caught early in the morning. In reality my parents didn't have the wherewithal to raise six kids and sometimes we were at a point of starvation. My brothers and I tried to supplement the scarce supplies by stealing from vendors and stores but were caught more often than not and got a pretty good thrashing. When we had food, we were happy but many times I cried myself to sleep at night because my empty tummy hurt so much. One day there was not a crumb of food in the house, and I had to quit school because my father couldn't pay the required fee. I ran away. I had the dream of going to university to become a famous scientist, getting rich, and buying all the food my family could eat. Instead, I ended up on a garbage dump in Bogotá after an odyssey that took me to many towns on the back of a truck or the roof of a bus. On the way I met kind people who would give me food and shelter for a night but always sent me on my way when day broke. They had enough problems of their own and couldn't feed another mouth.

"When I saw the skyline of Bogotá first time, I was sure I had reached the mystical place called Nirvana. Reality caught up with me in no time and I was lucky that a boy of about my age gave me some bread and allowed me to share his hole in the ground in the garbage dump. We turned it into a lean-to during the day when we lifted the corrugated sheet and supported it with a couple of sticks. We escaped the men in black uniforms and balaclavas who came to the garbage dump during the night looking for boys and girls to execute. As I said, we were the disposables of their clean society. Another problem was that many boys and girls sniffed glue and took drugs. Police and death squads came and executed the addicts for fun in broad daylight. It was a horrible sight. Many nights I couldn't sleep out of fear of suffering the same fate.

"I survived like that for about six months. I had become very skilful at dodging the cops and hiding until they were gone. I picked anything usable out of the garbage, polished pots and pans with fine sand, and sold them for a few pesos. I shared whatever I earned with my host, and we did better than most other kids but one day he didn't return to our shack. I don't know if he was killed or took off to greener pastures. Anyway, it was a few days later that my fortunes took a turn. I had sold one of my pots to an old man who invited me for a cup of tea. He told me about his posada where he gave shelter to homeless kids. His name is Germán Obejo. I was very suspicious of most strangers but him I trusted right away and followed him to his posada.

"He showed me the room I had to share with two other boys. When he pointed to the bed that would be mine, I was sure that he was a saint. I stayed for close to twelve years and he taught me to read and write, arithmetic, and the basics of biology, physics, and chemistry. We were a happy bunch of more than twenty boys and girls. All of us contributed to the upkeep of the orphanage with odd jobs in the neighbourhood and some goods we made in our workshop like wooden shelves and stools. But there were also some bad eggs among the kids. One of them showed me how to cut green beer bottle shards to make fake emeralds. Another one persuaded me to sell drugs. When Don Germán found out, I had to leave, also because I had reached the ripe old age of seventeen.

"I continued pushing drugs and selling fake emeralds to tourists, but territorial disputes pushed me out of Bogotá. I settled in Cartagena for a while and eventually moved to Barbados. I made a killing selling cocaine to tourists who couldn't get enough of the stuff. It made me wonder why so many Americans and Europeans who are well off and have everything going for them need drugs to enjoy life. What a bunch of fuckheads. But I didn't think too much about that side of my business. When I had enough money, I moved to the recently discovered tourism hot spot Costa Rica. Quickly I established myself as an entrepreneur of sorts and made a good living until I had the hot idea to suggest to Pablo Escobar what I am going to present to the Second Generation in about half an hour. You know the rest of my life's story to date intimately."

Vanessa is fascinated. She listens sometimes smiling, sometimes moved to tears. He checks the time, puts on his shoes and they leave the café to take their shopping up to their suite.

***

Oscar and Vanessa enter the conference room on the mezzanine floor a few minutes after 1:00 p.m. Alec welcomes them and introduces the other members of the group. They are Teresa Foméque, electrical engineer, Penelope Saenz, in charge of financial control, Pilar Estrepo, security analyst, Jorge Guzmán, business lawyer, Guillermo Urdinola, chemical engineer, Alberto Patiño, mechanical engineer, Maria Chacón, international law advisor, Leticia Cebállos, pharmacologist, Gerardo Restrepo, logistics specialist, Juan Carlos Quervo, computer scientist, Armando Rójas, physicist, and Alicia Arzáyus, political scientist. Vanessa and Oscar greet Sabrina and Ariana with warm hugs.

Igor stands in the far corner and is reluctant to greet them. He waves to them awkwardly and keeps his distance.

Alec can see that Oscar is quite nervous and he tries to calm him with small talk. Oscar can feel his stomach grumbling and wishes that he had followed Vanessa's advice and eaten the pastry. He gulps down four large glasses of tomato juice to keep his stomach quiet.

Some of the participants sit down at the oval table and slowly the gathering takes on the characteristic of a business meeting. Alec and Oscar want to sit down next to each other but Igor pushes Alec aside.

He hands Oscar a yellowed sheet of paper. "You recognise this?"

Oscar wrinkles his brow, looks at the letter, then smiles and nods. "Yes, of course. It's my letter to Don Pablo."

Igor's tone turns sharp when he points a finger at the relevant wordings of the letter. "You wrote that you gave the confiscation problem some thought and developed a plan to solve it with a global network of legal companies. We wanna hear the details. Is that clear?"

Oscar stays calm. "No problem. Should I start right away?"

Igor nods and goes to the other side of the table. He knocks on the tabletop demanding attention, points at Oscar, and barks in a sarcastic tone, “Here’s the guy who claims to have all the answers to the questions concerning our business. Let’s hear what he’s got to say.”

Oscar waits for Alec and Vanessa to be seated to his left and right. His mind is in turmoil not only on account of Igor’s obvious sarcasm but also because his plan is now almost two years old. He needs to get the priorities right and recall the details. He tries to remember what he thought of first on that fateful day in San José’s Mercado Central. He looks at his letter on the table and gives the impression of being a seasoned professional who takes his time before he starts to speak while actually trying to get his mind on track. Vanessa gently touching the back of his right leg is all it takes for him to calm down and focus. She knows all too well that this is make-or-break time for Oscar and lets him know in her way that she is there to support him. Sixteen faces are looking at Oscar in anticipation.

Finally, he clears his throat and begins, “Welcome to the new era of conducting your business. But first let me thank Igor for everything he has done to get Vanessa and me safely to Calí. He is a crisis manager of repute. Please give him the clap he deserves.”

Alec grins about Oscar’s unintended pun. The other participants slowly turn to stare at Igor. His sarcastic introduction to Oscar’s presentation wasn’t lost on anyone and they muster only lukewarm applause. Igor looks ready to disappear under the table. Oscar has taken the wind out of his sails.

Vanessa gives Oscar’s leg a gentle squeeze and suddenly he feels strong and invincible. He can follow a clear line of thought. “Igor told me that you want the details of the business plan I designed two years ago to bring cocaine to market without a loss.”

As soon as he utters the word ‘cocaine’, Alec stops Oscar’s flow of speech. Oscar bends down to hear Alec whisper, “Excuse me, Oscar, but we never ever use that word. We bring a product to market. Understand? It should have been explained to you before you launched into your presentation. Please, continue.”

Oscar nods and starts over. “Sorry about that and thank you for advising me to talk about a product. Okay, so let me tell you what I think should be done when there is a problem bringing a product safely to market. I thought about the root cause of the problem when I became aware of the seizures of tons of the product and millions of dollars of hard-earned cash. I sketched a diagram of bringing the product to market without a loss and eventually my business plan began to take shape.

"First I asked myself why the product is captured. Then I asked myself how the money that was earned in the underground economy is detected and thought of a solution to that problem.

"Right! Let's consider the seizure of the product. When you pack a product and want to ship it, you deal with net, tare, and gross weight. Net is the product, tare the packaging and weight of the carrier like a container, and gross is the total weight of product, packaging, and weight of the carrier. Our product is either loaded in containers as straightforward net goods or it is embedded inside another product. In either case the product is easy to find with the help of sniffer dogs. Coast Guard or Customs open a container and there it is - packages of our product. What they never check, unless it stinks of the product, is the container. Therefore, I suggest the product to be packaged odourless and become part of the tare, that is, the container.

"When the product has arrived at its destination there is the other problem of the wholesalers running an illegal business or a sideline of handling our product in a legal business. No matter what, we don't control the wholesalers except by means of threats and bloodshed, which is counterproductive. Therefore, I suggest setting up a global network of legal companies under our control for shipping and distribution of the product that will allow our business to disappear into a fog of legality.

"Once such a network is in place and we bring the product to market without a loss, we can tackle the next big problem, the seizure of hard-earned cash. My suggestion to solve that problem is cooperation with another organisation in a similar line of business. They have huge problems bringing their product to market but have never experienced any seizure of their earnings because they use an underground banking system. If we take over the shipping and delivery of their product in return for them to handle the transfer of our money, we kill more than two birds with one stone. You see, their transfer of funds has the added benefit of all money arriving in our bank accounts as legal payments."

Oscar pauses and reaches for a bottle of water. His throat is parched. He takes a sip and looks into the round of somewhat baffled faces. He realises that he will have to go into more detail to win over these youngsters who have to persuade their elders to cough up the dough that his massive change of doing business will cost. He looks to Alec who gives him a wink of encouragement and then to Vanessa who smiles happily.

***

Outside the conference room in the sparsely lit hallway loiters a dubious looking, pudgy figure of a man in a white dustcoat. It is Ramón Miranda, a hireling of José Santacruz Londoño, a Calí cartel drug baron, who has successfully cut into Pablo Escobar's business and could become the most formidable opponent if not enemy of the Second Generation, once they get their act together and get going. Ramón listens with a stethoscope pressed against the door. He has been spying for a while. When Oscar pauses to hydrate his throat again, he shrugs, takes off the stethoscope and leaves through a fire exit and into the parking lot outside.

Ramón gets into a car, takes out a cell phone, and places a call. "Hello, Don José, yes, it's me, Ramón. Basically, there's very little to report. Once that gang had settled down, I listened with my stethoscope to most of what this new guy had to say. The new guy? No, I didn't get his name. If he was introduced by name, it must have happened before I had a chance to listen. Anyway, I didn't get the impression that we have to take them seriously although it is possible that they want to set up a global network of legal companies to push drugs. What? Yes, that's the question. Where're they going to get the funds for such an operation? Okay, boss, I'll see you shortly and then you can tell me about your strategy and what we are going to do next."

20

Alec brings his BMW to a gentle stop in front of a five-star hotel. He hands a plain manila envelope to Vanessa in the back and takes documents out of another one. He turns to Oscar in the passenger seat. “Alright, here are the papers you need to get your identity cards, passports, and driver’s licences. There’s also a police report dated today, Wednesday, 28th August 1991, that states that you were robbed of your original papers, okay? All the data is verifiable, and the forms are bona fide documents. So, take good care of them.” He reaches into the envelope and gets out a map of Calí. “I got you a city map as well. I don’t want you to get lost.”

Oscar takes the documents and the map. “Thank you, Alec. But tell me, why are we here?”

Alec replies, “Oh yes, right. You will stay only one more night in your honeymoon suite. As of tomorrow, you will stay in this hotel until I’ve located a permanent residence for you. Show the police report at the reception and tell them that you will use the hotel’s address to receive your mail as long as you are looking for a house to purchase. Okay? Your suite is booked for a month. Pay for it in advance with your new credit cards that you still have to sign. One more thing, check the forms in the envelopes and memorise your names and personal data. Your names are Oscar Benito Pérez and Vanessa Lucinda Roa de Pérez.”

Oscar chuckles, looks at Vanessa, and repeats the names. “Oscar Pérez and Vanessa Roa de Pérez. Nice. We’ve been called worse names.”

Alec sighs. “Very funny. The instructions to get your documents are in the envelope.”

Vanessa leans forward. “Thanks, Alec. You’ve really gone to town to get everything so neatly organised.”

“I had hardly anything to do with that,” replies Alec. “It’s my father who pulls all the strings. He is incredibly well connected and did all of that in less than a day. I am very fortunate that I can rely on him although he thinks we are a bit crazy to listen to you, Oscar. That reminds me of your presentation yesterday. Excellent! You had the whole group in your hand and worked them like putty. However, you presented far too much detail. A rough outline would have been enough to win everybody over. And don’t worry about Igor. He and his father have an issue with you, Vanessa. I am certain that you know more about it than anybody. I'll have a chat with Igor and try to sort it out."

Vanessa looks doubtful and puts a hand on Oscar's shoulder. "Shall we go, Oscar? Will you wait for us, Alec? We shouldn't take too long."

As Oscar and Vanessa get out of the car. Alec leans over. "No, you are on your own from now on. Go out and get a taste of the city. I want you to feel at home here. We will contact you only as required for the next few days. See you soon."

***

Oscar and Vanessa finish the formalities in the hotel and take a walk. They end up strolling under the trees of a park in the Zona Verde in the centre of Calí.

They sit down on a bench and Oscar says, "Calí is quite a beautiful city, don't you think? It has so many parks."

She agrees, "Yes, it reminds me somewhat of home."

He asks her, "Home? Where is your home?"

With a faraway look in her eyes, she asks, "You mean my family?"

"Well, yes." Oscar touches her hand. "I know nothing about you."

Vanessa smiles bitterly. "Sometimes it's better that way. Oh well, here goes. I'm from the small town of Linares in the state of Nuevo León in the northeast of Mexico. My father was a cop, a corrupt and violent scumbag. He spent most of his time at the local tequila bar, a pulquería, got drunk, and caused a lot of damage. In short, he was the pride of the local police force that didn't care if he smashed up two or three police cruisers a year. His favourite pastime was to use my mother as a punchbag when he came home pissed as a newt. On my older sister's sixteenth birthday he came home to our little row house drunk and raging about the table set for the celebration. He grabbed the cake with sixteen lit candles and smashed it against a wall. Then he dragged my sister into the bedroom and raped her. My older brother Miguel and his cousin watched him fucking her, waited until he was finished, and then raped and sodomised her at the same time with double penetration. Worst part was that my mother observed it all with utter complacency probably out of fear. She took no action. My sister, sexually abused and bleeding, committed suicide. She hanged herself from the town's water tower.

"A few months later my father came home drunk as usual and saw me preparing dinner in the kitchen. I was chopping meat with a cleaver. He dropped his pants, seized me by the arm, and demanded that I suck his dick. In the ensuing struggle, I gave him a new centre parting. My brother heard the noise of the fight, stormed into the kitchen, saw our dead father with the cleaver stuck in his skull, and wanted to beat me up. I grabbed a butcher's knife and stuck it into his belly. He howled like a coyote before he croaked, and my mother came into the kitchen. She wailed at the sight of her dead husband and son, berated me, slapped me around the head, and threw me out. I waited until the police had investigated the murder scene and concluded that father and son had killed each other. My mother was dead scared of me and wouldn't let me back into the house.

"That's when things started to go really downhill for me. It was freezing cold, and I wore only a flimsy dress on that night in February. I ran to our church to ask the priest for help. I told him what the police had concluded and that my mother had thrown me out. Once he knew that my father and brother, who he feared, were out of the way, he led me behind the altar to receive the sacrament. He sat down, told me to kneel, put me in a headlock, pulled me across his lap, tore my dress up and panties down, and finger fucked me until he creamed his frock. That's how I was deflowered. I stopped believing in divine intervention after that because that big shit in the sky didn't strike that paedophile priest down with a bolt of lightning.

"The next few days were one long nightmare. I can't even remember how I ended up in the town of Piedras Negras. I spent a year working in a sweatshop, a maquiladora. I left for Monterrey with very little money. Looking for a place to stay, I wandered around the streets. In front of a nightclub a guy about twice my age sweet talked me into working for him and bought me a couple of nice dresses. He took me to his house, locked me up in a room, and rented me out to older men. One of them was Igor's father, Osvaldo Guttiérez. He took a fancy to me, paid the pimp to release me, and got me a passport. He gave me a couple of hundred bucks and promised two thousand more if I'd do an easy job for him. I agreed and he had about a kilogramme of cocaine packed in condoms shoved up my ass. He drove me to the border with the U.S. and I took a bus to San Antonio, Texas, where I was supposed to deliver the drugs. When the buyers who were supposed to wait for me didn't show, I took a bus to Houston where I sold the cocaine for the knockdown price of four thousand bucks. With that money in my pocket, I took a bus to Memphis, Tennessee, where an uncle, my father's younger brother lived. He and his wife were good people. They took me in and somehow wangled the system for me to go to school and graduate.

"These few happy days of my childhood came to an end when Igor's brother Vladimir turned up in my uncle's house about three years after my arrival. He claimed to have orders to kill me. My uncle jumped him and had a terrible fight until the police responded to my aunt's call. Vladimir was arrested for house invasion and the cops found cocaine in his car. Waiting for his trial, he was killed in jail by another drug dealer with a shiv. That's the issue Igor and his father have with me."

Oscar looks at Vanessa and is scared out of his wits. She had confessed as cool as a cucumber to the killing of her father and brother and a dispute with the family of one of the leading members of the Second Generation. He has to wonder who Vanessa really is and what she would be capable of doing to him if he ever had a disagreement with her. He raises a hand to interrupt her flow of speech. "Wait, wait, I don't understand. You didn't deliver the drugs of Igor's father. You sold it at a cut rate and kept the money. That means you are the catalyst of Igor's brother getting killed in jail. If that's the issue with Igor, then why did he hire you as my fitness coach?"

"He didn't," answers Vanessa, "at least not knowingly. He hired Amerigo's team. We had done some work for several of the families and came recommended. But let me finish. Then you will understand.

"After the Vladimir incident my uncle recommended that I leave Memphis. I moved to Knoxville where I studied Phys Ed and got a degree. But when the college tried to register my degree with the Department of Education, they found out that I was an illegal alien. They still gave me my degree papers, but officers of the immigration department came on graduation day, had me arrested and deported on a bus back to Mexico.

"A couple of years later, Amerigo saw me in Cancun giving fitness classes to obese tourists. He hired me to get security guards fit. They were in reality bodyguards of drug bosses. And again, some years later, Igor hired our team to get you fit. After the demise of Rafa, Felipe, and Amerigo he must have talked to his father about it and probably mentioned my name. Hearing it, Osvaldo very likely went nuts, told Igor about me, and ordered him to have me dispatched.

"I knew that something was up when Igor had not sent the heavies, he had promised for our protection in Boquete. Further evidence was provided when the driver had the order to pick up only you and let me face the police to have me arrested. I was so apprehensive to go with you because I hadn't realised that you had changed so much and would stand up for me. As long as we stay together, we have to look out for each other. Okay?"

Oscar looks shaken. "Holy shit, you've gone through hell already and now this. How do you keep your sanity?"

Vanessa shrugs. "I could ask you the same question. You've gone through hell as well like most people involved in the drug trade. Hey look, almost lunchtime. Let's go."

21

Oscar and Vanessa stand outside the government office near the Plazoleta de San Francisco on Calle 9 in the centre of Calí on Thursday, 5th September 1991. They received their new identity documents. The brand-new passport still crackles in its spine when Oscar opens it. The date of issue is the current day, an almost historical date for him. He reads his new name Oscar Benito Pérez with some apprehension and wonders when he can be Oscar Antonio Ortiz Acosta again. In the meantime, he will have to live with the fact that he has to memorise the personal data of name, place and date of birth as well as the family background of a stranger whose identity was imposed on him. At least he won't be mistaken for an American hot dog any longer he concludes with some glee and tucks the passport away.

Vanessa stands next to him and studies the city map. She is holding it upside down and looks confused. Oscar chuckles, takes the map, turns it right side up and traces the shortest route back to the hotel where he has an appointment with Alec.

Looking up, he gets a shock when he sees the Costa Rican drug baron Alfredo Calderón across the plaza talking to a young man. He watches them get into a Porsche 911.

Torn between keeping the appointment and wanting to find out what his old nemesis is doing in Calí, he checks his watch. He has only ten minutes to meet Alec punctually but decides to hail a taxi and follow the Porsche. He has to overcome Vanessa's resistance to get in. She doesn't know what is going on and would like to know why Oscar gives the driver instructions to follow a sports car. He doesn't answer her questions while clutching the dashboard.

The taxi can keep up with the speedy car in the heavy traffic along the narrow streets of the city centre but once they reach an open road, it almost disappears in the distance. Fortunately, the driver saw it turning off into a side road in Barrio Jardín. They follow the road that winds along a mountainside until they see the Porsche in front of a gate to a white marble palace. The taxi slows down to a crawl until the Porsche gets off the road and drives through the open gate into the front yard. The gate shuts, and the taxi moves slowly past the property. Oscar points to the building and holds his hand out in a questioning gesture. The taxi driver shrugs and mumbles the name Santacruz Londoño.

***

Alec leans against his BMW parked in front of the hotel. He checks his watch impatiently and looks up and down the road. He is ready to give up waiting for Oscar and gets into his car. He is angry and wonders what he should do. Oscar's presence is needed for a meeting he arranged with great difficulty. He can't go it alone and will be taken for an unreliable fool if he calls his contacts with a request for postponement and another date due to unforeseen developments. He picks up his cell phone and toys with the idea of calling someone when a taxi comes to a screeching halt next to him. Oscar and Vanessa get out.

Alec shouts, "You're late, damn it! We have to hurry, Oscar! Get in the car! We'll see you later, Vanessa."

Oscar gets in, and Alec speeds away with smoking tires. They leave behind an anxious Vanessa who is completely in the dark about the trip and the apparent urgency of it.

Alec drives as if obsessed sliding around corners, ignoring red lights and stop signs. Oscar fumbles with the seatbelt although he is convinced that it wouldn't save his life in case of a crash at the speed they are going.

Once they hit the highway to the airport, Alec weaves through the light traffic from lane to lane and asks, "What kept you, Oscar? You're half an hour late. I hope we're going to make it on time."

Oscar expects them to crash any second. A glance at the speedometer shows they are going at over two hundred kilometres an hour. He feels his end is near but manages to say, "Sorry, I'm late, but I had to find out what some slimeball is doing in Calí."

Alec asks through clenched teeth, "What slimeball is that?"

"A Costa Rican drug wholesaler."

Alec drives into the parking lot of the airport's private air service section, and they rush through the gates and onto the tarmac where a Lear jet is waiting. They get in, settle into the seats, and buckle up while the plane taxis to the runway and takes off.

Alec asks to see Oscar's new identity papers. He looks at the passport. gives it back and wants to know, "That drug wholesaler you mentioned. Who is he?"

Oscar explains, "His name is Alfredo Calderón. He helped the police to identify me when I got caught in Pablo's trap. He's Costa Rica's drug kingpin and as thick as thieves with the police."

Alec and scratches his head. “Hmm, what do you think he is doing in Calí?”

Oscar shrugs. “I don’t know. I spotted him getting into a sports car with some guy who drove him to a palace of a house with golden gates in Barrio Jardín. Do you know it?”

Alec smiles faintly. “Oh yes, I know the house.”

He picks up the aircraft phone and turns away from Oscar to prevent him from listening. He ends the call and looks thoughtfully at Oscar before he states, “Igor’s family used to supply that Calderón guy but for the past two years neither Pablo nor any of our families had any contact with him.”

Oscar perceives that as a warning and feels that he is suddenly standing on very thin ice. He is certain that he shouldn’t have mentioned Pablo and only mumbles, “Oh!”

His suspicion is confirmed when Alec asks, “Do you still bear a grudge against Don Pablo?”

He looks at Alec as innocently as he can. “What good would it do me to bear a grudge for something that happened over two years ago?”

Alec relaxes and reaches out to pat Oscar’s hand. “Atta boy.”

Oscar feels relieved about having averted a potential conflict and asks, “Where are we going?”

“Medellín,” is Alec’s short answer while he looks out the window.

“And what are we going to do there?” asks Oscar.

“You’ll see, you’ll see,” says Alec with a grin.

Once the plane has landed, it doesn’t take long for them to get into an open Jeep and onto a motorway. At the exit marked ‘Envigado’, they turn off and follow a south-eastern route.

Alec stops at a red light. Oscar asks, “Where are we going?”

“La Catedral, a.k.a. Club Medellín,” says Alec with a big grin.

It causes Oscar’s intestinal contents turn to water. He is ready to jump out of the car and run for his life when he says with a shaky voice, “That’s the prison where Pablo is held.”

“Indeed,” confirms Alec.

Oscar puckers up his rear and groans, “Oh, no!”

“Oh, yes!” counters Alec.

“Are we going to see him?” asks Oscar.

“Indeed,” confirms Alec. “So, act as if you’ve never met him.”

Oscar blubbers, “But I never have!”

“All the better,” Alec assures him.

Once the traffic light turns to green, he pulls away on a road leading into the mountains. At the gate to La Catedral, Alec and Oscar hand their identity cards to a prison guard who salutes and lets them pass.

In the white bungalow structure on the slope of the mountain they enter a living room.

Oscar tenses up when he sees Pablo Escobar sitting on a black leather sofa watching TV.

Pablo doesn't bother to get up but turns down the volume of the TV when he sees his guests entering and hears Alec greeting him, "Good morning, Don Pablo. How are you?"

Pablo addresses him with a big grin on his face. "Morning, Alec. How is my nephew, Gerardo?"

Alec answers with some pride, "Gerardo is doing very well. He has a Master's in logistics from a university in Holland."

Pablo looks satisfied. "And? Does he work for you?"

Alec is quick to respond, "No. He works with me."

Pablo chortles. "Are you trying to amuse me?"

He casts Oscar a suspicious glance, looks him up and down, and asks, "Who is that cat you dragged in here?"

In the manner of an overzealous used car salesman introducing a special offer, Alec holds out a hand. "Allow me to introduce Oscar Pérez, our director of marketing strategy. He has some bold ideas about our business we would like to discuss with you."

Pablo leans forward, reaches out, and shakes hands with Oscar. "Welcome. I had to deal with an Oscar once, a sack of shit, who tried to tell me how to run my business."

Oscar is certain that Pablo recognised him but keeps the peace since they were introduced to each other by a member of the Muñoz clan. Still, Oscar wishes that he could just disappear through the floor tiles and get away from here underground like a little mole.

Pablo pats the seat next to him and pulls Oscar onto the sofa. "Come on, man, sit down and let's talk. You want coffee?"

Oscar feels more like draining a bottle of a strong alcoholic beverage or popping a tranquilliser, but he nods.

Pablo bellows, "Juan! Three coffees and mineral water! On the double!" He leans back, looks at Oscar sitting on edge, chuckles, and slaps him on the chest with the back of his hand.

"Relax, man," he demands. "You can't think with your underpants in knots. I want to hear all your ideas."

Oscar slides back on the sofa and bides his time. He watches Pablo chatting with Alec who sat down in an armchair.

***

On the way out of La Catedral, Alec white-knuckles the steering wheel. Mad as a hatter he speeds down the mountainous road.

At the first lay-by he slams on the brakes, stops the car, and switches off the engine. He breathes so heavily that Oscar thinks Alec suffers an asthma attack. Within a second that assumption flies out the window.

Alec turns to him and yells, "I think, I'm going to puke! I'm the boss, you idiot! How dare you go against my instructions?"

Oscar falls almost out of the Jeep he is so taken aback by that verbal assault and asks, "What instructions might that be?"

At the point of total exasperation, Alec clutches the steering wheel and bangs his head on his hands making all the while the whinnying sound of a pygmy pony in agony until he belts out, "I told you to focus on the details of your business plan and not to talk about anything else! Single-handedly you destroyed our project before we even got started, you moron! What were you thinking, huh, when you ordered Pablo to hand over his operation and finance our project?"

Oscar takes a deep breath and says quietly, "That's a crock of steaming horseshit! I didn't order him to do anything. I told him that he had no alternative but to finance our project and let us run the business."

Still raging, Alec barks, "That's what I mean! Who are you to tell him? You are nothing but a pathetic drug peddler. Pablo built an empire!"

Oscar ignores the insult and responds, "Yes, he did, didn't he? And day after day he looks more like the emperor without clothes."

Alec is left speechless by that outrageous comparison and can only flap his jaw.

Oscar seizes the moment and continues, "Anyway, he agreed to consider my plan, at least in a way. He said that he would consider it as soon as his family was safe."

That remark has the stuffing knocked out of Alec and he asks in a normal tone of voice, "And? Is his family safe?"

Oscar answers nonchalantly, "I don't know. It's not important."

Alec flies off the handle and shouts, "Not important? Not important? His family is all-important to him! And he has to have the agreement of all of his lieutenants!"

Oscar dismisses that remark. "Ah, yes, and why wouldn't they agree?"

Alec dithers and gropes for words. "Because... Oh shit! Look, Oscar, there are families in our group that are openly hostile towards each other and Pablo. If his lieutenants get wind of that, they will reject the plan and instead terminate us with a wet job."

Oscar shakes his head and gives Alec a doubtful look. "And why would they want to do that?"

Alec tones down his voice. "Because there's no love lost in the entire drug trade. The different families and clans only cooperate and stick together for the sake of making money."

Oscar says in self-congratulatory tone, "Well, there you are!"

Alec is confounded by Oscar's manner and tone of voice and asks, "There I'm what? What are you on about now?"

Oscar gets tired of having to explain everything. "The families and clans as well as Pablo Escobar incur massive losses right now and are making hardly any money! That's what I'm on about. Pablo is bankrupt."

Alec belts out a laugh and vents his doubts. "Pablo bankrupt? You are bonkers, stark raving mad to think that he is bankrupt."

But Oscar carries on along his line of argument. "Yes, bankrupt! Do the arithmetic. All his properties, airplanes, guns, paste, laboratories, and transportation, does he get that for free?"

Alec shrugs. "Course not! That's business expenses."

Oscar is on a roll. "Aha! Now think of the money he spent on having hospitals, schools, and sports centres built. In Antioquia alone he spent more money on social housing than the Colombian government spent on social programmes for the entire country. And then the conversion of La Catedral into a five-star hotel, uh, prison that cost a reported eighty-five million dollars. He paid for it out of his own pocket! Add it all up and you'll see that Pablo has to be tottering on the verge of bankruptcy."

Shaken in his foundation, Alec mutters, "That's an assumption."

It is Oscar's turn for a sarcastic laugh and expresses his doubts. "An assumption? You got to be kidding! You're pretty weak in arithmetic for a guy with an MBA. He's virtually bankrupt, I tell you! And what does my business plan offer him? Retirement with free income and no expenses! Come on, man, Pablo is smart enough to realise that the days of 'plata o plomo' are over. Even he can't carry on as he did in days gone by."

Alec wants to argue Oscar's points but refrains from doing so. He starts the car and drives into Envigado. On the highway to the airport, Alec sees Oscar's lips moving and asks the obvious question, "Are you talking to yourself?"

Oscar looks at him with a mischievous grin and confirms, "Oh yes! I talk to myself whenever I have the need for a conversation with a really intelligent person."

"Interesting," mutters Alec thinking that Oscar is suffering some mental deficiency until his explanation hits him in the head like a football boot and he almost drives into the median.

Oscar gives him a sideways glance and smirks.

22

The next two weeks after the visit to La Catedral and the talk with Pablo Escobar pass quietly. Most of the days Oscar and Vanessa split their time between long walks in Calí and the fitness centre of the hotel except for a couple of days when they go on a visit to Bogotá. Oscar wants to show Vanessa his old haunts but most of them have disappeared in a building boom. It takes him a long time to find Don Germán Obejo's posada where he spent almost twelve years of his youth.

It is a tearful reunion. They find out that Germán has received an eviction notice. The city claims his property because he hasn't paid taxes for the past three years and doesn't have the money to settle the bill. It is an opportunity for Oscar to show his gratitude to the old man by paying the money owed and taxes two years in advance. It will give him enough time to sell the posada that will hopefully yield sufficient funds for him to purchase a house or apartment that can be maintained by a single person.

The visit leaves Oscar in inner turmoil about the injustice of Colombia's social system. Here is man with a heart as big as a wheel who took in probably more than a hundred homeless and abandoned children over his lifetime, gave them a roof over the head, a decent life and education and never got any recognition for it from the city authorities. Now they were trying to confiscate his property that has a value of several million pesos although he owes less than a hundred thousand of the inflationary currency. He wishes that he had the money to help Germán a bit more than just settling his tax bill and makes the solemn promise to himself that he will do so once he has enough money to his name.

On their return to Calí they find two notices, one that a fully furnished house is waiting for them to move in, and the other inviting them to come to the Muñoz residence the following day for an informal gathering. They spend the rest of the day packing their stuff and moving into the house just a block away from the Muñoz residence.

Oscar has a safe put into the floor of the game room in the basement of the house. Once the worker has finished his job of installing a hydraulically movable set of tiles that hides the safe, it is undetectable, and Oscar and Vanessa pile their valuables into it.

***

They arrive in the garden of the Muñoz residence late in the afternoon of the next day and join Alec at a table under a parasol.

He hands them the newspaper 'El País' with the headline, "Dispuesto a Retirarse Escobar" (Escobar Disposed to Retire). The photos of Pablo Escobar, his cousin Gustavo Gavíria, and the preacher Padre Rafaél García Herréros, the interlocutor appointed by Pablo Escobar, are splashed over the front page above the article of Thursday, 19th September 1991.

Alec smiles and says to Oscar, "I guess I owe you an apology for calling you an idiot."

Oscar chuckles. "Ahh, forget it. It was said in the heat of the moment."

Alec wags a finger and insists, "No, you were right, and I was wrong, and this report proves it. I talked to Pablo on the phone this morning. He told me that he talked to all the families involved in our project and assured me that we will get the initial funding."

Oscar rejoices, "See? I told you Pablo is smart. How much?"

Alec looks sternly at him. "Three hundred million."

"Pesos Oro or dollars?"

"Dollars, of course."

"Okay. That's a start."

Vanessa gets all fidgety listening to the two guys and chimes in. "Three hundred million? A start? Are you kidding? How much do you need?"

Oscar states, "For the entire operation? About five billion."

Irritated by his calm demeanour, she asks in a high-pitched voice, "You said billion? Five billion? That's crazy!"

And Alec pipes in, "Hold it! How do you arrive at five billion? You never mentioned that before."

"I know," replies Oscar. "I didn't want to scare the horses. But that's what we will need over the next three years for the entire operation."

Alec shakes his head. "You lost me. What's the entire operation? Come on, Oscar, put your cards on the table."

Oscar rests on his elbows, takes out a pen, and scribbles in the margin of the newspaper while he explains his calculation. "Alright, the entire operation includes the companies we have to purchase in Colombia and globally. Firstly, we have to get into partnerships with legal companies in Colombia because we can't buy them outright with the drug money. Then we have to buy machinery and build facilities for production and packaging under the umbrella of our legal partners. We also need a whole fleet of containers we have to convert to transport our product. That's for starters in Colombia. Later we need labs and pharma companies in strategic locations around the world to refine our product because paste is easier to conceal than the finished product. And don't forget that we need to control overseas distribution and sales to make it all work. Three hundred million is enough to get started and ship a trial load to market. But we have to invest our profits into the expansion of our operation for three years to achieve global control. What I mean to say is that we don't need more than the loan of three hundred million to get started. If our profits are invested properly, we can pay back the loan with interest, pay Don Pablo and all the investors the promised retirement share, and have sufficient funds for the required expansion."

A speechless Alec stares at Oscar who asks him, "When do we start?"

Startled by the question, Alec mumbles, "Uh, what? Oh, as soon as we can lay our hands on the money."

Oscar leans back to ask, "And when is that going to happen?"

All business, Alec replies firmly, "In a few days."

Oscar leans forward and says, "Alright. But there's one more thing I need to mention. We must have an accounting system to keep track of payables, receivables and cash on hand."

Alec wrinkles his brow. "You will run into some strong resistance to proper accounting. People aren't used to keeping track of their money. It is as if they have drawn a black line around the inside of a silo where they keep their money. As long as the black line is covered, they have enough. When the black line becomes visible, they run low. Be that as it may, why do we need an accounting system?"

Oscar smiles about the silo cash flow control and explains, "Besides the obvious requirement of paying the investors their share of the profits, I would like to know how much money you'll pay me for my work."

Alec waves a hand. "Ah, don't worry about that. We will pay whatever is due to you."

Oscar asks him quite innocently, "And how much is that?"

Alec is flustered by his persistence. "How much do you want?"

Oscar scribbles a few figures in the margin of the newspaper and explains, "Normally the fee for raising funds is between ten and fifteen per cent of funds received but I ask for only three percent of the first three hundred million because I will insist on legal funds to be paid into my account in the Cayman Islands. For the remaining four point seven billion dollars of investments over the next three years I make you the special offer of a one percent fee. Is that okay with you?"

Alec listens slack-jawed. He puts pen to paper and mutters, "That's fifty-six million over three years. A bit much, don't you think?"

"No," is Oscar's firm answer. "I've put my life and money on the line twice so far. My life will be on the line many more times in the near future when I make the deals to execute my plan, clean up the dealer network, and prepare the ground for our operation. And last but not least, your group will make a profit of more than three billion dollars in the first year of operation. That makes my fee look rather puny, wouldn't you agree?"

"Three billion in the first year?" asks Alec. "How do you come up with that figure?"

"With a pocket calculator," replies Oscar earnestly. "Look, there are an estimated twenty-five million habitual users in the United States according to the Drug Enforcement Administration. Let's say each user snorts about half a gram a day to satisfy their craving, which adds up to twelve and a half metric tons every day including Sundays and public holidays.

"Let's look at the present situation in Colombia. The Orejuela brothers and Santacruz Londoño with their so-called Calí cartel have carved out approximately forty-five percent of the market while Pablo and associates, let's call it the Medellín cartel, retain about forty percent with the rest going to minor operators. It is very likely that not every family will be happy to let us take over their operation for a share of the profit, but it is reasonable to assume that we can garner about thirty percent of the market. Okay, so far?

"Thirty percent of twelve and a half tons a day is three and three quarter or almost four tons a day. It is a huge quantity to produce, pack and ship covertly behind a screen of legal companies. So, let's bring that quantity down to one ton a day for starters. That's still a massive operation and we must find and purchase the facilities we need to achieve our initial goal without a glitch.

"Now let's talk profits. At a wholesale price of five bucks for half a gram, one ton a day or seven tons a week gives us a return of about seventy million dollars a week or three and a half billion dollars per year, if we use our own distribution system and can get all the money without a loss out of the United States. Three and a half billion less five hundred million for operating costs and business expenses leaves us with three billion in profit. Okay?"

Alec is overwhelmed and takes a while to speak. "Alright, Oscar, you have done your homework and then some. Let me make you an offer. Instead of a puny percentage of our investments, I offer you a share of our profits in perpetuity of say half a percent. That would give you more than fifteen million dollars in the first year if your prediction comes true."

The caveat 'if your prediction comes true' raises Oscar's suspicion. Although he appreciates the offer, he will have to reject it and be very diplomatic about it. He takes a moment to reply, "That is a very generous offer, Alec, but I can't take you up on it."

A quick-fire exchange ensues when Alec asks, "Why not?"

"Well, you have to divvy up the profits among the investors in the project and the members of your group."

"Okay. And?"

"I don't have the funds to invest in the project that would justify a payback of half a percent of the profit."

"Who cares? I make you a very generous offer and you reject it. Why?"

"I want to get paid only for my work - not more and not less."

"Okay, then explain what work you will do beyond your plan."

"Oh, come on now. My plan outlines very clearly that it is my obligation to set up the scheme that will allow you to bring the product to market without a loss and have your earnings transferred in full as legal funds. The plan was accepted by your group. I promised to execute my plan with all its inherent risks. I have to lay the groundwork. That demands a lot of detailed planning right from the word go, setting priorities and supervising activities. It will involve a lot more research and travel."

Alec weighs the pros and cons of Oscar's arguments and can see that he wants to keep a distance to the Second Generation. Yet, he doesn't understand why Oscar rejects the first year offer of an additional six million dollars and riches beyond his imagination in perpetuity. "So, you want nine million bucks in legal funds paid into your account in the Cayman Islands? Is that it?"

"Yes," is Oscar firm answer.

"Okay." Alec reaches across the table and shakes hands with Oscar to seal the deal.

Oscar gets up and turns to Vanessa. "Wanna go for a walk?"

Vanessa staggers out of her chair. "Yes, I need a walk to stop my head from spinning. Let's go."

"Wait a sec," objects Alec. "Don't you want to stay for dinner?"

"Oh, I didn't know we had a dinner date," replies Oscar. "Of course, we'd love to join you for dinner. Just let us take a walk for now. We'll be back in half an hour."

They turn and leave through the garden gate in the wall that surrounds the property.

***

Strolling along a quiet residential street, Vanessa takes Oscar's hand. "Holy shit! You sure know how to talk big figures. Three billion profit in the first year of operation? Are you sure of that?"

"Big figures?" asks Oscar. "You wanna hear some big figures? The US Department of Finance estimates that about three trillion dollars in cash are hoarded in Latin America. All of it was obtained in a period of fifteen years. Pablo alone had amassed over thirty billion in less than twelve years according to Forbes magazine that cited him as one of the richest men in the world.

"Now let me give you an even bigger figure that explains why the United States pursues its War on Drugs only half-heartedly. Every year an estimated seven trillion dollars in cash changes hands for the sale and purchase of illegal drugs in the United States. Just think what would happen to the economy if that underground cash flow would disappear from one day to the next. Thousands of retail companies that rely on daily cash transactions would go bankrupt, millions of people would be unemployed, and the entire economy would collapse triggering a worldwide economic recession."

Vanessa looks at him with raised eyebrows and absorbs what she heard. "Are you telling me that these hated and hunted drug barons actually prop up the American economy?"

"Yes," confirms Oscar. "And if these guys came to an agreement with the US Internal Revenue Service and paid taxes on their outlandish profits, they would probably be invited to become honorific United States citizens, notwithstanding their activities being condemned as illegal."

"Now my head is really spinning," mutters Vanessa. "What a crazy world we live in. But tell me something else. Why didn't you accept Alec's offer? You could have asked for a fandango dancing gorilla in patent leather shoes, and he would have agreed."

"I know," says Oscar, "but I have lots of reasons for rejecting his offer. I want to lay my hands on a payment for my plan as soon as possible. You see, although I didn't provide anything in writing, they have enough information to start the project and execute it. They know very well that I didn't tell them everything. They keep me on to avoid any hiccups but could tell me as well to piss off and not pay me a cent.

"Where would that leave me? I can't pick up where I left off before my time in prison. I would have to start afresh someplace and always fear that the Second Generation would have me eliminated because I know too much.

"With nine million bucks in the bank I can afford to hide in plain sight right here in Colombia where I have family and friends. I will also have enough cash at last to have a proper house built for my parents in Buenaventura and buy Don Germán's posada in Bogotá to provide for him for the rest of his days."

"Oh, that's so sweet," says Vanessa. "Germán will be pleased. But think how much more you could do with a bigger payout."

Oscar chuckles, "And when do you think I would get paid, if at all? The slightest mishap or not achieving the predicted three billion dollars profit in the first year would give them ample reason not to pay me anything. That's one side of the coin. The other is the lesson I learned that greed is the downfall of the best-intentioned man."

"What lesson is that?" asks Vanessa.

Oscar has that far-away look in his eyes when he explains, "It was that deal in Costa Rica that landed me in prison. My friend Bert..."

"Bert?" she interjects. "Who's that?"

"He was my neighbour. He's a writer, a reporter, a wordsmith of sorts. He roused the Second Generation to get me out of prison. He analysed why I had fallen into the trap set by Pablo. When I smelled what I thought were the big bucks, greed took over, dictated the day, and I switched off my brain and my instincts. That's what Bert told me, and he was right."

"No more greed for you then," comments Vanessa. "Where is Bert now? I'd like to meet him."

"Oh no! No way," is Oscar's instant reply. "I will never let you meet him. He has the habit of keeping my girlfriend warm during my absence, the dirty sod. His name should be Roger."

"Roger?" asks Vanessa. "Why should his name be Roger?"

"Then I could tell you with the last line of a limerick I heard a long time ago that he is Roger, the lodger, the dirty old codger, the bugger, the son of a bitch!"

Their laughter echoes in the street as they turn around and slowly go back to the Muñoz residence.

"I have one last question," says Oscar and casts Vanessa an affectionate look. "Have you ever had a million bucks?"

"No," she answers. "With the payout I got for getting you fit, I have barely enough to open a corner store in Linares."

"Would you like to do that? I mean, opening a corner store?"

"No!" she replies. "I couldn't do that."

"Really? Why not?" he asks.

"Because I couldn't sell junk food to kids, be responsible for their obesity, and say thank you every time they push their two pesos across the counter," says Vanessa.

Oscar looks at her and gives her hand a gentle squeeze.

When they stop at the garden gate, he murmurs, "I hope the Muñoz' serve something better than roadkill for dinner."

"Why should they? That's probably what they had for dinner before they made their millions," mutters Vanessa cautiously.

"What do you mean?" asks Oscar.

"Well, old habits die hard," she replies.

They enter the garden with broad smiles and their merriment raises a few eyebrows of the gathered Muñoz clan seated around an elaborately set dinner table in the garden.

23

It takes a little longer than the few days Alec had anticipated for the promised funds to be made available. Oscar uses the time to discuss logistics with Gerardo Restrepo and the required laboratory equipment with Ariana Andráe. He researches pharmaceutical, chemical, and food-packing companies in addition to container repair shops and shipping enterprises in financial straits that are looking for investors. Oscar goes to industrial exhibitions in search of the appliances needed to process paste and convert it to the finished product as well as packing machinery that doesn't require anyone handling the product.

In the process he gets to know most members of the Second Generation really well, appreciates their enthusiasm and engagement but is concerned about their lack of practical experience. All of them rely on the business savvy and practical experience of their fathers and blend it with the knowledge they acquired at university.

The exception is Alberto Patiño. He studied engineering, had received a polytechnical education and spent over half his time in workshops, where he got hands-on experience making and casting different alloys, as well as building and testing structures and machinery of his own design.

After four weeks of hectic activity, Oscar starts to wonder what happened to the promised funding of the project. He calls Alec a few times, gets noncommittal answers, and is told to be patient.

Over a month after Pablo Escobar announced his intention to retire, Oscar gets a call early in the morning of Wednesday, 23rd October 1991. Alec tells him to check his bank account in the Cayman Islands. In a roundabout way he conveys the news of having received the promised funding and that he deposited the nine million bucks in Oscar's account. He asks Oscar to come to the fourth floor of an office building in the business district of Calí on Calle 32 at ten o'clock. It is a large, modern building with a prominent advertising sign of an insurance company on its front and a coffee shop on the ground floor. He should bring along his most important plans and designs.

A phone call to the Cayman Island branch of his bank confirms the deposit in Oscar's account. He has breakfast in a happy mood and cheerfully explains to Vanessa that they will have to travel to Bogotá in the next few days.

***

Oscar arrives on the fourth floor of the business building where Alec is waiting for him in the hallway. He leads him to an office where a highly polished metal sign of the company 'Valle del Cauca Trading Ltda.' is screwed to the door. The office has a balcony and a small kitchen. It is outfitted only with the bare essentials of desk, filing cabinet, telephone, fax, a desktop computer with a printer, and a couple of chairs. Oscar puts his small briefcase on the desk and wonders what they are doing in the office of a company of which he has never heard.

Alec is in a jocular mood. "This is your orifice, Oscar. It is nothing spectacular but cheap. My father owns the building."

Oscar mutters, "That's very convenient."

He appreciates that a hole in the wall of a luxurious office building comes cheap but wonders about the company name on the door and asks, "What am I doing here?"

"You are trading carnations," says Alec. A brief ping of the phone signals a call and Alec asks, "Are you ready to receive the first order?"

He picks up the phone, listens, and puts it down. He pulls a face and mumbles, "That's funny. The line is dead."

He gets out his cell phone to call the number of the landline, but the telephone starts to ring before Alec has called the number. Oscar picks up the phone, hears a squawking voice, and presses the loudspeaker button before he puts the receiver down.

An angry voice blares, "...before you get started! I won't have you move into our territory! You little shit! Withdraw now or my hitmen will blow you up and send you to hell where you belong. This is the only and final notice. There is no place for you..."

Alec bends over the phone and interjects, "Good morning, Don Chepe! How are you today? I have to presume from your empty threats that you still pursue the old line of doing business. But what's with the quiver in your voice? You sound scared. What's the reason? Have you got your trousers full up to the belt?"

Heavy breathing and some unintelligible muttering can be heard before the line is cut.

Oscar is startled by the caller's threats. "Who is Don Chepe?"

Apparently unfazed, Alec smiles inscrutably. "That's the nickname of José Santacruz Londoño. He is the owner of the golden gates palace in Barrio Jardín." He scratches his head. "How the hell did he get this number? I have to call Pilar."

He punches a number on his cell phone and steps out onto the balcony. Oscar watches him pacing to and fro for quite a while and abruptly ending the call.

Alec looks worried when he comes back into the office. "Well, well, well, I think we have a real problem."

"What is it?" asks Oscar with a concerned look.

Alec plunks himself down on a chair. "Sit down, Oscar. Juan Carlos, our computer geek hacked the telephone companies' computers and Pilar our security specialist analysed the data. She told me that the data is proof of Santacruz' capability to intercept all electronic communications. Only the American and Israeli secret services have these systems at present. Juan Carlos is certain that Santacruz uses computers of Israeli origin, which could mean that Mossad is involved!" Alec leans on the desk and continues in a low voice, "What are we going to do, Oscar? And what the hell are the Israelis doing here getting involved in the drug trade?"

Oscar shrugs. "I don't know but I'm sure it's not to get cut rate cocaine for their troops. It's obvious they are in it for the money!"

Alec agrees. "Yes, and for the right batch of cash Mossad has probably supplied Don Chepe also with explosives that make TNT look like cheap Chinese fireworks. The threat of blowing us up is for real. We better do something and get out of here quick."

Oscar asks, "How does Don Chepe know where we are?"

Alec explains, "He gleaned that from the telephone company records. Every landline installation provides the exact location of street, building, floor, and even the room or office."

Oscar snaps his fingers and takes a newspaper clipping out of his briefcase. "I have an idea. Do you know how to use that thing there, the computer and how to write reports?"

Alec replies casually, "But of course."

"Good!" Oscar pushes the newspaper clipping across the desk. "Here's an Agence France Press interview with Don Pablo. Rewrite it as an exclusive with Santacruz Londoño. Add his claim of being the new King of Coke thanks to Mossad having installed a sophisticated computer system and supplying him with explosives better than TNT."

Alec wrinkles his brow. "And then?"

Oscar chuckles. "Send it out as a news release to security agencies including the Colombian Security Forces and Mossad, as well as every news agency except Agence France Press, of course."

Alec turns on the computer. "Hmm, that may send the security forces after Don Chepe but won't deter him from following up on his threat. We still have to get out of here as quickly as possible."

He asks Oscar to get coffee and starts to write the report.

Oscar enters the crowded café and patiently waits in line. He looks outside and sees a couple of white vans being manoeuvred into parking spots across the street right behind Alec's BMW. He is not concerned until he spots the sign of an office building maintenance company on the vans and sees men in green overalls and white safety helmets get out. They are busy getting holdalls out of the vans and look up at the building. Oscar starts to feel queasy and hopes that Alec is finishing the fake interview and sending it. Oscar gets two coffees and rushes back to the elevator.

Upon entering the office, he is relieved to see the mischievously smiling Alec feeding a report into the fax machine.

Oscar hands him a coffee. "There's a maintenance crew across the street. They are eyeballing this building."

Alec picks up all the papers, hands them to Oscar, and says, "Alright, that's it. I've sent my fake Santacruz interview to a slew of news agencies and secret service outfits. Let's get out of here."

Oscar doesn't have time to drink his coffee, stashes the papers in his briefcase and rushes after Alec along the corridor. They pass a fire alarm. Alec rips down the handle and punches the button. Sirens are blaring. He shoves Oscar through the fire exit door and tells him to go downstairs. People start streaming out of their offices and down the fire staircase.

Alec stands aside and watches the elevator. He sees four men in green overalls and white safety helmets stepping out of the elevator. They carry large holdalls and walk down the hallway towards the office of Valle del Cauca Trading. It is time for Alec to follow the crowd of people vacating the building.

On the sidewalk in front of the building, Alec spots Oscar and signals him to go across the street past the fire trucks arriving on the scene. He passes one of the vans, stops, and looks up. He is trying to listen to the driver who is talking on a walkie-talkie but the noise in the street drowns out whatever the guy in a green overall is saying. Alec walks slowly to his car where Oscar is waiting. They get in and drive away the moment a massive explosion on the fourth floor shakes the building. Glass shards and metal pieces are raining down. A piece of concrete comes hurtling down and gets stuck with a sharp point in the roof of Alec's car.

Alec says, "Hell has to wait for us a little while longer."

Oscar looks at him with raised eyebrows. "What're we gonna do now?"

"Plan B," answers Alec. "That office and the trading company was a fatuous idea. My father insisted that it was the right thing to do, and I obeyed his command to please him. It shows once more that we have to separate ourselves from our elders' influence and do our own thing. We should focus on your plan. So, what did you plan to do first?"

Oscar mulls the question. "Never mind my plan for a moment. The first thing we have to do is declaring Valle del Cauca bankrupt and have it struck from the register. Also, we have to switch to cell phone communication. Everybody has to use a pseudonym of his or her choice as the first step of going underground. As far as our business is concerned, we have to disappear out of the public eye. That is another reason we should not purchase companies but become silent partners. If we invest more than twenty-five percent of the company's current value, we have a free hand to impose any changes we want and need. The first company to look at is a manufacturer of generic drugs in Cartagena. The management is desperate for some cash infusion. You should contact the company and set up a date for a meeting. Shall we do that?"

24

Sean Murphy and his boss Dennis Adams are invited to attend the annual conference of the 'Global Commission on Drug Policy' in Washington, D.C., on Monday, 28th October 1991. The keynote speaker is Marion Barry, Mayor of Washington.

Sean walks into the conference hall of a large hotel where the event takes place. He signs the register and gets a nametag pinned on his lapel.

He looks for his boss in the conference hall. He can't find him and goes to the men's lavatory. He wants to relieve himself in preparation of having to sit through the number of speeches. He enters a cubicle since all the urinals are in use. It turns very quiet once the other patrons are leaving one by one. After a moment of silence, the main door is pushed open, and bangs shut just when Sean has finished his business. Two men are whispering. Sean peers through the crack between door and frame of the cubicle. In the wall mirror, he recognises Mayor Barry snorting two lines of cocaine off a little hand mirror held by an assistant.

Sean flushes the toilet and steps out. The assistant panics, pushes the mirror into Mayor Barry's face and stubs his nose. Sean walks to the sink to wash his hands. He looks over his shoulder and greets the mayor.

Barry crumples a rolled up hundred-dollar bill and replies, "Mornin'. Uh, do I know you?"

Sean chuckles. "I'm sure you don't, Mister Mayor." He cocks his head and adds nonchalantly, "I think you have some icing sugar on your nose from your breakfast muffin."

"Icing sugar?" asks the mayor and wipes his nose. "Oh yeah! Of course!" He sees Sean's nametag. "You're a delegate? I'm giving my speech in a minute."

Sean nods. "I'm looking forward to it, Mayor Barry."

Barry responds jovially, "Alright! I'll see you inside then!"

Sean leaves the lavatory pushing past two surprised beefcakes guarding the door. He sees his boss near the entrance to the conference hall holding two drinks. He joins him and together they enter the conference hall.

Before they sit down, Sean asks, "Do you seriously want to listen to the mayor's speech, Sir?"

Dennis gives Sean a sly look. "Marion Barry pontificating about drug consumption? Oh yeah, for sure, he's an expert on that topic."

Sean pulls a face. "I should think so. I saw him snort coke in the john."

Dennis is stunned and almost crunches the plastic cups he holds. "You what?" he shouts and then whispers, "And you didn't put the cuffs on him?"

"No, Sir," answers Sean with sheepish look. "I left them in the car. Didn't think I'd need them in this illustrious company."

"Okay, Sean, now remember," admonishes Dennis his young sidekick, "whenever Marion Barry is on the agenda as the keynote speaker or a participant you always keep your handcuffs handy. Just imagine the uproar you'd cause by stepping up to the microphone and announcing that you arrested Washington's mayor for the consumption of narcotics in public."

Sean starts to grin imagining himself up on stage. He turns and mutters, "There he is, the mayor with his entourage. The little guy on his left is the man who prepares the lines for Marion to snort."

"It figures," says Dennis in a tone of resignation. "He's the councillor for drug abuse. As the mayor always says, don't leave home without him."

"He does?" asks Sean.

Dennis chuckles, "I'm pulling your leg, man." He nudges Sean and says, "Let's get outta here. I can't stand Marion's blathering when he's full of drugs up to his eyeballs."

They leave the conference hall, go to a nearby lounge and Dennis says, "Will you finally take one of the drinks off my hands?"

Sean is quick to respond, "No, Sir. Thank you for the offer but I don't indulge this early in the morning."

Dennis looks caught between outrageous laughter and simple outrage. He flaps his jaw a couple of times before he belts out, "What the hell do you think this is, young man? Vodka or gin? I have you know it is tonic water. And don't let me catch you saying your boss is getting soused before breakfast. Understood?"

Sean shrinks back, daintily takes one of the drinks thrust at him and says, "Yes, Sir. Sorry, Sir. Thank you, Sir."

He takes a gulp of the carbonated drink and belches out a glass-shattering burp.

Dennis chuckles. "You got anything else to say for yourself?"

They sit down. Sean reaches into his jacket and takes out some folded pages. "Yes, Sir. I got information about strange goings-on in Calí. It confirms your suspicion of something big developing."

Dennis is suddenly all business. "What strange goings-on?"

Sean lowers his voice to say, "As you know, Sir, we intercept Santacruz Londoño's phone calls. He called the recently founded Valle del Cauca Trading company. It exports carnations, belongs to Alejandro Muñoz, and is managed by Oscar Pérez. Alejandro is the son of our old acquaintance Enrique Muñoz. His son exporting carnations could one lead to believe that the family has turned its back on dealing coke if it hadn't been for Santacruz' phone call. He threatened Alejandro to blow him up, if he didn't declare his withdrawal from the business. Now, it's a cert that Santacruz didn't mean the export of carnations with the business." He unfolds the papers and puts one page in front of Dennis. "But instead of Alejandro's declaration of withdrawal, this was issued one hour and thirty minutes after the phone call."

Dennis puts on his reading glasses and asks, "What's that?"

Sean whispers, "It's an exclusive Agence France Press interview with Santacruz Londoño. Among thinly veiled threats, he declares to be the new King of Coke thanks to the support of Mossad. Can you believe that?"

Dennis scans the interview. "Sure. Santacruz is certifiable, but this interview strikes me as fake. I mean, Santacruz is an idiot, but he is not that idiotic to announce his secret supplier of explosives and high-end electronics in public."

Sean is taken aback by his boss stealing his thunder. "Right you are! Half an hour after the report was issued, a powerful explosion blasted the offices of Valle del Cauca Trading. And this morning AFP issued a denial of having interviewed Santacruz. What do you make of that?"

Dennis rubs his chin. "The information is minimal. It's the tip of an iceberg. When I think of the drug barons and their families, then the comparison with a glacier calving an iceberg of massive proportions comes to mind. If my instincts don't fail me, that is exactly what we see - the tip of an iceberg."

Sean is confused by his boss' philosophical meanderings and asks, "An iceberg, Sir?"

Dennis waves the report about. "Yes. It's obvious that Santacruz found out the young Muñoz somehow wanting to get into the drug trade. That carnation export business is just a front."

Sean interrupts him, “I don’t know, Sir. This morning the Colombian government gazette announced that Valle del Cauca Trading declared bankruptcy and was struck from the company register.”

Dennis mutters, “Holy shit! The iceberg took a dive and disappeared. Did you manage to hack into Santacruz’ computer?”

Sean shakes his head. “No, Sir. The system experts in Colombia said that it doesn’t have a backdoor.”

Dennis orders Sean, “Leave that task to our computer hackers. They will find a backdoor and crack it open in no time.”

Sean nods. “Okay, Sir. There is one more thing. I contacted the business registration office in Bogotá and got the full name of this Oscar Pérez. It is Oscar Benito Pérez. Strangely enough, the only person in Colombia with that name and date of birth is a car mechanic from Cartagena, an alcoholic and drug addict who allegedly overdosed a couple of months ago. His body was never found but, surprise, surprise, he and his wife, that is the wife he divorced almost five years ago, turn up in a luxury hotel in Calí.”

Dennis gives him a jaded look. “Were you surprised?”

Sean shakes his head. “No, Sir, nothing to be surprised about. Hence, I ordered one of our agents onto their trail, but the couple had checked out of the hotel without leaving a forwarding address. They’ve just disappeared.”

Dennis gets up and repeats his question. “Were you surprised? But don’t give up. Okay? The picture will come together as we gain more intel. Come on, let’s go back to the conference hall for a bit of a snooze for the duration of Barry’s speech.”

25

A black limousine stops in the parking lot of Pharmagena, a generic drug company on Carrera 56 in Cartagena. Alec, Oscar, Leticia, and Sabrina get out of the car and are hit by an evil smelling cloud of dust from a nearby cement plant blown in by the prevailing wind.

The steel and glass structure of the pharma building, designed with the intention of conveying light, airiness, and clean environment of drug manufacturing, has lost its gloss under a crusty layer of grey dust. Alec gives Oscar a doubtful look before the foursome enters the building.

They enter the clean reception area. Alec is not convinced that they should continue with their enquiry about becoming silent partners. He turns to Oscar and whispers, "Are you sure about this company?"

Oscar nods earnestly, pulls a flat hand horizontally across his throat, and points his thumb in the direction of the cement plant.

Alec needs a moment to grasp what Oscar is trying to convey with his gestures. He seems to have understood and turns to the receptionist to inform her of the arranged morning meeting. A young woman in business attire, the secretary of the Managing Director and Chief Executive Officer, Hector Belgran, comes out to welcome the visitors. She leads the quartet into the boardroom where refreshments are set on the table.

Hector, an elderly man with thinning hair, glasses, and a weathered face joins them. They exchange greetings and business cards. Hector sits down and props up his head with one hand. It gives his face the look of a tired basset hound.

Looking from face to face and after a pregnant pause, Hector drops his hand and smiles. "You are quite the gutsy bunch of youngsters. You got a lot of spunk not to be deterred by Pharmagena's crusty exterior like everybody else before you. Today, the 16th December 1991 is a significant day for me. It was on this day forty years ago that my partner, Giovanni Buscetti, an Italian pharmacologist who is no longer with us, and I founded the company in this location. We did very well for thirty years until that cement plant next door outgrew its britches."

Alec looks worried and asks, "What happened?"

Hector chuckles. "As you know, we produce generic drugs for the underprivileged and those who don't want to pay the high prices of brand name medication. That puts Pharmagena right at the bottom of our government's ranking of companies. That cement plant across the road, a pissy little outfit that couldn't make ends meet until the mid-eighties, suddenly began to expand after it got a massive injection of cash, which is assumed to have been drug money. Its expansion coincided with the beginning of the building boom, which put the cement plant on one of the top rungs of importance because they could also afford to pay all sorts of kickbacks to government officials. When we tried to sue the plant for its unbridled pollution and the damages to our company, our lawsuit was thrown out of court, and we were told to move. Well, we are still here. So, tell me who you are and what raised your interest in Pharmagena."

"I will come to that in a minute," says Alec. "First give me your cost estimate for an environmental impact study and bringing charges against the cement plant for endangering public health."

Hector slaps a hand on his forehead. "I haven't got the faintest. I don't even know what an environmental impact study is. Never heard of it. But I can tell you that suing the cement plant through all the instances and appeals to the highest court could easily cost more than two million dollars excluding graft money for the judges, of course."

Alec nods. "Okay, an environmental impact study determines the degree of pollution of any kind and its effect on the environment. In the case of the cement plant, it is a matter of measuring the toxicity and heavy metal content of its smokestack output. Once the level of pollution has been established, the owners may be faced with a multimillion-dollar environmental clean-up or the installation of a scrubber. They will have the choice. Oscar, please take some notes."

He waits for Oscar to get ready and reminds him of the major points, especially the assumption that drug money financed the cement plant's expansion. He asks him for the offer for Pharmagena they typed up the night before.

"Mister Belgran," Alec begins. "We are a group of sixteen young Colombians who got together out of concern for the environment. Our company, Greenlief, is registered in Panama as an environmentally orientated organisation. We endeavour to promote the production of affordable medication and medicinal substances of plant extracts for therapeutic purposes. After his search for a potential partner, our business advisor, Oscar Pérez, concluded that your company came out tops for integrity, product quality, production, research facilities, and market positioning."

Hector listens intently and puts on his reading glasses when Alec gives him a copy of Oscar's appraisal of Pharmagena. He reads with raised eyebrows, nods a few times, and puts down his glasses.

"You have certainly done your research. It is a very sound assessment of my company. Let me address the point on which everything in business hinges - finances. According to your offer and your suggestion of bringing charges against the cement plant, I have to assume that you have very deep pockets."

Alec chuckles. "No, Sir, our financial resources are limited. They are actually equal investments by each member of our group. The moneys were either inherited or early inheritance payouts. Our financial statement will provide you with a clear picture."

He passes a three-page document to Hector and lets him study it for a while. "I expect you to subject our offer to due diligence."

Hector smiles and nods. "Yes, of course. Are all the investors in Greenlief progenies of the Mil Familias?"

Leticia raises her hands and pleads, "Please, Sir, don't ever mention or use that term again in our presence. We have had severe disagreements with our families. We don't want to pursue their way of doing business, which gave rise to FARC, ELN, and other guerilla militias. Our family feuds resulted in painful splits. We aim to bring positive and peaceful change to Colombia and wish to work free of family interference. Therefore, I ask you to refrain from contacting anyone of our families in your process of due diligence."

Hector looks at the four business cards in front of him and asks, "Miss Leticia?" She nods and he continues, "Your wish is my command. Should we come to an agreement then, I presume, you, a pharmacologist, would be working on our company premises and contribute directly to the turnaround of our fortunes?"

Leticia nods, thus confirming his assumption. Hector gathers up the papers and business cards and says, "Ladies, gentlemen, it is time for me to show you around our production facilities."

He guides his visitors through the administrative section and introduces them to board members and senior employees. After the brief and somewhat superficial encounters, they are getting down to inspecting the laboratories and manufacturing facilities. Leticia shows her mettle pointing out some outdated equipment and machinery and suggesting major improvements. Hector is impressed and becomes quite cosy with her. At the end of the visit, they shake hands and Hector sends them on their way with the promise of calling them within two days right after a meeting of the board that will discuss the offer.

***

Speeding along the coastal highway to the port city Barranquilla, Oscar is amused about Alec's presentation. He says to him, "That was a brilliant description of our product - medicinal substance of a plant extract for therapeutic purposes. We should try to get it classified as such and export it legally worldwide."

He turns to Leticia. "And you were brilliant, too. What a way to lay out family feuds and connect it to the rise of the guerillas. That will limit his due diligence to purely financial matters and stop him from investigating our identities."

The boisterous mood lasts until they arrive at Alimento Accesible, a dry goods packing company in a run-down industrial part of Barranquilla. It is housed in a decrepit building between two breweries and doesn't even have a parking lot for visitors. The space in front of the loading dock is blocked by trucks of all sizes delivering or picking up goods.

The mood of the foursome changes rapidly when they have to park their luxury limousine in the street and squeeze through the narrow spaces between the stinking lorries.

They are received on the loading dock by a fat guy in a sweat-stained shirt who claims to be the manager. Without looking at Alec's business card, he basically tells them to piss off. He hasn't got time to cater to visitors.

Quite outraged Oscar calls the company headquarters on his cell phone and asks if Alimento Accesible is in the habit of receiving all potential investors like that. First, he is informed that the company offices are not in the plant but located at the intersection of Murillo Toro and Olaya Herrera Streets. Then he is asked to pass his phone to the manager.

A barrage of insults emanates from the phone. The threat of being fired instantly unless the visitors are treated with a degree of courtesy gives rise to the manager turning pale and his eyes bulging out. He hands the phone back to Oscar and excuses himself to go for a dump.

When he comes back, he is very apologetic and hands out dust-masks to his guests. He even finds time to guide them personally through the plant. Dry goods including beans, peas, lentils, rice, sugar, and flour are filled into bags for retail.

The place is full of dust. Packing material is strewn on the floor. It is a chaotic situation. When Oscar shows the manager a couple of sachets and asks if the plant packs sugar for restaurants, the manager just shakes his head.

At the back of the building is an empty lot, part of the company property with access to a road. Sabrina takes note of it and the inspection tour comes to a swift end.

After a short ride, Alec parks the car opposite the company headquarters and they are received in the office building by Alberto Monge, the sole owner of Alimento Accesible. He is in his seventies, has a full head of white hair and a nose reminiscent of a hawk's beak. His facial countenance gives the impression that he is constantly sniffing. Yet, he is quite a jovial guy with a vocal range from rasping whispers to stentorian blasts.

He takes his visitors to his office, gives his only employee, an elderly woman, the receptionist-cum-secretary-cum-dishwasher the order to make coffee and bring it into the meeting room.

The story Monge conveys about his company is similar to the one they heard in Cartagena. Providing cut-price basic foodstuffs to the needy and all those who can't afford brand name products, his company is rated very low on the importance scale of local and federal politicians. He receives no support in the struggle against his two powerful neighbours, the breweries, who want to squeeze him out and take possession of his property.

The story Alec tells is also similar to the one he told in Cartagena but this time he presents the recently founded and Barbados registered company called Sanalimentos. It is a company that strives to provide healthy, organic food at affordable prices not only to the local and national market but also for export to neighbouring countries and North America.

Sabrina takes over and emphasises that food destined for export has to undergo a thorough inspection for purity and cleanliness. The Food and Drug Administration of the USA is very particular when it comes to imported foods. Therefore, she concludes, Monge's company has to undergo a thorough clean-up, repair and replacement of machinery, and the expansion of the facilities to accommodate a food-testing laboratory. She also assures him in case he should be agreeable to their investment offer that she would be working with him very closely in his spacious offices.

Upon hearing of the prospect of having Sabrina working in his vicinity, the old guy starts to drool and doesn't want to hear about or read reports and financial statements. He agrees to everything and tells them to visit his lawyer to finalise the deal. He even promises not to fire his receptionist. They part ways on the best of terms and Monge manages a smile that almost cracks his face.

Outside they share a laugh about Monge's quick agreement. Alec asks Sabrina if she really had an itch in her cleavage or rubbed her index finger up and down in it to get the old guy to drool and forget about any objection. Sabrina giggles and claims to have been completely unawares of such action. When Alec suggests that she should have given the old guy her panties as a farewell present to save them from having to see his lawyer, she punches him so hard that it almost floors him.

***

In the afternoon, the foursome meets Igor, Alberto, and Teresa in the customs controlled free port area of Barranquilla near the RepCon container maintenance company. The workshop gates are wide open. The visitors are issued safety helmets and heavy steel capped boots before they are allowed to enter the work area.

Alberto inspects the ongoing repair of a container. He talks to a couple of mechanics about reinforcements or the replacement of the base structure. They look sceptical but don't reject his suggestion out of hand. A welder joins them and draws a rough sketch in the dirt on the floor. The four men squat around the outline and agree that the welder's idea for a stronger and cheaper structure is sound. Alberto wants to discuss the upgrade of refrigeration containers, so-called reefers, but draws a blank because they don't handle those units in their workshop. Still, Alberto is sufficiently impressed with the mechanics and the welder to take their names.

All the while Igor and Teresa are checking the ceiling cranes and other electrical and hydraulic equipment. They take notes and Teresa suggests the replacement of most of the installations with modern and more powerful equipment and machinery. Briefly they discuss their notes with Alec and Oscar who have turned up in the company of the workshop foreman and a director of the company. Teresa asks if other buildings belong to the company. The foreman takes her outside and points to three adjoining buildings that belong to RepCon. One of them was a wharf, he explains, with a small floating dock that could take a fishing vessel via rails from the port basin into the repair facility, but it hasn't been used for some years and is in disrepair. The other two buildings are used for storage of parts and material.

The director still studies Alec's offer of the recently founded and Curaçao registered company FrutaSur. It specialises in chilled fruit mash and frozen concentrated fruit juice. Their offer is twofold - for one they would like to become partners in the container repair business and expand it to include the maintenance of reefers and for another they want to convert part of the RepCon facilities to a shipping warehouse for the recently formed and Barbados registered company Caribe Sur Maritime Shipping Company that will handle all of FrutaSur's exports to North America.

The director, Alec, and Oscar have an animated discussion. In the end, they are all smiles and shake hands. They have come to a mutual understanding. They part company on the director's promise to provide a final answer within a week.

***

Once their business in Barranquilla is concluded, the whole group heads back to Cartagena where they get together with their legal beagles Maria and Jorge and the financial wizard Penelope in Alec's hotel suite to discuss an action plan for the next few days.

Igor, their man of a thousand contacts, is given the task of investigating the investment source and ownership of the polluting cement plant and report back to Jorge who will initiate legal action.

Maria will check out the two breweries in Barranquilla and visit Alberto Monge's lawyers with Penelope to finalise their deal.

Alec and Sabrina will look for a fruit processing company to become a partner of FrutaSur and report back to Oscar who will have to prepare an offer.

Finally, Penelope will launder sufficient funds for the transfer of the agreed investment amounts.

Quite exhausted but content with the results of the day, Oscar excuses himself when the meeting winds down. He takes a taxi to his hotel on the seafront of Bocagrande and joins Vanessa who is relaxing with a drink on the terrace of the hotel's Café Jardín.

He joins her and they enjoy the mild sea breeze without saying much at first. She can see that he is exhausted and needs time to recover. She orders drinks. Once they are served and Oscar has had a sip, he recounts the events of the day in telegram style. It is sufficient for her to share his happiness about the results.

Both are surprised when Alec turns up and joins them for a quick chat. Essentially, he just wants to thank Oscar for his detailed research and business plans.

They share a laugh when he talks about Alberto Monge and does a spitting image of the old man's facial expression. He gets up, thanks Oscar once more for his marvellous job, slaps him on the shoulder, and leaves in a hurry through the hotel's lobby to get some shut-eye.

Although Vanessa listened to the banter, she watched the corner of the building where she saw the occasional glow of a cigarette and smoke being blown across the beam of a spotlight.

Ramón Miranda steps out. He stares into the hotel lobby looking for someone and then approaches Oscar and Vanessa.

"Good evening. Excuse the interruption, but wasn't that Alejandro Muñoz who just left?"

Oscar glances at Ramón. "Who wants to know?"

Ramón replies hastily, "Sorry, Sir. I'm his old friend Ramón Miranda. I wanted to say hello."

Vanessa squints at Ramón and scrutinises his jacket. She notices a bulge in the jacket under his left armpit and stubs Oscar's foot. Irritated, he looks at Vanessa who signals with her eyes that she has detected something suspicious about this guy.

Oscar ignores her signals and looks back at Ramón. "Ramón Miranda? I'll tell him later you said hello."

Ramón makes big eyes. "Oh, you're going to see him later? Is he around for a while? Where could I meet him?"

Oscar chuckles and wants to say something when Vanessa kicks his foot. He protests, "Hey, what's the matter with you?"

She gives him a stern look and another kick. "Sorry, that twitch in my leg is getting worse."

She puts her handbag on the table and addresses Alec's alleged friend. "Ramón, your friend Alejandro Muñoz has been in Panama for the past month and won't return for a couple of weeks."

Ramón wrinkles his brow. "Really...?"

Oscar makes big eyes. "What? But he..." he says and gets yet another kick.

Vanessa smiles apologetically, puts a hand in her handbag and the release of a gun safety is heard.

Oscar desists from saying anything when he sees a bulge in her soft leather handbag pointing distinctly at Ramón's belly.

She locks eyes with Ramón. "Yes, Ramón, really. That's all we know about the whereabouts of Mister Muñoz."

Ramón's eyes flit about between her icy stare and her handbag. He knows that she has an obvious advantage. Should he reach for his gun, she would shoot first.

By the sound of the gun safety release, he can tell as well that it is a large calibre gun. Her cold eyes indicate that she would not give a damn about a hole in her expensive designer handbag and shoot right through it.

He decides to retreat. "Very well, then excuse my intrusion."

Vanessa watches him waddle away and hisses at Oscar, "You turn into quite the chatterbox when you had a good day, don't you? Didn't you see that the guy had a gun?"

Oscar exclaims, "What? He had a gun? Oh, shit!"

Vanessa snaps the gun safety and takes her hand out of the bag. "Yes! Shit, indeed! You have to keep on your toes at all times."

Oscar asks with quivering lips, "What's that in your handbag? Is that a gun? Where did you get it?"

"Memories of Boquete," she replies. "What did you think it was? A hand puppet wouldn't be much use. We are in Colombia, remember?"

"Yes, sure," he answers. "But, but..."

"But what?" she snaps. "You have objections to protecting yourself? I don't rely on others to save my skin, and neither should you! Faced by an assassin, I'd hit back before I get hit or take the bastard with me, if he gets a shot off and it's time for me to go."

"Assassin?" asks Oscar. "How do you know he's an assassin?"

She responds in a sharp tone, "Because he carries a concealed gun and claims to be Alejandro's old friend. Yet, he asks for him by his proper name not Alec as all his friends call him."

Oscar blubbers, "Well, that may not mean a thing. It's just common courtesy to ask for someone by his proper name."

Looking exasperated, she needs a moment to respond. "Are you nuts? It's quite clear to me why and how you ran into trouble and ended up in prison. You are impetuous. You focus on only one task like a self-propelled boor driven by his flatulence and forget to keep your eyes open. For the past few weeks, you worked only on the development of your plan and did everything to protect your designs. And now that your plan appears to be working, you revel in its initial success and ignore protecting yourself against the inherent dangers of the Second Generation's business. You were lucky to escape a first assassination attempt due to Alec's astuteness. Yet, you of all people must know that you can't trust anyone. That includes assassins like this Ramón who was lurking in the darkness and observed us since the moment Alec arrived. I'm almost certain that Alec spotted him as well and made for a rapid exit through the hotel when the guy wasn't looking for a second. Why do you think Ramón checked the lobby first and then came to us? He had lost track of him!"

Oscar swallows hard and gives Vanessa a bug-eyed look. "So, uh, what do you suggest we should do?"

"Do you know how to handle a gun?" she asks.

"No!" he responds. "I've never fired a shot my whole life."

"Okay, Bud, tomorrow you will start, even if I have to take you at gunpoint to a safe area where I can teach you the basics. And we will get body armour you will have to wear wherever you go. And that's my final word in this matter."

26

It takes only a few days for all the deals, including the investment in a fruit processing company to be finalised. The offers are welcome and considered non-threatening or hostile because the management and workforce will stay to carry on with the business. The proviso that a professional member of the investment group will join the board of each company is also accepted as par for the course. The companies will undergo expansion programs that have to be supervised by an expert of the new level of activities.

Everything would have been well, had it not been for the environmental impact study initiated by an environmental group and the charges laid against the cement plant.

The Orejuela brothers and Santacruz Londoño are majority owners of the plant through a shell company and are royally peeved facing a potential multimillion-dollar environmental clean-up. Consequently, they have put their tracker dogs on the trail to investigate who is behind that action. Soon enough they find out who is responsible for their pains although Jorge kept a low profile and functioned only as a legal advisor to the environmental protection group. But his financial donation that enabled the group to launch the legal action gave him away. Jorge's close relationship with Alec and Igor lets Londoño draw the conclusion that Alec is the driving force behind it. He issues the order for his hired assassins to terminate these three guys and capture their advisor, Oscar Pérez.

Unawares of the looming danger, the Second Generation wants to celebrate the successful conclusion of the project's first phase. Alicia and Gerardo book the Café del Mar on Avenida Santander in Cartagena for Friday, 20th December 1991. They hire a popular local big band known for its hot salsa, merengue and ska rhythms and have several local radio stations announce the concert with the offer of entry free of charge and free beer to the first two hundred patrons to celebrate the band's release of its latest album.

The evening event is well organised and set to become a rousing success. Loudspeakers have been installed outside to appease the crowd of more than the first two hundred patrons. Dancing and a lot of chatter is going on in the parking lot. A section of the café's terrace has been cordoned off as a VIP area for band members and the hosts of this event.

***

Three limousines park a distance away from the Café del Mar. Six men in charcoal grey silk suits led by Ramón Miranda get out and walk towards the café's entrance. In the shadows of the building, they pull handguns from armpit holsters, load them through, and put them back. They nod when Ramón mutters the names of the guys they are supposed to dispatch but give him blank looks when he mentions the name 'Oscar Pérez'.

They enter the quiet section of the café, go into the gents' lavatory that they leave through the exit to the ballroom, and knock out a couple of guards on their way.

Alec and Sabrina are dancing until he needs to take a break and tugs her to their table. While he has a sip of his drink, he spots the men in charcoal grey silk suits who leave the men's lavatory and galumph along the perimeter of the packed ballroom like a troop of circus elephants without holding on to each other's tail, of course. They move towards Igor, Oscar and Vanessa on the dance floor and pull their guns.

Alec sneaks up on them, rushes Ramón and brings him down with a flying rugby tackle. He kneels on Ramón's back, wrests the gun from his hand and knocks him out with its butt. He reaches out and tears Igor down. Vanessa gets knocked over. Her handbag hits the floor with a thud. Shots ring out. The crowd panics and stampedes for the exit.

Vanessa rips the silenced Magnum .45 out of her handbag and holds it up to Oscar who is frozen in his motion and stares at Ramón. Igor snatches the gun from her hand and fires three shots at one of the assassins who collapses fatally wounded. Alec catches a bullet in the chest from one of the gunslingers and lays sprawled on the floor. Igor turns and kills another of the hitmen with a shot to the head. The crowd of patrons has cleared the entire dance floor in panic. Vanessa takes the gun from Alec's limp hand, fires at a hitman, and kills him.

The remaining two men of the six-pack shoot at anything that moves. Igor is fatally shot in the head. Seeing the hit, Penelope screams, crawls over to him. She is hit by several bullets and collapses on top of Igor. Jorge throws himself to the floor and tears down Oscar. Lying on her back, Vanessa kills one more hitman and wounds the last one. She runs out of bullets, picks up her

Magnum, gets up, and executes the wounded man when he lifts his gun.

Ramón regains consciousness, pushes Alec aside, raises his hands, and winks at Vanessa. She shoots him in the shoulder and the right leg.

She signals Oscar and Jorge to pick up Alec and get out. Knowing that the police will appear within minutes, the rest of the Second Generation leaves as well for the parking lot. They had parked their cars near the exit to Avenida Santander and get away quickly.

***

The digital clock on the wall of the Hospital Misericordia waiting room shows 2:15 a.m. Saturday, 21st December 1991. Teresa and Pilar are trying to comfort Ariana who is inconsolable. They heard that Alec underwent emergency surgery and is now in an intensive care unit. Pilar has found out that the one surviving assassin was also brought to this hospital and is recovering in a room on the same floor.

Inside the ICU, Alec is hooked up to an intravenous drip and monitoring equipment. Oscar, Vanessa, and Jorge stand at the foot end of the bed. Sabrina sits next to Alec and clasps his hand.

Their anxiety eases when he opens his eyes and mumbles, "What the devil happened?"

Jorge shrugs, "We really don't know. I think it was a commando sent to kill you and Igor."

Alec needs a moment to digest the message and muster the energy to ask, "How's Igor?"

Jorge wipes his face. "He's dead, and so is Penelope."

Alec is devastated hearing of his two friends' death. His face distorts in grief. He manages to mutter, "This has to stop. No more killings and bloodshed, you hear?" It takes him quite a while to control his sobs and ask, "Did the assassins get away?"

Oscar says quite composed, "No, not one of them. Five are dead and another is wounded. He's in the room next door."

Alec stares at the ceiling and asks no one in particular, "Six in total? Who were these guys? Who sent them?"

Oscar points a thumb at the wall behind him. "The assassin next door is your old friend Ramón Miranda. He could tell us."

Alec is stunned. "Ramón Miranda? I don't know anyone by that name."

Oscar nods. "Vanessa figured as much. He won't talk either."

Vanessa nods and sighs. "You have to give him a Coke."

Oscar is baffled, "What? Give him a Coke? Why?"

Vanessa rolls her eyes and leaves the room. She returns with a half-litre bottle of Coca-Cola and hands it to Jorge, "Give him this, and he'll tell you more than you ever wanted to know."

It is Jorge's turn to be baffled. "I don't understand. What if he prefers Pepsi? Will drinking Pepsi also make him talk? How about lemonade?"

Vanessa starts to wonder if Jorge paid for his law school tuition working part-time as a waiter in a greasy spoon. "No, it has to be Coke. Anyway, he's not supposed to drink it. You spray it up his nose into the frontal sinus where it converts to foam and expands. He'll think his head is exploding. It's an old trick of the Mexican police. He'll talk, you'll see."

While Jorge and Oscar still dither, she leaves the room and talks to the young policeman on guard duty in front of the room next door. She hands him a one-hundred-dollar bill and asks to fetch five large coffees. Happily, he pockets the money and is on his way.

Vanessa signals Jorge and Oscar that the coast is clear and sits down on the policeman's chair. After they enter the room, she can hear Jorge ask a question. It is answered by Ramón's cackling laughter and curses. Then a hissing sound and gurgling is followed by a scream and an endless stream of rapidly spoken words. A short while later, Jorge and Oscar leave the room looking satisfied.

The policeman returns with a tray. Vanessa takes it, hands him a cup of coffee and thanks him for his help. On his own again, the young cop looks into the room. He stares at Ramón who is muttering incoherently, occasionally lets out a brief shriek, and appears to have developed a nosebleed.

Jorge, Oscar, Sabrina, and Vanessa stand around Alec's bed. Jorge holds on to the headrest. "The bottle of Coke worked. The guy talked and is still talking. The killers were sent here by the Orejuelas and Santacruz Londoño. When they investigated who had laid charges against their cement plant, they found out my association with you. The commando was supposed to kill you, Igor, and me and kidnap Oscar. They spotted Igor and made their move, but your tackle of Ramón threw a spanner in their works and the shooting started."

Alec asks with a worried look, "So, what are we going to do about our project?"

Jorge looks pensive when he answers, “We have the companies we need in our fold. We could modernise and expand them and order and install the machinery. It’ll take time to get that done.”

Alec asks, “Yes, but what about Don Chepe? He’s not afraid of open warfare.”

Jorge agrees, “True, when I called Igor’s family with the bad news, Don Osvaldo assumed immediately that it was Santacruz. He wants to blow up his marble palace and go after the kids of the Orejuelas. There is no end in sight. That means we have to go deep undercover with our project.”

Oscar pipes in, “That’s what I’ve said from the start. Whatever we do has to be done covertly. We have to get fake identities and keep our cell phone calls to the bare minimum for safety.”

Alec looks to Jorge. “Can you organise that?”

Jorge assures him, “Yes, I will contact your father to get us fake identities. We’ll start our operation by moving you to a safe place.”

Alec protests meekly, “But this is a safe place.”

Jorge shakes his head emphatically. “Not safe enough. The cops know you’re here and very likely want to interview you.”

Alec questions the suggested action, “But how are you going to get me out of here? I could croak if I am taken off the ICU.”

Jorge dismisses that comment, “Don’t worry. We’ll take you out with the ICU. I asked the Special Forces to give us a hand.”

A knock on the door cuts him short. An officer of the Special Forces enters the room. A doctor and a nurse appear beside him followed by a detail of six soldiers. They follow the doctor’s instructions and take care of the IV, oxygen supply and monitors. Alec is moved out, down the hallway, and into a waiting elevator.

Oscar, Jorge, Vanessa, Pilar, Teresa, Ariana, and Sabrina rush down the stairs of the fire exit. A military medical evacuation unit is waiting outside. Alec and the ICU equipment are loaded into it.

The soldiers get into their trucks and Oscar and the others pile into their cars. Embedded in the military convoy, they are not stopped by the criminal investigation unit entering the hospital parking lot.

27

It is Friday afternoon. Dennis Adams yawns and stretches. A look at the wall clock tells him that it is 4:53 p.m., almost time to pack it in for the weekend and go home. He crosses out 17th January 1992 on his desktop calendar with a red pen, tosses the day's newspaper in his briefcase, and gets up. He locks his desk and leaves his office walking past the deserted desk of his secretary. At the elevator he presses the down button when he can hear someone come running along the hallway. He looks up and thinks, 'Please, don't let that be more irrelevant news about some failed drug investigation. I want to go home, play with my grandchildren and forget about this stupid War on Drugs.'

But no such luck. It is Sean Murphy who comes rushing along. He waves a folder and calls out just before Dennis steps into the elevator, "Sir! Would you have a moment?"

Dennis sighs. "Hi, Sean! You're out of breath."

In a state of excitement, Sean conveys breathlessly, "Yes, Sir! Right! I have received crucial information about activities that could indicate the whereabouts of the iceberg."

Dennis looks baffled. "Iceberg? What iceberg?

Sean cringes. "The iceberg you mentioned. Don't you remember the iceberg that disappeared when Valle del Cauca declared bankruptcy? It concerns Alejandro Muñoz! The report was sent a few minutes ago by Vern Cespedes, one of our field agents."

Dennis gives him a jaded look. "Ah yes, good old Vern. What is the date of his incredibly important information?"

Sean opens the file and says meekly, "Uh, 23rd December 1991."

Dennis chuckles. "Of course. I hope that good old Vern didn't pick up a disease celebrating Christmas and New Years with scantily clad conchitas and chulas on the beaches of Cartagena. What else could explain the delay of him filing his report?"

Sean blushes at the thought of Vern prancing around on a tropical beach with full bosomed, broad hipped women in micro thong bikinis. "His, uh, private life aside, Sir, I still regard Vern as one of our most reliable field agents. Perhaps his scantily clad conchitas are the source of his information."

Dennis sighs. “Uh-huh, interesting theory. And presenting his three-week old findings couldn’t wait until Monday?”

Sean inhales audibly. “Sir, I could just drop a copy...”

Dennis checks his watch - 5:05 p.m. He says with some resignation, “No, go ahead. Dump Vern’s breaking news on me.”

Encouraged by his boss, Sean replies, “Okay. Alejandro Muñoz was shot and Igor Guttiérez killed.”

Unimpressed Dennis asks, “Did they shoot each other?”

A smile creeps across Sean’s face. “No, they socialised. They were shot by hitmen.”

Dennis is stunned by one bit of information. “What? The sons of lifelong enemies socialised? That’s a switch. Let’s go to your office. Now I want the complete story.”

Sean leads the way to his office at the end of the hallway. Dennis takes in the notes and the array of pictures of all too familiar drug dealers’ faces stuck on a pin board connected by red cord. The diagrams of drug dealing bosses and their allegiance to various organisations drawn on a whiteboard are equally detailed.

Dennis turns to Sean and asks, “Who were the hitmen?”

Sean shrugs. “Vern couldn’t confirm that. Only one of the six survived.”

Dennis wrinkles his brow. “Only one of six hitmen survived? Who was hitting the hitmen?”

Sean checks Vern’s report and says, “Some witnesses stated that a woman shot and killed five of the hitmen in the shoot-out. She is assumed to be a bodyguard.”

Dennis grunts sarcastically, “Yes, sure, a female bodyguard. And? Has the surviving hitman been questioned?”

Sean stammers, “Yes, well, uh, no. He was questioned but appears to be of unsound mind. During questioning, when a cop opened a bottle of Coke, the hitman assaulted him and had to be subdued and tranquillised.”

Dennis assumes, “He must have something against drinking carbonated sugar water.”

Sean agrees, “That’s probably correct. He is muttering constantly about free beer in a nightclub and won’t respond to any question related to the shooting that took place.”

Dennis picks a marker pen, writes ‘Calí/Guttiérez’ and ‘Medellín/Muñoz’ on the whiteboard, and says, “Let me recap. Six hitmen enter a nightclub, kill one guy with Calí connections, and shoot another whose family has a Medellín history. In the ensuing shoot-out, the bodyguard, a woman, shoots and kills five of the hitmen but let's one of them live. Are you sure you got that info from Vern and not some deranged Hollywood scriptwriter?"

"I'm sure, Sir. As I said, Vern Cespedes is very reliable."

"It doesn't make sense."

"What doesn't make sense, Sir?"

"Sean, not in a month of Sundays would the Muñoz and Guttiérez clans, archenemies since forever, agree to hire one bodyguard, yet a woman, to guard both of their sons. Question is, who is that woman?"

Sean shrugs. "Nobody knows. She's supposed to look very attractive and not at all like a gunslinger."

Dennis grins sardonically. "Hmm, what does a female Colombian gunslinger look like, Sean? Fat, squat and with a face only a desperate mother could love? And why didn't she kill the sixth hit man?"

Sean raises his open hands. "Perhaps to send a message? Eventually he'll talk to his boss."

Dennis sits down on the desk. "Possible, but who is his boss? Something else doesn't make sense. Who would send six hitmen into a nightclub to kill one guy or two?"

Sean wags a finger. "Hold it. There was one more fatality. Penelope Saenz was killed as well."

Dennis jumps up. "What? Saenz? Penelope Saenz? Is she related to Benito or Jaime Saenz?"

Sean says, "She's a daughter of Jaime, the bean counter."

Dennis slaps his forehead "Jaime! Holy shit!"

He goes to the picture gallery and points to some connections shown by the red cord. He writes 'Valle del Norte/Saenz' on the whiteboard, draws lines that converge on a fat question mark underneath the three names, and turns to Sean. "You know, the killing of Jaime's daughter raises the key question, if the socialising of archenemies' kids means that the old guard has buried the hatchet to let the youngsters take over and create a new cartel."

Sean asks, "I see but why is the killing of Penelope key?"

Dennis explains, "Her father Jaime came to Miami a few days ago. He turned material witness for exemption from prosecution. If his daughter was involved with Medellín and Calí progeny then they are cooperating. What about Alejandro Muñoz? Has he been questioned by police?"

Sean shakes his head. "Uh, no, Sir. According to the policeman on guard of the nutty hitman, he was taken away by Special Forces before the criminal investigators arrived."

Dennis lets out a tortured grunt. "Of course! What next? Don't tell me! Our trails have turned cold and communication surveillance yields no more results. Right?"

Sean looks embarrassed, "Yes, Sir. Sorry, Sir."

Dennis looks close to tears, "Yes? You said yes, didn't you? Is this the DEA or the Keystone Cops? Never mind, Sean, never mind. Anything else?"

Sean mutters, "Yes, Sir. Your assumption about a new cartel may be right. Vern had received information about a phone call of Santacruz Londoño with one of his henchmen. It concerned a meeting in a hotel in Calí of the sons and daughters of sixteen different drug families. But before Vern could track them down, they had vanished."

Dennis is perplexed. "Vanished? What do you mean they vanished? Like a fart in a pigpen?"

Sean smirks. "Yes, Sir, that's a very apt description."

Dennis groans. "Chrissakes! Just what we need! Sixteen families establish a new cartel that vanishes before it starts to operate. Is that it or do you have any other news?"

Sean shrugs, "No, Sir, that's it."

Dennis drops the marker pen. "Okay, Sean. Instruct our field agents to check unusual activities in Bogotá, Medellín, Cartagena, and Calí. Purchase of companies, port movements, and so on are of interest. Also, I want you to go to Miami and talk to Jaime Saenz. See what you can get out of him. And, please, don't bother me until Monday. My grandchildren are visiting. Have a nice weekend."

Dennis picks up his briefcase and walks away a bit hunched over and looking quite dispirited.

28

Gerardo's rough estimate of three months for the renovation and expansion of buildings and delivery and installation of machinery and equipment to start their intended production is spot on. Sabrina signs off the finished work at Alimento Accesible on Thursday, 2nd April 1992, and walks with Armando through the plant. Dust masks are no longer required. She shows him the clean work environment and the expansion for packing chilled fruit mash with some pride and satisfaction. At the end of the plant is the entrance to his exclusive place of work. The legend on the door warns that entry to the 'Dust-free Food Inspection Lab' is strictly prohibited to unauthorised personnel.

Armando opens the door and steps into the new annex. The strong smell of mortar and paint still permeates the air. Painters and electricians are busy with their final touches.

The workshop is divided by a glass wall. The smaller section houses an office and massive rolls of plastic lined white packing paper for sugar sachets. An air lock large enough for a forklift carrying one of the rolls of packing paper to pass through is the entrance to the larger section. Units of machinery bearing the shiny stainless-steel letters and logo of the Italian manufacturer stand in the centre of that section and are still covered in clear plastic sheets. Two humongous coffee makers stand to the side and are ready to produce gallons of a strong brew.

The painters are folding up drip sheets and carry out paint buckets and ladders onto a loading ramp outside. The electricians run a final test on the air filtration unit, a high-volume German made HVAC, which controls humidity and temperature and removes any smell. Armando passes through the airlock in the glass wall, hands the workers plain brown envelopes full of cash, and thanks them for their excellent work. He watches them load tools and material onto a couple of small trucks and leave on the freshly asphalted back road. Once they are gone, he shuts the heavy steel gate to the new loading dock at the rear of the building as well as the workshop gates and takes a closer look at the stainless-steel machinery. Satisfied he gets out a cell phone and calls a number.

Armando waits patiently for his call to be answered and says, "Hello? Your Excellency, Senator González here. How are you coming along? Your speech is ready? That's very good news. I look forward to you delivering the goods tomorrow."

He ends the call, takes the cell phone apart, and drops the SIM-card into a garbage bin.

***

Ariana and Guillermo observe several labourers wearing gas masks in the new 'Research & Experimental Laboratory' of Pharmagena. The masks are not really necessary because the HVAC's steady, sustained dull rumble indicates that all chemical smells are removed when barrels of acetone are lifted by ceiling crane and poured into a vessel. Crumbled blocks of coca base are dropped into the agitated solvent. The resulting thick soup is pumped into a second vessel where hydrochloric acid and more acetone are added. Salt crystals form and are filtered out. They are dried on a slowly moving conveyor belt. The cocaine crystals drop into large plastic barrels. Once a barrel has been filled with forty-five point five kilograms, an insert of four point five kilograms refined sugar is placed on top. Then the barrel is sealed and moved to storage. The entire process is controlled by a real-time computer system.

Ariana and Guillermo sit in their office and watch the activities in the lab through a large window.

Ariana wonders out loud, "Do we have enough for a trial run?"

Guillermo is certain. "More than enough, I'm sure. But let me check." He turns to the desktop computer, opens a file, and points to the screen. "We have almost two and a half tons according to our register."

"Is that enough?"

"More than enough. Remember, our trial run is limited to about one ton. Armando is ready as well. I should call Alberto to let him know that we're ready. I have to see how much capacity he has in the containers. And I have to call Sabrina as well to see how she is coming along with the legit export goods."

He sighs. "Shit, I can't remember their names and titles."

Ariana admonishes him. "You have short-term memory loss, Memo. Alberto is Minister Benítez, and Sabrina is Deputy Alvárez."

Guillermo shakes his head. "Bloody hell! Minister! Senator! Deputy! Oscar has made damn politicians out of all of us!"

He picks the number for Minister Benítez and places his call.

***

In the cavernous hall of RepCon, a telephone is ringing. Alberto, usually calm and in control, is nervous. He is behind schedule. He rushes around in search of the phone and stubs his toe on a heavy tool lying on the ground.

The welders and mechanics see him hop around on one foot, start to snicker, and point to a sign depicting steel-capped safety boots and helmets that should be worn at all times.

A welder reaches into the container and hands Alberto the phone. He presses the answer button and barks, "Yes! What? Sorry, you got a wrong number. I'm Alberto Patiño. Oh, damn it!"

He smashes the phone throwing it to the floor. The workers around him look stunned. Alberto takes another cell phone from his jacket and leaves the workshop.

He looks up the quick dial contacts and presses the call button, "Hello? Yes, I'm sorry, I forgot. I'm as busy as a one-armed paperhanger with hives. Problems with the supply of materials, failing machinery, and on and on. What? Tomorrow? I don't know. Only one is ready. Okay, we'll try to finish one more. Yes, okay, I'll see you tomorrow."

He sighs, puts the phone away, and goes back into the hall. He gathers the workers in a circle and points to the reefer where the refrigeration unit still has to be installed and to the skeleton of a second one that he wants to have finished today. All the containers have to be built to his exact specifications, which means that they have to use new material only and cannot cannibalise two old ones.

Once the mechanics and a refrigeration technician get to work, Alberto turns to the two painters. He points to their work and speaks in a sarcastic tone.

"Now look here, Salvador and Dali or whatever you call yourself. You have to remove the entire pile of crap you painted on the side of the container. Whatever gave you the idea that a vulgar looking mermaid with breasts like coconuts is our company logo? My instructions were clear enough. You are supposed to paint only C-S-M-S-C in sixty-centimetre-tall dark grey letters in italic Optima font with a blue shadow on each side of the containers in the centre. Bold triple blue lines depicting waves are supposed to underline the letters. Below it you will paint the legend Caribe Sur Maritime Shipping Company S.A. in the same width as the letters above. On the doors you will paint in black Helvetica the ownership and reference codes for transport control as written on the note that's stuck to the door of the container and required by international standards. I don't want to see that nude mermaid with a face like Frida Kahlo that will scare every sailor shitless. Is that clear?"

The two painters with artistic ambitions look bedraggled in their spotty overalls. They pick up buckets of paint remover and mops, and reluctantly tackle their artwork of a chubby mermaid. The buzz they get from inhaling the fumes of the paint remover is their only bonus.

29

At dawn of Friday, 3rd April 1992, a forklift loads sealed blue plastic barrels onto a truck at the loading dock of the research laboratory of Pharmagena.

The original inscription of "50kg Refined Sugar" on each barrel is covered with a biohazard sticker. The legend "Sustancia Experimental Peligrosa" warns that the barrels contain a dangerous experimental substance.

Guillermo watches the loading of the truck and checks two sets of shipping documents. They appear to be legitimate papers for police or military control posts along the route to Barranquilla. The first is for the shipping of biohazard material to an incinerator and the second for the delivery of refined sugar to Alimento Accesible. He thinks about all the paperwork and rubs his chin.

He wonders what Oscar was thinking when he came up with this scheme of two sets of shipping papers. In case the police or military wanted to search the truck and demanded that the truck driver leave the cab, the game would be up if two sets of papers were found and the barrels were probed to any depth.

The sticker would not prevent an ignorant but nosy soldier or police officer from ripping open a barrel. Finding sugar when it is supposed to contain hazardous material would come as a great surprise. After all, sugar is not a biohazard as even the thickest of uniformed official knows.

Guillermo foregoes calling Oscar and getting a long-winded explanation. He tears up the biohazard shipping documents, climbs into the back of the truck, and removes the stickers from the barrels. He hands the sugar documents to the driver when twenty-two barrels have been loaded and wishes him a safe trip.

***

The steel gates of the new loading area of the building extension at the back of Alimento Accesible open up when the truck arrives. Cautiously it backs up against the loading dock and the gate shuts.

The truck departs once it has been unloaded. All gates are shut, and the 'Dust-free Food Inspection Lab' is hermetically sealed.

Oscar, Armando, and Gerardo in white hazard suits and gas masks as well as a few trusted labourers stand around the gleaming machinery. Two rolls of packing paper are already installed, and the coffee makers have produced enough of the brew to fill the first vessel at the end of the machine. The second vessel is filled with a milky liquid. It will fix the coffee pigments to the sugar sachets. The entire setup is in its experimental stage upon the instructions of Guillermo, the chemist.

Armando activates the HVAC. A couple of labourers open the first barrel and remove the inset containing the sugar. The barrel is lifted with a small hydraulic crane and emptied into the machine's funnel. Armando activates the machinery.

The packaging machine pushes out a broad band of twelve endless strips of sealed sachets. The strips move through the vibrating tubs before they pass through the drying unit. The strips are cut into units of 120 sachets, folded into bars, and wrapped in heat shrunk plastic foil.

Oscar pushes his gasmask up, picks up a bar of sachets, and sniffs it. He puts the bar back on the table and watches a couple of labourers packing twelve bars into flat packs, wrap them in plastic foil, heat seal the packs and put them on a trolley. Armando and Gerardo pick up two packs that weigh six and a half kilos each and leave together with Oscar through the airlock. In the adjoining office they shed their masks and protective clothing.

Oscar lifts one of the packs. "That looks very good. But why do we pack the sachets into flat parcels? They won't fit into a container support frame."

Gerardo nods. "That's right, Oscar. We've discarded your original idea of stuffing bars of sachets into the support frame. Packing the flat parcels into the insulation material of the refrigeration containers is more efficient and less likely to be detected. Also, each sachet contains three and a half grammes of hydrochloride."

Oscar looks at him critically. "Why? What's the reason for the change? And what's hydrochloride?"

Gerardo chuckles. "Hydrochloride's the academic term for our product. It's also called HCI. Logistics demand the change in packing our product. First, we fill each sachet with three and a half grams, an eighth of an ounce called an Eight Ball. It's easier to handle by retailers and street dealers and the consumer gets a product of highest purity. Second, loading the container frames with individual bars is cumbersome and not as efficient as replacing insulation material of a reefer with the packages. It allows us to carry up to one ton of our product in one container. Stuffing the support frame with bars of sachets can carry a maximum of only fifty kilograms. Big difference. Get the picture?"

Oscar pinches his lower lip nervously. "Yes, of course, but the risk is much higher. We could lose a ton of the stuff with just one container."

Armando listens to Oscar's questions and objections and barks angrily, "Will you shut up! Your ideas were given consideration, but this is not your task. Don't argue with packaging and logistics you know nothing about. That's our territory. So, shut up, okay?"

Surprised by the verbal onslaught Oscar takes a step back. "What's the matter with you? Have you sniffed too much of the merchandise or what? You don't tell me what tasks I have!"

Armando barks back, "I told you to shut up! We have other things to worry about and don't need your stupid objections. Come on, Gerardo. Let's go. We'll leave this asshole here."

Oscar is stunned and watches Armando pick up the packs and turn to leave. Oscar grabs him by a lapel and lands a punch in his face. Armando crashes to the floor. Blood drips from his nose.

Oscar grabs him by the front of his shirt and pulls him halfway up. "Is this the only language you understand, you little wanker? You don't call me an asshole, you hear me?"

Armando shoves a hand into his pocket. Oscar sees it and says calmly, "Digging for your piece, Armando? You wanna shoot me? Go ahead! Start the cycle of violence all over again. If you kill me, you'll be next to die and then Gerardo, 'cause he's a witness, then Alec, 'cause he didn't stop you and on and on it'll go until you have an all-out war. That's what you want?"

Oscar slams Armando to the floor in disgust and turns to put on his jacket. His shirt has slipped out of his trousers at the back and Armando and Gerardo can see the body armour he wears. They give each other knowing looks but don't say a word.

Armando gets up, dabs, and plugs his nose with tissue paper, and dusts himself off. In silence, he puts the cocaine packs into a travel bag and leaves the office together with Gerardo.

Oscar follows at a sedate pace, watches them drive away in Armando's car and calls a taxi on his cell phone.

***

Armando parks his car in front of the container repair workshop. Oscar's taxi is stopped at the gate of the free port. He walks in and greets four customs officers of a K-9 unit. They are standing by their pickup trucks with dog kennels on the back holding German Shepherds, the sniffer dogs.

Oscar whistles and Armando approaches the officers with his travel bag. He is in a state of heightened anxiety being fearful of dogs and dreading the worst outcome of their noses still detecting traces of their product.

He drops the open travel bag on the ground and stands aside ramrod stiff. The customs officers put the yelping canines on leashes and let them sniff the bag. After pawing it for a while, they settle on their haunches with tongues lolling.

Oscar is happy and tells Armando to cough up the dough for the customs officers. He hands over thick envelopes with his arms outstretched to stay away from the dogs. The handlers count their cash, salute, put the dogs back in the kennels, and depart.

Inside the workshop, Alberto shows Oscar a reefer. He lifts the outer aluminium cladding and props it up. He points to fifty square indentations in the insulation material, takes the two packs, and presses them into the cut-outs. He covers the packs with a layer of insulation material, lowers the cladding and explains that a fixative will be sprayed on the inside of the cladding for a firm attachment to the insulation material.

Oscar is impressed and whistles softly. He asks Alberto how he came up with that ingenious idea.

Alberto declares with some pride, “I got my Engineering Master’s in Germany. What you see here is German precision work and ingenuity. Just like our product.”

Oscar is stumped. “Our product is German?”

Alberto smiles. “Don’t you know the history of our product? You should read up on it. It’s interesting.”

He retrieves the packs of sachets while he keeps on talking. “I’ll give you a summary to save you some time. The coca alkaloid was first isolated by the German chemist Gaedcke in 1855, and the purification process we still use today was developed by the German chemist Niemann in 1859. He also gave our product its name based on the Quechua word ‘cuca’ plus the suffix ‘-ine’, which in chemistry forms the names of alkaloids. In short, cocaine is actually a German quality product. No wonder it’s so popular in America.”

They share a laugh and leave the workshop to join Armando and Gerardo who watched them from a distance.

Armando faces Alberto in a state of agitation and bellows, "I counted only fifty cut-outs for a total of one hundred. That's room for half a ton. We agreed to carry one ton. What the fuck is your game?"

Alberto waves him off and says calmly, "No game, Armando. If you ask for a one-ton capacity, you can also ask pigs to fly. One ton is too much to carry in the insulation of one container. I will not put our project at risk."

Armando is incensed and spits, "Put our project at risk? You're cutting our income in less than half!"

Gerardo who has been very quiet since the incident in the packaging plant speaks out, "Aw, shut up, Armando! This is a trial run! We can clear almost five million bucks with the half-ton load of one container. If we overload it and it bursts open, our scheme goes down the toilet and we lose it all. Will you cover the loss? Of course, you won't! Your father would kill you. Leave your ego at home for once and don't argue!"

Armando stares at Gerardo. "I thought you were my friend."

Gerardo stands nose to nose with him and barks, "I am, you dickhead! That's why I'm telling you to shut up, do your job, and pack our product! Everything else is none of your business!"

Oscar and Alberto look on with raised eyebrows. Oscar tut-tuts their argument and says, "I leave it to you to sort out your differences. I'll be on my way."

He walks to the gate of the port and gets into a waiting taxi. He instructs the driver to drive to the hotel in Cartagena where he will pick up Vanessa for their flight to Calí.

30

It becomes clear that it will take a few more days than anticipated to pack the product into the cut-outs of container insulation, load tons of chilled tropical fruit mash and get the two containers ready for shipping. Oscar cautions everyone not to rush the trial load process but to check and re-check every step to assure the containers will pass the customs inspection in the port of Miami.

Alec takes charge of the contacts in the United States, invites the key players to come to Barranquilla to sample fruit mash, place their orders, and get all the documents in order. He is also working out the travel schedule for Oscar and Vanessa, which is quite a daunting task. They will travel around the globe according to Oscar's detailed plan. First, they will conduct their business on the east coast of the United States, then in Europe, Asia, and finally on the west coast of North America before returning to Colombia.

Oscar trusts Alec to have everything under control and takes the opportunity to keep the promise he made to himself of purchasing Don Germán Obejo's posada and secure the old man's retirement.

The brief visit to Bogotá turns into a complex affair. The old man tells Oscar and Vanessa that paying the property taxes was of little consequence. Real estate vultures are now claiming his property. A complicated legal process was initiated by a lawyer, Ernesto Castillo, who claims that the posada had been owned by one of the claimants' ancestors when Germán's grandfather bought it over a hundred years ago. The lawyer asserts that not all potential heirs had agreed to the sale of the property, a common legal requirement all over Latin America at the time. Thus, the purchase is declared invalid, and the present resident is a squatter who has until the end of the month to vacate the premises. Fortunately, the letter is just the shyster's assertion and not a court judgement.

Vanessa urges Oscar to take action and file an injunction in a court of law against the claimants. Yet, his experience with the judiciary hems him in and casts a shadow over the suggestion of talking to a judge.

Germán mentions a law firm that could file the injunction or talk Ernesto Castillo out of dropping the claim in return for a generous fee. It takes a lengthy telephone call to the law firm for a junior partner, Vicente Cordero, to be assigned to their case and they meet on the street outside Castillo's office.

Vicente looks at Germán's ownership documents, the tax bills, and the letter he received. He expresses his surprise about a law dating back to the year 1839 being cited as the main argument for the claim to the property. He is not quite sure if such a law of almost fifty years before the founding of the Republic of Colombia is still on the books and applicable. He mentions that it may be irrelevant if Germán is willing to pay Ernesto Castillo an amount larger than fifteen percent of the amount in dispute, which is the nominal lawyer's fee. Oscar agrees immediately to pay the bribe and they proceed to visit Castillo.

Vanessa waits in the reception area and listens to what turns into a heated discussion in the lawyer's chamber. She can discern the voices of Oscar, Germán, and Vicente who does most of the talking. She can't make out what is being said but notes that most of Vicente's talk is answered by Castillo's mocking laughter.

After less than fifteen minutes the three men leave the chambers looking disappointed and frustrated. Vicente wants to follow up on filing an injunction, excuses himself, and goes to see a judge about it. Oscar suggests an early lunch in a nearby restaurant and a discussion about any alternative approach.

While she is eating a shrimp cocktail, Vanessa learns that Castillo considered a bribe of thirty percent of the dispute amount hilarious because the market value of two million dollars for the posada is not even ten percent of its value once the property is redeveloped. That means that the claimants want to replace the historic building with an extravagant office structure.

As soon as Oscar finishes his discourse, she excuses herself to get some medication for stomach cramps at a pharmacy.

Out on the street Vanessa checks her watch. It is 11:55 a.m., almost lunchtime for most office staff. She rushes back to Castillo's offices and seeing the reception deserted, storms into the lawyer's chambers.

"Hello, Ernesto," she addresses the lawyer. "How are you?"

"Who are you?" he barks. "How dare you barge into my chambers?"

She asks, "Don't you remember me? I'm Martha Ortega, one of the claimants for Don Germán Obejo's posada in Alcazares. I ran into your receptionist, and she told me you had visitors who offered you lots of money to drop our claim."

"Wait!" he shouts. "Your name is Martha Ortega? Never heard of you."

"That's outrageous!" she fires back. "I'm one of the top claimants. Check the list of names in your file. You'll see that my name is right at the top. You are quite negligent if you don't remember the names of your clients."

He opens a file and looks at a list of names. "There's no Martha Ortega on my list. Who are you and what do you want?"

Vanessa puts a hand into her handbag. "Actually, I wanted to ask you only one question."

"Oh, yes? What's the question?"

Vanessa gives him a sweet smile and releases the gun safety. "Are you familiar with the old term 'plata o plomo'?"

Ernesto recognises that metallic sound, rips open a drawer of his desk, and grabs a Smith & Wesson revolver. But before he can lift it, Vanessa has taken the silenced Magnum out of her handbag and aims it at him. He lets the gun drop back into the drawer. His hands start to shake and a bead of sweat appears on his forehead.

He stares at Vanessa and asks quietly, "What do you want?"

Calmly she walks around the desk to stand on his right side and says, "You were offered 'plata' to the tune of over three hundred fifty thousand dollars to drop the claim against Don Germán Obejo. Since you cited laws almost two hundred years old, you should know as well that since the time of the conquistadores the prevailing law is 'plata o plomo'. You rejected the offer of 'plata', consequently, you get 'plomo'."

She pulls the trigger and blows his brains out. She stows her gun back in her handbag, takes his Smith & Wesson revolver out of the drawer, presses it into his right hand, and fires a shot into the plush carpet of his office.

She picks up Germán's file, stashes it under her waistband, and buttons up her jacket. She leaves the office and takes the fire exit staircase to leave the building through the parking lot at the back. Five minutes later she joins Oscar and Germán in the restaurant.

"Do you feel better now?" enquires Oscar.

"Oh yes," Vanessa assures him. "It was just gas. That walk really helped firing off a couple of shots."

Germán chuckles and Oscar says, "I have a new plan."

Vanessa looks surprised. "You have? That's nice but may be irrelevant. You know, while you were arguing with the lawyer, I developed a really good understanding with Castillo's secretary.

She saw me walking past the office where she was waiting outside for the police and told me that Ernesto Castillo committed suicide."

"Whaaat?" is Oscar's shocked response and Germán almost drops his dentures into the bowl of soup in front of him.

Oscar mutters, "That's a game changer!"

Germán shakes his head slowly. "No, no, it may not change anything. The claimants just take the case file to another shyster and go to court to get a judgement against me."

Vanessa unbuttons her jacket and pulls out the file stuck in her waistband. "Case file? You mean these papers?"

Oscar grabs the file and opens it. "Where did you get that?"

Vanessa puts on her most innocent look. "Oh, the secretary gave it to me. She figured it wouldn't be of much use just collecting dust in a dead lawyer's office."

Oscar flips slowly through the pages of the case file. He sees bloodstains on the list of claimants and looks at Vanessa full of doubt. "Are you sure the lawyer took his own life?"

Vanessa shrugs, locks eyes with him and smiles. "I can only convey what the secretary told me."

"Of course," responds Oscar sarcastically.

He doesn't believe a word of her alleged encounter with the receptionist. "What else did that gasbag tell you in her encounter of less than five minutes with you? Did she enlighten you why Castillo committed suicide?"

"Oh yes. It was a matter of honour."

"Really? And since when do lawyers have honour?"

"When they realise that they were offered twice the amount to drop a case they were offered to pursue the case."

"That makes sense," says Germán. "When it comes to grabbing money, any lawyer will feel a pinch of honour tweaking his soul."

Oscar gives Germán a bemused look and wants to say something when his cell phone rings. He answers the call, listens, and puts the phone down. "That was Vicente Cordero. A judge has refused to consider his request for filing an injunction."

"Do we need an injunction?" asks Germán. "The lawyer is dead, and we are in possession of the case file. If we let it disappear, there won't be a case against me."

"Right," says Vanessa. "Call Vicente and request an urgent meeting for the sale of Don Germán's posada."

The two men look at her surprised and Oscar turns to Germán. "You want to sell your posada?"

"No," replies Germán. "I want to live in my house in peace and not be bothered by the trumped-up claim of being a squatter."

"There you are," says Oscar to Vanessa. "He doesn't want to sell his home. What are you talking about?"

Irritated by his short memory, she drums her fingers on the tabletop and groans audibly. "Why are we here, Oscar?"

"To have lunch?" he asks hesitantly.

"Oh, I see," she bawls sarcastically. "We came all the way from Calí to Bogotá to get food poisoning in a run-down restaurant. Let's go back to Calí. Right now. I'm longing for a healthy, home cooked meal."

Vanessa gets up and both men give her a puzzled look. Germán waves his hand for her to sit down again and smiles cunningly. "Let me finish my black bean soup, please. It's actually quite tasty. Now tell me why you came to visit me. It's wonderful you want to help me keep my home. But that wasn't the only reason for your visit, was it?"

Vanessa sits down and holds out an open hand. "Oscar? Don't you want to answer Don Germán's question?"

"Right, uh, yes," he answers. "What was the question?"

"For crying out loud!" shouts Vanessa and raises eyebrows all around. "What's the reason for us visiting Don Germán?"

Oscar stares at his empty plate for a moment and mutters, "But he has already said that he doesn't want to sell."

Vanessa looks ready to strangle him. "Perhaps because you haven't presented an offer yet? Don't you want to buy the posada, have it renovated, arrange for a housemaid, and provide the guaranty for Germán to stay at his home rent free for life?"

Oscar blushes with embarrassment and Germán looks earnest. "That would cost millions. Do you have so much money, Vanessa?"

"No, I don't," she says, "but Oscar has."

"He does?" asks Germán and turns to Oscar. "Where did you get that kind of money? You are not in the drug trade, are you? I don't want to have anything to do with drug money."

"No," Vanessa assures him. "It's Oscar's consulting fee for a trade deal exporting plant extracts to North America."

"And that's worth millions?" asks Don Germán.

"Yes," confirms Vanessa. "It's worth billions. Isn't it, Oscar?"

Oscar blushes some more and nods. Vanessa continues, "But never mind that. Don Germán, would you be agreeable to sell your posada to Oscar in return for living there rent free for life and having a housemaid to look after your every need?"

Germán grins. "A housemaid? Is she pretty?"

"That's up to you," answers Vanessa. "You will hire her."

Germán chuckles and gets up. "In that case, I would consider selling my posada to Oscar. Come on, let's go, and talk to Vicente to get all the paperwork out of the way."

It takes the whole afternoon for Vicente to register the sale of the posada to Oscar Antonio Ortiz Acosta, who is absent and represented by his proxies Oscar Benito Pérez and his wife Vanessa Lucinda Roa de Pérez. The money transfer from the Cayman Island to Germán's bank account for the purchase of the property as well as an exorbitant fee for Vicente's legal services poses no problem and the deal is done.

By early evening a bottle of champagne is popped in the posada to celebrate the event.

31

Upon their return to Calí in the early morning of Tuesday, 14th April 1992, Oscar and Vanessa are informed that they will have to leave for Miami that afternoon.

The trial reefers are on board ship since Sunday. The arrival is slated for Wednesday. The disembarkation, unloading of legit goods into a customs warehouse, and transport of the 'empty' reefers to a container inspection and repair shop should be observed by Oscar and Vanessa. Also, the product's distribution to wholesalers and collection of cash must be conducted by them since there wasn't enough time to set up a trustworthy system in Miami. The good news is that eight more reefers are being prepared for shipment to Baltimore and New York where a distribution and cash collection system is in place. The only remaining problem in these ports, as well as New Jersey, is the old guard of drug dealers. They are feeling pushed aside and unwilling to give up territory. That will take some persuasive action to sort them out.

In anticipation of their departure, Oscar and Vanessa had packed their bags before their trip to Bogotá and are ready when Alec picks them up at noon for the drive to the airport. Near the entrance to the departure hall, Alec hands them their airline tickets as well as new passports, identity cards, driver's licenses, credit cards, and business cards in exchange for their old identity papers.

Oscar checks his passport and reads Oscar Uribe Gonzalo. 'Damn it, yet another name,' he thinks, 'how am I supposed to remember my name and date and place of birth?' He signs the passport and credit card with an awkward scrawl and hopes he can repeat it whenever needed.

While Alec has a discussion with Vanessa, Oscar goes to the lavatory. His brief absence is the opportunity for Alec to hand Vanessa a note. He reminds her that it is her job to protect Oscar and sort out any disagreement with wholesalers and retailers who stubbornly refuse to accept the new terms of business.

Alec wishes them good luck. Oscar and Vanessa check in, get their boarding passes, pass through migration without a problem and settle down to wait for the departure of their flight.

***

Sean Murphy stays at a hotel in Coral Gables, Miami. He is handed a lengthy note and puts his portfolio on the reception counter while he reads it.

Oscar arrives by taxi from Miami International Airport, enters the lobby, lifts his briefcase onto the counter, and knocks Sean's portfolio to the floor. Papers spill out. Oscar and Sean bend down simultaneously to pick them up and knock heads together.

Sean rubs his head. "That's how one meets by accident."

Oscar sees the DEA logo and reads the name on the business cards he hands to Sean. "I'm sorry, Mr. Murphy. Please accept my apologies."

They straighten up. Sean still rubs his head. "Thank you. You wouldn't have an aspirin on you? You have a hard head."

Oscar is a bit baffled. "No, I don't. I mean, I have no aspirin."

Sean grimaces. "But you have a hard head, Mister, uh?"

Oscar whips out a business card, and they shake hands. "Oscar Uribe Gonzalo. Pleased to make your acquaintance, Mr. Murphy. I see that you are with the DEA. That's interesting."

"Yes, but it's more frustrating than interesting. What do you do, Mr. Uribe?"

"I'm a manager of Caribe Sur, a Barbados shipping company."

Sean wrinkles his brow. "Then you are a Barbarian?"

Oscar stares at him. "Pardon me?"

Sean realises that denizens of Barbados are probably not called barbarians. "Uh, I mean, you are from Barbados."

"Oh no, I'm from Colombia."

"Really? Do you have many contacts in Colombia?"

Oscar waves a hand in a grand gesture. "Yes, of course!"

Sean locks eyes with Oscar and rubs his chin. "Hmm, you wouldn't know the businessman Oscar Pérez by any chance?"

Shocked to hear his previously assumed name, Oscar quickly looks down to the left, pinches his lower lip, and mumbles, "Oscar Pérez, hmm, no, I'm sorry, I don't know anyone by that name."

Sean observes Oscar's every move. "Pity, well, it was just a shot in the dark. Anyway, it's nice meeting you, Mr. Pérez."

Oscar is stunned and stares at Sean. After a few seconds that feel like an eternity, Oscar regains his composure. "Pérez? No, no, my name is Uribe."

Sean manages a tortured laugh. "Of course, Mr. Uribe. I'm sorry for that slip of the tongue. I am very tired after a long day's work. We should get together for drink, Mr. Uribe."

Oscar is relieved. "Yes, that would be nice, Mr. Murphy."

They shake hands once more and Sean leaves looking back at Oscar who turns to the receptionist and hands her his reservation.

***

Vanessa steps out of a small hotel in Miami's Little Havana district on West Flagler Street. She reads Alec's note, walks down the street, and enters a restaurant and bar. Even in the dim light of the establishment, it doesn't take her long to recognise the Cuban with a craggy face she is supposed to contact. He grins a lot showing off his distinguishing mark of a shiny golden incisor. He joins her at the bar and drives her to distraction with his constant grinning while she outlines her desired purchase. She takes five hundred dollar bills from her purse, tears them in half and pushes a half pile to him with regards from Enrique Muñoz, Alec's father. Hearing the name, the Cuban's face drops. He nods and hurries out.

Vanessa is waiting in the parking lot behind the hotel when the Cuban drives up in a garishly painted '85 Chevrolet Impala. He backs up and opens the trunk of his car. Vanessa inspects an arsenal of handguns on display. She points to a subcompact Glock, a silencer, a carton of ammunition, and two spare magazines. She loads a magazine, clips the silencer on the gun, and fires a couple of rounds into the wall of the hotel. The gun functions perfectly. Vanessa is satisfied, hands over the other half of the five hundred dollar bills and the rest of the agreed purchase price, and the Cuban leaves in a rush.

In her room, Vanessa stows the gun and spare magazines into her suitcase when she spots a two-inch Texas cockroach crawl out from underneath a pillow. Calmly, she takes sugar sachets and pours a line on the blanket and into a plastic waste bin she laid onto the bed. It takes a while for about twenty of the big insects to crawl into the bin. Vanessa pulls a plastic laundry bag over it, takes her luggage and the waste bin, and leaves the room.

Vanessa wakes up the dozing receptionist by slamming the room key on the counter. He raises a hand in a questioning gesture. Without uttering a word and before he can ask a stupid question, she pulls the bag off the bin and tosses the cockroaches at him. He is suddenly wide-awake with the insects crawling all over him. He swats them with his bare hands in a state of frenzy.

Vanessa walks out without settling her bill and hails a passing taxi to join Oscar.

32

At first light of the morning on Wednesday, 15th April 1992, Oscar and Vanessa drive in the light traffic of Miami's NE 5th Street towards Dodge Island. Oscar presents a business card and his passport to the security guard at the gate to the free port of Miami and they are waved through. He follows Port Road until they are near their container ship. Nervously he watches the two Caribe Sur reefers being loaded onto waiting carriers and customs officers with sniffer dogs opening them for an inspection. It is with great relief that he sees their signal to release them.

Oscar and Vanessa follow the carriers at a considerable distance to a bonded customs warehouse. The containers are unloaded and transferred to a couple of commercial trucks. 'Empty' they leave the free port without further checks.

The trucks drive along Dolphin and Palmetto Expressways to a container inspection and repair company in the suburb of Hialeah. The reefers are moved by crane to the back of the large workshop.

Oscar talks to the owner and local distributor of nose candy, Bill Pedroso. He explains to him how the cladding has to be lifted to get at the packages of cocaine. Bill admits not to have the millions of dollars to pay for a ton of cocaine that was delivered. He has contacted four retailers to come and pick up their load. They know they have to pay cash and will bring bags of money.

Vanessa enters the workshop and stands in a dark niche. The truck of a drugstore chain and three SUVs arrive in the workshop. The truck driver agrees with the new form of handling the goods in Eight Ball sachets. He drags a holdall full of bundles of dollar bills out of his truck. It takes a while to count the money with a banknote counting machine. It is enough cash for sixty-four parcels that are loaded into the truck. Oscar receives a travel bag with over three million two hundred twenty-five thousand dollars.

The SUV drivers and their passengers look at the remaining pile of packages. One of the drivers, a guy in shorts and T-shirt, picks up a package, breaks it open, and rips out one of the sachets. He turns to Oscar waving the sachet and shouts, "What the fuck is this? You tryin' to sell us sugar, you fuckin' son of a bitch?"

Oscar smiles inscrutably and asks, "Why don't you open the sachet? It's an Eight Ball of pure, uncut merchandise."

The burly guy crumples the sachet and throws it to the floor. "Oh yeah? Then how am I gonna cut it, asshole?"

Oscar gets riled up by the verbal assault. "You don't cut it! Each sachet is an Eight Ball, and you sell it as such! Understand? And don't call me an asshole!"

The driver and his dogsbody draw their guns. The driver barks, "Okeydokey, then I'll call you a cocksucker. Open the sachets and pack the stuff the traditional way! You hear me, cocksucker?"

Vanessa watches the development and steps out of the shadows. When the driver's assistant points his gun at Oscar's temple Vanessa says firmly, "Yes, I heard you."

She shoots the gunslinger in the leg. He screams, collapses, and writhes on the ground. The driver spins around on his heel to hear Vanessa say, "We don't do business with scumbags. I recommend that you fuck off! Pronto!"

He stares at her in utter disbelief and asks nobody in particular, "Who the fuck is this? Where'd the cunt come from?"

He raises his pistol. Vanessa shoots him. Making sure they won't get up again, she executes him and his dogsbody with shots to the head and pockets the driver's gun. Oscar and Bill are aghast.

Bill whimpers, "What the fuck are you doing? Are you nuts? That was my best customer! How am I gonna clean up this mess?"

Vanessa snaps, "Don't ask me. You invited the scum! You get rid of it!"

Oscar tries to calm her. "Vanessa, you shouldn't have..."

Outraged about his spinelessness, she barks, "On the contrary, I had to, or you would have ended up with a slug in your noodle."

Oscar twists awkwardly. "Aw, come on now..."

Vanessa glares at him. "What's the matter with you? You have a death wish? Just let me know. I'll be glad to oblige. Now get this business done! I want to get out of here!"

Oscar can't believe what he heard but her dispassionate stare convinces him that he is on death's door unless he gets back to the business at hand immediately. He turns to the two drivers who watched the action completely unmoved and are ready for a deal.

He asks if they have any objection to the merchandise packed in Eight Ball sachets and how they want to split the remaining parcels. They are agreeable and divide the goods. Once their cash has been counted, Oscar gets his six million four hundred fifty-one thousand dollars and releases the goods. Since the price of the sale to wholesalers is set by the distributor, Bill Pedroso is left with almost one and a half million bucks. Oscar and Vanessa pack their bags with cash into the trunk of their car and leave.

Driving along Okeechobee Road, Oscar says, "You killing those two guys, Vanessa, it scared the shit out of me."

Vanessa snaps, "What about them wanting to kill you?"

Oscar answers, "Alright, but did you have to kill them?"

"Yes, I'm under strict orders to protect you."

Oscar suspected as much and wants to make sure that his hunch is not just a hunch. "Under orders? Who gave you those orders?"

"Alec," is her curt response.

"And did he order you to kill me, if I don't toe the line?"

Vanessa stares at Oscar. "Look, there are several things you don't seem to understand. You got your nine million bucks and can disappear whenever you want. So far, I got nothing of that magnitude. Alec promised me a payout of point one percent of whatever we realise on this trip. And another thing: you either don't know or ignore the difference between friendship and business. There is no friendship in business. The maxim of business is 'I'll kill you before you kill me'. Remember we are on a business trip and not an excursion to establish friendly relations with drug dealing scumbags. If you don't want to bring your plan to fruition, what choice do I have?"

It takes time for Vanessa's words to sink in. Oscar can't think of anything else but to ask, "Where did you learn to shoot like that?"

"Twice a week on a shooting range in Memphis. My uncle insisted that I had to become a sure shot to defend myself."

Oscar gives Vanessa a sideways glance. "I thought of having lunch after dropping off the cash at Alec's trustee. But I've lost my appetite. If it's okay with you, we'll skip lunch, pick up our stuff at the hotel, and catch the next plane to Baltimore."

"That's fine with me," agrees Vanessa. "Let's get out of here. I don't trust Bill Pedroso cleaning up the mess without the fuzz catching on it was a drug deal gone sideways. And who knows if he can control his tongue when the cops apply the third degree. More likely he will start singing like a canary."

33

Sean returns from his trip to Miami. He is tired from working long hours processing the information he gathered and preparing a report to present to his boss on Friday, 24th April 1992. He yawns while walking along the corridor and bumps into Dennis.

Dennis growls, "Hey, careful, young man! I tend to go ballistic when someone steps on my corns."

Sean gives him a bleary-eyed look. "Sorry, Sir. I wasn't looking."

"Funny you should say that. You look like a somnambulist."

"A what?"

"A sleepwalker. You came to see me?"

"Yes, well, actually I was going to make a copy of my report, drop it off, and go home to get some sleep."

"Your report about your trip to Miami? How did it go? How's our friend Jaime Saenz?"

Sean waves a limp hand. "Jaime is fine but more tight-lipped than ever. I think he is stalling. However, if he signs an affidavit, we could force the Colombians to deliver Pablo Escobar to our care."

Dennis seems satisfied. "Well, that's something. Follow up on it. Anything else?"

Sean cocks his head to the left and appears doubtful. "I don't know, Sir. Maybe. I ran into a Colombian in Miami, name's Oscar Uribe Gonzalo, manager of a Barbados shipping company. I checked him out and pulled a blank."

"Did you check out his connections?"

"Of course, Sir. His employer is the Caribe Sur Maritime Shipping Company. One of the directors is Muñoz, first name 'A'. If 'A' stands for Alejandro, then Oscar Uribe and this Oscar Pérez of Valle del Cauca Trading, the company that was blown up and declared bankrupt, could be the same guy. Suspecting as much, I even tried the old trick of addressing him by the name of Pérez to see how he would react. But he kept his cool."

Dennis ponders, "Hmm, interesting. Come to my office for a moment. I have to show you something."

In his office he takes a mugshot out of a desk drawer. "This is the Colombian dealer Oscar Antonio Ortiz Acosta who was caught in Costa Rica in eighty-nine and sentenced to life for murder. Eighteen months later, he was busted out and disappeared. Does this Oscar look like the Oscar you've met?"

Sean gives the photos a look and shakes his head slowly. "Sir, I can't swear it's the guy I met. He was slim and athletic. His face was gaunt. That guy in the photo has jowls like shopping bags. He's of the same ethnic group and there's a similarity in the eyes."

Dennis gets excited. "Similarity in the eyes? Eyes can never be changed. Look at the photo again and tell me how similar."

Sean shrugs. "Impossible to say, Sir. We talked less than five minutes. However, when I asked him, if he happened to know Oscar Pérez, he looked down to the left. It was a sure sign that he was lying when he said that he didn't know anyone by that name."

Dennis agrees. "True, true. Looking down to the left in response to a question is usually an indication that a big, fat lie is going to be dished up. Hmm, Oscar Ortiz, Oscar Pérez, Oscar Uribe, you know, Sean, we should haul this Oscar Uribe in for questioning. You kept track of his moves?"

Sean confirms, "Yes, Sir. At present he and his wife are staying at a hotel in Battery Park, New York. By the way, he travelled from Miami via Baltimore to New York and coinciding with his visits in these cities as well as in Newark, New Jersey, five major drug dealers and seven hitmen were shot and killed."

Dennis sucks air through his teeth. "Five big-timers and seven of their hitmen were shot and killed in four different cities. Actually, we should be elated that someone is taking some work off our hands. But in this case, it's an indication of a major clean-up. And Oscar Uribe was in those places with his wife? Could she be the Colombian gunslinger? What's her name?"

Sean shrugs. "I don't know, Sir. He always signed in under his name only."

Dennis scoffs, "Clever bastard. Let's haul him in anyway. Call New York for a lockdown. We'll nail Oscar and question him."

Sean cocks his head to the left. "Could it wait until Monday?"

Dennis hesitates and scratches his head. "No, it can't. But it's alright. I'll do it. They won't leave by train or bus, I'm sure. So, it's the airports and the hotel. You go home and get some sleep. Okay?"

***

Oscar and Vanessa sit at a small table of the hotel's Rise Terrace and look out at the Liberty Statue. He rubs condensation off his glass. Leaning forward, he whispers, "I wonder how police profilers come to a conclusion about the looks, behaviour and predictability of a serial killer."

Vanessa leans back. "Oh, that's what you think of me now."

Oscar shakes his head. "That's not the point. I am concerned about police profilers' investigation of drug gang killings. Can the police tie them together and come up with a profile that allows the conclusion they were committed by one and the same person?"

"I see," says Vanessa. "As far as I know, profilers start by looking for a pattern of preferences of a killer that includes type of weapon used, behaviour, location and time of day. It allows them to predict if the killer is a professional hitman or an opportunistic amateur with a grudge. Now consider the following. In this grand nation of the brave and the free more than a hundred people, including pregnant women and children, are killed every day by gunfire and nobody seems to suspect that several of these murders were committed by a serial killer because a preference pattern cannot be detected. If you kept your eyes open, you would have noticed me picking up the piece of one victim in every location and using it in the next location such as a large workshop, a tiny office, a quayside, and a deserted sports plex at different times of day and night. In short, a preference pattern of type of weapon, behaviour, location and time of day cannot be established."

Oscar takes a deep breath and says, "I hope you're right. Anyway, this was our last stop in the States. Next stop London, then Berlin, and on we go to Bangkok."

She looks at her watch. "We should get going. Our flight leaves in less than four hours."

***

The Yellow Cab stops at the international airlines terminal of New York's JFK International Airport. Oscar and Vanessa scramble out, get their luggage out of the trunk, and walk into the building. They check their tickets and look at the departures board. Slowly they proceed towards the check-in counters. Outside, a bus comes to a screeching halt, and several men and women in DEA-jackets spread out in front of the terminal entrances.

Lisa del Carmen, a woman in the departure hall who could pass for Vanessa's sister, nervously rushes around, and looks at the people queuing up. Behind her, on a bench not too far away, sits Oscar's brother Benigno. Lisa spots Vanessa and Oscar, and gestures to Benigno.

Lisa touches Oscar's arm and whispers, "Oscar? Are you Oscar?"

He looks at Lisa who stands next to Vanessa and does a double take. "Who are you?"

Lisa points to Benigno who stands behind him. Oscar turns and stares at his brother, a bit shorter but of similar looks. "Benigno? My brother?" He spreads his arms and hugs his brother.

Benigno gets moist eyes and holds on to Oscar's arm. "Oscar? Is that really you? How many years has it been?"

Looking over Oscar's shoulder, Benigno sees the DEA officers checking the papers of anyone entering or leaving the terminal building. Several of the DEA officers come inside and randomly check people's identity papers.

Benigno takes out a passport-size wallet and signals Lisa to follow suit. In an urgent tone he tells Oscar, "Give me your papers, passport, driver's license, business cards, ticket, all of it. Your Oscar Uribe tickets were cancelled. You and Vanessa are booked on the flight to London under your new names."

Oscar reaches into his jacket. "New names? But why?"

Benigno hisses, "Never mind - quick, quick!"

Oscar hands his wallet over and takes the one held out to him.

Benigno exhales audibly and mumbles, "You are Benigno Benavides. Remember my date and place of birth. You arrived two days ago, okay?"

Oscar nods and both of them turn to watch Lisa and Vanessa still swapping papers. Vanessa ferrets through her handbag to dig it all up and drops the bag. Lisa is very quick picking up Vanessa's current papers and exchanging them for the new ones. When they straighten up, they face the DEA agent Hank Wallace who paid scant attention to the two women gathering the contents of a handbag.

Hank addresses Benigno, "DEA, Sir, and where're you off to today?"

Benigno answers with a cheerful smile, "New Jersey."

Hank gestures helplessly. "New Jersey? You kiddin'? You can't fly to New Jersey. You hafta take the bus or a taxi."

Benigno chortles. "I know. My wife and I live there. Our friends here are off to Europe."

Hank turns to Oscar. "Uh-huh, I see. Your passport, please."

Oscar obliges and Hank flips through it, scrutinises the identity page, and looks for the entry stamp.

He looks at Oscar. "What's your name?"

Oscar without hesitation, "Benigno Benavides."

"When did you enter the United States?"

"Two days ago."

Hank turns to Benigno. "And you are...?"

Benigno says with pride, "Rafael Nieto, pharmacist from Newark."

Hank scrutinises their faces. "Mm-hm. You two are related? You look like brothers."

Oscar looks down to the left with an embarrassed smile. "No. No relation, just good friends."

And Benigno adds, "We darkies all look the same, y'know."

Hank pulls a face. "Is that so? You say you live in New Jersey? May I see some identification?"

Benigno reaches for his wallet. "Yes, of course. Is my green card and driver's license alright?"

Hank nods. "Yeah, sure."

He takes the green card and driver's license, jams a loupe in front of his right eye, and scrutinises the cards. Satisfied, he gives them back to Benigno.

He hands Oscar the passport with the words, "Here you go. Have a safe trip, Mister Benavides."

34

In the morning of Tuesday, 5th May 1992, a Mercedes taxi does a full turn on Berlin's Pariser Platz east of the Brandenburg Gate and comes to a gentle stop in front of a hotel displaying six stars. Oscar and Vanessa get out, enter the lobby, and to their great surprise are welcomed by Benigno and Lisa. Oscar wants to know what brings them to the capitol of the recently unified Germany. Benigno informs him of their reliable contact in the National Security Agency who raised the alarm about a DEA agent tracking him, recommended Alec to send him and Lisa to the USA and provided all the documents. They are not fake but genuine as are more new identification papers for them that are necessary because the German secret service exchanges lots of information with other agencies. The supply chain of genuine documents from birth certificate, green cards to passports was a result of Don Pablo's forward thinking by paying a retainer in the millions of dollars to willing participants in the American security system.

Before he lets them go, Benigno shows him a current newspaper. On the title page is a report about the Colombian government's plan to extradite Pablo Escobar to the United States on the strength of an affidavit by the former accountant of a drug cartel. An American prosecutor is cited to have said that Pablo is wanted for almost every crime imaginable short of parking tickets. Pablo will face life in prison if not the death penalty.

Oscar expresses his doubts about the plan and will discuss it with his brother once he and Vanessa had a chance to freshen up.

The two couples meet again for lunch in the hotel restaurant with a view of the Brandenburg Gate. Their conversation centres on the newspaper report. Benigno considers it sensational, but Oscar discards it as a canard at best and intentional misinformation at worst. He explains that Pablo Escobar stated on several occasions that he'd rather be buried in Colombia than rot in an American prison cell. He will never agree to an extradition and put up a fight to stay or simply walk out of prison and disappear among the thousands of friends he has in and around Medellín.

Benigno is not convinced that Pablo could simply walk out of prison in Envigado. Oscar chuckles and mentions that he visited the five-star hotel where Pablo is held prisoner, saw the security measures, and got to know him quite well during a lengthy discussion. He assures Benigno that the alleged drug kingpin is not the bloodthirsty monster he is made out to be by his antagonists. He is an ardent patriot with a social conscience and has huge support among the beneficiaries of his philanthropy. The War on Drugs has practically nothing to do with drugs but is a fight for the billions if not trillions of dollars the drug trade has amassed in less than twenty years. The United States is the real culprit in this dispute because they do nothing to curb the drug abuse of millions of addicts in their country.

He adds that the extent of drug addiction in any country is like a thermometer up the arse of society. It serves as an indicator of the extent of its social ills. Also, one should not forget that there are over ten times more people addicted to legal, that is, prescription drugs than there are users of illegal drugs.

In the course of his monologue in defence of Pablo Escobar, Oscar got quite hot under the collar and raised his voice considerably. Three businessmen at the next table stopped their conversation and listened to him. The one sitting closest to Oscar clears his throat and in typical Berlin beer table fashion butts into the discussion and voices his opinion in bad Spanish, but nevertheless in Spanish. He questions the implied demand and supply facet of the drug trade and states that these criminal drug dealers cannot get away with impunity for causing immeasurable harm to the American and European societies. When the man adds that any defence of Pablo Escobar sounds like the statement of a drug dealer, Oscar scoffs.

Vanessa fixes the man at the next table with an icy stare and asks, "Have you quite finished or do you need to regurgitate more mainstream media opinion you glean from your gutter press?"

The three men are stunned by her sharply voiced question. One of them tries to tone down what threatens to become a heated argument. "Listen, lady, in my opinion..."

Vanessa cuts him off. "I'm not interested in your opinion, Sir. I don't know who you are or what you do and don't want to know, either. But you have made it quite clear that you know nothing about the illicit drug trade. For your edification let me tell you what we do. We are representatives of the Colombian judiciary investigating the drug money investments into your country that you so desperately need to alleviate the financial double hernia you suffered with the heavy lifting of buying East Germany."

She looks at Oscar, Lisa, and Benigno and gets up. "Are we finished? Let's go. The atmosphere in here has become quite repugnant."

She and her companions leave the restaurant without another look at the three men and go for a walk under the linden trees of the appropriately named 'Unter den Linden' avenue.

Benigno is full of praise about Vanessa's intervention and putting that obnoxious loudmouth in his place. Her bold lie with respect to their quartet being representatives of the Colombian judiciary still amuses him. Only Lisa is concerned that these three guys could be police or even from the secret service. Should that be so, they might use their authority to snoop around and investigate her claimed representation of the judiciary. But Oscar tells her not to worry. He can't imagine that policemen or secret service agents would have lunch at such an expensive restaurant. Also, he and Vanessa will stay at the Hotel only one night. He anticipates having to inspect the properties he intends to purchase and will have to travel around the former East Germany for a number of days. He and Vanessa could register in any of the hotels during their journey under the new identity Benigno has on hand for them. But he agrees with Lisa that they should avoid any further clashes with members of the public.

They continue their walk along dilapidated buildings under repair and one construction site after another. Benigno wonders how Berlin compares to London. Oscar shrugs and says that they hardly saw anything of London except the area of Canary Wharf where they wasted a lot of time waiting to talk to a banker. He opened accounts with a British Virgin Island bank for Pharmagena, Alimento Accesible, RepCon, and Caribe Sur Maritime Shipping Company. He organised the acceptance of over five hundred million dollars in cash to be brought to the Caribbean Island by private plane from the United States and requested the money to be deposited into the four companies' new accounts. Fortunately, the British banker with whom he struck a deal was happy to accommodate the request and laundered the drug money for a couple of million bucks shoved into his pockets.

***

Early in the afternoon, Oscar enters the lobby of the 'Treuhandanstalt', the trust agency on Alexander Platz in charge of the privatisation of formerly state owned East German companies and lands. He meets with a representative in charge of industrial properties and presents the portfolio of Pharmagena. They review a range of pharmaceutical plants on offer and agree to earmark two of them. When Oscar expresses his interest in agricultural cooperatives and forested land, two other representatives are called.

The negotiations take longer than Oscar had expected but by five o'clock in the afternoon a ten percent deposit for all the earmarked properties has been received in Berlin and the deal is done. He has four weeks for a final decision to purchase them. Oscar is given a general survey map to help him find and inspect the objects. The representatives shake hands with Oscar, accompany him to the door, and call a taxi on his behalf.

***

Oscar joins Vanessa, Benigno, and Lisa in a cosy café a couple of city blocks from the Hotel. He conveys the news that he conditionally bought two pharmaceutical plants and the huge acreage of land and forest of a farming cooperative for a song. He states that the trust fund has a fire sale going on and orders a bottle of champagne to celebrate.

Benigno wants to know how much that song will cost. Oscar stuns everybody when he mentions the figure of two and a half billion. Vanessa wants to know how he is going to get that amount of dollars to finalise the deal.

"Dollars?" asks Oscar. "No, they want to see Deutschmarks. That halves the dollar figure more or less. I have four weeks to come up with the cash to finalise the deal."

"And how're you going to do that? One and a quarter billion bucks in four weeks? That's impossible."

"Not at all. Look, in just over two weeks we amassed half a billion with twenty-seven tons. Increasing shipments to fifteen tons a week with expansion to New Orleans and Houston we will garner an additional two billion bucks in four weeks. The only problem I foresee is sneaking all that cash out of the States to the British Virgin Islands."

"Shit," mumbles Benigno. "I wish I had that problem."

"You may think so," asserts Oscar, "but it's a bigger problem than you think. Just one confiscated load of cash can throw our operation in disarray. Think of the production and shipping costs. The suppliers want to get paid. And then there are the pilots and package handlers that ship the cash. As soon as they get wind of what they are handling, their rates go sky-high. That is our greatest weakness and the reason I have to visit Thailand as soon as possible to arrange a meeting with the Golden Triangle bosses and see if they are willing to cooperate with us."

"Okay," agrees Benigno. "But Alec wants you to go to Russia first and finish all your purchases."

Oscar looks at him critically. "Why does he want me to go to Russia?"

Benigno shrugs. "I guess he wants to know how much the total expansion in these two European countries will cost."

"And then?"

"From what I understand, he has some complicated formula he uses to pro-rate the cost of expansion into other countries in Europe, the Middle East, Africa and the Americas."

"That's beyond me," mutters Oscar. "Russia it is then. Okay, Vanessa?"

"Yes, of course, but before we inspect your purchases here in Germany, we should get the visas for Russia."

"Smart thinking," says Benigno and gets out two wallets. "Here are your new identities."

Oscar waves him off. "Keep them. I don't want another identity. I can hardly remember my present pseudonym. I take the risk of travelling with my present identity."

"Have it your way, but Alec won't like it."

"Piss on it," scoffs Oscar. "I don't care if he likes it or not. Vanessa and I do the fieldwork and we have to feel confident about our names. You know, Benigno, these border guards are not stupid and often highly trained. One hesitation or mumbling the wrong name and our cover is blown. For now, we better leave things the way they are."

35

The inspection tour in Germany and the purchase of chemical and pharmaceutical companies in Russia took much longer than anticipated. It is almost the middle of July when Oscar and Vanessa finally touch down in Bangkok.

Their patience is put to a test when none of the arranged meetings with furtive Thai contact men come to pass for two weeks and they have no way to call them.

Oscar is on the phone with Alec almost daily to find out when one of the contacts will finally show up. Both of them start to doubt the reliability of Asian operators and the viability of cooperation with Khun Sa, the Golden Triangle head honcho. It takes a crash landing of one of their transfer planes in Puerto Rico and the confiscation of fifteen million dollars of their funds to convince Alec and Oscar to stay the course.

It is Saturday, 25th July 1992, and after two weeks of idleness, Vanessa and Oscar start to feel homesick. They don't look forward to another boring weekend in Bangkok. The Thai cuisine and cultural offerings don't hold any appeal for the Latino couple. They consider the sex shows of girls smoking cigars with their vaginas appalling. Also, the harassment by she-males inviting them for exciting times is a bother every time they step out of the hotel. Consequently, they stay mostly in their suite and order the one palatable meal they found on the menu - steak and garden salad at a price ten times what they would ladle out for it in Colombia.

Oscar watches manipulated news on TV and Vanessa reads an English language newspaper. Suddenly she voices her surprise and holds up the paper for Oscar to see.

"Here, look at this, Oscar. Pablo walked out of prison."

Oscar actually bothers to sit up. "What? Pablo escaped?"

"Well, I wouldn't call it an escape," replies Vanessa. "It says here that while the guards watched the front gate like hawks, he and his lieutenants walked out the back and disappeared in the forest. Gone in thirty seconds."

Oscar is amused. "That's Pablo alright. Does it say why he walked out?"

Vanessa reads the explanation. "The government wanted to transfer him to another prison."

Oscar scoffs. "Why would they want to that? The government had a deal with him."

Vanessa cites the report. "Yes, but he is alleged to have broken his part of the bargain. It's claimed that he tortured and killed four of his lieutenants including his head lieutenant, Sean Sauer."

"That's nonsense," comments Oscar. "Pablo wouldn't do that. Why would he?"

"You may be right on that score," agrees Vanessa. "The report gets a little murky. Evidently, the lieutenants didn't like a deal Pablo had struck with families associated with competing cartels and revolted."

"Oops," mutters Oscar. "That's cutting close to the bone. It concerns us. I'll have to talk to Pablo when I get back."

Vanessa puts down the paper. "You know, Oscar, there's something that puzzles me. Lately you've said a lot of good things about Pablo. You've even defended him of not being the bloodthirsty monster he's made out to be. Yet, he was the guy who conspired against you, even gave orders to have you killed. The horror you experienced in prison is fully on his slate. Don't you feel at least some animosity towards him? Wouldn't you like to get even with him?"

Oscar smiles, folds his hands behind his head, and looks up at the ceiling. "I will, Vanessa, I will in my own good time."

***

A Thai gentleman dressed in a business suit is waiting in the lobby of the hotel. The receptionist makes a phone call and a few minutes later Oscar steps out of the elevator. The receptionist points to the Thai gentleman.

He and Oscar shake hands and take the elevator up to the club lounge where they sit down by a window away from other guests, place their order and Oscar hands him his business card.

The Thai reads the name and smiles. "Is that your real name?"

Feeling a little uncomfortable, Oscar says, "It's my name."

The Thai nods. "Of course."

A waitress serves a cocktail for the Thai and coffee for Oscar.

The Thai looks at Oscar's coffee. "You do not indulge?"

Oscar tries to match the Thai's smile. "No. None of us do."

The Thai nods. "Oh, very good. Who is 'us'?"

Oscar explains curtly, "The owners of my company and I."

The Thai nods again, takes a sip and puts down the glass. "Is it you or the owners who seek cooperation with us?"

Oscar stirs his coffee calmly. "Who is 'us'? Can you provide proof that you are the legitimate contact I have been waiting to see for over two weeks?"

The Thai stares at Oscar. "Don't you trust me?"

Oscar sniggers. "No, and why should I? Unless you provide proof of being the legitimate contact, this meeting is over."

The Thai sighs, gets out a cell phone, and talks to someone for quite a while. Then he punches a lengthy number into the phone, listens briefly, and says, "One moment, please."

He hands the phone to Oscar who is surprised to hear Alec's voice with such clarity as if he was talking to him locally.

Alec assures him that the Thai is the legitimate contact. Only he and his associates know how to intercept an Australian government safe land line. If that weren't so, then Oscar would be calling from the Australian prime minister's office in Canberra.

Satisfied but still not convinced, Oscar ends the call. He gives the Thai a wary look. "Okay, let us continue although you should know that I still don't trust you. I will explain our intention only in very general terms. Getting back to your question, it was my idea to cooperate with you, but my partners established the contact."

The Thai leans back with a serious look. "Very good. How do you expect the cooperation to work?"

Oscar explains in a business-like tone, "We bring your goods to market without a loss, and you transfer our money without a loss."

The Thai moves forward in his chair. "Aha, and how will that work in detail?"

Oscar takes a serviette and a pen and scribbles while he talks. "In detail? On a trial basis, we buy a fifty-million-dollar stockpile of your merchandise and pay for it in cash in the States. We package and ship it to ports of your choice and deliver it to your retailers. As they receive the merchandise, they transfer their payments and additional money we assign to them to accounts of our choice. I have the greatest respect for your banking system and trust that the suggested cooperation will be of interest to you."

The Thai drains his glass and looks fondly at Oscar. "Thank you for your expression of respect. I appreciate that."

He and Oscar get up. The Thai bows and they shake hands.

The Thai holds on to Oscar's hand with both hands. "I will see what I can do for you. In the morning fly to Chiang Rai, a small town in the north, where I will book a suite for you at the Teak

Garden Spa Resort and Hotel. It's very nice. You and your companion will enjoy it. I will contact you tomorrow afternoon."

Oscar bows slightly. "Thank you, Mister, uh?"

The Thai smiles. "It's my pleasure, Mr. Ortiz. Good-bye."

Oscar is stunned about this mysterious Thai referring to him by his real family name and, quite correctly, to Vanessa as his companion. Mouth agape he watches the Thai step into the elevator.

36

The Teak Garden Spa Resort & Hotel in the community of Chiang Rai is indeed very nice just as the Thai gentleman had promised. A downer is the hotel's restaurant only serving traditional Thai dishes. Another upset is the fact that the nameless Thai doesn't contact Oscar as promised on Sunday but only on Monday at 5 a.m. He promises that a car will come to the hotel to pick him up before noon. When nobody turns up, Oscar is ready to throw in the towel and return to Bangkok. But then he gets another call at lunchtime from a stranger who swears on his mother's grave that Oscar will be picked up the next day in the morning.

On Tuesday, 28th July 1992, a Toyota pickup with a tarpaulin over the deck drives up to the hotel's entrance at 6:30 a.m. The driver walks inside and returns with Oscar who is dressed for the jungle in cargo pants, cotton shirt, vest, and sturdy hiking boots.

Oscar gets into the back of the pickup. He is shocked to face three boys and a girl of about twelve years of age wearing battle fatigues and carrying Kalashnikovs. They sit on planks that are screwed to the top of the wheel wells. The girl pushes him onto a seat against the back of the driver's cabin and pulls a black jute bag over his head. She ties his hands and straps him to his seat.

Oscar can only guess where they are going. His sense of orientation tells him that they follow a relatively smooth road due north for almost an hour.

The ride gets very bumpy when the car turns off the road and goes west. The tell-tale noise of the car labouring through rough terrain is the giveaway that it grinds its way through creeks and shallows and over hillocks along a path that leads generally uphill.

The car stops. The engine is turned off. Oscar can make out the driver talking to three men. The slight noise of hands slapping on rifle butts lets him presume that the men are armed. One of the men lifts the tarpaulin and looks at the boys, the girl, and their passenger. He laughs, drops the tarpaulin, and bangs his fist on the side of the pickup. The three men let the car pass and it enters the border area of Burma, Laos, and Thailand.

The ride continues on narrow paths through jungle terrain. They stop at the headquarters of the drug overlord Khun Sa almost smack in the centre of the Golden Triangle.

The girl unties Oscar, pulls the bag off his head, and leads him towards a building with a pagoda style roof. She motions him to bend down, ruffles his curly hair, and wipes the sweat off his face with a clean handkerchief. She takes him by the hand, leads him to the bottom of the building's stairs, and giggles when she gives him a slap on his backside.

Two grim looking guards frisk him and take his cell phone and a package from his vest pockets. One of the guards holds up the two items and shouts at him in a language Oscar does not understand. Calmly, Oscar takes the package from his hand, unwraps it, and opens a gift box to reveal a solid gold cigarette case. The guard grins showing off a row of golden teeth, pockets the cell phone but lets him keep the gift. He leads Oscar up the stairs, opens the door, and shoves him into the house.

Oscar stumbles into the spacious room where a gaunt man wearing battle fatigues stands by a side-table under a window. It is Khun Sa, chief of the Asian heroin trade, who pours juice into two glasses, turns, and holds one out to Oscar.

He looks sternly and says, "Welcome to my humble abode, Oscar."

Oscar takes the glass, thanks him and they sit down, Khun Sa in a peacock chair and Oscar on an ottoman. The seating arrangement is a statement in itself with the host looking down on his guest.

Oscar presents Khun Sa with the gift he salvaged from the guard's clutches. His host opens the solid gold cigarette case, takes out a cigarette, lights up, and inhales.

He takes a few puffs. "My favourite brand. How did you know?"

Oscar is pleased that his gift has hit the spot and asks, "How did you know my name is Oscar?"

Khun Sa nods. "Oscar Antonio Ortiz Acosta. Correct?"

Dumbfounded, Oscar whispers, "Yes."

Khun Sa appears to be pleased and says, "There you are. We have a way of finding out your real name and you my favourite cigarette brand. Let's keep it a secret how we do that?"

He chuckles, stubs out the cigarette, and takes sip of juice. "You are a smart man, Oscar. I like your proposal. When can we start?"

Oscar turns an open hand towards his host. "We are talking to each other. So, you could say we have started already."

Khun Sa nods. "Indeed. But where do we go from here?"

Oscar replies, "Once I have received your commitment to cooperate with us, it would take one phone call to start the operation."

Khun Sa wants to hear more details. "One phone call to whom? And what are you going say?"

Oscar inhales deeply before he starts his lengthy explanation of having to call his chief of operations to allocate the funds for setting up shop in Bangkok. Their cooperation would require an even split of the costs between the Second Generation and Khun Sa for the purchase of legal companies exporting frozen seafood, the packaging equipment, and the conversion of containers. The merchandise itself would be purchased by the Colombians, of course, who would pack it, ship it, and deliver it without a loss to any destination. He points out the considerable investments required to ensure a flawless operation and the help they would need for the hiring of reliable personnel. He explains once more the procedure of the risk-free deal for Khun Sa in return for the legal deposit of all their proceeds in selected bank accounts.

Khun Sa gets up and Oscar follows suit. They shake hands and the host wants to say something. He is cut short by the distant sound of gunfire and helicopters. Khun Sa dives and is flat on the floor while Oscar still looks at the window wondering about that noise of a bullet ripping the window screen. He hits the ground a split second before the door bursts into splinters under the impact of a grenade exploding on the staircase.

Looking out through the breach, Oscar sees guards on their bellies firing high-powered rifles into the dense jungle on the perimeter of the open place.

He is horrified by the sight of screaming child soldiers storming towards the undergrowth of the forest firing their guns. Several of them are hit fatally by snipers responding to the onslaught. Three helicopters hover at a distance over the jungle firing their large calibre guns until one is shot down by missiles, explodes and crashes into the thicket. The gunfire subsides.

A moment later four boy soldiers and the girl that accompanied Oscar step out of the jungle. Each one carries the grisly trophy of a severed head of an enemy soldier.

The girl is inconsolable and wails incessantly. She tosses the head at the foot of the steps to the pagoda and drops to her knees.

Khun Sa gets up and takes in the bloody mess of corpses and badly injured guards screaming. He walks cautiously down the damaged stairs, squats next to the girl, puts a hand on her shoulder, talks to her, and spits on the head lying at her feet.

He straightens up, walks up the stairs towards Oscar waiting in the doorway and tells him, "That's the head of her father. It was hacked it off when he tried to crawl away. Sad, but shit happens in the heat of battle."

He stands next to Oscar and spots the cell phone on a ledge. He squints at Oscar who signals that it is his and reaches for the phone.

A woman's voice can be heard calling a name. Calmly, Khun Sa listens for a moment, switches off the phone, opens his holster, and pulls out his HK UCP pistol. He turns to the guard who took Oscar's phone and executes him with one shot to the forehead.

Oscar is horrified watching the coldblooded execution. He struggles to stay calm and not scream out the terror he feels.

Khun Sa hands the phone back to Oscar and leads him down the stairs. On the open place, he shouts commands, and two of his mercenaries rush to the back of the pagoda to get the pickup.

Then he returns to the business at hand. "Before we were so rudely interrupted, I was going to give you my agreement for a trial run of your plan. We will have to communicate every step of the way, but you can't call here."

His hand sweeps around over the bloody mess at their feet. "This is the result of one careless call by one man to his girlfriend. The location of every phone can be triangulated. The result is what you see. We will have to leave this place today and move to a new location. I'll give you a number to call in Bangkok."

Oscar nods and swallows hard. The stench of the blend of cordite and blood chokes him to the point of wanting to throw up. The two men keep on exchanging their points of view. They shake hands once more when the Toyota pickup arrives.

Two armed boys and Oscar get into the back. Without a black jute bag over his head, he looks back at the devastation.

He is relieved to leave this place of horror and grieves for the little girl as well as the child soldiers who were killed or injured.

Then the jungle swallows them up.

37

Pablo Escobar and his flunkey Juan Diego Arcila Henao sit on comfortable chairs on the porch of a low wooden house. It is hidden in dense forest only a couple of kilometres from Envigado on a mountainside in Antioquia, well camouflaged, and not visible even from a short distance.

Pablo stares into the valley below through a gap in the undergrowth. He sighs. "We've been hiding here for so long, I can't even remember what day of the week it is."

Juan is ready as always with unsolicited advice. "We've been here for forty-eight days. It's Tuesday, 8th September 1992."

Pablo groans. "Thank you, calendar man. I wish you wouldn't rub it in that we are in a self-imposed exile for seven weeks already. When I look down into the valley and can see people working in the fields or driving by, I wish I could join them, you know, go shopping, have a coffee, and have a chat with old acquaintances like a normal person."

Promptly Juan replies, "Yes, but you are not normal."

Pablo turns on him and hisses, "I'm not normal? You think I'm crazy?"

Juan leans back to be out of reach of Pablo's looming backhander and hastens to say, "No, not crazy but a celebrity. If you were a normal person, the French press wouldn't have sent that hack for the interview a couple of weeks ago."

"Hey, that wasn't a hack," protests Pablo. "She looked very pretty and took nice pictures of me."

"Yes," agrees Juan. "And now you can't even sneak into Envigado for a cup of coffee and a chat. Because of the pictures she took the whole world knows that you gained almost fifty pounds and grew a long beard."

Pablo dismisses that comment with a wave of his hand and wants to say something when a cell phone rings. He picks it up from under his chair and bellows, "Yes? Speak to me! Oh, hello, George! How are you? How's your campaign for re-election?"

He switches the phone to speaker and listens to the nasal blathering, "Fine, Pablo, just fine. I will be a shoo-in for my second term. That hick from Arkansas doesn't stand a chance. Anyway, how are you? Where are you right now?"

Pablo looks at Juan, tips his temple to indicate what he thinks of the caller. “I’m in beautiful Colombia, George, keeping busy.”

Pablo’s thumb is ready to end the call when it takes the caller a moment to respond, “Keeping busy, yes, of course. Now listen, Pablo, I’m a bit pissed about you walking out. Do you think it was a wise move? I don’t think so. I gave you ironclad assurances.”

Pablo cuts into his flow of speech, “Yes, George, of course! Were your assurances as ironclad as your ‘Watch my lips - No new taxes’?”

Pablo and Juan chuckle, and Pablo continues, “Listen, George, your assurances are not worth a monkey’s wet fart.”

It takes the caller a moment to swallow that epithet before he objects, “Just a minute, Pablo. I gave you a personal assurance. That’s quite different from political campaign promises. Let me reiterate my offer. Give yourself up to our judiciary and I’ll get you the best lawyers money can buy. You’ll be treated with all the respect we have for our CIA agents...”

Pablo cuts him off by adding, “...and still end up in prison. I told you before that I prefer a grave in Colombia to a prison cell in the United States of America.”

It takes again a moment for the caller to speak. “That’s about the most stupid thing I’ve heard. Look Pablo, you and I go back quite a long way to the early eighties. We’ve had interesting discussions and I always respected your point of view.”

Pablo butts in, “Hold your breath, George. You’re wasting time to let your boys with all their electronic gear find my location. Nice try. Good luck with your re-election. Don’t underestimate that hick from Arkansas. He’s quite popular with the ladies.”

Pablo presses a button to switch off the speaker that sounds identical to the connection being cut. He leans forward to hear what the caller says thinking he was cut off. “Shit! That broccoli eating, motherfucking, tit sucking, three-balled son of a bitch is too smart for this charade. We’ll have to try another route to trap or kill him.”

Pablo giggles and shouts, “I hear you, George! Now that was an assurance, I’d call ironclad!”

The phone at the other end is slammed down and Pablo and Juan have a good laugh.

Pablo takes the cell phone apart, breaks the SIM card, and tosses it into the bushes.

He looks at Juan. “We have to think about making a move. Perhaps we should consider hiding in plain sight in Envigado.”

38

Unexpected hiccups with the purchase of legal companies in Bangkok and delays in the delivery and installation of machinery and equipment give rise to frustration, arguments, and cost overrun for the Second Generation's cooperation project with the Golden Triangle. Jorge, Alberto, and Guillermo are summoned to help supervise the work.

It provides the opportunity for Oscar to take a few days off to 'square some accounts' as he tells Vanessa. She doesn't need to trudge along because he has to speak only to his bank manager in the Cayman Islands.

She doesn't believe his mealy-mouthed explanation and would like to know the reason for him booking a flight via Los Angeles and Costa Rica to his alleged destination. Yet, she leaves well enough alone and books a flight for herself to Mexico to spend time on home territory and check out investment opportunities since she has received a chunk of her promised payouts.

***

Oscar arrives in San José on Thursday, 17th September 1992, rents a car at the airport and takes a leisurely drive past his old haunts. He doesn't enter the posada in Moravia but affords himself the treat of a baguette, ham and cheese, and some smoked salchichas. He sits in his rental car and munches his sandwich in the vicinity of the posada in the hope of seeing Bert. His patience pays off when he sees the dented old Mazda lurch into the side road and park near the entrance to his old home.

He gets out of his car and shouts, "Bert! Hello! How are you?"

Bert turns, looks at him, shrugs, and wants to enter the posada.

Oscar shouts again, "Bert! Don't you recognise an old friend?"

Bert walks towards Oscar, scrutinises his face, and speaks in a low voice, "Is that...? That's not you, Oscar, is it?"

Oscar puts a finger to his lips. "Benigno, my name is Benigno Benavides."

They stand face to face and hug briefly.

Bert holds Oscar by the shoulders. "Man, you've changed a lot and not just your name. How are you doing? Everything alright?"

"Yes, more or less."

"And what brings you back to this place? I'm sure it's not the happy memories."

"You're right, it's not. Listen, do you have a bit of time for a coffee and a chat?"

Bert pulls a face and shakes his head. "No, I'd love to hear your story, but I'm really pressed for time. I have to meet a deadline in an hour and finish a report. Can we meet another day?"

"No, I'm afraid I won't be here for another day. I want to square some accounts and I'm off again. But we should stay in touch. Here, I'll give you my address in Bogotá. Anytime you come to Colombia you'll be welcome to stay for as long as you like."

He gets out a pen and notepad and writes down the posada's address and telephone number. "Call ahead before you come to Colombia and mention my old name in case I'm not at home."

Bert takes the note and stashes it in his wallet. "Thanks, I appreciate that."

He kicks a small stone off the sidewalk and says, "You mentioned squaring accounts. Are you here to take revenge or to see Silvia?"

"Oh, I'd love to see Silvia," confirms Oscar and asks, "Do you have her address and telephone number?"

"Yes, sure," replies Bert and dictates both for Oscar to scribble down. "Okay, now let me give you some advice. Don't go visit her. Her home is under surveillance. She did some deals bypassing Alfredo Calderón and now his stooges and the cops are waiting for her to trip up. It doesn't look good for her. So, give her a call and lure her to a neutral place where you can meet and reminisce. Okay? Sorry, Os..., uh, Benigno, I got to go. It's great seeing you again. Take care, will you? And forget about squaring accounts. Please!"

"I'll keep that in mind and thanks, Bert. You take care as well and I hope to see you soon in Bogotá."

***

Oscar calls Silvia from a public phone booth and persuades her to meet Benigno Benavides. She has no idea to whom she is talking but agrees to see him in the late afternoon after he conveys greetings from his best friend Oscar.

He books a business suite in the five-star hotel where he intends to meet Silvia. He settles down and writes a list of the names of people with whom he wants to square accounts. Right at the top is Alfredo Calderón, the local drug boss, followed by the cellmates

Bernardo, Mario, and Raúl, and the brothers José and Ricardo León. The list also includes the corrupt judge Juan Cordero and his ally, the prosecutor Antonio Arías.

Shortly thereafter Oscar drives along Avenida 2 in search of a saloon owned by a couple retired pimps from Vienna and Berlin who got away before the police could nab them for tax evasion and settled in Costa Rica. He spots the bar with its wide-open front and sees one of the owners, an Austrian by the name of Heinz. He parks the car and enters the tavern.

Heinz doesn't recognise Oscar and is surprised to be addressed by his first name. When Oscar whispers something about an interesting business proposition worth a bucket of money, Heinz wants to know how much and is told that he can name his price once he has assessed the extent of the required work.

He invites Oscar to discuss the proposition in the office upstairs. Oscar comes straight to the point, presents a list of candidates he would like to see whacked, and asks if Heinz could be of assistance in this matter. Heinz looks at the names and whistles softly when he sees the names of the drug boss, the judge, and the prosecutor.

"These five wannabe gangsters are no problem, but the other three have protection." He looks up sternly and asks, "What's your beef with the guys on your laundry list?"

"They are all connected to a case of a guy getting framed for murder he didn't commit," states Oscar calmly.

"I see," mumbles Heinz and pauses for a moment before he asks, "Can you cover the cost?"

"Name your price," is Oscar's brief reply.

Heinz mutters to himself for a while until he concludes, "Okay, that's five large each for these three, seven and eight for the brothers, and fifteen, twenty and fifty for the rest. That's a total of a hundred fifteen grand in U.S. currency, of course."

"No problem," says Oscar. "I can have the full amount transferred to your account with the proviso that I have to be in the vicinity when the dispatches take place."

Heinz rocks to and fro in his chair and pulls a face. "That will require additional coordination and ups the total to a hundred and fifty large. Do you need physical evidence?"

"No, my visual account will be fully trusted. Do we have an agreement?"

"Yes, sure. What about the payment?"

"I can transfer the amount via phone with one instruction. Do you want it here or do you have an offshore account?"

Heinz happens to have an account in the Cayman Islands like every smart criminal. It makes the money transfer all the easier. After the calls for the payment order and deposit confirmation, Heinz and Oscar shake hands and seal the deal. Heinz asks him where he can be reached, and Oscar gives him his phone number.

Heinz sees the country code and wrinkles his brow. "That's a Colombian number. Are you from Colombia?"

Oscar nods and smiles when Heinz scrutinises his face and says, "You look vaguely familiar. Have we met before?"

Oscar shakes his head. "You have met my brother."

Heinz searches his memory for a similar face and asks, "Is that the fat cat who sold inhalers filled with cocaine?"

Oscar chuckles. "Yes, but don't call him fat."

Heinz nods. "Right, like all fat cats, he doesn't like to be called fat. How's he doing? Is he still selling inhalers?"

"No, he's not pushing inhalers any longer. He's got bigger fish to fry. He's doing alright."

"Good for him," says Heinz as he gets up. "He'll always be welcome in our joint. Listen, I have to make a few calls to set up the schedule for my dispatchers to get the job done tonight. I'll call you within a couple of hours to let you know place and time. You better be ready."

***

Oscar sits in the coffee shop of the hotel where he booked a suite, orders a cup of java, and watches the people entering the lobby. He is nervous and annoyed with himself for being nervous. The excitement of seeing Silvia has a firm grip on him.

Thinking of the few weeks he spent with her, he concludes that it was the happiest time of his life. And it wasn't only because of the wholly satisfying, sexual encounter. He had given up some of his established routine, a small part of his life and received so much more in return.

Silvia gave up her way of life for him and became a great partner. He can only wonder how his life would have turned out had he not fallen into Pablo Escobar's trap. Could he have lived in peace with Silvia by not demanding or expecting too much personal gain? Would he have pulled out of the drug trade and fulfilled his dream of owning a small hotel on some tropical island to get away from the constant threat of being caught for his illegal activity or even getting killed by some competitor? Will he still get away from it all now that Vanessa has come into his life?

Thinking of Vanessa, he starts to drum the tabletop with his fingertips. Vanessa is a very smart and self-assured woman. He respects her and likes her a lot for what she has done for him. But since he got to know her darker side, he fears her more than he respects or loves her.

Deep in thought he stirs his coffee when he spots a lady with an ample bust entering the hotel lobby. Her sight immediately awakens most impressive memories. He can't see her face since it is partially covered by a wide-brimmed hat and oversized sunglasses.

The woman walks into the café. She takes off her shades slowly and Oscar recognises Silvia. He gets up and waves to her but is ignored. Puzzled, he sits down again and watches her talking to a waitress and scanning the café.

It strikes him that she appears to ignore him on purpose and wonders if that is her tactic to distract attention from the meeting with him. After all, Bert had warned him that she is under surveillance by Alfredo Calderón's stooges and the police.

He keeps an eye on her when she sits down two tables away. The waitress serves her coffee and a piece of cake. There is no sugar bowl on her table. She snaps her fingers to draw the waitress' attention.

Oscar gets up, hands Silvia the sugar from his table and says, "There you are, madam."

She looks up, gives him a glance, and thanks him. Oscar smiles at her and asks, "Are you here to meet someone, madam?"

She stuffs her mouth with a forkful of cake and nods.

Encouraged he continues, "Silvia Robles?"

Instead of answering, she signals a young man in a dark suit to come closer. He puts a hand in his jacket when he stands next to Oscar and the familiar sound of a gun safety release can be heard. Silvia leans back, gives Oscar a stone-faced stare, and asks, "And you are?"

"I'm Benigno Benavides," he responds hastily. "I called you to discuss a business proposition. We shouldn't do it in public, though. I have a business suite where we can discuss everything in private."

She takes a scant look at his face and asks, "Do we know each other?"

He bows slightly with a big grin on his face. “Yes, madam. We’ve met some time ago.”

The thought occurs to him that her bodyguard may be more than that knowing her penchant for expressing her gratitude for services rendered in a physical manner and preferably in bed. Perhaps he should let sleeping dogs lie and relish the memories of her. But then he gives her the number of his suite and adds that he will be waiting for her should she be interested in discussing his proposition. He walks away and steps into the elevator.

It doesn’t take long for a knock on the door of his suite. Silvia’s bodyguard pushes past him without a word, inspects the rooms, and even looks under the bed and behind the curtains. Not having found anything, he leaves the room to wait outside.

Silvia enters, takes off her hat, unbuttons her jacket, and sits down. Oscar stands in front of her and spreads his arms wide. When she makes no move to get up, he takes her by the hands, lifts her to her feet, and embraces her.

“Hey, what are you doing?” she protests.

“Don’t you recognise me?” Oscar lets his hands slide under her jacket and up her back.

“No, I don’t. You said we met before, but I can’t remember everybody I’ve met.”

She tries to wriggle out of his hold but notices that he has already unhooked her bra.

“Stop that,” she demands and pauses. “I don’t remember your face but, uh, I have a vague recollection of that large banana in your pocket.”

Looking into his eyes she asks, “Is that you? Oscar?”

“Are you joking? You don’t remember my face but recognise the large banana in my trousers. Can anyone top that?”

Thus, the renewal of their affair takes its course.

Once they take a break, she asks, if he has come for his money. He assures her not to want any of it and asks how her business is going.

She is reluctant to talk about it until he lets on to have heard about her problems with Alfredo Calderón. Then she tells him how it came about.

When Calderón had refused to supply her business, she had sent her guys to hijack one of his trucks. But what she thought would have been a heist of perhaps a hundred kilograms of cocaine was a load of over two tons. Consequently, she carried on her business without begging Calderón for supplies. She switched from retail to wholesale deals, which let him smell the rat of her being the perpetrator. While Calderón visited Londoño in Calí to ascertain that she wouldn't get any merchandise from a Colombian source, her gang unburdened one of his warehouses of another fifteen tons of nose candy. That was tantamount to a declaration of war. He sent his stooges and policemen after her. Rapidly she had to enlarge her troop of bodyguards and convert her property into a fortress. It is a bitter dispute which only one can win.

Oscar contemplates what she told him and wants to discuss a solution to get her out of the mess when his cell phone beeps. It is Heinz who gives him the schedule for the dispatches and adds that the judge is out of the country. They will have to wait for his return to chambers.

He asks if Oscar is ready to be in Santo Domingo de Herédia for the first dispatch. Oscar assures him that he will be there and is given the addresses and times for the execution of all the jobs.

He invites Silvia to see some fireworks and promises that her business problem would be resolved by the end of the day.

They take a shower together to save water. Consequently, it takes much longer than planned also on account of Oscar not wanting to let go of her and swearing that he wants her to be with him for all time. She is touched by his declaration but evidently has developed a keen business sense and puts a stop to the fooling around by showering him with cold water.

Oscar, Silvia, and her bodyguard arrive at the given address in Santo Domingo de Herédia just in time to see three heavies enter a small house near the Parque Central.

Oscar lets the car roll forward until they have a good view into the house and can observe the fight of Bernardo, Mario and Raúl getting knocked out. Two of the dispatchers lift the heavy concrete lid of the septic tank in the backyard for the third guy to drop their victims into it. They put the lid carefully back in place and leave the house. Calmly they walk to a black SUV with dark windows and drive away on the road to the suburb of Tibas as fast as traffic permits. Oscar follows them at a distance and has to jump red lights a couple of times to keep up with them.

On the way Silvia asks where the fireworks will take place. What they watched in Santo Domingo really stank in her opinion. Oscar agrees with her and explains that fireworks don't start with a big bang. That is reserved for the grand finale.

In Tibas, one of the heavies rings the doorbell of a large house. Ricardo León answers the door and is given a note. He thanks the guy and leaves the house a moment later. His head is blown away with a dumdum bullet fired from a silenced assault rifle out of the backseat window of the SUV. Oscar asks if the muzzle fire was a good start to the fireworks and Silvia agrees but is not impressed.

They follow the SUV to the suburb of Guadalupe where they pass the prison and come to a stop near the gate of the Rapid Reaction Force barracks. Night has fallen and they have to wait patiently for fifteen minutes before José León rushes out talking on his cell phone. He runs to the parking lot and gets into his car when the SUV stops next to it. A window is lowered, a hand reaches out and knocks on the window of the car. José turns down his window and a hand grenade is tossed in. The SUV takes off with smoking tires and gets out of the parking lot just before the explosion rips the car apart. Silvia and her bodyguard appreciate the fiery display.

Oscar keeps up with the black SUV on its way to the suburb of San Pedro. The heavies park a block away from the stately home of the prosecutor Antonio Arías. The property is surrounded by a seven-foot-high wrought iron fence and guarded by police as is appropriate for a corrupt member of the judiciary with plenty of enemies to worry about.

Oscar has stopped not too far away in the darkness of a quiet street. He sees two of Heinz' dispatchers enter the front yard of a darkened house two houses down from the stately home. One carries a gas cylinder and the other a large package. After twenty minutes they reappear and get back into the SUV. Slowly they drive into a side road when a massive explosion blows out the windows and the front door of the stately home. Flames engulf the house. The policemen get out of their cruiser and stare at the inferno.

Oscar follows the SUV in the dark and switches the headlights on once he is some distance away from the scene of the crime. They turn onto Highway 39 and then a road into the suburb of Alajuelita at a leisurely pace. Silvia recognises the area and gets visibly nervous. She asks Oscar where they are going and is puzzled by his mysterious answer that they are on their way to her freedom.

It becomes clear what he means when the SUV stops, one of the heavies comes to shake hands with Oscar and advises him to turn around and park out of sight of the estate of Alfredo Calderón amongst some bushes by the side of the road.

The SUV moves slowly towards the estate and stops. One of the guys gets out with a map in his hand and approaches the guard. A moment later the guard is shot and dragged into the guardhouse. The other two heavies rush to the gate carrying what looks like a bundle of sticks of dynamite and a roll of cable. All three of them put on black balaclavas, climb over the wall, and disappear in the darkness of the estate. Only one of them can be seen once ducking between cars of the fleet parked in front of the main house.

A moment after the three heavies return to their SUV and disappear in the dark up the road from the estate, a police motorcade arrives and stops at the closed gate. An officer is calling someone on a walkie-talkie.

Alfredo Calderón is leaving the house followed by his entourage of stooges. He waves to the officer giving him a signal. He and his stooges get into their cars and Alfredo starts his. All eight cars blow up together apparently linked by wire. It is a massive firework display.

Oscar turns to Silvia. "You're free now. I can arrange a deal to set you up as overlord, if you are interested."

She reaches for his hand and presses it against her cheek. "You are incredible. What do I owe you?"

"Owe me? What for?"

"The fireworks. It must have cost you a wad."

Oscar smiles and says, "Two things, Silvia. First, you don't owe me anything, and second, one can't put a price on deep satisfaction." He pauses for a moment and then continues, "Excuse me, I have to make a phone call."

He calls Heinz and thanks him for the military style execution of the task. He tells him to cancel the last dispatch and split its fee among the three henchmen. Heinz invites him for a celebratory drink to his watering hole and expects to see him within the half hour.

Oscar lets the car roll out from behind the bushes and down the road into Alajuelita until they are out sight of the police motorcade. As he starts the engine and switches on the headlights, he notices they are being followed. He hopes that it isn't one of the police cars. Paying scant attention to anything else he doesn't catch what Silvia's bodyguard asks him, but he hears the familiar sound of the gun safety release.

He asks in the direction of the backseat, “Is there a problem?”

The bodyguard snarks, “Yes, I asked what deal you are talking about. I mean, you claim you can arrange a deal that’ll make Silvia the overlord. Then you must be the head of a cartel.”

Silvia says, “Listen, Bubba, Oscar isn’t the head of a cartel. That deal is between him and me and none of your business.”

“You think so, do you?” The bodyguard points his gun at her head. “But if I blow your head off, I’d be the overlord. Right?”

“Wrong,” barks Oscar and again looks at him. The car swerves, he steadies it and adds, “You’d have nothing and be nothing for the hour you may have to live after killing Silvia.”

The bodyguard scoffs and points the gun at Oscar’s head. “I guess then I have to blow you away first, you stupid bastard.”

Oscar can feel the cold steel of the gun in his neck. He wiggles the steering wheel pretending to have a problem with the steering, takes the foot off the accelerator, and switches the hazard lights on. The car comes slowly to a halt. Oscar is relieved to see the black SUV passing. It stops in front of them. One of the heavies gets out, waves to Oscar, walks up to his open window, and asks if there is a problem with the car.

“Yes, there seems to be a problem with the steering.”

Oscar gets out swiftly and conveys the trouble with Silvia’s bodyguard.

The henchman appears to be highly amused. He goes around the car, opens the door, and helps Silvia to get out. Casually they go to the SUV where he has a word with his partners. They get out and point a submachine gun and the silenced assault rifle at Oscar’s car. Silvia’s bodyguard jumps out holding his gun. It takes two shots to kill him and his body slumps into the ditch by the side of the road.

Problem solved. Silvia faints. Oscar carries her back to the car and lays her down on the backseat. He waves to the dispatchers and continues his ride into the city.

Silvia regains consciousness shortly before they arrive at the saloon. She doesn’t remember anything and asks what happened. Oscar tells her that the guys in the SUV persuaded her bodyguard to stay in Alajuelita. She vows to talk to him until Oscar says that he quit his job and moved to happier hunting grounds. She doesn’t understand that it means he was killed and wonders who would offer him better conditions than she does including pension fund, dental plan, and thirty vacation days a year.

Later that night, after she has been fêted as the new coke queen, she entices Oscar to quit the hotel and move in with her. She owns her luxurious home after all due to him persuading her to switch from picking pockets to a more lucrative form of making a living.

Once they are in her house, they hash out a plan for her to receive all the merchandise she needs to assure her position as the number one wholesaler in the country.

As a first step though, he asks her for stacks of cash. He fills a batch of plain envelopes with banknotes and goes outside in search of police cars. He sees one and hands an envelope to each police officer with the words, "The king is dead. Long live the queen."

Having heard of Alfredo Calderón's demise, the cops accept the graft gladly, and call their officer about the new development. Within a few minutes Oscar has handed out all the envelopes to the policemen of four more cruisers that appear out of nowhere. They promise the new queen all the protection she needs in return for weekly handouts of cash.

Oscar calls Calí early in the morning. Pilar answers the telephone to his great surprise, and he asks her what happened to Alec. He decided to go into politics and run for election as a senator, she tells him. She is sitting in for him and asks how she can be of help.

In response to his request for a steady supply of merchandise to the new head of operations in Costa Rica, she informs Oscar that the quantity of merchandise consumed in the target country in one month is equivalent to one week's consumption in the city of New Orleans alone. It is too small to bother with a delivery. That puts a crimp in his plan.

He suggests the alternative of using the country as a transhipment point for deliveries to the US west coast because it is cheaper and quicker than paying part of the fee for passing through the Panama Canal. Then the desired quantity of goods can be extracted at a safe container repair shop in San José.

After some deliberation and clarification of details, Pilar agrees with Oscar and assures him that it will be done.

He informs Silvia of the arrangement and plans to stay for the next three weeks to supervise the new procedure.

39

The setup of a trouble-free transfer of reefers across the isthmus from Limón on the Caribbean coast to Puerto Caldera on the Pacific and the delivery of drugs to Silvia takes longer than the three weeks Oscar had envisioned. But the extended stay with Silvia suits him fine. He is pampered, cared for, and has a fitness studio at his disposal. He feels well, is happy and satisfied, and almost forgets about his expected return to Thailand. If Pilar and Vanessa had not called him from time to time to remind him of his duties in Bangkok, he quite probably would have dropped out of his involvement with the project. He even thinks seriously of turning his back on the entire drug trade, although he is planning and executing every detail of his current work thus assuring the drug delivery for Silvia. But in view of her potential arrest and a long prison sentence, the thoughts of a total withdrawal from the business remain an important part of his reflections.

Prison would destroy Silvia spiritually and her ruin would destroy him, too. His concern for her welfare has the consequence of his impetuous linear thinking changing to comprehensive lateral considerations of the overall scheme of his work. In addition, he doesn't see Silvia just as a sex object any longer. He has recognised how smart she is, a woman who stands on her own feet and does not need a man to tell her what to do and how to do it. In this context, he wonders if his view of her will change with age when her face will be wrinkled, and her physical attributes yield to the strain of gravity. He is sure to love her all the same no matter how much the tooth of time gnaws at her because he sees her as a person who gives him a zest for life by simply being the woman she is.

It takes more than eight weeks for the transfer of reefers and the delivery of drugs to function perfectly and until Oscar's departure is on the agenda.

His last action, before he sets off, is a visit to Delgado Miranda. He orders a passport with valid exit and entry visas for Silvia in the fictitious name of Marta Figueres Sabadell. He transfers the demanded ten thousand dollars to Delgado's bank account in Panama and is assured of the delivery of the documents upon a call with the password 'Cacique', which means roughly translated 'Noble Chieftain'.

Oscar lets the cat out of the bag of leaving her the next morning, Monday, 16th November 1992. It turns their last evening together into a melodrama. She did not expect his departure and becomes quite hysterical. She begs him to stay, and he has no choice but to tell her in confidence about the Second Generation's project.

He must return to Thailand to ensure the proper operation and observe the loading of heroin for the west coast of Canada and the USA. He implores her to remain calm, since he will return in a few weeks. Then he mentions quite casually his plan to give up the drug trade once he has finished his work and has been paid. She is completely confused to hear him talking about a future without selling nose candy and wants to know what he intends to do instead.

Taking her by the hand, he walks with her into the garden of her property situated in a quiet street of the suburb of Escalante.

He puts an arm around her shoulders. "We live in a wonderful world, apparently. We stroll in the expanse of your garden, see the enchanting blossoms of the bushes, smell the intoxicating fragrance of the flowers, and don't hear the noise of the city. Evidently sublime peace holds sway. But outside the wall that surrounds your property, everything can quickly come to a bitter end. You are currently enjoying the protection of a corrupt police force, but if the next government fights corruption, you could end up in jail. I cannot bear the thought of being separated from you by prison walls. I want to take a stroll with you anywhere in the world and not be threatened with arrest, go through endless interrogations, suffer torture, experience the monkey business of court proceedings, and then die in jail. I want to live with you in peace, wherever we live. Do you understand? It is my biggest fear, never to see you again."

During his monologue, he looks down at the city in the valley. He turns to Silvia and can see tears streaming down her cheeks.

She leans her head on his chest and sobs softly. Suddenly she pushes away and clutches his arm. He has the strange vision of not seeing an adult woman, but a crying girl who needs warmth and security when she howls, "Do you love me?"

He nods and she clings to him. When she calms down after a while, she says, "I will always stay with you as long as you love me, but I need to know what you want to do in the future."

They sit down on a bench. Oscar tells her of his dream of owning a hotel in the tropics and continue Don Germán Obejo's work for homeless and abandoned children in the posada in Bogotá.

After his long-winded story, he informs her about her new identity papers under the name Marta Figueres, which will be delivered to her upon the password 'Cacique'. Silvia does not like the name because it would connect her to one of the first families in the country and swears to herself, never to ask for the papers.

They spend the night together, during which they barely get any shut-eye. When it is time for Oscar to hit the road early in the morning, they say farewell at the gate of Silvia's estate, and he heads for the airport after promising to be back before the end of the year.

40

Oscar and Alberto walk along the fence of Bangkok's harbour on Thursday, 19th November 1992. They stop opposite the workshop of a company where trucks deliver empty reefers. The refurbished ones with the lettering South East Asia Shipping Company are trucked to a frozen seafood company down the road. A bit further down the harbour front the loaded reefers are lifted onto a container vessel registered in the African country of Liberia.

Alberto looks at the hectic activity. "You know, Oscar, you have really started something incredible. The entire process is virtually undetectable, but it has the drawback of being very labour intensive. I was wondering if you cooked up any other ideas."

Oscar mulls the somewhat backhanded compliment before he responds, "It would be unwise to come up with a different or new idea when the original process has barely gone under way. What I mean to say, I want us to achieve our goals first and be absolutely certain that we hit every target of delivery and money transfer. So far I haven't spent any time thinking about improving a process that is not yet entirely proven to work flawlessly."

"I understand, but could you give it some thought?"

"Of course, but it's a matter I can't force. When the time has come, it will bubble up from the depth of my mind."

They walk on a few steps when Oscar abruptly stops. "Actually, on my flight back here I read an article about using plant extracts and even food waste as a base material for producing fibres, foils and compostable plastic. If we could convert the coca paste and opium to foil or fibres, we could ship our merchandise as well as smack in the form of rolls of yarn, textiles or foil and be really on top of the game."

"Brilliant," mutters Alberto. "That's a great idea, Oscar."

"Okay, but it is just an idea. Also, consider the additional outlay for the acquisition of chemical plants we would need to reconvert the fibres and foil to our merchandise."

"Of course. In which magazine was that article? If it contained the names of scientists researching and developing the materials, Ariana and Guillermo could contact them to get started."

"It was the inflight magazine of an airline. What raised my interest was the strange headline, 'Would you wear a suit made of yoghurt?' I thought the idea was original. You know, like wearing a suit that keeps you cool and can be eaten in an emergency. But it turned out to be the manufacture of fibres from milk residue and plant extracts for making textiles. Totally unfit for human consumption. Pity."

Alberto chuckles and they part ways on the confident note of having touched upon a further method of making their merchandise undetectable once they have figured out how to do it.

Oscar goes to a warehouse near the Chao Phraya River in the Kheha Phatthana district. Standing on the roof, he waits patiently until the container ship is ready to leave Container Terminal 2. The hawsers are pulled in and the vessel is towed down the river by two tugboats. Oscar is satisfied to see the first shipment of undetectable pure heroin on its way to sail across the sea.

He returns to the President Palace Hotel with a heavy heart knowing that he will face a grumpy Vanessa. He hasn't told her that he met the love of his life again and is planning his future together with Silvia.

Vanessa had stumped him with the question what took him over eight weeks for a chat with a bank manager in the Cayman Islands. He totally forgot his original little white lie about the reason for his trip. He claimed squaring accounts with people in Costa Rica took a long time and started to spin a long yarn about hunting down and killing the villains who had caused him so much grief in the past.

Vanessa looked at him askance not believing one word. How could he possibly have learned to handle a silenced assault rifle with a scope and fire it accurately at a moving target or for that matter lift an enormously heavy concrete lid all by himself to drop three unconscious villains into a septic tank? And how about wiring packs of dynamite sticks into the ignition system of eight cars when he can't even point out the alternator under the hood? What happened to him, she wonders, that he started to suffer from Munchhausen syndrome, the habit of telling preposterous lies embedded in phantasmagorical stories.

Vanessa knows that their personal relationship is over, finished, and no longer salvageable, although he still treats her with all the courtesy becoming a person he respects. She is hurting from his rejection, yet it never occurs to her that it may have something to do with her threat of shooting to kill him if he doesn't toe the line. She had voiced that threat in Miami and implied it again during a conversation in New York. It was a threat Oscar had not forgotten.

His inherent fear of Vanessa's gun handling skills and readiness to kill lets no scruples arise when he books a single room and moves out of the shared quarters. Yet, sleeping alone for the last few days in Bangkok he misses her.

No matter how annoying her loud snoring was, it was also reassuring to have her by his side. She gave him comfort and warmth and sometimes reason for hilarious scenes like that night in Moscow after she had borscht and dark rye bread for dinner that caused her to fart so loud that it woke her up and she asked him what that noise was.

Having no companion in his bed is an experience that takes him back to the days in the bungalow of the health resort in Panama.

One morning he gets up and storms to the window in a daze to see if Vanessa is outside doing her calisthenics waiting for him to go for a power walk. Seeing the skyline of Bangkok saddens him and makes him think that her care and effort made him the healthy and athletic man he is and never was before.

***

The day before Vanessa and Oscar depart Bangkok for Vancouver on Canada's west coast, he invites her on a city tour. Despite their prolonged stay they haven't seen much of the tourist attractions.

He would like to come to terms with her, his bodyguard, who is ready to kill him if she would see him endangering the project.

He calls for a limousine with a tour guide and they are shown what passes for attractions. Soon both Vanessa and Oscar are pretty bored. When they pass a public park along the banks of the river, he asks the guide to stop so they can go for a walk.

They haven't talked much during the tour, and it comes as a surprise to Vanessa when Oscar asks her out of the blue if she has a gun in her handbag and wants to see it. It is with great hesitation that she gets the gun out, a Glock 17, and hands it to him. It is only her certainty that he doesn't know how to release the safety and use it on her that she lets him handle it.

Stunned and mouth agape she watches him take on the stance of a baseball pitcher and fling that deadly firearm as far as he can. It twirls like a boomerang and Oscar fears for a second that it could come back and hit him in the head. But it skims the water surface twice and disappears in the middle of the lazy river.

Unable to interfere, Vanessa just shouts, "Are you nuts?"

Oscar is relieved to have got rid of the gun, pulls a funny face and squeaks, "Yes, ma'am, I'm nuts. Wanna see my certification?"

A moment later he asks, "Do you have any more guns in your bag or the hotel?"

She shakes her head. "No and I don't know what to do with the carton of ammo I have for the piece you threw away."

He suggests with a smirk, "A ambulant vendor of roast meat on a stick has his open barbecue near the hotel. Toss the carton in the fire when he doesn't look and run away quickly."

She mutters, "You are nuts! You crazy bastard!"

Her anger gives way to amusement, and she giggles about him pulling faces.

Oscar sees her smiling face with some relief and says, "I like you so much better when you are smiling and don't carry a gun."

She tries to object, "Yes, but..."

He cuts her off, "No more killing, you hear? We have to find a peaceful way to achieve our objectives. Tomorrow we are off to Vancouver. Then we have to scurry down the west coast to Seattle, San Francisco, and San Diego, observe the deliveries of smack and we're done. What are you going to do? Will you go back to Calí?"

She shrugs and says, "I'm not sure. I'd like to follow up on my business prospects in Mexico, but I don't even know if Alec will let me go."

"Oh, he will," he assures her. "He has already abdicated from the position of project leader and runs for election to the senate."

"What?" Vanessa is lost for words. "He in politics? How do you know?"

Her questions untie his tongue. He tells her a truthful version about his trip without mentioning Silvia. He explains why he called Pilar and was informed about Alec's political career dream.

Vanessa accepts his new version of events and understands why he spent almost eight weeks in Central America. When she asks him what he is going to do once his job for the Second Generation is done, he tells her that he will recover his original identity and carry on the work of Don Germán Obejo. He adds that hiding in plain sight under his real name is the best cover. The Second Generation will never find him should anyone of them ever bother to look for him.

Their amiable chat is almost a long farewell, but they still have to finish their job. They return to the hotel and get ready for the flight to Canada.

41

The Liberian registered container vessel is docked at the Burrard Inlet terminal of Vancouver Harbour on the night of Wednesday, 2nd December 1992. Oscar and Vanessa sit in a car opposite a terminal gate and observe the unloading.

Ten South East Asia Shipping Company reefers destined for Vancouver are checked for drugs, are given the all-clear, put onto trucks, pass through customs, and hit the road in different directions. Oscar follows a convoy of three trucks going east.

In the neighbouring city of Burnaby, the trucks drive into the large warehouse of a seafood import company. Oscar gets out of the car and takes a casual stroll past the building. From the other side of the street, he observes that the reefers are taken off. The trucks are loaded with empty containers and depart. The sliding wooden gate is shut.

Oscar crosses the street and peers through a crack in the gate. He is astonished about the organised work with military precision in the warehouse. A crew of Asian labourers unload the frozen shrimp and fish and move them to cold storage. The cladding of the containers is lifted, and the flat parcels of heroin are retrieved.

A man with a batch of papers goes along orderly rows of plastic tubs on wheels and sticks a sheet on each tub. The workers put heroin parcels into the tubs and cover them with packs of frozen seafood in accordance with the order sheet. The tubs are wheeled into a fleet of refrigerated delivery vans.

Oscar moves a few steps back and watches the vans leave the warehouse rapidly. In less than an hour the work is done and not a trace of heroin could be found in the warehouse.

Oscar and Vanessa follow the last of the delivery vans going west to the seedy section of East Vancouver. The van pulls up at the back of a 24/7 convenience store. A young store employee unloads one of the containers and pushes it into the back of the store.

Oscar walks slowly along the side road past the open back door. He sees the young man pack the seafood into a freezer, put five packages of heroin onto a scale, and take them to an adjoining office. He returns a moment later and hands bundles of cash and a bill of sale to the driver of the delivery van. The driver stuffs money and bill into a plastic bag, pushes the empty container back into his van and takes off in haste for the next delivery.

Oscar enters the convenience store and greets an elderly woman behind the counter with a friendly smile. She eyeballs him with suspicion. He takes his time reading the list of ingredients on bottles of juice and asks the woman for juice without added sugar. Oscar doesn't understand her squawked response and keeps on looking.

A skinny man wearing a black silk bomber jacket emblazoned with 'Go Big or Go Home' enters the store. Oscar steps aside to let him pass. The man knocks on the office door and a young woman opens it. Oscar pretends to search for items while he keeps an eye on the man who hands over four rolls of cash and steps into the office. Oscar picks a couple of bottles and turns to pay for them when the man comes out of the office holding a small white plastic bag filled with sachets and rushes out of the store. Oscar bids a friendly farewell to the stone-faced cashier and leaves. He waves to Vanessa to come to him and follow that skinny man at a distance on the other side of the road.

Standing in a doorway with a clear view into a back alley, they observe the skinny man extract a brick from the wall of an old building. He takes a couple of sachets out of the white plastic bag, stashes the bag in the wall, and puts the brick back in its place. He leans against the wall on the corner of the back alley until a young couple stops and talks to him. He takes a sachet out of his pocket.

The young man and woman dig into their pockets and count their money. They hand over everything they have and receive the sachet. They go into the alley, squat near a dumpster, and prepare a fix with a spoon, a small bottle of water, a burning candle, and two syringes. The skinny man watches them shoot up and slump over a short while later. He goes to the young couple and feels for the pulse on their necks. He walks away with a sombre expression and calls the 911 emergency number on his cell phone.

Oscar and Vanessa see two police cruisers and an ambulance arrive at the alley. Two paramedics check the drug utensils, inject the young couple with a medication, and apply cardiopulmonary resuscitation. They give up and cover the woman and the man with white sheets.

Oscar and Vanessa walk away. After a few steps she holds on to a lamppost and throws up all over the sidewalk.

***

The following day Oscar sits on a sofa in their hotel suite and watches the TV-news at noon. The female newscaster, blonde and with a big, fake smile more suitable for flogging used cars, presents the main news items including, "...and in Vancouver the police reported a rash of drug victims. Eighteen drug addicts died from an overdose of pure heroin last night. More details in a minute after these messages."

Oscar switches the TV off. He has seen enough and can hear Vanessa's heavy breathing behind him. He turns his head to face her.

She looks pale and sways a bit. She holds on to the backrest of the sofa and whispers, "Eighteen? We killed eighteen people last night?"

Oscar shifts around and reaches for her hand. "No, we didn't kill anyone last night. They committed unintentional suicide with an overdose. They didn't realise or heed the advice that they had purchased pure, full strength, uncut heroin and gave themselves the golden shot."

She rips her hand away and shakes her head. "That's a lousy excuse. We delivered the stuff."

Oscar is in denial mode and dismisses her comment. "You can put it that way if you want, but we, that is you and I, the Second Generation or Khun Sa didn't tell them to shoot up. They're victims of their upbringing and a pretty well fucked up society that doesn't provide any perspective for them. If you want to blame anyone, blame their parents, churches, schools, and society at large for conditioning them to become obedient little robots that fit into the little boxes meant for them. They tried to escape a meaningless life and started to take drugs. Nobody asked them or told them to do that."

Vanessa looks at him horrified and mutters, "You can say whatever you want to justify the supply of deadly drugs. I don't want to have anything to do with that any longer. I'm out, Oscar. You hear me? I'm out!"

She staggers away. Oscar sighs and asks in a low voice, "How many people have you killed in your lifetime starting with your father and brother? Nineteen? Twenty? That was all hands on. And now you get wobbly knees because some drug addicts overdose."

She turns, comes at him furiously, and shouts, "Yes, I killed people in self-defence and blowing away assassins and drug dealing scumbags. You told me a few days ago, 'No more killings.

We have to find a peaceful way to achieve our objectives.' Is that your peaceful objective killing hundreds if not thousands by letting them overdose?"

Oscar turns away from her. "You're confused. Why don't you take a rest and think about what I said? You will see that the society in which these drug addicts live is to blame for their addiction. It is a society promising that hard work will be rewarded no matter what job you do. Once they realise that they do useless jobs they hate, lead useless lives and that nobody gets wealthy with hard work, unless, of course, you consider daylight robbery of your customers, or kicking or tossing a ball to be hard work, they start taking drugs from one day to the next to escape the reality they can't handle. In most cases they are aided by their doctors who prescribe opiates as if it was candy and put them on the slippery slope of drug consumption. And don't believe the bullshit that evil, no-good bums lurking around schoolyards entice little kids into smoking, snorting, or shooting up. The majority of druggies are the thousands of adults who are upstanding members of society one day, suffer burnout and take to drugs."

Vanessa has turned away and slumps onto the bed in the adjoining room when Oscar mentions 'society' again. She doesn't want to hear the rest of his argument and buries her head amongst the pillows. Oscar gets up, mumbles something about grabbing a bite to eat, and leaves the room.

He gets back about an hour later and is taken aback by seeing a bellhop in their suite loading Vanessa's suitcases onto a trolley. He asks where she is going. When she says that she has to catch a flight to Mexico, he asks if he can accompany her. It takes her a while to agree.

They say their final farewell in the departure hall of Vancouver International Airport, Canada's Pacific Gateway.

42

Oscar completes his trip down the west coast of the United States and observes the successful deliveries of a total of thirty tons of heroin in Seattle, San Francisco, and San Diego. He leaves hyperventilating politicians and baffled police forces in his wake who can't explain and don't know what to do about the sudden onslaught of overdosing heroin addicts. 'Something has to be done' and 'somebody ought to do something' are the chorus lines heard up and down the coast. Naturally, the opposite of any effective measure is taken by state governments. Harsher punishments are legislated for any drug user that happens to get caught by the strong arm of the law. Enforcement of the new laws doesn't do anything to abate the number of drug victims but fills prisons with screaming addicts who have to go cold turkey. Not receiving any help, they go back to their old habits as soon as they are released. In effect it is proof of a broken system run by politicians who suffer a total disconnect with the population at large, refuse to understand the root causes of the drug problem, and are not willing to stand up for the urgently needed social reforms to reduce, if not eliminate drug addiction of every kind.

The resulting west coast mayhem is of no concern to Oscar. It is a demand and supply situation in the best of capitalist traditions. All he supplies are commodities craved by millions of users in the U.S. alone, albeit illegal and expensive or perhaps because of it. Dealing cocaine and heroin is a growth market of immense proportions thanks to the failing social structure. It is becoming a global phenomenon due to the American tycoons' unrelenting effort to foist their model of capitalism upon countries around the world where the rich get richer, the middle classes shrink, and the masses of impoverished people are growing and kept in their place.

Oscar is certain that both substances, cocaine and heroin in all their forms, would probably not only be legal but also highly recommended as an antidote to all sorts of ailments, if the USA was the country of origin. After all, American companies are the suppliers of noxious and highly toxic substances ranging from unregulated herbicides and pesticides to deadly defoliants that are traded around the world and thrust upon unsuspecting users by the manufacturers' all-powerful lobby. The same can be said for the military-industrial complex that supplies banned armaments like land mines and cluster bombs to anyone willing to pay the price and is guilty of the death of hundreds of thousands of civilians who have nothing to do with whatever conflict is conjured up by militarists of every shade.

No, Oscar has no scruples about the perpetually increasing wave of death and the consumption of illicit drugs in North America or any other country. It is a problem the countries wailing about drug addiction have brought upon themselves.

***

The fourteen men and women of the Second Generation give Oscar a hero's welcome when he returns to Colombia on Tuesday, 8th December 1992. The shipping of merchandise from Colombia and Thailand works flawlessly. The money transfer into the accounts of their companies was eyed with suspicion at first because there were no big deposits that corresponded to the shipments. It took a few days for it to become clear how the Asian system works. Thousands of small deposits ranging from just over a hundred dollars to less than a thousand paying for the receipt of legal products or services pour into the accounts of the more than twenty companies Pilar has registered in every known tax haven. Not only does the Second Generation literally swim in money but also the money they have received is legal. The original loan of three hundred million dollars has been paid back with interest and the shares of the profit are paid out on a regular basis.

The success of the project does not go unnoticed by others who start to feel the pinch of being cut out of deals they thought they had secured. It is impossible for them to track down the culprits who cause them so much pain because the Second Generation is working under the cover of its network of legal companies. They have captured more than sixty percent of the market in the eight months since the first trial load was shipped to Miami.

Competing drug lords try to recapture their market share with aggressive methods as for example with special submarines that carry bigger loads. It proves to be a disaster with stockpiles of drugs captured off the coast of the United States and in Colombia.

Yet, all the quantities captured amount to less than five percent of the total amount of drugs consumed around the world thanks in large part to the successful delivery system that was planned and realised by Oscar.

The Second Generation's Colombian companies have been purchased and underwent huge expansion programs. They hire a vast number of qualified and experienced professionals in every sphere of their activities. The new employees are tasked with any required activity in their field of expertise except the actual production and shipping of the original merchandise. That is reserved for a tight little circle of trusted technicians and engineers who design completely new methods of concealing the merchandise and pack it yet better in less labour-intensive forms.

The logistics expert Gerardo has come up with a delivery-on-demand system he adapted from crude oil deliveries. Similar to oil tankers floating on the seas waiting for a call for their load from the nearest port, he has containers loaded on a range of vessels that can respond to a call from Europe, the Middle East, Asia and, of course, North America in the shortest turn-around time possible to meet any emergency. This system will be expanded until such time when the chemists have managed to convert cocaine paste and opium to foil or fibres and the final product can be manufactured in the recipient countries.

Guillermo and Ariana travelled to Europe and Asia for discussed with relevant scientists the novel approach of converting almost any natural plant extract to useful, environmentally friendly, and harmless base products. Their team is working under immense pressure. Its progress gives rise to hope that a finished product will be ready for shipping before the end of the coming year. In expectation of this event one of the recently employed business consultants sets up partnerships in the Middle East with chemical companies in Lebanon, Jordan and especially Saudi Arabia, the biggest growth market for the consumption of illegal drugs. The chemical plants Oscar purchased in Germany and Russia as well as those acquired recently in Spain and Italy are in the process of being refurbished and geared up to handle and process foil or fibre for reconversion to coke and smack.

These developments leave Oscar with nothing to do. He was paid the promised amounts and could turn his back on any further involvement with the illicit drug trade if it weren't for his desire to persuade Silvia to stop trading drugs as well as the nagging impulse to get even with Pablo Escobar.

'One step at a time' is his credo as he plans his next move. He averts any suspicion by informing Pilar about a visit to his former teacher in Bogotá and spending the festive season with his spouse.

***

He hardly recognises his posada despite the renovation work still going on. The colourful design of flowers and animals on the front wall is impressive. The old wooden gate nobody could open any longer has been replaced by a master craftsman's piece of work that can swing open at the lightest touch. Oscar is introduced to the housemaid Griselda, a very friendly woman with a round face that matches her figure. She and her husband were farmers in the south of the country. Their crops were destroyed, and livestock killed by the repeated spraying of Agent Orange. She responded to Don Germán's small ad in a daily newspaper. He hired the couple and thus provided a home for the entire family.

Oscar's reunion with Germán is one of joy when the old man tells him that the renovations were more than he ever dreamed of having done to his home. Oscar is immensely pleased to see that his old room and bunk bed has been preserved. The kitchen is a bit of an anachronism with one half housing the old wood stove and oven, the rickety cupboards and table that Germán had insisted should stay and the other half a modern setup of the latest available technology for food storage and preparation.

When they sit at the old kitchen table to discuss the future, Germán is emotionally overcome by Oscar's wish to carry on the work of providing shelter and education for homeless and abandoned children that had benefitted him for so many years. He had never expected Oscar to be so taken in by his humanitarian work to want to continue with it. When Oscar asks him if he happens to know how many of his former residents had taken to drug consumption, he proclaims proudly that not one had ever gone down that slippery slope. That's the reason for him wanting to continue the work, explains Oscar. It is the only way to prevent youngsters from being sucked into this deadly maelstrom. He doesn't reveal that he witnessed suicide, murder, and outright war during his travels around the world on behalf of the drug trade but says that all the bloodshed related to drugs can only be stopped by reducing the demand for drugs to an absolute minimum. That is the reason for him wanting to continue the work done with great success for many years by his old teacher. They part on the best of terms and Oscar is on his way to Panama.

***

Loaded down with the gifts he purchased in Panama City, Oscar decides to buy a car and drive to San José.

After crossing the border into Costa Rica without problems, it is only a matter of avoiding an accident on the curvy mountain road and in the rush hour capital city traffic until Silvia receives him like a long-lost lover. It has been only five weeks since he left, yet she can't stop pampering him as if he'd been absent for five years.

Together they go to deliver presents to his friends. Heinz and his partner get bulletproof hunting vests, and Bert one of those newfangled laptop computers with all the gadgets to access the Internet. The gifts are much appreciated.

Silvia sends her staff home for a two-week vacation. She wants to be alone with her lover. When she unwraps her presents, she is impressed by a diamond necklace and earrings he got for her. She puts the jewellery on, looks in the mirror, and takes it off again. In contrast she is totally taken in by a bolero jacket Oscar had made for her by Panamanian native women of the Kuna tribe in their mola fashion.

***

It takes Oscar almost until the end of the second month of 1993 to return to Colombia. It is in response to a message from Alec to meet him in Cartagena. He has no idea why Alec wants to talk to him but welcomes the opportunity of a meeting to explain that he has essentially turned his back on the drug trade.

It is a quiet Tuesday morning, 23rd February 1993, when he sits by a window of the Café del Mar in Cartagena and enjoys a cup of the finest Colombian coffee. He thinks he is seeing things when a green motorhome stops in the parking lot. It has a humongous photo of a smiling Alec plastered on its side.

A moment later Alec walks in and greets him. "Welcome home, Oscar. It's been a long time. I'm glad to see you."

Oscar gets up and they shake hands. "Yes, Alec, it's good to be back. Have a seat."

After ordering a cup of coffee, Alec whispers, "I must congratulate you on realising the project. You did a bang-up job."

Oscar looks down. "Yes, right, bang-up job, indeed."

Alec is surprised and asks, "Hey, Oscar, I congratulate you for a job well done and you scoff at it. What's your problem?"

"My problem?" asks Oscar and avoids Alec's gaze. "You said some time ago the killing and bloodshed has to stop. But it hasn't and is going on unabated. Since I decided to start a family, it made me think of the danger we are facing. I can't bear the thought of wife and children getting killed because I'm in the trade."

“Not to worry,” says Alec. “You know how your wife takes care of imminent danger. You’re safe with Vanessa by your side.”

“Vanessa isn’t my wife,” mumbles Oscar. “She never was. We put on the pretence to stop Igor from hounding her.”

“Is that so?”

“Yes, and you could have spotted my little lie because the pilot of a plane has no authority to perform a wedding.”

“I see,” mutters Alec and concludes, “So, you want out.”

Oscar shakes his head. “I didn’t say that. I want the killing to stop. It isn’t just dispatching unreliable dealers. I’m talking about the thousands of innocent people in Colombia who refuse to get involved in the trade and are ruthlessly killed by your suppliers.”

Alec stirs his coffee and ponders what Oscar just said. “That is not good, I agree, but we have no control over the activities of our suppliers.” He takes a sip and asks, “How is Vanessa?”

Oscar shrugs. “I have no idea. She didn’t want to have anything to do with us any longer after we saw a young couple overdosing on smack on the first night of delivery in Vancouver and learned the next day that eighteen addicts had died. She left for Mexico.”

Alec raises an eyebrow. “So, what does she do now?”

Oscar shrugs again. “I don’t know. I haven’t heard from her since she left me high and dry to finish the job. She said that she wanted to pursue business opportunities in Mexico.”

Alec asks instantly, “Like what? Helping our competition to ship their merchandise through Mexico to the US?”

Oscar shakes his head. “No! She would never do that!”

Alec squints at him. “But she poses a real danger. She knows how we operate, our companies, shipping, delivery method, and names. She could blow our entire project right out of the water.”

Oscar shrugs. “She could but she won’t, I assure you! I know her better than anyone and I know she would never do that!”

Alec retorts in a sarcastic tone. “Yes, right! Just wait until one of her friends or relatives overdoses and watch her change her mind about keeping shtum. She will prattle and spill the beans to anyone who cares to listen. Mark my words.”

Oscar gives him a sly look. “That’s an assumption. Instead of speculating what Vanessa might or might not do, I’d rather hear what we can do to stop the killings related to our trade.”

“Give me a break, Oscar.” Alec finishes his coffee, and sighs. “You have to put things into perspective. Tell me what kills more people - religious fanaticism, prescription drugs, junk food and tobacco or our business? Well, it isn't our business, is it? If it were, I would fight it as a scourge that has to be stopped. Therefore, I will not only continue trading our product, but also fight for its legalisation. It's the only way we can stop the killing."

"And how are you going to do that?"

Alec points to the parking lot. "Look outside. That's the first of a whole fleet of vehicles I will use in my campaign to get elected. I'll be running for a senate seat."

Oscar dismisses the idea. "As a senator, you'll hardly be in a position to legalise narcotics."

Alec nods. "I know but an avalanche always starts with one small snowball that gets bigger and bigger and picks up flake after flake until it is unstoppable. Sounds just like the senate, don't you think? Flake after flake?"

Oscar is amused about the comparison. "You got a point there. Just don't mention it in the election campaign."

Alec nods. "I won't, and I want you to help me in this endeavour as my campaign manager."

"Me?" Oscar almost squeals that question and takes a sip of his cold coffee. "I have to think about that."

"Go ahead but what's there to think about?"

"Very simple," says Oscar. "It's good to know what you can do but it's far more important to know what you can't do and be honest about it. I'm not a campaign manager."

Alec scrutinises Oscar. "I trust you don't say that on account of unfinished business. You have to learn to let sleeping dogs lie, Oscar. Your exploits in Costa Rica marked you as being vindictive. If you still harbour a grudge against Don Pablo and think about getting even, I suggest to you as my friend to drop such a plan."

Oscar takes a moment before he rasps, "Really? And what would you know about what you call my exploits?"

Alec chuckles. "Come on, man, you initiated the transhipment route through Costa Rica. Every day several reefers pass through San José and some of them stop at a repair shop to drop off a delivery for the new wholesaler. Everybody wondered what had happened to this Caledon..."

Oscar interrupts, "Calderón, his name was Alfredo Calderón."

Irritated Alec continues, "Whatever! They wondered what had happened to him. Slowly it filtered through that the Colombian friend, lover, stud service guy of the new coke queen had financed a big clean-up to dispatch him and his flunkeys, a state prosecutor, two DEA contact man and three petty criminals. All of them were somehow involved with the capture and jail time of a certain Oscar Antonio Ortiz Acosta. Some people are starting to wonder if Oscar and Benigno Benavides who serviced the coke queen for two months isn't one and the same person. How long do you think it will take that country's authorities to get wind of it and nail the coke queen? She has become a liability! And as far as you are concerned, I recommend that you never return to Costa Rica. We can't get you out of the slammer a second time, no matter that I consider you my friend and how much you have done for us."

Alarm bells go off in Oscar's head. He stares into his coffee cup and mulls the threat of having Vanessa and Silvia eliminated and letting him hang out to dry. The only way out is taking Alec up on the 'invitation' of becoming his campaign manager. But now even more so, Oscar will be damned to take him up on the job offer.

He decides that attack is the best defence and nails Alec with an icy stare. "It's a done deal then that you will have Vanessa terminated as soon as you can locate her, dispatch Silvia with a wet job and have me blown away unless I accept the invitation to work as your campaign manager."

Alec squints at him. "What the fuck gives you that idea?"

Oscar leans back. He has Alec on the ropes. "This is the first time I hear you say 'fuck'. You have changed more than you will ever admit. Just like the politician you aim to be, it isn't what you say, it is what you don't say that gives away your plans."

Alec wags a finger of denial, but Oscar doesn't let him get a word in edgeways. "Don't try to deny that you will have Vanessa terminated because she knows the entire project and could blow it right out of the water. Your words, Alec!

"Don't try to refute that you will have my future wife Silvia dispatched because she has become a liability. Again, your words!

"And as far as I am concerned, you have no more use for me except as your campaign manager. If I don't accept the invitation, I will be another liability and have to be blown away. Right?"

Alec raises a handy and gives up. "If you want to see it that way, be my guest. What we might do to a person who poses a danger to our operation is just a pathetic assumption on your part."

Oscar scoffs. "Alec, you are the born politician. Your verbal contortions of denying your evil plans qualify you for the diplomatic corps. Permit me to point out the real threat to your operation. It is you, Alec, for two distinct reasons. For one, greed has a firm grip on you. You want to amass more and more money. Soon you will start to suffer from a severe case of megalomania that'll make you think you're omnipotent and above the law.

"For another, your fear of Vanessa and me knowing too much and Silvia being a liability is proof of your lack of trust in the abilities of your team to create completely new production, packaging, shipping, and delivery methods of your product not anyone of us knows anything about. Your mistrust in your most trustworthy people is the real threat to the project.

"I don't have your education with a degree from the London School of Economics. I have only street education, but I have maintained my instincts for survival and those instincts permit me to give you as my friend some sound advice. Rein in your greed, be happy with what you have, and use it wisely. And finally, learn to trust your people. You have some really smart, creative, and skilled members in your team. They are already working on the conversion of the product to something nobody can tell apart from cling wrap. Neither Vanessa nor Silvia nor I know anything about that. So, let us go and leave us in peace."

"Have you finished?" asks Alec quite superfluously. "Now let me give you some advice. Bring Vanessa and Silvia to Colombia where we can keep an eye on them, and they will be safe."

Oscar shakes his head and cuts off Alec before he can spew more assurances. "You are confirming my worst fears. I guess Silvia and I will be safe once we settle in Colombia. But Vanessa? You have just confirmed her death sentence. How can you expect me to work for you under those circumstances? Please, look for someone with experience in campaign management or politics. Ask Alicia Arzáyus to become your campaign manager. She is a political scientist. I'm not your man for that job."

Alec knows that he might as well bang his head into a brick wall. Oscar is too smart and experienced to fall for any promise he will make. He gets up and asks, "So, what are your plans?"

Oscar responds, "There's a hotel project on the island of San Andrés. I was thinking of becoming a part owner. Also, a mobile phone company in Medellín provides an opportunity to get into that line of business on the ground floor. But otherwise, I have no plans except bringing Silvia here and raising a family."

"Sounds good," says Alec. "Good luck."

"Thanks, and good luck to you, too," says Oscar, shakes hands with Alec, and watches him leave.

43

The DEA is in upheaval since several other federal agencies got involved on an unforeseen scale and manner in the War on Drugs. But instead of fighting the scourge, some of these agencies are alleged to actively transport tons of cocaine from an interim storage in Venezuela into the United States. It is claimed the drug is sold to the highest bidder and the proceeds are used to finance the Central Intelligence Agency's covert activities, that is to say its dirty work. If proven it would confirm that the official claim of waging a War on Drugs is but a blatant lie.

The federal agencies' drug smuggling has been going on for some time without ever having been confirmed or denied by any of the agencies. This dirty business was started by President Ronald Reagan's administration in the 1980s to provide the CIA with funds for the Contra rebels' dirty war against the leftist Sandinista regime in Nicaragua. Thus, it is nothing new and the DEA should be used to it by late March of 1993. Yet, what is new about the recent activity is the CIA's alleged collaboration with the so-called Calí cartel, officially the most wanted criminal gang in the Americas.

Another frustrating development is the cooperation of the Colombian government and its security forces with the Calí cartel in its unquenchable desire to hunt down and destroy the Medellín cartel and deliver Pablo Escobar to the United States. Evidently, they are not aware or ignore that the Medellín cartel had ceased to exist several years earlier, and Escobar had declared his retirement. He is alleged to run the cartel's drug business from a hideout in the larger area of the district around the city of Medellín.

The other federal agencies' activities interfere with the DEA's ongoing work. The administration's management in general and Dennis Adams in particular are furious about it. Dennis gets piecemeal information at best, if any. Even his field agents are often hindered or prohibited by CIA agents to conduct their work under the pretext of 'national security'. Hence, the DEA's cartel investigators have to make sense out of the bits and pieces of information handed to them as well as the rumours and gossip spread at the water cooler by bumptious know-alls.

When a field agent's comprehensive report trickles in, it is frequently a piece that doesn't fit into any of the various puzzles. That holds true for a report Sean Murphy receives from an agent in Costa Rica. He tries to fit the information into his elaborate cartel charts but can only cross out Alfredo Calderón with a red marker pen. When he enters the name of the alleged new queen of coke, Silvia Robles, as a search argument into his computer, he draws a blank. She doesn't have any connections to drug cartels or a major dealer and has no criminal record. Everything stated about her in the report amounts to conjecture. Also, her Colombian contact man by the name of Benigno Benavides, although suspicious, is as clean as a whistle. The third part of the report claiming that the isthmus has become a major transhipment route for cocaine destined for the US west coast cannot be substantiated because no shipment has ever been found and confiscated.

Sean sticks the report on the board and draws a line connecting it to the big question mark drawn by his boss in reference to his assumption of a new cartel formed by the Second Generation of Colombian drug bosses. Sean looks at the white board and sighs. It is all inconclusive and highly unsatisfactory. He goes to see Dennis in the hope of an informed chat.

"Hello, Sean," says Dennis. "Did you receive another piece of information that doesn't fit your charts?"

Stopped dead in his tracks before he can even greet his boss, Sean can only mutter, "How can you tell?"

Dennis grins. "Your face is an open book. When you look excited, you have solved a puzzle. When you look down in the tooth, you received info that doesn't fit. What is it this time?"

Sean is amazed and wants to say something to that effect. He admires Dennis' skill not only for recognising connections that others fail to see but also his willingness to discuss any problem and maintaining his sense of humour. But Sean refrains from gushing. It would make him appear to be a brown-noser. Instead, he talks about the problem at hand.

"I received a report from our new field agent in Costa Rica about what looks like a clean-up. The drug boss Alfredo Calderón and all his flunkeys were terminated."

Dennis is amused. "That's good. Scratch him off your list."

"I've done that, Sir. However, it is alleged that Calderón has been replaced by a new drug boss, a woman by the name of Silvia Robles. Yet, she is as clean as the driven snow, has no criminal or police record, no connection to a cartel and none to any of our agencies. Question is, where does she get her supplies to become the alleged wholesaler?"

"Second Generation."

"Yes, Sir, a valid assumption, but we have no evidence of its actual existence. Anyway, there's more to that clean-up operation. Two of our informants were killed as well."

"Oh, that's not good. Who are they?"

"The brothers Ricardo and José León."

"That's no loss. They were useless, never supplied any information, but raked in our monthly fee. Good riddance."

"There is more, Sir. The prosecutor Antonio Arías, brother of our murdered agent Miguel Arías, was killed with his entire family when his house was blown up. Three minor criminals were killed as well in that same operation in one night. They were dumped into the septic tank behind their house where they drowned."

Dennis makes big eyes. "That's original. Texas should adopt that as a method of execution. It could prove to be very popular letting murderers drown in their own human waste."

"That would be cruel and inhuman punishment," objects Sean.

"True," agrees Dennis, "but think of the alternatives. Frying, gassing, hanging a convicted criminal or injecting him or her with lethal chemicals isn't any less cruel."

"Certainly, Sir, you are right. Permit me to finish. All the assassinated victims were evidently linked to the life sentence for murder of this drug dealer Oscar Antonio Ortiz Acosta."

"Oh, I see. Wasn't he one of the three Oscars, the last one we failed to apprehend in New York?"

"Yes, that's him alright," confirms Sean. "The last one, Oscar Uribe I met in Miami, but we couldn't connect him to any drug deals. The shipping company he represents proves to be absolutely clean. Its deliveries of frozen food stuff to seven ports on the east and west coast are beyond reproach. It's all clean and without a trace of illicit substances."

"Interesting but what has all that got to do with your investigation of the cartel activities?"

"I have absolutely no idea. That's why I came to see you. There's one last bit of information that possibly could shed some light on the link of the new drug boss with the Colombian cocaine trade and the Second Generation. It's the lover of Silvia Robles, a Colombian by the name of Benigno Benavides."

"Lover of a drug queen, hmm," mumbles Dennis. "Sex and drugs and no rock 'n' roll? Benigno Benavides? Who is that?"

"That's a good question. He appeared first on our records after a two day stay in New Jersey. He travelled to London, Berlin, Moscow, and Bangkok where he spent several months. His stay in Thailand was only interrupted by a visit to Costa Rica at exactly the time in September of last year when the clean-up operation occurred, and the new drug queen took over."

"September of last year?" interjects Dennis. "That's half a year ago! What took our field agent such a long time to file his report?"

"He's Costa Rican, Sir. I questioned him in this regard and await his reply. Yet, there is a bit more to this case. Benigno Benavides also travelled to Vancouver, Canada, Seattle, San Francisco, and San Diego after he left Bangkok. In his wake our west coast was flooded with heroin. He moved on to spend more time with Silvia Robles and returned to Colombia. Since February his trail has turned cold, and we have lost track of him."

"Holy shit and derision!" shouts Dennis. "Isn't it always the same? We have a trail, and it turns cold. Yet, I bet my bottom dollar that the CIA knows exactly where this Benavides could be found."

"Why do you say that, Sir?"

Dennis gets up, pushes his hands deep into his trouser pockets, stands by the window, and says, "I will let you in on a little secret. Keep it a secret until the time of a formal announcement. The head of the DEA, Bob Bonner has decided to quit. The reason for his decision is simply that for years other federal agencies have been interfering in the work of our agency. The CIA has transported tons of narcotics into the United States without notifying us. It nullifies all the excellent work your team has done. Your work has provided insights into the operation of the cartels, which resulted in the confiscation of hundreds of tons of cocaine and millions of dollars of drug money. Yet, there has been a steady increase in the influx of cocaine and heroin into our country. Two years ago, it was estimated that the cocaine consumed on our shores amounted to about four thousand tons a year. That estimate has risen to over six thousand tons while the confiscation of drug money has dropped to almost zero. I guess the work of the Second Generation is done not only with the tacit agreement but also the support of the CIA or the Second Generation has simply outsmarted us.

"Your detail of information about tracking Benigno Benavides and the flood of heroin that followed in the wake of his global trip tells me that the Colombians are cooperating with the Asian heroin bosses, ship and deliver their deadly cargo and in turn have all their loot transferred by the Asian's underground banking system, which we haven't been able to crack. In summary, I can say that the DEA has been reduced to the role of nabbing petty street dealers and that the work of our cartel investigation unit has been rendered null and void. Therefore, and for reasons of unpredictable future developments, the administrator of the DEA has decided to quit his post before the end of this year, and I have handed in my request for early retirement at the same time."

The revelation of his boss quitting his job hits Sean badly. He can feel an electric shock going through his brain and down his spine that paralyses him. What is he going to do without the advice of the man he regards as the most capable department head of the DEA? What will become of his work? He sits down and tries to absorb the effects of the bombshell his boss dropped on him.

Dennis turns and sees his shattered team leader, head down, and clasping hands. He steps to his side and puts a hand on his shoulder. "I'm sorry, Sean, to break the news to you so suddenly but I felt that you of all people deserved to be informed. You have uncovered ninety-nine percent of the intricacies of the Colombian drug dealers as well as the heroin trade. You have gained insights that our politicos will prevent from ever being publicised. If you persist in carrying on your work, you will end up a frustrated old man whose work has yielded nothing in this so-called War on Drugs.

"May I suggest you hand in your resignation and start looking for a job in an organisation that will appreciate your skills and doggedness to dig up facts. The United Nations Office on Drugs and Crime comes to mind. I have good contacts there and I would give you an excellent letter of reference."

Sean gets up slowly. He shakes hands with Dennis and nods when his boss says, "Not a word to anyone. Okay?"

44

In the course of the six months that follow the conversation with Alec in Cartagena, Oscar is taking trips to Buenaventura, Calí, Bogotá, San Andrés, and Costa Rica. It is all in preparation of securing a safe place for Silvia and himself that is out of sight of the Second Generation while maintaining a public presence on a limited scale. It is a shell game he plays - with Alec in particular.

His first clandestine trip takes him to his hometown where he looks up his brother and receives the passport and other identification documents Benigno held for safekeeping since they met in Berlin. Checking the name, his identity for all trips abroad will be Pablo Montalban henceforth, but he will continue to conduct his activities in Colombia under the name of Benigno Benavides. Then he goes to the local Buenaventura authorities in the company of his parents who present his birth certificate to apply for his original identity papers in the name of Oscar Antonio Ortiz Acosta, which he receives a couple of weeks later. Fulfilling a twenty-five-year-old promise, he purchases a large piece of raised land by the riverside and has a house and workshop designed that is to be built for his parents by a local contractor. The workshop will be his father's domain to build small vessels. But to be on the safe side, a boat designer and a couple of craftsmen are hired who can help him build boats that won't sink upon launching.

Oscar's engagement in Buenaventura is concluded with the standing order of the deposit of funds in his parent's bank account.

***

Oscar goes to Calí to clear out his personal belongings. He is not surprised to see the house Alec had purchased for them occupied by people who claim to be servants of the Muñoz family. All of them are armed men. They had already stuffed Oscar and Vanessa's belongings into cardboard boxes and stored them in the garden shed. Fortunately, the new occupants of the house have not detected the safe in the basement. It takes a few days for Oscar to be left alone in the house and open the safe. He retrieves his papers and valuables and puts his correspondence, designs, and plans, into another plain cardboard box that he stores inconspicuously among the other boxes in the shed.

The cash he found in the safe comes in handy for the purchase of a van under the name of Pablo Montalban. It will make his departure less perceptible as a disappearance but let the van appear to be a rented moving vehicle for his relocation to nearby abodes. The servants even help him load his van and wish him happy times in the furnished condominium he rented in a nearby high-rise.

Before he leaves the city, he pays the apartment rent for one year in advance. He sends the servants of the Muñoz family the note that they are at liberty to stay there whenever he is absent and that the key is under the doormat. Then he hits the road with the intention of never returning to Calí.

***

Oscar drives all night and arrives at the break of dawn in Bogotá. It takes Griselda a moment to recognise him, and swing open the big gate. He drives the van into the inner yard, unloads his boxes, and stores them in 'his' room. The box with papers of his Second Generation activity is now well hidden and under lock and key.

Germán gets up around 7:30 a.m. and is overwhelmed when Oscar presents the van as a gift to the posada. Griselda's husband is assigned as the designated driver and to airbrush the name 'Lyceo Humanitas' on its sides. It may persuade those street urchins who happen to be sufficiently literate to trust the offer of a safe home, good food and an education in the posada.

The next four weeks is spent interviewing teachers and hire two of the applicants. A curriculum is prepared and classrooms set up.

His last activity in Bogotá for a while is to accompany Germán in his search for homeless and abandoned children. They return to the posada with two girls and one boy whom they managed to persuade to accept their help. The kids are of course very suspicious until they are told that the door is always open. If they want to leave, they can do so at any time. One of the girls, filthy and wearing only a torn dress, scurries out. She seems to have disappeared but returns a few hours later to everybody's surprise with three more girls and a boy in tow. They go through the same routine as the first girl and boy, take a shower and pick clean clothes out of the storage room before they undergo a medical exam and are given a welcome meal.

Oscar is satisfied with the arrangements. Before he bids farewell and is on his way to San Andrés, he hands Germán an envelope for safekeeping. It contains his Oscar Ortiz identity papers.

***

On the island he is received by the owners of the site for a new luxury hotel. The property is located near the airport in the north of the archipelago. The structure of an old hotel is half torn down. The wrecking machinery and equipment is damaged and stands idle. Oscar absorbs the sights in silence and doesn't ask any questions.

It takes him a few days to locate a labourer who participated in the demolition. The man admits openly to have damaged some of the machinery and provides an explanation. The labourers had not been paid for a couple of months after the major investor pulled out of the project. The present owners blamed the workers for the project delay and massive cost overruns. A labour dispute ensued, and the workers downed tools when they were not paid their wages. He adds that the project has stood idle for a couple of months and reacts bitterly upon hearing the "workers are on vacation" claim.

Oscar hires an architect, a quantity surveyor, and a lawyer for the upcoming negotiations. They are islanders and confirm what the labourer had told him about the project. Well informed and supported by his team of experts, the present owners' fraud is quickly established. They embezzled the funds of the major investor with exorbitant consulting fees and kickbacks. Long and arduous negotiations over several days follow to determine the actual value of the property, reject the original design of the hotel as impractical, and the estimated construction cost to be excessive.

Oscar's team works overtime to come up with a new design, a detailed cost estimate, and a resolution to the labour dispute. After two months of tough negotiations an agreement is reached. Oscar deposits fifty-one percent of the project cost into an account and his partners the balance. He assigns his lawyer as a co-signer for every payment and withdrawal of money. The workers return, repair the machinery, and the project is back on track.

His mind at rest, he rents a safe deposit box at a bank for his Benigno Benavides identity papers and takes a flight to San José under the name of Pablo Montalban.

***

He enters Costa Rica as an innocent looking tourist. He takes a taxi into town and thinks he can safely go to Silvia's house. When he notices that he is tailed by an unmarked police car, he redirects the taxi to the Mercado Central. He tells the driver to wait for him on the other side. He rushes along the aisles between the stalls in a zigzag course and is almost at the exit when a man in civilian clothes puts a hand on his shoulder and addresses him as Benigno.

It turns out to be a police officer, a member of the troop of corrupt cops providing protection for Silvia. He recognised Oscar at the airport and followed him. He informs him that it is not safe to visit Silvia. The DEA recruited several new agents and pays big bucks to some policemen for the continuous observation of her house and her every move. He thanks the officer, pays him a handsome fee for the information, and turns back into the market.

Oscar buys an overall, work boots, a hat, and a set of gardening tools, goes to the taxi waiting for him and instructs the driver to drop him off at a hotel in the vicinity of Silvia's house. He asks the driver to wait, rents a room for a week, drops off his luggage, and then instructs the driver to go to Delgado's address in Tibas. It takes Delgado only half an hour to produce an entire set of fake identity papers that identify him as a gardener from Limón.

All set Oscar returns to the hotel where he holes himself up for three days to grow stubbles and create an unkempt look. He can't call Silvia because her telephone conversations are in all likelihood traced and she would respond with jubilation hearing his voice.

Instead, he writes a note offering lowest rate gardening services in the early morning hours by a landscaper with international experience gained in Colombia, the suburb of Moravia and Southeast Asia. The bellhop of the hotel receives a reward for its delivery to Silvia's address.

In the morning of his fourth day in the hotel, Oscar gets dressed in overalls, work boots and the hat, puts the gardening tools in a jute bag, and slinks out of the hotel through the backdoor. In a small park he takes handfuls of moist dirt and smears it on the knees, sleeves, and backside of the overalls for a more convincing look of an active gardener.

Along the street where Silvia's house is located no police cars are in sight. A black van and a delivery truck that doesn't deliver anything stand along the curb. A jute sack slung over the shoulder, slightly bent over and with heavy steps, Oscar trudges along the sidewalk and rattles the garden gates with a small trowel.

He is stopped by a policeman who gets out of the van and demands to know what Oscar is doing and where he is going.

In the best Limón-accent he can muster, Oscar states his business and shows the guy his fake identity card and the contents of his bag. He is let go and bangs on the steel gate to Silvia's property. A guard opens a little window, recognises him, opens the gate wide enough for Oscar to pass through, and slams it shut.

It turns out to be a critical moment when Silvia walks towards him. He pulls his hat deep to his brow and when she is close, he says, "Give me instructions of what you want a gardener to do."

She recognises his voice, gasps, and wants to hug him. He fends her off, grabs her by the wrist and whispers, "Psst, don't talk! Let's walk to the rose bushes behind the house."

Silvia yells, "What the hell is the matter with you?"

Oscar answers just as loud, "I only asked, if you want me to trim your bush, ma'am."

He points a thumb back at the gate and a parabolic mirror with a microphone aimed at them from across the street.

She looks at that contraption and asks, "What is that?"

He takes her by the hand and says loud and clear, "That's a hearing aid, ma'am. Shall we go have a look at your bush?"

He has to overcome her resistance to drag her behind the house. At the back he insists on entering the dining room, puts a finger to her lips to be quiet and whispers, "The DEA is outside your house. The agents are listening to every word spoken in here but hopefully they can't pick up what I am saying. Your telephones are also tapped, and every call is traced. Please, be quiet or whisper."

She seems to cotton on at last. Without a word they go up to her bedroom where she shuts the windows and closes the heavy brocade curtains. He explains to her that the DEA and the police are on to her. She is in danger of getting arrested and thrown in jail. She doesn't appear to listen to him while she strips him of his overalls and gets undressed herself. They don't need to say much while they engage in her prolonged welcome home session.

He can't stay for very long to avoid raising the eavesdroppers' suspicion. Before he leaves, he warns her once more of the danger of being arrested. He insists that she has to leave her home but to do that unseen she should be transported out in the trunk of one of her larger cars. He will arrange a clandestine flight out of the country to the island of San Andrés where she will be safe. She finally agrees to do it for him and their future together and tells him that she will let the house to her parents although they will likely turn it into high-class brothel or a school for pickpockets.

Unhindered he gets back to the hotel and immediately starts his hectic activity to organise Silvia's escape. He asks Heinz for help with the booking of a private plane, gets Silvia's fake papers from Delgado and informs Silvia that her departure is fixed for today.

After an uncomfortable escape in the trunk of a car to the Caribbean lowlands near the town of Siquirres where a twin-engine airplane is waiting for her on a rough airstrip, she has a smooth flight and is reunited with Oscar in San Andrés.

***

They get to Bogotá at the beginning of September 1993. On the day of their arrival, rain comes down in buckets, which doesn't help Silvia to get a positive impression of the city.

Also, the bare apartment, reserved for them in the posada, is not conducive to lift her spirits. Making matters worse is the muddy, barren lot, supposedly the garden of the property. The lack of flowers, trees, and greenery downright depresses her.

An extensive shopping spree lasting several days improves her mood. She can purchase whatever she likes or deems necessary for a cosy home. Once they have settled into their new abode, Silvia insists on hiring a maid and a gardener.

Oscar is only too happy to comply with her wishes. The landscaping will keep her busy and let her get over his announced absence for the next few weeks.

***

In Medellín he contacts the struggling cell phone company in need of a financially strong partner to survive and prosper in the competitive market. But instead of becoming a partner, he buys the company outright and changes its name to CelMed. Although he is now the owner and president, he gets in on the ground floor and does any job to get a complete picture of the company's functions.

Within a couple of weeks, he can see that he has to hire specialists to negotiate transmission rights with the government and sign contracts with cell phone manufacturers.

The first shipment of phones arrives quickly, and the company has an impact on the market when Oscar gives cell phones away to anyone signing up with CelMed.

Despite all his work and involvement in the day to day running of the company or perhaps because of it, he did not forget the actual purpose of buying it.

Under the name of Pablo Montalban, he contacts the U.S. embassy and requests to meet a DEA agent, which is denied.

He writes a lengthy note outlining his plans and asks for it to be forwarded to the DEA, which is granted. The plan is welcomed and a few days later Vern Cespedes turns up at CelMed pretending to be a computer consultant. Without identifying himself as a DEA field agent, he helps to set up a phone register that will be useful to him and his continuing investigations.

Oscar likes to get out of the office and promote his company in public. He gets permission from a shopping mall to 'pitch his tent' on the edge of the parking lot to give away phones. On Thursday, October 14, 1993, he sets up his displays under an awning of the colourful company van and puts on a red and yellow company bib. He doesn't have to wait long for curious shoppers stopping by to have a chat with him about the offer of a free cell phone. Many sign up and leave with their new communications device.

A green motorhome decorated with national flags passes slowly on the street and stops near the van. Alec gets out and saunters into the crowd surrounding Oscar. He watches him and has to smile about Oscar's tall claims and humorous asides in response to people enquiring where the phones can be used and for how long the service is free of charge.

Alec stands to the side, picks up a display phone, and asks, "What's the price of one of these?"

Still talking to a couple, Oscar interrupts the conversation to say over his shoulder and to the amusement of the bystanders, "If you have to ask the price, Sir, then you can't afford it."

Alec's reply is instant. "Where the hell are we here? You sound like a poncy shopkeeper on bloody Regent Street in London."

Oscar turns, recognises the aspiring politician who looks pissed off, and says, "No, we are on Calle 44 in Medellín, and you get a free telephone when you sign up with CelMed. How are you?"

They shake hands and Alec says, "Oscar, what's going on? I haven't seen you in months."

Oscar points to the crowd of people around his stall. "See for yourself. I bought CelMed and our campaign keeps me very busy."

Alec looks glum and mutters, "Hmm, so you've become a campaign manager of sorts after all. What's with the bib?"

Oscar strokes the bib and says, "It gives the people confidence to talk to me. I mentioned this company as an opportunity to get in on the ground floor of this business. It's my turn promoting it. I give away phones in return for signing up with CelMed."

Knowing that the location of cell phones can be triangulated, Alec squints suspiciously and asks, "Handing out free phones, huh? Where? Only in Medellín or in Envigado as well?"

Oscar overcomes his initial shock upon hearing the name of Pablo Escobar's reputed hide out. He raises his eyebrows in an expression of surprise. "Envigado? You mean the rural areas around Medellín? You know, we haven't thought of that but that's a very good idea. Yes, we should spread out into the surrounding communities that haven't got reliable public phone service."

"You haven't thought of it? I don't believe you. You should forget about Envigado! Okay? All phone calls are traced."

Oscar wrinkles his brow. "What are you getting at?" He pauses and smiles. "Oh, I see what you mean. Pablo uses cell phones. They will have traced him already. I want to achieve our goal of thirty thousand new clients before we spread into rural areas. It's impossible to trace that many phones."

Alec sneers. "You don't keep up with the latest computer technology, do you? The snooping agencies can trace the location of millions of cell phones at the same time."

Oscar is quick to reply, "Is that so? Amazing! But don't worry, CelMed doesn't collaborate with any snooping agency."

"You don't have to, they've already got your number, rest assured. Thanks to the big chief supporting our project you've become a rich man. Enjoy your wealth and use it wisely. Isn't that the advice you gave me not too long ago?"

Oscar nods. "Yes, indeed, I did."

Alec whispers, "There you are. Follow your own advice and don't stir up old animosities. I have firm plans and won't allow you to fuck it up."

Oscar pulls back his head in surprise. "Harsh language for a senatorial candidate. What firm plans do you have?"

Alec points to his motorhome. "What do you think? The election is still a few months off, but I can't afford to have my name dragged into a flare-up involving Pablo."

"Of course, I understand," replies Oscar in an amiable tone. "But as I said, don't worry. I'm not interested in a flare-up. Now, if you will excuse me, please, I have to take care of my customers."

Alec watches Oscar turning to the crowd of man and women clamouring to sign up. He shakes his head, gets into his motorhome, and slowly drives away.

***

A few days later Oscar returns to Bogotá. Two surprises await him. Silvia looks a little more zaftig than he remembers her from five weeks earlier and her smile is serene. Looking out the window tells him that the hired gardener worked a miracle with that barren patch of land. It is a gorgeous rock garden with trees, bushes, flowerbeds, a fishpond, and a fountain. He thinks that gardening must be doing Silvia a world of good to become a more homely looking woman until she tells him that she is pregnant.

Overjoyed he wants to celebrate the exciting news with her, but she takes him by the hand and knocks on the door of one of the guestrooms.

The door opens slowly, and Bert shows his sleepy face. After a warm welcome, Oscar wants to know for how long Bert plans to stay. Probably for quite a while, answers Bert and asks for a coffee.

They settle in the garden and Bert tells them the reason for his visit. He had been found out as the author of the reports that had been a thorn in the flesh of the government of Costa Rica for some time. He stood accused of having ‘insulted’ former heads of state with his reports about corrupt politicians and fraudulent environmental practices. Facing arrest and a prison sentence, he preferred to flee.

It was the laptop and the Internet service, Oscar’s generous festive season present that had put the National Journalism Institute, the national censorship authority on his trail. As long as he had used the old teleprinter to distribute his reports, they could not be traced back to him, but modern technology and the Internet Service Provider made it possible to track him down as the originator of a report about three former presidents making millions with the sale of arms to terrorists, the illegal logging of protected species of trees and export of its lumber, and robbing the national emergency fund, respectively.

That report had been too much for even the most lenient members of parliament. The elected windbags called on a task force to find the hack who insulted three ‘dignitaries’ and threatened ‘national security’. Before the police ransacked his abode, Bert escaped in his clapped-out Mazda in the dark of night. He made it in the old jalopy through the mud of a banana plantation to the border with Panama and got out of the country of friendship and peace with the help of smugglers. He can never return or will end up in a jail cell next to the three former presidents who had been detained for their crimes that were detailed in Bert’s report.

“That’s ironic,” says Oscar. “You dig up some facts, write a report about criminal activities of former heads of state who got arrested, and instead of being lauded for your investigative work, you are now a wanted criminal. You think it may change, if these three turkeys end up in prison?"

Bert scoffs. "No, Oscar, they won't go to prison. At worst they'll get a slap on the wrist."

"But what about you? Won't you go free if they are found guilty?"

"No, once your name is entered in what they call the big book, you're tainted as a wanted criminal forever. Don't forget, I committed the unforgivable crime of insulting three former heads of state, regardless of them being criminals."

That puts a damper on their conversation. It takes a while for Silvia to ask what Bert is going to do now that his main source of income is history. Bert shrugs and mutters something about enough dirt to be dug up in other countries. Then he asks Oscar to tell him about his exploits and fill him in on missing details.

Oscar has no scruples talking about the Second Generation, the deal with Khun Sa, the shipping and delivery of merchandise through a global network of legal companies and transfer of money with the help of thousands of merchants. When he is finished, he wonders if Bert couldn't strike pay dirt with a report about the Second Generation in general terms. Bert nods in agreement and has already taken some mental notes.

Finally, Oscar invites Bert to join him on his next trip to Medellín to witness a historical event. Bert wonders what that event might be and agrees to accompany Oscar also because he would feel very uncomfortable to be left alone with Silvia.

45

It is a cool, rainy day in Richmond, Virginia, on Thursday, 28th October 1993. The drizzle seems to affect the prevailing mood in an auditorium where Dennis Adams stands at a lectern and faces the gathering of DEA agents. A list of phone numbers, frequencies, and addresses is projected onto a silver screen. Sean Murphy and Vern Cespedes in the front row listen intently to what Dennis has to say.

After briefly introducing the topic of his speech, Dennis comes to the point of the display on the silver screen. “The list you see provides detailed information about the location and frequencies of the cell phones distributed by a telecommunication company in Medellín. It was a very fortunate circumstance that the owner of the company, Mr. Pablo Montalban, came forward with a plan to help us in the hunt for Pablo Escobar. We didn’t question his motives once the search of his name and persona revealed that he is a businessman without a criminal record. He is proof that most Colombians are hard-working citizens who wish for peace in their country and are willing to cooperate with us. We accepted his plan of distributing free cell phones to anyone who signs up as a customer with CelMed, Mr. Montalban’s company, and provide us with a list of the customers’ addresses and cell phone frequencies.

“One of our field agents in Colombia, Vern Cespedes designed a register for the company that lists all incoming and outgoing calls of the phones, especially those in the town of Envigado. We have reason to believe it is part of the area where Pablo Escobar presently hides out. The register shows the frequency of every cell phone in use. The frequencies in conjunction with constant voice pattern recognition will pinpoint a phone that may be used by Pablo Escobar. Once he is identified as a caller or a called party, we can triangulate his exact location in the region of Antioquia. It is the breakthrough we worked to achieve for the past four years.”

A murmur of approval is going through the crowd.

Dennis waits for the audience to calm down. “Please, let me finish. Now that we have achieved a breakthrough, the CIA has been assigned to finish the task and will be glorified for capturing Escobar, if their agents manage to do so. However, no matter if he's captured or not, the drug war in Colombia will go on while our War on Drugs should be abandoned. It could never be won. It was a futile undertaking our federal government initiated on purely racist grounds. The Nixon administration assumed that only Afro-Americans consume drugs and could be brought to heel with widespread arrests. This turned out to be a huge fallacy.

"As it turns out, drug addiction is a social problem of the entire population strata and unless we come to terms with the reality of the drug problem starting at home, drug consumption will continue to grow. If we can't control, reduce, and to the largest extent eliminate the demand for narcotics, there will always be somebody eager to supply the drugs.

"In short, the War on Drugs was a fiasco from the start. Not only was the horse saddled back to front by fighting the suppliers of illicit drugs instead of tackling the root cause of drug consumption at home, but also, we are given a budget that amounts to less than one percent of the money the drug cartels are raking in. To put it bluntly, we are condemned to fart against thunder."

Vern whispers to Sean, "How can he say that? Isn't he afraid that it will negatively impact his career?"

Sean mutters, "No, why should he? He's retiring."

Vern is stunned. "He is? What about you and the big cheese?"

Sean gives him a jaded look. "You mean the head of the DEA? He is stepping down. That's why Dennis has handed in his request for early retirement. As for me, I have a job lined up in New York starting in January."

In shock about the news, Vern isn't listening to Dennis any longer. He doesn't hear him announcing his retirement and doesn't participate in the question period that brings the presentation to a conclusion.

He wonders about his own future and career. What is going to happen to the cartel investigation unit? Can he continue his work as a DEA field agent? Will he ever return to Colombia, the country and its people he knows so well and loves dearly?

Images of him cavorting with scantily clad conchitas on the beaches of Cartagena briefly twirling around in his mind disappear into the far distance.

He surmises that his colourful life in Colombia is all in the past and his future looks bleak.

46

Bert accompanies Oscar on his trip to Medellín, but after two weeks of inactivity, he starts to wonder what historical event he is supposed to witness and write about.

Based on Oscar's quite detailed portrayal of the flourishing drug trade under the guidance of the Second Generation, he wrote a report that hasn't found any takers. It was plainly regarded as fiction by news agencies and papers around the world because he didn't mention any names, which was the main reason for the lack of interest shown. His description of the delivery of drugs, money laundering and acquisition of companies useful for the manufacture for drugs under the protective screen of a global network of legal companies was confirmed only by the Italian secret service, SISMI.

The Italians supporting his claims may have been the other reason for Bert's report finding no resonance. The prejudice against Italian investigative work is very common. When SISMI's documentation of the Colombian drug barons' fifteen-billion-dollar purchases of property and companies in the former East Germany through a global network of legal companies is published as a centrefold in the newspaper 'Corriere della Sera', it is not only doubted but also condemned as counterproductive by other secret service and some drug agencies.

Although Bert appreciates the unexpected support the Italian secret service provides to lend credibility to his report, he feels that something far bigger has to happen for his work to be taken seriously and published.

He observes CelMed's activities, and wonders about the frequent visits of American consular officials. It is upon the advice of one of these officials that Oscar expands his activities to Envigado on Monday, 22nd November 1993.

***

After a few relatively quiet days in the centre of Envigado, Oscar is puzzled about the denizens' lack of response to his generous offer. Most of them look at him from a safe distance and listen to him offering free cell phones as though he is touting warm beer on a hot summer's day. They scoff and walk on. Very few of the local residents who have the reputation of being modest and cautious actually enquire about the service and even fewer sign up and get their free phone.

Oscar notes that all of the signees are merchants or businessmen. None of them are from the lower echelons of society, that is to say, direct beneficiaries of Pablo Escobar's philanthropy of financing the construction of houses and amenities that were built for them. Oscar wonders if word got out that every cell phone call can be monitored and will be traced by security agencies. Have the people conspired to protect their benefactor? Or is it a matter of them prioritising their privacy over the convenience of a free mobile phone and service? Anything is possible in this town.

Oscar puts his questions to Bert and gets the advice, 'If the mountain won't come to Moses, then Moses will have to go to the mountain.' Consequently, he decides to move to another part of town on Tuesday, 30th November 1993, and park the van on an open space near the small forest Bosque el Chuscal close to the row houses that were built for low-income earners.

Oscar goes from door to door along one of the streets on this cool day in a light drizzle. He talks to the residents and demonstrates the cell phones he gives away. His friendly and trustworthy demeanour lets most people, in the majority housewives sign up. They accept the gift of a free phone and use it right away when he gives them the phone number of a friend or neighbour they enquire about.

Meanwhile Bert holds the fort under the awning of the van. Besides the phones, he offers free coffee and pastries to anyone stopping by but still has very few takers. He jots down his impressions of Antioquia, Medellín, and Envigado to alleviate his boredom.

His train of thought is derailed by the distant rumble of diesel engines shortly before midday. He can see a number of military vehicles under camouflage nets parked on a path through the forest.

When Oscar returns for his lunch break, Bert asks him if there is some military exercise under way and if they shouldn't move to a different location. Oscar assures him that they are in the best spot to watch the historical event unfold.

A short time later, just when Oscar is ready to get going again, Vern Cespedes comes trudging out of the forest. He sees Bert and pretends to be a prospective customer. He tries a phone and asks

Oscar, if he has had any takers. Oscar winks, takes a couple of lists out of a pouch, folds them, and puts them into a pamphlet that he hands to Vern.

***

Vern walks back into the forest where he gets into a black delivery van parked among the military vehicles. It is stacked with communications equipment and computer terminals. Vern passes the lists to an operator who keys the data into a computer. Every time he hits the 'Enter' key, the record is transmitted instantly to a US Air Force E-3 Sentry Airborne Warning and Advanced Control System, an AWACS plane circling high above Antioquia, where the record is slotted into a file of all distributed cell phones.

A couple of Technical Sergeants in the communications observation section of the plane listen to the telephone conversations they pick up. They observe two screens each showing voice pattern graphs. One shows the constant Pablo Escobar voice pattern and the other the voice patterns of scanned conversations of all the cell phones in use in Envigado at that moment. A third small screen provides the percentage match of the voice patterns.

Suddenly there is an alert of a perfect match and the Technical Sergeants signal to the System Technician, a Staff Sergeant, to start the triangulation of the phone call. But before the coordinates of Pablo's exact hideout can be established, the phone call is ended. It lasted only long enough to narrow down the area of the sanctuary to a district of Envigado. That information is transmitted to the Colombian Security Forces with a request for a house-to-house search to take Pablo alive.

47

On Wednesday, 1st December 1993, soldiers in full battle gear spread out in the district where Oscar is going from door to door. One of his customers, Maria Ortega, a petite woman in her mid-twenties, enters her two-storey row house. She puts a shopping bag and a square carton on a shelf in the hallway and hangs up her coat.

The front door is still ajar. She looks out and sees soldiers marching past. A police car drives up and stops across the street. She locks the door in haste and whispers, "Don Pablo?"

She picks up the bag, rushes into the kitchen, and draws the window curtains. She goes upstairs and is relieved to see the bedrooms empty.

In the bathroom she looks up to the ceiling. The cover plate of the hatch to the loft is out of place and the frame is scuffed.

She grabs a towel, stands on the bathtub rim, wipes away the scuff marks, moves the cover plate into its proper place and whispers, "Don't worry, Don Pablo. I'll keep the cops at bay."

In anticipation of an unwelcome visit by the police or military, she gets undressed in the bedroom and puts on a bathrobe. She musses her long black hair, dabs some clear cream on her nose, grabs a handful of paper tissues, and rushes downstairs.

She stands in the small living room and peers through the curtains when someone is banging on the front door.

Maria shuffles along the hallway, puts the safety chain on the door, and opens it a bit. Two young soldiers and an older policeman stand outside.

Maria blows her nose and asks, "Yes? What do you want?"

The policeman says in a friendly tone, "Please, open the door, lady. We have to conduct a house-to-house search for a fugitive criminal."

Maria looks scared. "A fugitive criminal? In my house? That's impossible. I'm sick and all alone."

The policeman is very calm and friendly. "I understand, lady, but we are under orders to search every house. You must open up. I assure you we won't be a minute."

Maria sighs and fumbles with the chain to open the door. Her bathrobe slides open and provides the soldiers with a full frontal.

They stare and snicker. Embarrassed she pulls the bathrobe close and opens the door. While the three men check the downstairs quarters, she goes upstairs to the bathroom.

She sits on the toilet when a Soldier barges in. She tries to keep him out by pushing against the door and shouts, "Get out! I'm having a dump!"

After a quick peek, the soldier pulls back and shuts the door. Maria hears him and the other two banging on the walls of the bedrooms.

At last, they stop, and the policeman is heard to say, "We're done. Thanks for your cooperation. I'm sorry for the disturbance. Get well soon."

Maria listens to them trampling down the stairs and the front door slamming shut. Silence reigns in the house.

She takes a broom, pushes the cover plate up a bit, and whispers, "Don Pablo? The soldiers and the cop are gone. You can come down in a minute."

She flushes the toilet, goes downstairs, and gets the shock of her life when she sees the two soldiers loitering in the hallway. She lets out a sheet glass shattering scream, grabs a butcher's knife from a sideboard in the kitchen and shouts, "Out! Get out of my house!"

The soldiers grin at her. The shorter one of the two unbuttons his pants, takes steps towards her, and says, "Come on, girl. We've seen your assets. Here, have a look at mine. How about a quick fuck for the fatherland?"

Maria waves the knife in a threatening gesture and shouts, "One more step and I'll cut off your fucking assets. Get out of my house!"

The soldier scoffs at this delicate woman waving a knife, grabs her wrist, and unperturbed by her screams he pushes her onto the kitchen table. He wants to rape Maria when the front door is pushed open.

Maria's husband Juan rushes into the house. The soldier standing in the hallway tries to stop him. Juan can see what's going on in the kitchen, struggles past, grabs a cast iron skillet from the stove, and whacks the soldier who is maltreating his wife in the side of the head. Knocked out, the soldier rolls to the floor. The shouting and screaming attracts other troopers loitering outside. They push into the house and see the unconscious soldier with his genitals exposed. Maria lying on the kitchen table screaming hysterically and Juan holding a skillet complements the picture for even the thickest of recruits.

An officer wants to have Juan arrested, changes his mind, orders the comatose soldier picked up and his men to clear out.

The front door slams shut. Maria gets up, pulls her bathrobe closed, leans against the sideboard, and sobs. Juan looks at her aghast and asks quietly, "What the hell is going on here? Why are you dressed like that?"

Tears streaming down her face, Maria sniffles, "I had to distract the soldiers and pretended to be sick."

Juan puts the skillet on the table and says, "You distracted them alright. You look like a cheap slut."

Maria clasps her hands and begs, "Please, Juan, understand. I had to act fast to stop the soldiers from looking in the attic."

Juan pulls a face and mocks his wife. "Of course! And what stops a bunch of horny soldiers faster than a woman strutting around naked in front them? Only a woman can think of that! Slut!"

They can hear footsteps on the stairs and Pablo Escobar comes into the kitchen. Juan and Maria greet him devoutly, "Hello, Don Pablo."

Pablo smiles at them. "Hello. Don't call your wife a slut, Juan. She's a good woman. You should be proud of her."

Juan nods and looks embarrassed. While Maria rushes to the hallway to pick up the carton she left there, Juan mutters, "Thanks for your phone call to let me know of the ruckus in our home."

Pablo winks. "Think nothing of it. But I lost my cell phone. It slipped out of my pocket and down a hole between the boards."

Maria hears his lament and says, "Don't worry, Don Pablo. You can use mine."

Pablo looks at her surprised. "You have a cell phone? They are very expensive. How can you afford one?"

Maria chirps, "I got a free phone just yesterday. This new company CelMed hands them out as a promotion."

She puts the carton on the table and opens it. "I got something for you, Don Pablo." She shows him a chocolate cake with a red and white heart decoration and a Happy Birthday wish.

Pablo is deeply moved when Maria and Juan sing the birthday song with subdued voices while holding his hands.

Maria starts to weep quietly. "I only wish your family could be with us. I'll make some coffee. Please, sit down, Don Pablo."

In silence they enjoy their coffee and cake until Pablo helps himself to a third piece and mumbles, "This is good cake. Where did you get it, Maria?"

She answers with pride, "I made it myself. Only the decoration was put on by the baker."

Pablo nudges Juan. "See, Maria is not just a smart woman. She's a good housewife, too. You're a lucky man."

***

At dusk more military trucks arrive and line up on a clearing in the small forest. Hundreds of soldiers mill about. General Adolfo Fernández is on the telephone inside the rear of a communications truck.

He barks in his familiar style, "You didn't find him? What the hell are you saying? He's in Envigado! I can practically smell him! Have your men searched every house, basement, loft, and air duct? What? No, the people are on his payroll and protect him! Damn it! Arrest everyone and check the empty houses. That will flush him out... What? No, you don't arrest him. You shoot him on sight! Understood? ... What? You have strict orders the gringos want him alive? Fuck the gringos and fuck the CIA! I give the orders here! I want him dead, and his arse served on a platter when it's still warm! That's an order! ... What? You can't do that in the dark? Then encircle the entire area and do the big run tomorrow morning at dawn!"

He slams down the field telephone, struts away in a huff, and kicks an empty beer can.

48

At dawn of Thursday, 2nd December 1993, Oscar drives his van to the subsection of Envigado where he distributed the cell phones the previous day and stops at a spot near the path through the forest where military vehicles are parked. A military patrol orders him to move. Oscar has to stay out of the way of all military movements. He drives along the edge of the forest and stops at a spot where he can watch the soldiers milling about. It looks quite disorganised the way they walk hither and yon apparently without clear orders. Oscar turns to Bert who is asleep and gently taps his shoulder.

Startled Bert sits up, looks at a soldier staring at him through the windscreen, and asks, "What? Who is that? Where are we?"

Oscar responds laconically, "Envigado."

Bert checks his watch. "Shit! Ten past six! Why are we here so early? I thought we were going to have breakfast and take it easy."

Oscar lifts a paper bag filled with goodies. "Don't worry about breakfast. I got sandwiches and coffee."

Bert eyeballs the bag. "Okay, but why are we here so early?"

"I got a call at four this morning," says Oscar with a grim expression. "I was told that the historical event is about to happen. Look at the troops encircling the entire subsection. And we are in the front row centre to see the event unfold. When they have Pablo pinned down, I want to face him and shout, 'I am Oscar Antonio Ortiz Acosta, you son of a bitch! I hope you'll end up in prison and get fucked in the arse until the day you die!"

Bert raises a hand. "Wow! Oscar! Slow down! So, the historical event is only the capture of Pablo Escobar?"

Tears well up in Oscar's eyes when he says, "Yes!"

Disappointed Bert sighs and speaks in a calm tone, "I understand how bitter you must feel. But that is a bit much vitriol you are spewing there. Think of yourself for a minute and don't let bitterness dictate your life. You could end up with a heart attack."

Oscar wipes his eyes. "If only you knew..."

Bert puts a hand on his shoulder and says, "I know. I know what you've gone through. Remember that I was the only guy who ever visited you in prison? You have to look on the bright side as well. Thanks to Pablo arranging the financing of the Second Generation's project you are filthy rich. You have friends and family who love you. And most important you have a lovely spouse who is expecting your child. Man, you are a lucky sod! You have everything you can wish for. Once Pablo has been caught, you can be Oscar Antonio Ortiz Acosta again without fear and live a happy life with your wife. You can live in the beautiful posada in Bogotá or any other place in the world of your choosing - except Costa Rica, of course. That's off limits for both of us."

Oscar's spirit improves and he asks, "Do you know that Pablo once wanted to buy Costa Rica by offering to pay its entire national debt?"

Bert nods. "Oh yes, I remember it well. The discussions they had in parliament showed that the six families who have the country in their back pocket don't give a shit about the welfare of the people. Of all the parliamentarians, a communist had to bring the discussions to an end by threatening to make the entire dirty affair public. And he did!"

They laugh heartily about that tidbit of history and fall silent until Bert asks, "Do you think they'll take Pablo alive?"

Oscar rubs his chin and says with aplomb, "They have to. I have it on good authority that the Americans want him alive."

Bert scoffs. "And since when does a prick like General Fernández listen to what the gringos want?"

Oscar opens a thermos flask and pours two cups of coffee. He watches the troops moving about and says quietly, "We'll see, Bert, we'll see."

Bert sips his coffee. "And if he's captured alive - then what?"

Oscar watches several heavily camouflaged soldiers with sniper rifles sneaking past the van and spreading out in different directions. "He will be extradited immediately. His capture is the historical event you are here to observe. You will write a report about it, won't you?"

Bert is noticeable disappointed. "Yes, of course! But I thought... Oh, never mind."

"Never mind what?" asks Oscar. "Come on, out with it."

Bert mutters in a pensive mood, "I thought, or better, I hoped the historical event would be the government bringing Colombia's bloodshed to an end by declaring cocaine a regulated substance. Even peace negotiations with the guerrilla movements would be truly historical."

Oscar chuckles. "You're an incorrigible futurist, Bert. It will come but you'll have to wait another forty or fifty years for that.

For now, we just have to wait for Pablo to be captured and be satisfied with that."

***

In Maria's house a percolator bubbles on the stove. Maria fries eggs. Juan comes downstairs and pours himself a coffee. A moment later, Pablo joins them at the table and is served breakfast.

He pats Juan's shoulder and Maria's hand. "You're wonderful hosts. I will never forget this."

Juan responds meekly, "It's the least we can do for you, Don Pablo."

Pablo wags a finger. "No, you've done much more than the least. You've done everything you can with your limited means. Once this affair has blown over, I'll set you up in business. Would you like that?"

Juan cocks his head and smiles. "That would be a dream come true, Don Pablo. But what can we do for you right now to get you out of here?"

Pablo eats his breakfast and says with a full mouth, "Don't you worry about that, Juan. I'll call some of my guys to pick me up. May I use your phone, Maria?"

Maria assures him, "Yes, of course, Don Pablo. It's upstairs on my bedside table. Shall I get it?"

Pablo shakes his head, "No, Maria, sit down. Eat your breakfast. I'll go up as soon as I have finished my coffee."

A minute later, he bounds up the stairs and picks up Maria's cell phone.

***

A sergeant in the communications truck hidden in the forest Bosque el Chuscal receives coordinates over the headphones. He confirms them and enters them into the computer showing a map of Envigado. The coordinates pinpoint Juan and Maria's house. He prints the image and rushes outside.

The commanding officer looks at the printout, gets on his walkie-talkie, and instructs jeeps to be moved up the side street and positioned near the house. He orders two snipers to move to the back of the row houses and check their rifles. He wants them to climb up some trees and shoot Pablo on sight to disable him should he try to escape on foot. A detail of Special Forces soldiers is waiting for the signal to storm the house.

***

Pablo is upstairs still on the telephone when the front door is kicked in. He hears the screams of Maria and Juan trying to prevent the invaders from storming into the house. Pablo slips away into the attic through the hatch in the bathroom. Silently he puts the cover plate back into place, picks up his Sig Sauer handgun, and silently crawls to the attic of the adjoining house. He gets from one house to the next until he reaches the end of the row houses where the solid concrete block wall of an older building obstructs his way. He peers out through a skylight and can't see any soldiers or policemen at the back. He climbs out onto the roof, clambers onto the older building, and rushes along the ledge towards a fire door.

Two shots ring out. Pablo is hit in the left arm and shoulder. He grabs his pistol with his right hand, puts it to his ear, and fires a shot without hesitation. His body slumps, rolls over the ledge, drops into the backyard of the building, and hits the ground.

***

Oscar and Bert have heard the three shots and see soldiers lifting their rifles in jubilation. They get out of the van and are taken by surprise about the number of press photographers and hacks running up the street. They pass a weeping Maria and her husband Juan who holds her close. They rush around the building and see a group of men in the backyard posing with Pablo's corpse to have their picture taken. General Adolfo Fernández goes as far as putting his right foot on Pablo's midriff in a victory pose.

Oscar can't restrain himself and shouts, "Take your foot off! You were under orders not to kill him!"

Fernández takes his foot off the corpse and barks, "Arrest that man! He is one of Escobar's auxiliaries!"

Vern walks up behind Oscar, holds up his DEA-badge for everyone to see, and says firmly, "No, he isn't. This man is under the protection of the government of the United States of America. Don't you dare touch him!"

Oscar watches the general's expression change from victor to wet poodle with grim satisfaction and turns to thank Vern. But he has disappeared in the crowd of newsmen. In his place stands a sniper in his heavy camouflage and says quietly, "We didn't kill him, mister. We shot him in the arm and shoulder to take him alive. The fall killed him, or he committed suicide shooting himself."

Oscar nods and watches Bert who gets all fidgety listening to the general getting all pompous again. Bert shouts, "Why don't you show us where and how you killed Pablo Escobar?"

The general proclaims, "That's a very good idea. Follow me and I will show you exactly what happened."

He leads the reporters, photographers, and a TV crew into the building and up a filthy staircase to the platform in front of a fire door. There he re-enacts his claimed hand-to-hand combat with Pablo, how he escaped Pablo's poor marksmanship, shot him in the head, and how Pablo escaped through the fire door despite his fatal injury. He earns laughter when he fails to open the door and insists that somebody must have locked it since his dramatic struggle.

Bert comes out of the building and talks to Oscar. "What a bloody liar. This asshole of a general should be demoted to clean toilets with his toothbrush."

Downcast and oblivious to Bert's commentary, Oscar mutters, "That is not what I wanted. I didn't want Pablo to be killed. Despite everything, he didn't deserve to die like this."

Bert shrugs, "Well, there's nothing we can do about it. But tell me what really happened."

Oscar relates what the sniper told him, and they depart the scene. They return to their van to leave this surreal place and drive to Medellín and on to Bogotá.

Aftermath

Oscar never returned to dealing drugs. He lived happily with his wife Silvia and had three children with her. He was splitting his time between his humanitarian work in the posada in Bogotá and running his hotel on the island of San Andrés. His friendship with Bert lasted until his untimely death in 2011.

Oscar was hit in the head by a bullet that killed him instantly while sitting in the garden of his hotel. It was never determined if it was an assassination or an accidental death from a stray bullet of a gunfight that took place between alleged drug dealers on the street.

Silvia handed the posada over to a humanitarian organisation that continued the work started by Germán Obejo who had died in his sleep some years earlier. She sold the hotel and the cell phone company and returned with her three children to Costa Rica, her native country. She was never investigated or prosecuted.

A couple of arsonists torched her house on her orders after she saw that her mother had turned it into a high-class brothel. She had a new house built on its site that she called affectionately 'Casa Oscar' and started to provide shelter for orphaned and abandoned children.

***

It took almost five years for Bert's report about the Second Generation to be taken seriously and published worldwide. His report about Pablo Escobar's life and death was published but scorned for painting too humane a picture of the drug overlord.

It took close to twenty years for his Escobar report to be vindicated by a French documentary crew that followed Pablo's trail and interviewed his widow and son who had moved to Argentina. The TV-documentary presented a truthful chain of events and matched Bert's assertions.

Disgusted with all the lies and deception about the drug trade spread by the media and government officials around the world, Bert turned to environmental protection. He was appointed press officer and worked for many years with an international organisation fighting the pollution of the oceans.

***

Vanessa Camacho went belly up with a nationwide chain of fitness studios in Mexico. Low on cash, she offered her services as a personal trainer to a drug boss in the north-western state of Chihuahua. She was taken hostage by a competing drug gang, and it is assumed that she was killed when her boss refused to pay the demanded ransom. Yet, her corpse was never found. It is quite possible that she was of assistance to her kidnappers with her thorough knowledge of the Second Generation's business model and is still alive.

***

Alec Muñoz never succeeded in his attempt to go into politics, possibly because he lobbied for the regulation of cocaine. Instead, he pursued an academic career and became a professor of business administration at a university on Colombia. He teaches the advantages of going global with a business. He should know.

***

Since its inception in September 1991and in the course of the next twenty years, the Second Generation gained control of roughly 80% of the Colombian drug trade and effectively disappeared into its global network of legal companies. A few credible reports claim a third generation had taken over the business in 2014.

Contrary to all pronouncements from official government sides, the trade of illicit drugs is flourishing and expanding. It will do so until governments take decisive action to battle the root cause of the steadily increasing drug consumption, namely the social ills that give rise to this problem. The needed social change is unlikely to happen as long as the avarice of the 'haves' is given free reign and austerity is imposed on the 'have nots' of society.

***

The United Nations Office on Drugs and Crime estimated in 2008 that the worldwide trade of illicit drugs had a value of over US$ 500 billion a year and a growth factor of over eight percent per annum, which proved to be correct. The global drug trade had doubled by the year 2015 and exceeded US$ 1 trillion.

***

Drug control organisations around the world agree with the DEA that illicit drugs seized by customs, coast guard and police of all countries never exceed five percent of illicit drugs traded and consumed.

***

During the Summit of the Americas in Cartagena, Colombia, in April 2012, several presidents and representatives of Latin American countries, most notably President Juan Manuel Santos of Colombia, President Otto Pérez Molina of Guatemala, and President Felipe Calderón of Mexico called for an end to the US initiated War on Drugs. They suggested a worldwide debate to decriminalise and regulate illicit drugs, specifically cocaine and heroin.

These steps were reiterated during the United Nations Summit on Drugs in New York in 2016. Yet, a serious discussion on a worldwide scale is not going to happen as long as the governments of the biggest drug consuming nations around the world refuse to consider it.

***

Word had got out about the Second Generations original cocaine and heroin shipments by reefer container. But the copycats quite evidently had not considered how it was done. 16.5 tonnes of cocaine hidden in seven regular containers were detected in the port of Philadelphia, Pennsylvania, in June 2019.

Also, some drug lords not associated with the Second Generation have not abdicated from using violence and brute force. It resulted in the hunt for and arrest of Dairo Usuga, aka "Otoniel", boss of the "Clan del Golfo". He was extradited to the USA in May 2022 facing 122 charges for drug trafficking, criminal association, murder, and money laundering.

The global cocaine production and processing initiated by the Second Generation was confirmed by the European Monitoring Centre for Drugs and Drug Addiction (EMCDDA), The Hague, Netherlands, in May 2022. The reconstitution of apparently harmless substances into cocaine takes place within 27 European Union countries where more than 214 tonnes of cocaine were seized in 2020. This applies in particular to Belgium, Spain, and the Netherlands. In addition, Europe has increasingly become a "transit zone" for cocaine destined for the Middle East and Asia it was stated.

www.ingramcontent.com/pod-product-compliance
Lightning Source LLC
Chambersburg PA
CBHW061056100726
47911CB00012B/259
* 9 7 8 0 9 6 8 7 7 1 1 7 4 *